# the
# promise
# box

# the promise box

## vanessa craddock

BALTIMORE

smartgirlspublsh@cs.com

**SmartGirls**
PUBLISHERS

P.O. Box 11492
Baltimore, Maryland 21239


ISBN # 0-9760515-0-8
Printed in the U.S.A.
Library of Congress Control Number 2004099556

Cover and Page Design by Eunice Corbin


**smartgirlspublsh@cs.com**

To Wallace Beauford, Jr.,
November 15, 1939 – November 21, 1976

And

To Florence Williams "Susie"
July, 1955 – April, 1976


*Your spirits live on through my words*

# Acknowledgments

Thanks to the people who support me in every way:

Edwin Craddock, my husband, for being my heartbeat, my drive, and the rock that made this book possible.

Eric Carmichael, my son, for being a lifeforce as important to me as the air I breathe, and for letting me pick his brain any time I need information.

Tia Craddock, my daughter, and my little pumpkin pie, for being the spice of my life, and undoubtedly the inspiration for many more stories to follow.

Thanks to the people who read through this in various stages and gave me the feedback I needed to keep at it: Richard Valentich, Angela Bragg, Gertrude Nobles, Terita Williams, Clara Diggs.

Thanks to the Booking It Graduates (BIGraduates) who attended the Philadelphia seminar in June of this year, for the emails and experiences they shared.

Thanks to the Sunday Brunch Book Club, my reading group, especially to Patricia Mc Coy, for the years she listened to my plans for this book.

Thanks to La Rita C. Haynes, my sister, who never ceases to surprise me.

And a big thanks, of course, to these people without whom this project would not have come to life: Charlyne McWilliams, my editor, Eunice Ellis, my graphic designer, Robin Green for her literary know-how, and Allegra Bennett and her step-by-step approach to doing what you have to do.

# Bernadette

## *one*

"Beeaaaatriiiiiiiiiiiiiiiiiiiiice!!!!"

Bernadette's voice exploded from the bottom of her lungs, piercing the frigid October morning loud enough to wake the whole block. For good measure, she jammed the flat button doorbell one more time, and promptly broke the nail on her index finger.

"Damn!" she whispered as she watched a line of blood form quickly at the top of her nail. Now, she was livid.

All that beating against the solid wooden door of her sister's row-house had yet to get Beatrice's trifling butt up. And Bernadette knew her sister was in there, too lazy to get up to see what the commotion was about. By now, someone could be lying dead on the front doorsteps, and her sister was too nonchalant to even look. If it weren't for the letter inside the pocket of her fatigues, Bernadette wouldn't have come back to Baltimore. Not at this time.

Backing down the three marble steps that led to the front door, she stared at the upstairs windows of her sister's house and thought about hurling a stone. A good crack in a pane that size would send her out screaming. Maybe. It was a safer bet that if Beatrice were locked upstairs in her bedroom with some new boyfriend, which was Bernadette's guess, nothing short of a bullet would interrupt her.

An icy blast of wind hit the side of Bernadette's face, blowing her hair over her head, and she turned sharply, brushing away dirt that blew with it. For the tenth time she asked herself why hadn't she asked the cab to wait? How could it be so cold here with fall just beginning? It couldn't be more than 40 degrees, and she'd been standing outside in it now for at least an hour. She glanced at her watch. Over an hour.

Bernadette frowned as a touch of fear pricked the back of her neck. "You're being silly," she told herself as she thought of the letter. What if

Beatrice couldn't come to the door? She reached in her back pocket with stiff, frozen fingers and pulled out the tightly folded note, opening it slowly to stare again at the puzzling message:

> The color of cream, white and just right
> The color of butter, so yellow and light
> The color of coffee, smooth and so brown
> The color of chocolate won't keep you around
> The color of honey, I want you to know,
> Is dark as they like it, as far as they'll go
> And if you can't meet it, or match it to boot
> You won't get invited to share in the loot
>
> To love you, you must be the person they want
> The color that they would be happy to flaunt
> To bring them attention, to give them their due
> Or they may be willing to sacrifice you
> Remember they go by the number of three
> Remember they never want you to be free
> They do want to kill you, you simply must know
> That you will be next if you move on this slow
>
> First Danny went missing, they hid this just fine
> 'Til it was way too late to help solve his crime
> Juanita was second and look what they did
> I know you wish you could have helped her instead
> They don't want to see you; you're not what they like
> You simply can't press them to treat you just right
> It's what you can't shed, something you cannot be
> So they'll pick you all off in two sets of three

There was no signature, no return address, and the handwriting was barely legible. Why would someone send her something like this after all the years her sister and brother had been dead? Juanita died last, just shy of age 16, and that was 15 years ago. And as far as she knew, Juanita died of pneumonia, in her mother's house. Nobody killed her.

And her brother Danny hadn't even been in Baltimore when he died. He was barely 19, just getting out of boot camp down in Fort Bragg when he was in a car accident. Bernadette's first thought was the letter was a joke, then she checked and saw the Baltimore, Maryland postmark, and that stopped her. Someone from home tracked her all the way to San Diego to warn her. Now what the hell did that mean?

A wave of weariness hit her so hard it was all she could do to stumble over to the steps and sit. She held her hand to her forehead, squeezed her eyes shut and sighed. Her head pounded like a tom-tom. If she could just find her Tylenol... she reached deep inside her black duffel bag for the bottle, eyes still closed. Just three or four of those 500 mg pills and a cigarette would surely take the edge off. Then she would walk up the two blocks to North Avenue and hail a cab to Mama's.

She popped off the cap, dumped three capsules into her frozen palm, and swallowed each separately without water. They clumped together at the base of her throat, and she squeezed her eyes tightly swallowing hard until they moved down. She never traveled without the three things that kept her running, Tylenol Extra Strength, Virginia Slims, and her MP3, filled with every song that Gladys Knight had ever sung. She had to have a daily dose of all three or she was as good as dead.

A window behind Bernadette finally went up, and she swung around to see who had answered. She squinted when she saw it was just an old woman with a tight gray bush from the house next door who leaned on the windowsill and looked down at her.

"Baby, you can save all that energy. They had a party in there last night, and just went to bed sometime 'round two or three this morning. Ain't nobody going nowhere from that house today. You can believe that."

Bernadette stood up and faced her.

"What do you mean? There's a little girl in there who has to go to school?"

The woman looked Bernadette over a minute.

"You must be her sister the Marine she talks so much about."

"Yes ma'am," Bernadette answered in surprise, tugging at her fatigues. She couldn't believe her sister had actually remembered the branch of service she was in, let alone mentioned it. Would she remember what she did, running computer programs on a multi-million dollar computer system for the government? Most important, would her sister remember that Bernadette was up for a higher security clearance and make sure she wasn't smoking weed or drunk if the government came to ask questions about her?

The old woman leaned over the sill and pointed up the street.

"See that car?" she asked as Bernadette stared at a bright red Cavalier. "When that car ain't moved by now, they in there for the day. Don't nobody go nowhere, not even that little girl when he don't get up and move that car."

Bernadette pursed her lips, and shook her head. How had she guessed? It was always a man involved with Beatrice. She grunted, then bent and grabbed her cell phone from her bag, flipping it open and jabbing numbers.

"Well thanks for telling me, because I'm calling the police. A child needs to be in school everyday, I don't care how many parties they have." It galled her the way Beatrice just did things without a second thought. She'd even changed her phone number sometime this past week and hadn't even bothered to tell Bernadette. She made no sense.

Just then both women heard the latch draw back with a loud snap and Beatrice's front door opened. Bernadette watched as the top of a man's head peered around the door edge and a pair of very red, unfriendly eyes settled on her.

"Can I help you?" His voice was thick with sleep.

"Yes, you can tell my sister that Bernadette is here."

The man hesitated, opening the door a bit more. Bernadette stood straighter, clutching the phone and glaring back, and in a few seconds he left, the door still open. Without pause, she grabbed her bag, stuffed the phone in her pocket, and started up to the house when the door flew wide open and her sister Beatrice fell out on top of her.

"Bernadette! I didn't know you was coming here, girl! Come on in. I can't half hear that bell."

Yeah, right, Bernadette thought as her sister roughly pulled her inside and slammed the door behind them, taking her down a long hall and into a large, dim living room. Through the semi-darkness, Bernadette tried to get her bearings, smelling stale smoke as Beatrice bustled around gathering trash from the chairs and piling it on the table.

"Sit down, I wish you would have told me you was coming, but that's all right. Excuse this mess, but we had a little party last night and I didn't clean it all up yet. This is a real surprise, Berni."

"You had a party on a Wednesday night?

"Yeah, we got a new business starting, and you do what you have to do," Beatrice laughed, giving Bernadette a once over. Bernadette could tell by her sister's lingering stare that she liked what she saw. She should.

She'd just had her thick, unruly, dark brown hair freshly permed and stylishly bobbed chin length to frame her perfect oval, honey brown face. She was a little taller than Beatrice and athletically firm, like a poster for a fitness club. Her sister's body, on the other hand, had seemed to explode since Bernadette last saw her.

Beatrice was dressed in a pair of tight black leggings, covered with a million white lint balls, and a tight Barbie pink sweatshirt which just did cover her waist.

"Witt? You want to come back in here and meet my baby sister Bernadette. The one that's the Marine like you. He used to be a Marine too, you know."

Witt's footsteps were heavy as he came to the dining room doorway and stopped. From there he nodded, lifting his chin up as he said, "What's going on?"

Bernadette sucked her teeth and walked over to him extending her hand. How could you meet somebody clear across a room? A bit of eye contact and a touch of his hand would tell her what her sister was dealing with, so she watched his face as she reached to give his hand a firm shake.

"Glad to meet you," she said, a full smile showing the deep dimple in her left cheek. But barely had their hands touched before he let hers go. He clearly did not like her coming over and touching him.

"You too," he mumbled and disappeared back into the dining room.

Bernadette raised her brow, then turned to her sister, who waved her back over to the couch.

"Sit down Berni and tell me about California. It must agree with you girl, you looking real good."

Bernadette hesitated. She didn't want to sit. She wanted to talk about this letter in her pocket to see if any of this could be true. She wanted her sister to be alone, not attached to some new man the way she seemed to be all her life, like it was some addiction. Beatrice was 29 years old now, with a nine-year-old daughter to raise. Hell, when was she ever going to grow up and set the bar for her child?

"California is okay," Bernadette said, turning and looking around critically. "It's definitely a place you can get used to," she added, then quickly glanced over her shoulder. Something wasn't right. She'd learned to get a feel for situations and people, and she could tell that something was not right in this house. She could hear the morning sounds of the house next door, the TV announcer going over traffic and weather updates, voices screaming back and forth. There was nothing moving in here. Where was her niece?

"Toukie still asleep?" she asked casually, still shivering as she decided to perch her rear on the edge of the cracked vinyl couch. Bad enough the house looked like a barn, did it have to be as drafty too?

"No. She'll be down the minute she know it's your voice," Beatrice said through a wide grin.

Bernadette remembered the way she'd left them four years ago, when the Marines moved her to California. Beatrice had just moved to Baltimore County into a new townhouse of modern furniture in an up and coming industrial area. She had a typing job with the government and was doing well. Bernadette forked over $1,000, all the money she had saved for a new Toyota RAV 4, to buy her sister a living room set and new bedroom furniture for Toukie. Where was it all?

"Isn't Toukie going to be late for school?"

Beatrice hesitated.

"Not today. She was coughing too bad last night, so I told her she wasn't going nowhere. All of us was coughing bad. I thought I even heard my baby cough."

Bernadette's mental inventory stopped as abruptly as if she'd pushed the escape key on her computer keyboard. She stared at her sister's lips.

"My baby?" she repeated.

Beatrice stared back. "I know Mama told you I had a baby boy in August."

"No. And neither did you."

"Well, I did. I have a new baby."

"But why?"

"Why what?"

"Why would you have another baby?"

Beatrice's full lips parted. They heard Witt drag something big across the floor in the next room, as Bernadette watched her sister's eyes widen in surprise. Maybe she was just embarrassed for Witt since he could no doubt hear them, and this baby was probably his idea. He didn't know Beatrice like she did, and this little domestic scene was going to blow out quicker than a candle in a hurricane.

"What you mean asking why I had another baby?" Bea's smile evaporated.

Bernadette stared. Was Beatrice kidding? Did she really not understand her own limitations? She was a magnet for men, and the way she attracted them, why would she have a baby? What made her think Witt was the man? None of them made her happy for long.

Bernadette took her eyes off the stricken look on her sister's face, and saw that Bea's hands were firmly planted on both arms of the chair, nails first. Uh oh. She was clearly pissed. Trying to think of a way to take her words back, Bernadette thought about taking out the letter, the reason she was here anyway, but before she could, a loud scream from upstairs caught them both off guard.

"Aunt Bernadette!" They looked up in time to see Toukie sail down the long stairwell, a blur of blue in thermal underwear and a tight blue scarf. She didn't stop until she landed in Bernadette's lap.

"Look at you!" Bernadette laughed, grabbing Toukie close to her chest. "You are so long."

Toukie grinned and stood up as if to show her aunt just how long. She was a real picture. Her baby face look had matured into one of an attractive, young girl. Toukie had just lost her first tooth when Bernadette left for San Diego, and now all the girl's adult teeth were grinning back at her, almost too big for her face. Of course now she wouldn't have those thick wavy plaits Beatrice used to make that strangers would grab and tug, but her eyes were still as big, clear and beautiful as her mother's.

"She was only five when you left," Bea said as though she could read Bernadette's mind.

Bernadette stared at her niece. Toukie's look was identical to Beatrice—with Bea's flawless copper skin, long dark lashes and perfect kewpie doll lips.

"And you're how old now?" she teased.

"Nine! You know I'll be 10 in May."

"Of course. Nine." Bernadette repeated. But she stared at her niece, noticing how mature she looked, with little round knots swelling on her chest already. That seemed awfully fast.

"Ain't she big though," Bea said. "Every time I turn, I gotta buy her some clothes she can fit. Look at her behind. It's growing big as mine! They grow up fast these days, child."

Bernadette stood to see how close in height Toukie was, and pulled her niece's soft hand into hers to squeeze when she looked down.

Toukie's nails were bitten almost to the cuticles, and the tips were big and puffy. She lifted Toukie's hand just as Witt came back and stood in the doorway. At that moment, Toukie snatched her hand and gazed up at him. Beatrice too snapped her head around to watch him.

Maybe it was his stance. The way his shoulders squared and chest poked out like a proud peacock. Without saying a word, the mood in the room changed. It made Bernadette stare at him too.

"Toukie?" Bea asked. "Where did you leave the baby?"

Toukie covered her mouth.

"Sleep on your bed."

"On my bed? You know you can't leave a baby on the bed," Bea said, her voice rising with each word. "He could flip over and fall to the floor…" Toukie turned abruptly and started toward the steps when Witt's voice stopped her.

"You stay down here with your Aunt Bernadette. Beatrice can go up and get him."

Bernadette waited for fireworks. Who did this man think he was talking to? If Beatrice wanted to go, she would have gone. She turned her body around to make sure she could see Witt's expression when Bea lit into him with her sassy tongue. Only it didn't happen.

"Yeah," she heard Beatrice say. "Let me get him all cleaned up for you, Berni. He must be out like a light, or he would be crying by now," she added as she swept past and started the long climb up.

Bernadette stood frozen. What just happened here? She turned her eyes to Witt and noticed how keenly he eyed Beatrice. With his attention diverted, she quickly checked him out. He was tall, easily six feet, and muscular. His arms were tight, his thighs were thick and his stomach was washboard flat. He would definitely draw attention with his looks.

He had smooth milk chocolate skin, and light brown eyes, making Bernadette wonder if they were contacts. Then her eyes fell on the gold that topped the V-neck of his white undershirt, and she frowned. A ring dangled from a gold chain, and she picked up the three point diamonds that glistened back at her from the thick gold circle. It was a unique piece; definitely something you wouldn't see everyday. Yet she'd seen it.

Toukie had not budged from the spot where she stood when Witt stopped her from getting the baby. She stood silently looking up, and Bernadette realized they were all standing like statues, listening to Bea move around upstairs and talk to the baby. It was a relief when Beatrice's footsteps came back in the hall, and they heard her approach the steps. Her flip-flops slapped each step loudly all the way to the bottom, where Toukie bounced over to wait. Toukie reached out to straighten the blanket around the baby, but Bea didn't slow down until she stopped in front of Bernadette, her arms extending a chubby lump covered in a Winnie-the-Pooh receiving blanket.

"I don't want to hold him," Bernadette said.

Beatrice met her eyes, and looked at Bernadette as though she were crazy.

"You going to have to learn what it's about sooner or later. You damn near 30 years old."

Bernadette could feel Toukie watching her, and she could also feel Witt's eyes.

"I'm 26, and I don't ever have to know about it. You mean you actually woke him up?"

"He'll go right back to sleep. I had to dry and feed him anyway." Bea's eyes pleaded, as she moved the bundle back to her sister so Bernadette could see the baby's big, Charlie Brown head that turned when Toukie stuck her finger in his hand. He had the littlest hands that were so pale, the skin seemed translucent. In fact, his face was just as pale, a trait that ran here and there in her family. Her eldest sister Marietta looked damn near white. There was more pigmentation in his ears, and he had a sharp little straight nose and very pink lips.

"Having a problem finding your feminine side, Bernadette?" Witt asked and gave a small laugh as he strolled over to the hall closet. She felt her skin prick and fought the urge to say, 'it must have all seeped into you,' choosing instead to say, "You can't be too careful with germs these days, but congratulations on having such a fine baby."

They all watched him pull out a flannel shirt, which he slipped into quickly, saying "Thank you, he is that." Beatrice, baby still in her arms, hurried over to him. She whispered something.

"It's all right; I'll be back in a bit. Get Toukie to finish upstairs."

"But if somebody call me about the money?" Beatrice asked, a bit louder.

"Take a message! They can call me back." He pulled on a leather bomber jacket with fleece lining, then slammed the closet door.

"Nice meeting you," he said in the general direction where Bernadette stood, and she replied, "Likewise," turning her back to him. She heard Beatrice whisper one more time, then heard him yell "No!" so loudly, it reverberated throughout the hallway. His heavy footsteps went off down the hall, then out the front door, slamming it hard behind him. Bernadette smiled to herself.

Where did Beatrice find that piece of work?

# *two*

Beatrice stood frozen by the hall closet.

"Bea?" Bernadette hurried over to her sister, Toukie following closely. "Now what the hell was his problem?"

Beatrice turned.

"His problem? Bernadette, I am not in the mood today, so don't come back home to start up with me. Okay? I just don't feel like it." She turned the baby so that he fit snugly over one shoulder, then walked away. Her round rear end bopped up and down with each slap of her flip-flops through the hall, and her long, black curly ponytail swung from side to side with each step. She marched through the dining room, and into the kitchen where she stopped at the refrigerator and opened it.

Bernadette trailed behind, surprised at Beatrice's outburst, feeling her niece stepping on her heels.

"Fine, I won't. Just let me ask you one thing, then I'm done. Why would you let that man holler at you like that in front of Toukie?" Bernadette stopped just inside the kitchen door. Where was the fight in her sister?

Beatrice took out a bottle of formula, jumping when some of the liquid spilled from under the loose top. She balanced the baby, went to the sink and maneuvered around a stack of dishes to pick up a saucepan. Sighing loudly, she turned and walked around the kitchen table to Toukie, taking the baby from her shoulder and handing him over.

"Take him back upstairs, and wash him up for me."

Toukie stepped back, crossing her thin arms. "Aw, Ma," she whined, sighing loudly. "I want to stay down here with you and Aunt Bern."

Beatrice took a second to flick her eyes up and down Toukie's long body in a warning gaze and Toukie promptly reached out and took her brother, rolling her eyes in the process and stomping loudly out of the kitchen.

Then Bea turned back to Bernadette.

"Witt did not holler at me."

"Oh? He uses that tone of voice to talk to you all the time? I was in his presence for all of 30 minutes, and I can see that man has no respect for you and probably not much more for Toukie. And since I've been here, not one of you has coughed. So, why isn't she in school, and he at work? You can take that screaming off Witt if you want, but I can't have him scaring Toukie like that."

"Bernadette, Witt loves that girl. You don't know the first thing about him, so don't come back here acting like you do."

"I know enough. How could you let him control you like that? It was killing him that I wasn't falling all over him like you were, and I can't believe you were. You never used to let a man tell you to do anything, and now you're all up his ass!"

A warning look crossed Beatrice's face. She left the bottle and the saucepan in the sink, marched over to the table, and stood before Bernadette.

"I'm all 'up his ass' and every place else he need me to be 'cause he take good care of me. I was working myself crazy trying to keep up that townhouse payment, and Witt told me I could quit. So I did."

"You mean you don't even have a job?"

"I don't need one. Witt take care of me. He didn't want me all stressed out, and he said wasn't nobody else babysitting his son."

"And you're depending completely on him?"

"Witt got it all worked out. Right now I get checks, for Toukie and the baby. And food stamps. So, that give Witt more money to save for our business."

"As in welfare checks? Is that what you mean?"

"If you would just be quiet one minute, Bernadette, I swear. I can't even explain! You got to understand Witt."

Bernadette bit back her response, watching Beatrice's hands fly up close enough to her face to smell the baby's formula. Their eyes held a few seconds before Beatrice went back to the sink to fill up the saucepan. Bernadette watched, gazing at the mess around her. There were dirty plates everywhere, stacks of pots and pans piled high in the sink, and the heavy smell of fried grease hung in the air. Beer and wine bottles lined up on the table, along with balled up napkins and overflowing, stinking ashtrays. It looked like a hell of a party for a Wednesday night.

The running water reminded Bernadette she had to go. She jumped up. "Your bathroom upstairs?"

"Or down, take your pick."

She hurried down, not wanting to disturb Toukie who had gone stomping up each one of those steps that led to the second floor. At least not until she had a one-on-one with Bea about this letter. She stumbled at the bottom of the basement steps, right into a table nearly knocking over a lamp. She reached out and turned it on.

Whew... Bernadette thought staring around. What was all this? There was a long brown suede sectional couch and armchair with several large leopard floor pillows on thick, beige carpeting. A glass coffee table held a stack of CDs, and more beer bottles and men's clothes were strewn across the floor. Against the wall were two of the largest stereo speakers Bernadette had ever seen, part of a serious sound system set inside a black cabinet with smoked glass front doors and a wrought iron tower of CDs. And to the right of the music stood one of those huge, as in 50-inch or so projection television screens with a cable box on top.

This was clearly Witt's pad.

Bernadette made her way to the back where a small enclosure contained a single toilet in a little room, set against the cement wall. When she came out, her eyes were drawn to the wall, where shelves of books were lined from ceiling to floor. Curious, she went over. Many books were on law enforcement and criminal justice, but most were books of classic black literature. She stared at the authors' names—Richard Wright, Langston Hughes, Amiri Baraka, Ralph Ellison, W.E.B. DuBois, Malcolm X, James Baldwin, and August Wilson...no women. Then there was a row of cookbooks. Cookbooks?

She returned upstairs, going first into the living room to get her cigarettes, then back into the kitchen, where she lit one, wrapped her arms around her body, then sat at the table in search of an empty ashtray. With no luck, she pulled an empty beer bottle in front of her where she plucked her ashes and waited for Bea to finish at the sink.

"Okay, you want me to understand Witt, tell me what I need to know. I'm listening." Bernadette inhaled deeply, letting smoke curl from her nose and mouth. She crossed her legs, her black combat boot kicking up and down as she impatiently waited for her sister to speak.

It was killing her to try to reason with Beatrice when she had already put together a picture of Witt, and it was not good. He thought he was smart, and maybe he was, but he had no manners, he could barely watch his temper, and he had to have control. She was ready to move him out, but it was going to take patience to convince Beatrice, and patience she did not have. Bernadette was a mover. She'd make up her mind about something and take action, risks and all. She was a left lane driver all the way, with gas pedal to the floor. Right or wrong, she was what she was.

Patience took time, and she had no time to waste. The women and men on base were often surprised when they saw how gorgeous her thick brown hair was that she usually pulled back into a severe ponytail on workdays, because she had no time to primp. Time is precious, was a banner she had pinned to the wall over her desk. That was her motto, and it served her well.

Beatrice, now that the bottle was warming in the pan, finally came over to the table and stood a moment before settling in the chair next to Bernadette.

"Berni, why did you come back?"

Bernadette stared. She didn't expect a marching band to welcome her home, but to have her own sister ask her why?

"I mean, I'm just getting up on my feet. This is the first time in my life I have the chance to make something work, and this ain't the time for no mess." Beatrice sighed loudly. "I'm with Witt 'cause he's taking me to Daddy, and I need to see him."

Bernadette's broken nail started throbbing as she stared incredulously, trying to link that lunatic who screamed at her sister and slammed out of the house, with the man she used to call Daddy, who left her when she was only four.

"I found Daddy," Bea continued, "even though I know we promised Mama we wasn't ever going to look for him because she did not want us to, but I been thinking real hard about things, and ain't nothing or nobody going to stop me from seeing him now."

Bernadette pushed to the edge of her seat. "So, you got one of those crazy letters, too?"

"What letters?"

Bernadette paused, seeing her sister was clueless. "Why else did you find Daddy? Where?"

"He's in this business club that Witt is about to get into. Only Daddy don't know I'm with Witt. And Witt don't know my father's in the club that's going to help us."

Bernadette frowned. "I guess I don't understand. Why are you finding Daddy? He didn't want to find you, and finding you would have been easy."

"You don't understand, Bernadette. You don't remember at all what it was like when Nita died, do you? You don't know Mama blamed me, and still don't have nothing much to do with me."

"And you think Daddy is going to care?"

"I know it. I was only seven when he left, but I know Daddy loved us, and I know if he was here, I wouldn't be treated like this. Mama want to blame me for Nita dying, but I'm wondering why she want to put it on me so bad. Why she want to make everybody hate me? The more I think about it, the more I wonder what she got to hide?"

"How could she blame you? Nita died from pneumonia. Didn't she?"

"Eventually."

Bernadette pressed her fingertips against her forehead and asked, "So, what does Witt have to do with all this?"

"Honestly? Just a coincidence. I mean, we just happened to be hanging one night at the Raven's Sports Bar, me and my girl Mae—remember crazy Mae?" Beatrice's moist, perfect lips curled up in a daydream smile, "...when Witt came up to me. Witt had them broad shoulders, remember I told you 'bout how a man holds his shoulders tell just what you going to get in bed. We got to talking, and at first, I just thought he looked good, that it was going to be a good, long night of loving."

"I'm feeling you there, Bea. Witt is fine."

"He told me he worked at the Westinghouse plant, but had his own business on the side. He makes fancy pieces of furniture out of wood—you should see the baby's nursery. Anyway, he said that he had been saving to get in this business club with his uncle. It's all men, and you have to have a certain amount of money to even get interviewed. If you get in, they help you out, guarantee you loans and help you get customers and advertise and everything. And I didn't know 'bout Daddy being in this same club 'til that night, when Witt came home with me, and we was in the bed. I saw that ring he wear round his neck and couldn't believe it. That's the same club ring Daddy used to wear."

Bernadette's eyes opened wide.

"Daddy had a ring like that?"

"Just like that. And Daddy was in this business club."

"Why does Witt already have the ring if he isn't in the club yet."

"It's his uncle's ring. His uncle is a member. Or was. His uncle got put out the club for cheating on his taxes, but he told Witt how to get in, how much to save, and who to contact and everything."

"But Daddy was a teacher. He wasn't a businessman. What kind of business club could a teacher afford to be in?"

Beatrice snapped.

"Daddy was in a damn business club Bernadette, what the hell else you want me to explain?"

"And you believe that Witt just came up to you in a nightclub, and just happened to mention that he needs to get in a business club your father is already in?"

"Why? What you think?"

Bernadette had long stopped smoking, dropping the butt of the cigarette in the beer bottle. She sat with her chin in her hand, foot kicking up and down as she looked at her sister's shining, excited eyes. Her mind was clicking and putting everything she heard in order.

"I guess the question is, why did Witt come up to you in that bar? How did he just happen to pick you out, the very girl who has a father in the very club he wants to be in? No other woman there would have had a father in that club."

"You think he know Daddy already?"

"I think he knows something. And why would the club let Witt in if they had to put his uncle out for cheating?"

"Cause they don't know it was Witt's uncle. He won't tell them. His uncle don't have the money to help Witt out, but he told him how he could get some help. Daddy's club is supposed to have some real important and well-to-do black folks in it. Witt said he'd be set for life."

Bernadette drummed her short, clean, evenly clipped nails on the table and said, "It's all too coincidental. I don't know about this Witt. But it's funny you've been thinking about Juanita and what happened to her, because I got this letter in the mail and that's what it's about. Here, you read it and see what you think."

Bernadette pulled the paper from her pocket, unfolded it and handed it over. She lit another cigarette, thinking about Beatrice's story while her sister sat hunched over the table reading with her fingers following every word. How did people read like that?

After she finished, Beatrice laughed, and shoved the paper back at Bernadette.

"That's so stupid."

"Stupid? Do you think it could be true?"

"No. Nobody killed Nita."

"So, why send this around? Did you get a letter like this?"

"No."

"Who would play with something like this?"

"I don't know. It's stupid."

"What if it isn't? What if Witt didn't just happen to come up to you by accident? What if it is something else going on with our family? What if it is murder?"

"Who would be killing us then?"

"I don't know. Maybe it's someone who wants to get even with Daddy over a business deal. Or maybe it's Daddy, having us killed and collecting life insurance. Who knows about Daddy? I do know that two of us dying young, in separate accidents, is some really bad luck."

"You know, you make me so mad. Why would you say Daddy?"

"Because he's the one that's missing, Beatrice. And since he left, we did lose two siblings. Because I don't believe Witt just found you in a bar. And because it's possible that whatever broke Mama and Daddy up is not over. Something had to happen to them. If Daddy really cared about us, no matter what Mama made us promise, we would have heard from him."

Beatrice leaned over and nervously stacked some dirty dishes in a pile.

"What you plan to do 'bout that letter?"

"Find who wrote it. I'll bet our father knows who wrote this, and I only have until tomorrow evening to find him. I don't understand it, but he probably would."

Beatrice jumped up. "You can't do that! Who else would believe some letter like that but you? First of all, it just sounds crazy. That letter don't tell you nothing. What's all that about being different colors? We getting killed because of our skin colors? If they want to say something, tell me who the hell to watch out for. Tell me what to watch out for.

"Second, we ain't been killed in threes. Only two of us is dead, and it's been years since Nita died. This letter is a joke."

Both sisters turned to look at the hissing pot on the stove. Beatrice rushed over and turned off the burner. She took out the bottle, and let it sit in the sink to cool.

"How can I prove that?" Bernadette asked. "Now that you know

Daddy is in this club, I have to find him. I can't have this kind of mail coming to me in the military—whoever wrote this could keep me from getting the security clearance I need for my promotion. And nothing from the past is going to ruin this for me."

"Maybe it came from somebody over in California that you done pissed off to no end like you doing me today."

"The first thing I checked was the postmark. It came from Baltimore."

"Bernadette, you don't need to go talk to Daddy 'bout this and mess nothing up for me. After I get my business straight, and we start making money, you can ask him anything you want, but I don't want Daddy mad at me over some stupid letter you got."

"Mad at you?" Bernadette nearly choked. She smashed out her half-smoked cigarette in a plate of gravy, then said, "Beatrice, he doesn't know that you exist! When was the last time you saw or heard from him? What birthday did he acknowledge? What Christmas present did he ever send you?"

"Mama wouldn't let him! We had to promise Marietta and Mama--"

"Marietta? I don't remember promising my sister anything."

"Well, you did. We put it in that jewelry box the day of Nita's funeral."

"Why?"

"Why you think? We had to promise NOT to talk to Daddy again."

"But why would talking get us in trouble?"

Beatrice threw up her hands.

"Go ask Mama. She the one that put Daddy out. She the one that made up the rule we can't talk to him. Or ask Marietta. She the one know why Mama put Daddy out. Show them that letter and see what they say."

Bernadette's eyebrows went up.

"You think they would know about this letter?"

"Of course, but I don't know what they might tell you."

Bernadette moved the empty beer bottle in a circle on the table, considering. Then Beatrice moved close to her.

"I think Mama got a reason to keep Daddy away from us," she said in a low voice. "Mama put Daddy out, but it was something Mama did wrong. She didn't want Daddy to know."

Bernadette shook her head. "That was our mother. She did the best she could."

"I'm just saying…"

"Beatrice, Daddy was the one who did nothing for us. Mama may have been secretive, and made mistakes, but she's the one who stuck with us. She took care of six children, four girls and two boys, all by herself, without any word or money from Daddy—who just loved us so much, he couldn't stand to see us, talk to us, or be with us."

"I guess you think I'm stupid. Yeah, I dropped out of school, and I don't have your college degree or nothing, but I'm far from it. Daddy don't have nothing to do with that letter. I don't know who wrote that, but if you want to get on the right track, show it to Mama and hear what she got to say."

Bernadette stared at Bea in disbelief, then stood up, feeling like she was in a scene from the Twilight Zone."

"I can't stay here and listen to you tear Mama down. Not the only person who was ever there for me."

"You still want to believe in Mama, then go ahead. Try that letter out on her."

Bernadette reached down and snatched her pack of cigarettes off the table. "I can't believe you," she said and then stalked out the kitchen to get her bag, her sister close behind.

In the living room, both sisters faced each other. "I can't believe you're saying this about your own mother," Bernadette whispered. "Witt must have literally fucked your brains out for you to say that."

"What the hell did you just say, Bernadette?"

Bernadette threw her bag over her shoulder and posture straight, walked down the hall and out the house. When she got to the sidewalk, Beatrice was in the doorway, screaming.

"You want to say that to me again, Bernadette?"

Bernadette glanced at Beatrice one last time, shook her head, and walked away. She couldn't believe the names her sister screamed after her.

It wasn't until she neared North Avenue that she stopped. Damn, she thought. She should have gotten the name of Daddy's club so she could find Daddy tonight. She certainly couldn't go back and ask now.

Adjusting her bag, Bernadette stuck out her hand for a cab. She'd just have to find Daddy on her own, and get to the bottom of this.

# three

*Daddy was next*, Bernadette decided, as she sat in a Fells Point diner at the bottom of Broadway on Thames Street enjoying a large bowl of hot cream of wheat, toast and bacon. She had ordered a large cup of black coffee, and surreptitiously added a finger of vodka from a miniature she'd stashed in her duffel bag. If she had to talk to her father about this letter, she needed fortification.

She had thought of going straight to Mama's, but decided she might as well get some food and make some plans first. Too bad the only other family she had left in Baltimore was her mother. Her other sister, Marietta, now lived in New York and her brother, Corey, in North Carolina. She really didn't want to do this alone. One thing she knew, she was not leaving Baltimore until she could get her hands on the person who had the nerve to put this mess in a letter and send it to her.

She had torn out the listings of Windsors from the city telephone book in the library just up the street, and was working up the nerve to dial the first D. Windsor from the wrinkled white page. She sighed, quickly punched six of the numbers, and sat there. *What is your problem? He can't hurt you through the phone.*

She jabbed the final digit and took a deep breath.

"Hello?"

She was at a loss. It was a woman's voice.

"May I speak to Daniel Windsor please?"

"Who's calling?"

Bernadette opened her lips to say Bernadette Windsor, then thought quickly. "This is a courtesy call concerning the warranty on his vehicle which is about to expire."

"Oh, you definitely have the wrong number. First of all, his name is David Windsor, not Daniel. And second, he doesn't own a vehicle of any kind. Nor much of anything else."

"Oh, well, I'm sorry for wasting your time. Thank you," she said, and hung up. That was hard, and she wasn't going to do that again. No way. She was just going to have to go home to Mama and ask her where Daddy was. This was just ridiculous.

"Will there be anything else?" the waiter asked again, for the third time. Bernadette looked over when she noticed a nice little line forming, and all the tables full.

"No, I'll take the check now, please," she answered, and pulled out her wallet. This whole trip was neither in her budget, nor in her time schedule, and she knew there'd be hell to pay when she got back to California. She had to make this time here count!

Walking back up the street to the library, she looked up listings of business clubs in Maryland and stared fruitlessly, having no idea what kind of business her father was in. Maybe it made no sense to waste time this way; after all, she hated wasting time. Why didn't she just ask Mama what she knew?

*Because of the jewelry box.* The thought jolted Bernadette. After Beatrice brought it up, Bernadette absolutely did remember Marietta forcing her to write up some promises that they put in a jewelry box. A box that belonged to Juanita. What was it she promised? With a deep sigh, Bernadette gave up on searching for clubs and decided to go home to Mama. She would just have to help.

******

When Bernadette opened her eyes, it took a minute to see in the semi-darkness that she was back home in the familiar surroundings of her old teenage bedroom. The objects of that period surrounded her: the double bed, the blue Care Bear lamp, the white chenille spread she'd had for years. The black and red pom-poms from Western High School still hung across one side of the mirror, while the black, yellow and red pom-poms from the University of Maryland, College Park hung on the other side. And there were red and black stuffed Terps, Maryland's mascot, on every empty space.

The charcoal sketch of herself at age 18 on the Atlantic City board-walk stared back at her over the bed, the eyes direct and unrelenting. Not a lot had changed.

As she turned her head back, a whiff of baked macaroni and cheese hit her. It meant that Mama was home and cooking, and she was hungry again. She jumped up and pulled out her duffel bag to find the jeans and tee shirt she'd packed.

This was quite a switch. Usually she spent her free time back home with her sister Bea, swapping dating adventures. Beatrice was full of stories, discarding men left and right for this and that, she would have Bernadette riveted while she explained what had happened on her dates, detail by detail. She did no editing. Sex was her adventure, and when Beatrice talked about it, she made it seem like fun. The things she did to men would make Bernadette's toes curl. With Bernadette, sex was always basic and quick. Get on top, get it going, get it over. She had no adventures, and certainly no time for relationships. Normally she enjoyed the hell out of Bea and her stories. Now she'd be stuck home with Mama as her entertainment.

Smelling her vodka breath on every exhale, Bernadette rushed in the bathroom and brushed her teeth, then splashed a cup of Listerine around in her mouth until her breath smelled better. She couldn't do anything about the red veins in her eyes from her vodka-laced coffee. Oh well, she thought, running a comb through her hair and pausing. She stared, turning slightly, and saw a strong resemblance to Beatrice. When had they begun to look alike?

Beatrice was a goddess. Her skin was flawless, a tinge lighter than Bernadette's, her features strong and evenly proportioned. She was just perfect. Bernadette felt her own best feature was her lips, full and perfectly shaped. She liked her mouth. But men always seemed to like her eyes. Exotic, they told her, and commented on them before her hair or her long, shapely legs. Would Mama see any difference?

She took a deep breath then went off to find her.

Mama was sitting in the dining room still in her nursing uniform, where she'd eaten dinner. Chicken bones were on the plate centered on the mat before her as she leaned her broad forearms against the table and looked up from her reading of the Baltimore Sun. When Bernadette appeared around the corner, Mama leaned back and a huge grin split her face as she opened her arms.

"Mama!" Bernadette greeted, running over to her and holding tightly as she was crushed in a smothering embrace. For a few long moments they held each other tightly, then her mother stared in her face, wiping the hair back from Bernadette's forehead.

"You didn't tell me you was coming home today!"

"I didn't plan it," Bernadette said, staring back at her mother. She never changed. The same large chocolate brown square face with Beatrice's slightly slanted eyes stared back. Mama's long black silky hair was tied up in a tight ponytail and just graying at the temples. Otherwise, she looked the same, her body short, stout and strong.

"Well, what's going on with you, girl? You grown enough to leave and stay gone. You ain't married yet, are you?"

"You would be the first to know."

"Well, something is new. Pull up a chair and tell me. Do you want to eat?"

"Do I? I could smell your baked macaroni and cheese in my sleep. And you made chicken? For me?"

Mama nodded. "How long you been in town? I was surprised to see that room door closed, and when I opened it and saw you, I knew you needed a whole dinner."

"I just flew in this morning, and went straight to Bea's."

"Mmm. And you're not spending the night with your sister? What happened? I never see you your first night in town."

Bernadette twisted her lips. "Well…nothing happened. I just couldn't stand being around Beatrice another minute today."

Mama burst out laughing and just as she asked why, Bernadette held up one finger and walked through the swinging French doors where the food smells grabbed her. She reached up into the cabinet for a plate and started with a huge helping of macaroni and cheese, dipped up some string beans with strips of ham hock and slipped a baked chicken leg on the edge of the plate. In seconds she rejoined her mother in the dining room.

She mumbled a quick grace and dug in.

"Ma, I think something is going on over at Beatrice's. When was the last time you saw her?"

"I ain't seen her since Lord knows when. She don't come 'round here and I don't go there. Beatrice don't want to hear nothing I got to say to her."

"She said you knew she had another baby. Why didn't you tell me?"

"She didn't call you?" Mama leaned back and her chair sent up a loud creak in protest. "She called me from her hospital bed to tell me about that baby. Lord, was she happy. He must be bout 2 or 3 months now, and she ain't brought him around yet. I asked her to."

"What about that boyfriend? You met him?"

"No, I don't ever see those men your sister hook up with. What's wrong with this one?"

"There's something about him that's not right. The whole while I was there, Bea was acting strange, and kept looking over at him. He loves giving orders, and she seems to love following them."

"Beatrice?" Mama snorted. "Since when?"

"That's what I'm saying. When did she change, 'cause she has. Drastically. She is so big now…and so…obedient. Tame. Like somebody's trained pet or something."

"Beatrice ain't changed. She must call herself in love with this man and want to show him how she loves him, but I guarantee you, she ain't listening to nobody for long. A tiger can't change his stripes, baby."

Bernadette ate more of the macaroni while her mother continued to complain about how stubborn and selfish Bea had been since birth. "How many times did the doctor threaten to cut me open 'til she finally burst out? How much did she fight against me when I tried to get her back in school? When I tried to get her to come back home and do right? I don't believe Bea changed for that man. She ain't changed a bit."

When her mother paused, Bernadette looked over at her.

"Mama, do you think Beatrice is all right mentally? When you talked to her at the hospital, did she sound like she was all right to you?"

"She sounded fine. Like she was real happy about everything that day."

"Did you speak to Witt?"

"Who?"

"The boyfriend."

"No, I just talked to Bea. I guess he didn't have nothing to say to me." Her mother turned the newspaper page, her short fat arms shaking with her movements. Bernadette chewed slowly watching her mother, then she put her fork down on the plate.

"Mama, I hate to bring this up but I need to ask you something important."

She saw Mama shift in her seat, then look up from the newspaper, a squint in her eyes and a frown in her forehead.

"Did Nita really die from pneumonia?"

Mama paused a beat.

"Well, that's what the doctor said."

"But was it pneumonia?"

"Yes Bernadette. I don't have a M.D."

"And she got it from the flu? From lying around too long in bed?" This time Mama leaned back.

"You must know something, if you asking me that. I'm sure your sister done told you everything she know about it."

*What was she saying?* "Bea never told me anything, Mama. Was it pneumonia?"

"That's what they said. After she had that abortion and got sick from *that.*"

Abortion? Is that what Mama was so scared to say? Bernadette knew when her sisters were sneaking out with boys, but not what they were doing. And all that time she thought Juanita was sick with bad cramps, the red water bottle wrapped up in Mama's big white towels with the huge black-eyed susans all over them pushed up against her stomach. Nita's eyes as big as those flowers. It was a bad abortion.

"Did you tell Daddy about it? Did you tell him what was going on?" Her mother pushed back her chair and turned toward her.

"Why would you ask me something like that? Of course."

"Because I didn't know you ever told Daddy anything. I never could ask you anything about him, so I'm asking now. As far as I know, Daddy wasn't at the funeral."

"He didn't come to the funeral I had for Nita. He went at another time."

"You mean there was another funeral?"

Mama slapped her newspaper closed. "You know it was."

"I didn't." Bernadette wiped her lips. "So who came to the other funeral?"

Her mother stared. Hard.

"You know good and well who them daggone people are, and why in the world would you ask me about that now? All that stuff happened a long time ago."

"What daggone people, Mama? Why would anybody have two funerals?"

"Lord, Bernadette," Mama said, with one eyebrow cocked up in a warning. "If you don't know what I went through with your father at that time, you sure ain't going to find out tonight."

"Why?"

" I'm not going through all that on this night! I'm not up to it! That what you and Bea had to talk about today? No wonder she sent you back here with me."

"Well, we did talk about Nita. But she talked about Daddy mostly. Bea said she was planning to see Daddy again."

"Well." Mama paused. "Far as I know he's still in Baltimore."

"I know we promised you we would never see him."

Mama asked in a quiet tone, "Where is she seeing him?"

"At his club. Bea's boyfriend is joining Daddy's business club, and she's going to surprise him."

Mama looked at Bernadette. Her eyes had a bright glow.

"She's joining a club your father's in with a boyfriend? He must have some money."

"I couldn't see much." She remembered Witt's part of the basement and the books of literature then hesitated. "He was driving Bea's car, and they live on Broadway with next to no furniture, so I don't know. But he did speak very well, and he had a polished look. Even his teeth looked like he'd had them straightened. I have no doubt he's well educated. I just don't see him connecting with Bea."

"Why not? Your sister can hold her own; she ain't no dummy. She may be stubborn as hell, and don't always act like she got good sense, but she ain't dumb."

Bernadette let Mama's words buzz over her as she puzzled over Mama's remark about money. The letter upstairs mentioned sharing in 'the loot'. Did that mean Daddy had money?

"Ma, why was Daddy in a business club? Wasn't he just a teacher?"

"He was a professor of journalism at Howard, and the only club I knew about was a social club some professors were in. They did help people in certain careers to get started. So maybe now it is a business club. That was a while ago."

"And did the club give Daddy a ring?"

Mama looked blank. "Not that I know of. The only ring he wore, other than his wedding band was a ring his mother gave to him. It was a thick gold band, with…"

"Three diamond studs. The gold band was shaped to look like a rope."

"You remember that?"

Bernadette looked at her mother. "Where did his mother get that ring?"

"She had it made. And he loved to wear it."

Bernadette looked down at her plate. It was no coincidence that Witt

ran into Bea. Witt was wearing Daddy's ring. A shiver ran through her.
Mama saw it

"What's wrong? Was Toukie okay? You didn't mention seeing her."

"She's beautiful. It's just that boyfriend. Even Toukie acted like she was scared of him."

"I wouldn't worry about that. Beatrice ain't going to let no man hurt that baby. She loves her daughter, that much I can say."

But Bernadette couldn't agree. If they were in trouble, it was because of Witt. He was wearing Daddy's ring, it had to mean something. Maybe Mama would know if she saw the letter. Biting on her bottom lip, Bernadette pushed back from the table and faced Mama.

"Mama, I got a letter that I need to show you."

"From who? Look, if your father wrote you, I don't want to know. Like I said, all that stuff was a long time ago."

"The letter is not signed, and yes, it is about what happened a long time ago."

"You know what? I live my life for tomorrow, not for yesterday. I'm past yesterday and I got more important things to do. I thought you came here for something important. Do you know what tomorrow is?"

"October 12th?" Bernadette sat thinking. Certainly Mama didn't mean Columbus Day, did she?

"It's the day your sister died. I went to the cemetery today to put some flowers on her grave, after work. You ought to go."

"Ma, I'm not too good with the cemetery thing."

"You should go and pay your respect. I don't understand my children. They never go out there to remember their sister or brother. My parents died when I was sixteen in that car accident in South Carolina, and before I left, there wasn't a year I didn't go to spend some time with them. I do that now when I go back home."

"It's not a respect issue. I just don't like cemeteries."

"You don't have to stay there. I just thought you might visit, being that you are home, and it is the very day she died. It's good to remember her on her day."

"I DO remember her, Mama. Not just on that day."

'But you don't show her."

It's not like she can see us, Bernadette wanted to say, but Mama was serious. She knew what she wanted.

"What time do they open tomorrow?" Bernadette asked.

"'Bout seven, seven-thirty. They close the gates at five."

"Okay. I'm going to spend some time with Toukie, I didn't get the chance today dealing with her crazy mother, but after Toukie, I'll go there. I promise."

Mama folded her newspaper, turned down the small radio on Aretha Franklin singing *Chain of Fools*, then drained a huge glass of ice water.

"I got to be up early, so I'm going to bed." She grabbed her plate.

"But it's barely 7:30!" And I'm here, Bernadette added silently.

"I got to get my rest. They 'bout to do a shift change, and I never know what I'm going to get."

Mama walked into the kitchen, and Bernadette hollered after her, "Just leave your plate in the sink Mama. I'll get it with mine."

As she came out, Mama walked over to Bernadette and rubbed her head, then, as a second thought, she grabbed a handful and pulled her head back gently, forcing Bernadette's face up.

"You been in love yet, Bernadette?"

"Ow, Ma," she said in a small laugh, reaching up to loosen her mother's fingers. When she couldn't, she looked at her mother and wondered if it was a trick question. "Nooooo," she finally answered, trying again to pull away. " Not yet."

Her mother let go of her hair. "I know you haven't. Whenever you do, you can come back and ask me about your father. I'll be ready to tell you all about him."

Bernadette listened to her mother climb the steps, rubbing her scalp where her mother had pulled her hair. What the hell did that mean? She loved Daddy too much to talk about him? Or was it that she wouldn't understand until she let a man break the shit out of her? Why wouldn't Mama ever just say what the hell was going on?

Long after her mother had gone up and closed herself in her bedroom, Bernadette sat listening to the small radio play old R & B tunes she hadn't heard in years. When Al Green came on singing *Love and Happiness*, Bernadette kicked back in the chair and rolled her eyes up to the ceiling. Al Green had it all wrong. There was no such thing as both love and happiness, at least not in the same package with the same person. There was either love, and the soul connection that matched you to somebody and made you want to go through a lot of crap with them through thick and thin, or there was happiness, and that fleeting mind-blowing sensation that came with it and put you in another time and place. She made that distinction long ago and chose happiness every time, not expecting anything more than the pleasure of the moment.

Did Mama really not know the difference?

*four*

"Bernadette, what in the Sam Hill are you doing tearing up my house, with a cigarette in your hand?"

Bernadette looked up from the floor at her mother standing over her in the dining room in a wide blue terry cloth bathrobe, head tied up in a black scarf, eyes blazing.

"You're right." Bernadette said getting up. "I know how you feel about smoking." She banged through the French doors into the kitchen with her cigarette and put it out in the kitchen sink.

"What are you doing in my things?"

"I'm just looking for that jewelry box Juanita used to have," Bernadette called out from the kitchen. "I didn't want to wake you up, but I have a plane to catch at four today, and I have to finish up--"

"Finish up what?" Mama stepped in the kitchen, arms crossed.

Bernadette set her extinguished cigarette on the counter and turned to her mother. "I tried to tell you about this letter I got, but you didn't want to hear about it. Somebody thinks Nita did not die from pneumonia, and I just want to see."

Mama uncrossed her arms and walked over to the counter taking the cigarette and heading over to the trashcan where she dropped it.

"If your father want to start sending out letters to my children about me, and my children want to start checking up on me, then do what you want. I know you wouldn't be where you are now if it wasn't for me, neither would Marietta or Corey, so what else could I do?"

"This letter is not about you."

"Then why send it? Far as I'm concerned, my children are grown, and they can believe whatever they want to believe, but I'm through with it. The past is over." With that, Mama turned and banged through the doors.

Bernadette stood still, wishing she hadn't touched Mama's things. It seemed like it was a good idea last night and early this morning to look for the jewelry box full of promises, and find out what this letter was hinting about, but she didn't expect Mama to explode.

Damn, Bernadette thought as she went back to start replacing Mama's dishes and other keepsakes to her china closet and server.

By the time Mama came back down, Bernadette had almost completed putting the room back together. Mama glanced over at her but went straight into the kitchen where minutes later, the smell of sausage and eggs filled the rooms.

"Help yourself, I gotta get out of here," Mama said coming into the dining room. "You said you have to leave at four?"

"Yes ma'am, but I'll be back, Mama. I don't think I want to stay gone for so long anymore."

Mama hugged Bernadette, who squeezed back tightly. "Now, you taking a cab to Andrews Air Force Base or what? I don't get off until 4:30."

"I called my friend Dina last night and she said she could take me out there, so I'll be fine. I have to go to her house- her mom wants to see me- but I'll make it."

"All right Bernadette," her mother said, and she went to the hall closet and pulled out her coat. After Bernadette gave her one last kiss, she watched her mother slam out.

In the kitchen, Bernadette was surprised to discover Mama had fixed two omelets along with the link sausages, and warmed some small biscuits on a saucer. Coffee dripped in the coffee maker, and she grinned. "God bless you, Mama," she said as she fixed her plate and sat down to eat. "But you still didn't have to throw out my last cigarette."

Bernadette glanced at the clock, wondering what time Toukie would be leaving for school. At that moment the telephone rang. Reaching back to pick up the lime green trim phone on the wall, she swallowed the half-chewed biscuit.

"Hello?"

"Hello, Berni?"

"Nancy?" Bernadette's voice rose up an octave. Nancy was her roommate of two years in San Diego, and also an officer in the Corps working in social work.

"Don't get upset," Nancy said, Bernadette's mind already spinning, picturing Nancy curled up in bed under her shelves of green leafy plants hanging on every available space in her bedroom. It was only 4:30 on the west coast.

"Why, what's wrong?"

"Colonel Chisholm just called here for you, at this time of the morning, telling me you promised to get him some special report by 1500 hours today, and he hadn't heard anything from you. I should mention he called like, four times last night for you, wanting to know where you were, but I didn't tell him because you hadn't, so I thought you didn't want him to know."

"Oh shit! I did forget that report." Bernadette stood up, twisting the telephone cord in her hand as she started to pace. She could not afford to blow this. It was her job to program the reports that the senior officers wanted, so that they could send the information to the Pentagon to spit out the stats that were needed to report the war. Things were getting really tricky when it came to getting the budget the military needed, and a special task force, which included her, had been put together to do this right. She wasn't wasting her six years in the Marines to come out stuck as a lieutenant because she screwed up a report.

"I know who could run the reports I already set up—Nancy, if he calls again, give him Pvt. Winnie Sugar's number. Look in the address book on my dresser. She's excellent, and she can get it to him on time."

"Berni, he called here at four in the morning. I'm telling you, he is tracking where you are, not that report. I think he has a crush, and you can call it fatherly, but I know better."

"Trust me, you make a much better friend than my mother. I can handle the Colonel, okay?"

She heard Nancy sigh into the phone. "Okay, but remember, I warned you first. And also, will you be in some time tonight? Remember I'm giving Lonnie a birthday party tomorrow at the club, and there was a special request for your company."

"For me?"

"Remember that guy you were locking eyes with at the club last week? Reggie Taylor? He comes to La Jolla to see Lonnie's band quite a bit, and he's been asking some very interesting questions about you."

Bernadette felt her heartbeat quicken. She had allowed herself a night out, wanting to meet this dude Lonnie her roommate was raving about every breath she took, and also wanting to unwind from weeks of work on the Colonel's new program she was helping to set up. She hadn't expected to find anything, because it was a fact known to Bernadette that you could never find a man if you went looking. Men found her all the time, but it was always the same old song: a few well placed compliments, a movie and dinner if she were lucky, then came the moves for her to pay up. The company was usually shit. Men these days seemed to expect the world, and she didn't have time for it. As a Marine, civilian life was a luxury she couldn't afford. The Corps was her life and she knew she couldn't have both. Still, there was something about this Reggie...

She wasn't looking for him. Lonnie's band had just completed a set and when the lights went up, Bernadette was just thinking what a great keyboard player Lonnie really was when she let her eyes roam the room. They landed on a long, lanky form that rose from a front table, clad in a dark brown leather jacket, jeans and a green bandana. It was the way he moved, his sexy walk up to the stage caught her attention, and she didn't realize she was staring. Reggie slapped hands with another band member, and when his face turned, Bernadette saw the most beautiful smile she'd ever seen on a man. He was the most delectable thing she'd encountered in California in the four years she'd been there.

By then, a lot of the crowd had thinned out to the halls where the restrooms were, and his eyes had met hers. It was the biggest zing she ever felt that went through her, and when he continued his lingering stare, she sent him a silent message. "Yes, I feel it, and I know you feel it too." It was another second later that the vocalist, a tall, rail-thin girl jumped down in front of Reggie and broke the connection.

"He asked about me, huh?" Bernadette asked, and she could hear Nancy smile through the phone.

"I wouldn't lie about that. He even noticed your dimple, which is how he described you to Lonnie. I told him you'd be there."

"Well, we'll see," Bernadette responded airily.

"I'm sure we will," Nancy said. "By the way, any progress on that crazy poem?"

"Not much. I'll have a report for you by tomorrow."

Nancy laughed. "Tell your Mom and everyone I said hello, and call if you need me."

****** 

It took Bernadette a good hour to clean up the mess she'd made in her own bedroom, then she took a long, hot shower thinking crazy thoughts about Reggie, and his sexy smile. What would be different about him? He was probably from the same old tired mold.

When she came out the steamy bathroom, she paused. She had

looked everywhere in Mama's house for Juanita's jewelry box except in Mama's room. What if it was in there? Besides, Mama had made a very curious statement in the kitchen that kept playing in Bernadette's mind: 'Your father is sending letters about me...but the past is the past.' Yes, but what did you do in the past? was Bernadette's question.

Next thing she knew, she was in Mama's room searching among dozens of knick-knacks, bottles of medicines, perfumes, lotions and sprays. Mama had too much stuff in too tight a space—everything was packed in there: television, stereo, movies, and albums. Everything but that jewelry box.

Again, Bernadette was frustrated. Something had to be in here. She turned and then noticed a file cabinet with a tablecloth draped over it by the window. A large philodendron sat on top. She moved the plant and the cloth, and to her surprise, found a blue trunk.

In seconds, Bernadette pulled the trunk down flat and opened it only to find stacks of school papers. Picking up a handful, she noticed they were graded tests and reports by all her sisters and brothers. Childhood mementos, but no jewelry box. Just as she started to repack, she noticed something under the papers. Tugging, she pulled up a small quilt, a gold and maroon plaid, with long gold fringes. And in the center, there was a picture of her dead sister, smiling coyly in her Dunbar High cheerleading uniform. Bernadette flipped it over, and there was a tag with a signature: A Charlene Coleman Creation. That's when she noticed the stacks of condolence cards, and picked up some. All were poems about losing a daughter. Just as Bernadette gave up, she noticed another quilt. When she pulled this one up, she saw it was an old Tinker bell pajama set that Juanita used to wear. That's when she turned it over and noticed the big, dark patches of hard, dried blood, and nearly screamed.

Blood? On Nita's pajamas? Yet she died from pneumonia? Stuck to the material by a piece of duct tape was a large yellow envelope, which Bernadette turned over. Nothing was written on it, but the seal had been taped shut. Bernadette shook it, turned it over, and felt through it. There were small books inside, like the size of those little pocket calendars. Or...she felt again, the size of passports. She laid the envelope on the floor and spread the books out with her fingers to count them. There were six, one for each of them. Were they indeed passports?

\*\*\*\*\*\*

It was almost nine o' clock by the time Bernadette got out of the cab in front of Toukie's school, and hurried inside, duffel bag on her shoulder, seeking the office. She knew it would be a bad morning if she tried to pump Beatrice about Witt, so she got Bea's permission to see Toukie before she left.

Bea had called in permission for Bernadette to see Toukie and in the office, the pale and very pimpled secretary was expecting her.

"Ms. Alston, please send Anissa Dent to the principal's office. Anissa Dent to the principal's office," she called into the PA system, and motioned for Bernadette to wait.

Bernadette walked over to the bench where she had been motioned, but paused to peruse the teacher's boards. Her mind was still on the contents of the trunk. She had decided to keep the bloody pj's and packed them in her bag, but still she wondered about the passports. What were they for? Did Mama know they were in danger? Why hadn't she used them? If only she didn't have to fly back so soon. Every piece that she needed to understand was in this city, and she had no time to put it all together so fast.

She wanted Toukie to know she hadn't forgotten her, and she would be back. She wanted her to know most of all that she would never let Witt hurt her. Ever.

Mama wouldn't miss those bloody pj's, Bernadette hoped, and maybe she could find out what all that blood was from. Bernadette grabbed the zipper, opened her bag, and found a pen, and started jotting down her questions. She would find out what happened to her sister.

After making notes for at least 10 minutes, she glanced at her watch. Where was Toukie? Was she even in school today? She got up to go back to the secretary, but at that moment, the woman said, "Oh, there you are, your aunt's been waiting here for you."

Bernadette turned and stared at the slender young black woman with shoulder length black hair who stood looking at her, then the young girl beside her who was smiling widely. Bernadette blinked.

Was that Toukie? Bernadette's eyes zoomed to her head. Her hair! What had happened to it? It was cut so close to her head in such an uneven fashion that when she turned, Bernadette could see her scalp showing through, in two separate bald spots. Almost like two eyes in the back of her head.

She grabbed her niece and held her tightly in a hug.

"Dang, they let you come here to see me?" Toukie said with a little laugh.

"I got special permission," Bernadette said and hugged her again thinking, Oh God. What was happening to Toukie? She pulled Toukie over to the bench to talk, noticing the skin tight black jeans she wore that hugged her behind way too much, and the dirty, runover white tennis shoes. She looked like a street urchin.

The woman with Toukie followed them to the bench, then introduced herself as Toukie's teacher, Ms. Alston.

"I wondered if I could just talk to you a moment," the teacher said, "I've never gotten a response from the letters I sent to Anissa's mother."

Bernadette nodded, reminding herself that Toukie's given name was actually Anissa, and allowed the teacher to usher them to a back conference room. With the door closed, Ms. Alston engaged Bernadette in a litany of problems she was having with Toukie's attendance, and she felt that if someone could address this early, it would give the girl a chance. There were some other problems, which Ms. Alston said could indicate some 'domestic issues', "like how tired she always is. It's almost like she has an evening job," the teacher said with a frown. "And then there are the lies. I don't know if Toukie would know the truth if it hit her. Yet, she is one of the brightest students in my class."

When Ms. Alston left them, Bernadette looked at her niece wondering where to start. She stared at the ill-fitting clothes, and opened her duffel bag, pulling out her wallet and revealing a new pack of cigarettes she'd bought.

"Oooooo cigarettes. Can I have one? I won't smoke it until I get out of school."

"No, you can't. And I hope you're joking."

"I'm not."

"Look Toukie, I'm going to give you $40," she said handing Toukie two twenties. "Buy yourself some new jeans and a CD or something. You deserve something."

"Dang! Thank you Aunt Bern," Toukie said with a wide, pretty smile."

"And this is just the beginning. We have a lot of catching up to do. First of all, what is this about being tired in class?"

"Ms. Alston is boring. Everybody is tired in her class."

"Toukie, this is not a game. Why are you late everyday, and absent so often?"

"That's not my fault. I have to do my chores in the morning and the night, and Witt won't let me go to school until I finish."

"What chores?"

Toukie sighed, reached in the pocket of her tight jeans and pulled out a piece of notebook paper.

"Here. I had to write them down."

Bernadette stared at the childish script, read quickly, then frowned.

"I don't think you meant to give me this note." She handed it back to Toukie, who looked at it and covered her mouth laughing out loud. "Sorry. That was from my boyfriend Raymond. He want me to 'do it', and I don't even know if I like him like that yet."

Bernadette's mouth fell open. "Do what?"

"You know what, Aunt Bern. Dang, don't be acting like you don't think I know. I'm almost 10."

Bernadette leaned back. "Surely you're not having sex?"

"Not the real sex. You know, the other kind. I mean, the ain't-no-way-I-can-get pregnant kind." Before Bernadette could say another word, Toukie snatched back the note and gave her the right paper, which Bernadette opened slowly eyeing her niece, then read:

*Morning - make my bed, put up my books and clothes, wash up, put baby's clothes in washer, change and clean baby, clean dishes, pick up market note and money.*

*Evening- do homework, help Mom fix dinner, watch baby, do dishes, clean kitchen floor, wash baby clothes, iron my jeans and wash my socks, read my books.*

"Who gave you all these chores?"

"Witt. Then, I got to look in the newspaper and see what kind of stuff to do on the weekend. Witt takes everybody to stuff, like the railroad museum, Port Discovery, fire museum, art gallery. And then, he makes me read a book a month…a biography, and I have to tell my mother what I read. He said I have to know this stuff so I can tell the baby when he gets bigger."

"Witt assigns all this work?"

"Uh huh."

"And what about your homework. Does he let you do both?"

"I gotta do my reading from Witt first. I can get into trouble if I don't. But, he don't give me punishment if I don't do my school homework."

"What kind of punishment?"

"Just...no telephone. No music. No dinner. No television. I can't do nothing and I can't talk to my mother and she can't talk to me. And sometimes, no school."

"Mmhmm. And what does your mother say about this?"

"She tells me to listen to Witt. He's my father."

"Toukie, I have to ask you, has Witt ever hit you? Or your mother?"

"No."

"Ever touched you? I mean touched you. Like, in your private areas."

"NO!" Toukie laughed. "No way."

"Then why are you afraid of him? I know you are. You just clam up around him."

"I don't like to get punished, so I don't say stuff that might get me punished. And I don't like him fussing in my face, 'cause he gets real close and talks and spits when he talks."

Bernadette could feel her blood boiling. "Yeah, I don't like that either. But you know what Toukie, you still should not have to live in fear. You still should not have most of those chores on that sheet. We have to make you happy again."

"I am."

"Well, maybe, since I see your mother lets you do whatever you want with your hair and clothes. That's a pretty radical hair cut you have there."

"Oh this? I didn't cut this. My mother said it was something that happens sometimes, 'cause it happened to her when her sister died. My hair just fell out."

"Fell out?"

"Yeah. Most of the bald spots are gone now."

This time when Bernadette hugged Toukie, she found herself fighting back tears. Something was terribly wrong. How could this happen? Was she being poisoned? Didn't arsenic work this way? Bernadette gave Toukie her phone number at work as well as home, and promised her it was going to be okay. She would come back and make sure of it.

******

All Bernadette wanted was to go back and confront Beatrice, but she promised to stop at the cemetery and put down some flowers, then she had a plane to catch.

She made a quick stop at the cemetery office where she bought a wreath of white carnations and picked up a map which directed her to the gravesites of the children of Daniel and Ruth Ann Windsor. Then she went to fulfill her promise to Mama.

When she found Juanita's grave, it was all cleaned off and neat with Mama's fresh roses from yesterday. Bernadette moved the flowers to the side and read the metal plate on which was printed: Juanita R. Windsor, November 18, 1969 – October 12, 1985.

A cold chill washed over Bernadette. Even though the city bustle surrounded the walls of the cemetery, inside everything was tranquil. The sounds did not filter completely. Here, time was a minute, or a million years. Juanita was a part of infinity.

Bernadette covered her face with both hands and wondered what her father had to do with all this. Or, was it her mother? If only her father had been able to stick around, none of this would have happened to them. Juanita would not be here. Fathers guarded their daughters. That's what they did. They kept their families safe, and when he left, they were unsafe.

Maybe someone did mean for all of them to die. And she was the one who had to find out for sure, because the letter came to her. Did someone think just because she now knew an M-16 inside and out that she could avenge this?

She turned slightly when a breeze caressed her cheek. She thought she would feel scared or depressed sitting here, yet she didn't. She felt a calmness she never felt, a complete peace and serenity. Mama was right. She did feel a connection, like Nita knew she was here and was happy to have her. She closed her eyes and let the feeling absorb her. When she opened them, she looked down at the map in her lap. There were two other red X's on the map. Bernadette frowned. There was the one that directed her to Nita's grave, which is where she was. Then she got up and made her way over several feet, in the same quadrant. A second X placed her in front of Daniel's. She stared down, where she could see Mama had been and cleaned off his name, leaving him several white roses. She tried, but she could not remember enough about Dan to feel him personally.

Then she looked at the map for the third X.

This one was a good walk from the other two graves, across the cemetery grounds. So, she followed the map and walked it. She had her duffel bag on her shoulder, and she felt the distance as she kept her eyes focused on the grids and kept her direction. She stopped in a different part of the cemetery, where there were mausoleums, and crypts. The outside burials had huge, fancy tombstones. Bernadette read a few, frowned, then looked down at the spot which the X indicated. She found herself staring at a tombstone that read 'Michael Robert Windsor, blessed child of Daniel James and Ruth Ann Windsor, February 17, 1960 born and died.

They had another brother? Whoa…she stared in surprise. There was a child that no one mentioned to them, or spoke of, ever? Could this be true?

Suddenly she understood. The letter was right. There were 3 of them already dead. It was not a joke. Three were dead, and three more were to go? There were other stones with the name Windsor on them. Unknown names and very old dates. Tremendous, marble slabs with long Bible verses. Who were these Windsors?

They had a brother they knew nothing about! Her heart pounded in her chest. This was big, and she would have to find out why Mama never told them. But she couldn't now. She had to get back home, or be charged AWOL.

She rushed down the hills, over the winding paths until she was out the gates. The next cab ride she took was to her friend Dina's, where she sat, shaking all the way.

Dina and her mother Mrs. Monterey greeted Bernadette like she was a POW, with big hugs and kisses as they settled her in the living room. She had to go through what she'd been doing the past four years in 15 minutes. She was still feeling that out of body sensation that had started at the cemetery with her discovery, and it was hard to focus on them.

"Who is he?"

Bernadette jerked her eyes up to Mrs. Monterey, who was staring at her closely. "Cause you are just positively glowing," she added, and Dina laughed. Bernadette touched her cheek, knowing the flush she must be seeing was due to the excitement of her find. But Mrs. Monterey was waiting to hear about a man.

"Nobody. I'm not ready for that yet," Bernadette laughed.

Mrs. Monterey had a lop-sided grin on her gaunt face as she leaned forward to listen, her little short, red wig perched on her head as she sat fully made-up. She'd always worn wigs, different colors, always stylishly maintained. It was the same look she'd had for as long as Bernadette had been Dina's friend after she'd gotten a few drinks in her. Bernadette could see things hadn't changed. Dina's Mom had always been a drinker, and she was always giving Dina's friends something to drink, it hardly mattered their age. She said she hated drinking alone, but as Bernadette could see, it never stopped her.

This afternoon was no different. Bernadette was forced to accept a glass of Bristol Cream, and a vegetable cracker with something squeezed on top from a tray of pickings set out atop the baby grand piano.

"It's too big a field to choose from. I wish you could come out to help me."

Dina's Mom guffawed. "I know that's right. You don't rush through anything, because you probably got all the time in the world to get the best one."

"Well," Dina broke in, not to be outdone. "You didn't ask, and Mama didn't mention, but," she held up her hand.

"Dina?" Bernadette looked at the manicured hand and with a lot of effort located the tiny diamond on her good friend's ring finger. "When did this happen?"

Dina launched into a winding story as Bernadette looked at the clock thinking of her flight home. She heard snippets about a boyfriend named George, majoring in international business, and Dina finishing her Master's degree in telecommunications at Morgan.

When Dina wound down, Bernadette checked the clock again and told her they would have to eat on the run. "I was just asking my Mom," Dina said, "if we should pack up this food to take." She jumped up. "It is a long ride out there. I'll be right back."

When she got up, Mrs. Monterey moved closer.

"If I had it to do over, I would do everything different. Date everybody I could until I found the right one. You will, Bernadette, and I'm proud of you." Bernadette didn't know what to say when Mrs. Monterey talked about men like that. She always did, as though she wasn't married, with Mr. Monterey right under the same roof, coming and going in his own understated way. Anyone could see he wasn't what Mrs. Monterey must have wanted. Or felt she deserved. He had taken good care of her, but she had little to do with him. Ms. Monterey had been a housewife, baking all day, home with her children, except for the two to three days a week when she'd done some part-time work teaching piano lessons to some very well-to-do clients.

Mr. Monterey, it seemed, was the black sheep of a family of achievers, and Mrs. Monterey had picked the wrong one. Bernadette remembered Dina bragging about her grandfather and uncles being bankers. Her father never seemed to break through. He did some work in banking, but that didn't work out for him. He ended up working in some antique shop his father owned, restoring and selling something Dina called Negro paraphernalia, and must have done fairly well at that. They were still living here.

Mrs. Monterey reached up and refilled Bernadette's glass, and asked about the rest of her family. Mrs. Monterey always did. She was the mother Bernadette sometimes had to go to when her own was too busy or to tired to give anything of herself. And Mrs. Monterey was there to listen. She always had a drink with her, but she calmly listened and provided guidance.

Abruptly Mrs. Monterey downed her glass, leaned back in her chair, and surprised Bernadette.

"Your father is writing again you know? He did a long article in *Black Enterprise* about the Affirmative Action debate, and it was good. Like the writing he used to do for *The Crisis* magazine. I couldn't believe it."

Bernadette's attention, which had been wandering around the spacious living room and staring at the piano she never remembered seeing anyone play, suddenly focused and her eyes widened.

"Your mother didn't tell you about it?" Mrs. Monterey shook her head. "I don't understand it. Your mother had a good man, though not perfect, and she put him out to raise six children on her own. I couldn't do it. And she did a good job. But ...you can't keep a father away from his children. No matter what he does, you can't do that."

Bernadette tried to work the look of surprise off her face. If Daddy was good, why did she do it?

"Well, as you said, Mama did very well without him."

"Of course, but I always felt that you should show children what it means to forgive. You don't have to forget, if you think you shouldn't, but children today have got to know that it's about forgiving. It's about moving on"—

Dina swept into the room, her eyes shooting darts at her mother.

"Bernadette, do you want me to wrap up some of these little apple turnovers Mama had sent in? They are the best, but I didn't know about diet, or whether you liked pastries."

"Please. I love apple turnovers. Thank you, Mrs. Monterey."

"That's nothing. I miss you, Bernadette. I miss you being around Dina. Now it's just that George, and some other girl I wish she would leave somewhere."

"Mother? Do you mind? Why don't you put that sherry away and go lay down?"

"Because I'm talking to Bernadette, and you're interrupting. Don't be so rude."

Dina left again, and Mrs. Monterey rolled her eyes and turned to Bernadette.

"You have a strong personality, you know. Stubborn and willful like your mother, and determined and passionate like your father. I think you are more your father's girl than your mother's. And that's not a bad thing."

Bernadette frowned. Mrs. Monterey knew them well at one time, back when Mama and Daddy moved on this street after the birth of Marietta, when her brother Danny was just a year old. But when Mama and Daddy broke up and Mama gave up the house, that was it. After 14 years, Mama moved on, but Bernadette stayed friends. To her, Mrs. Monterey was a hoot. She was funny, dressing up in costumes in the mid-afternoon, letting them dress up and do skits as little girls. She had never really changed.

This time when Dina came in, she didn't hold her tongue.

"Mom, what are you doing? Did Bernadette bring up her father to you? What makes you think she wants to hear you talk about him?"

"What? I have to pretend she doesn't have a father? Like her mother wants to do?"

"Mom, would you please? Bernadette, come help me in the kitchen. I don't know what you want to drink with these sandwiches and I can use two more hands."

Bernadette's interest was sparked, and she looked expectantly at Mrs. Monterey who said no more. She glanced over at Dina, who looked like she could fry a couple eggs on her head if someone cracked them over her right now.

"Your mother knows something I don't. I take it as a compliment, to say what she did. And thank you, Mrs. Monterey, for the drinks."

She got up and followed Dina into the kitchen, picking out a lemon-lime soda to add to the bag of goodies.

"She's a drunk. She is my mother and I love her, but she talks out of her head. That's why I don't come here that much any more. I stay with George out Federal Hill, and when I stop by, I bring a friend so I don't have to listen to her. Mama hates them, because they keep me from listening to her. I can't take her."

"You used to. We both used to talk to her. She does her best, Dina. She always did."

"Well, now, all she does is drink and ramble. It makes no sense."

"She's a mother. They never do." Bernadette said, and they both laughed.

"She's bitching about what your mother did, but look what I have? She doesn't treat my father any better, and he enjoys it. He wouldn't know how to breathe unless my mother was tearing him down. I don't understand them, but guess what? I don't have to."

"It's okay. They're our parents. We're not supposed to understand until we step into their shoes. Don't even try."

Mrs. Monterey joined them in the kitchen, her goblet refilled. "All ready?"

Bernadette went over and hugged her tightly. The woman almost fell, leaning into her. She was well on her way to being totally sloshed.

"Thank you," she whispered to Mrs. Monterey, and when she let go, she noticed tears in the woman's eyes. Mrs. Monterey may not be perfect, but she always tried.

"It's just the sherry," Dina said in exasperation. "Mom, we have to go. Why don't you go back upstairs and lay down?"

"It's good to see you Mrs. Monterey. Thanks again for the drinks," Bernadette said.

When Bernadette slammed the door of Dina's Dodge Stratus, she stared down the block at the old clapboard house where her family once lived. She thought of the three of them already dead, and felt an electric current humming through her body. She wasn't going to be able to stop the humming until she found out what had happened to them and what was happening to Toukie.

It wasn't until she was almost at the airport that she realized, she never did find the promise box.

# Marietta

*five*

Marietta fingered the letter from her baby sister Bernadette in her left hand, staring through empty eyes at the swatch of pale yellow paint she held in her right hand. She felt as though a train had just hit her. For a minute, it was as though Bernadette was in this room, demanding answers. This letter could only mean one thing. Trouble.

How much did Bernadette know?

Marietta rose slowly from the Bellini swivel chair and walked over to the picture window that faced the south side of her New York apartment in the Paramount Towers. The swirl of people bustling below caught her attention momentarily before her thoughts were jerked back.

This just could not happen at this time. Who wrote the poem?

She pushed aside the drape and leaned her forehead into the window. The glass was cool against her skin. Funny how things had worked out for so many years. She was now 36, and how quiet and normal life had been since she hadn't seen or heard from any of those people in her family. She thought she had finally closed the door on all the pain of the past. And she had, after they had made that promise box.

Marietta smiled. Leave it to Bernadette to name the box. Whatever it was, it had worked. It held them up, and moved them past that awful afternoon of Juanita's funeral.

Just look, Bernadette was already a first lieutenant, gunning for captain. Beatrice was in an actual committed relationship. She now had a steady man, a son and a daughter. She was going into some kind of business venture—hell, that was pretty good for somebody who had dropped out of high school, strung out on any drug she could get.

The promises had done what they were supposed to. Now it was time for them all to move on and let the past be. What was it that Beatrice hoped to prove telling Bernadette stories about her and Daddy? That she, Marietta, knew why Daddy had to move? What was it Beatrice thought she knew? Her facts were absolutely wrong, but her feeling was absolutely right. She must have heard something, or found something. This just could not happen now, of all times.

Marietta repositioned the long white drapes framing her bedroom window, then turned her lithe, well-toned body away from outside distractions. She pulled off her khaki blouse and skirt, compliments of the U.S. Navy. Black fingerprint smudges stained the blouse front, courtesy of her job as an editorial assistant where she worked in public affairs as a warrant officer in the Foley Building, in South Manhattan. She was lucky enough to be have been appointed from the enlisted ranks as a specialist in the printing field, which she later parlayed into various editorial functions. Not as lucky as Bernadette who found herself a program, that NROTC, to pay for her entire college education so she could become a fully commissioned officer. But that was Bernadette.

Down to her white mesh Warner's bra and taupe pantyhose, Marietta walked over to her favorite seat, her chocolate leather armchair with matching ottoman and sat, propping her feet up.

What to do, what to do? Bernadette was not about to mess up for this family, not after all this time, and all Mama had done. The best thing to do was let Bernadette think she was solving that poem, but manipulate what she was solving. Make sure she did not go after Daddy. Call Beatrice and ask about the boyfriend, like Bernadette advised. Find out about Daddy's club, and show Bernadette it was legitimate. Witt had every reason to try to be in it if he thought it would help. Then she would tell Bernadette the bottom line: Daddy was gone, thank the good Lord for that, and leave him be.

But there was still that poem. Marietta bent forward, wrapping her arms around her waist, until her chin touched her chest. Painful cramps gripped her gut. Obviously, somebody knew something and wanted to start some trouble for Mama. If anybody had proof that Danny or Juanita had been killed, they would have taken their evidence to the police. So, someone just wanted to be hurtful.

Kicking up just a little bit of dust could start a panic, and Bernadette was reacting just like they wanted, worrying over nothing. She had to be calmed down, or this could get very ugly.

Beatrice was the key to keeping Bernadette calm. Marietta knew that Bernadette looked out for Beatrice, for some strange reason. A cooperative Beatrice could make Bernadette back off, but Beatrice was anything but. She had to do something about this, but it was not going to be easy.

"Mari!"

Marietta jerked her head up as Del, her boyfriend, walked in the bedroom and looked at her.

She smiled cautiously when their eyes met, marveling in that way of new couples when just the sight of each other still sparked amazement. He had a classically handsome face, evenly proportioned features, with the exception of a long narrow nose. He was cutest when he would screw it up, as he habitually did in worry or confusion, and run his hands through his short cut brunette hair with prominent natural blonde streaks. If she teased him about the faces he made when he was thinking, his ears would get red, and she would stop.

"We gotta move if you still want to pick out that paint tonight."

"All right," she answered, more subdued than she meant.

"What's wrong?"

"Nothing. I was just going through the mail and reading it."

"Yeah, I noticed you picked up the whole stack and brought it back here. Didn't I get anything?"

Marietta paused. "Well, I guess." She picked up the stack and gave it to Del, putting Bernadette's letter on her lap. "I was just reading a letter from my baby sister."

"Now, which one is she?"

"Bernadette."

"Something wrong?"

"Well, she said she went to Baltimore last weekend and she didn't like what she found going on at my other sister's house. You have to understand Bernadette, she wants to guard everything and everybody so that nothing ever changes, and that's impossible. Things change. My sister in Baltimore is living with someone new, and Bernadette isn't happy with him. She's worried about how he treats my niece."

"How do you know she doesn't have a right to?"

"I don't. I know Bernadette, and right or not, she's going to raise hell until she knows everything about this man, from head to toe."

"What's wrong with that? If it makes her niece safe."

"Nothing, if she was going to take care of it herself. She's stationed in San Diego, so she writes me to take care of it."

"Well, when was the last time you saw your sister in Baltimore?"

"It's been a while."

"I know. You don't write or call anybody but your mother, do you? Maybe you should go home and see what's going on." Del squeezed in beside her on the chair, his legs nudging hers over.

Marietta sighed. Then laughed.

"That's what Bernadette says. I should go home and see Beatrice. I should check on things. Be a sister."

"You don't believe her?"

"It's just, what if this man is crazy? He might be a raving lunatic, to use Bernadette's words, and if Bea loves him, what can I do about it?"

"If it's a problem, you can do plenty."

"But how will I know? He won't do anything in front of me."

"The niece may tell you, if you ask her. Or your sister may tell you. You won't know unless you go."

"Okay. I see that I'm outnumbered here. I have no choice but to go. My sister pretty much dumped it in my lap."

Del paused, then Marietta felt his arm around her shoulder. "You don't like your sisters very much, do you?"

She paused a beat, then turned to look at him. "How can you think I wouldn't like my sisters?"

"Then they don't like you. Is that it? They never call or write. Unless, I guess, there's a problem that they don't want to handle. Then they dump it on you."

Marietta balled her fists in her lap tightly.

"We're just very different, all of us. We don't mix. Our lives are all over the place, so I just let things be. When all is quiet in my family, it means all is well."

"Don't you miss them?"

"I have. But over the years, if there ever was a problem, I was there. I think now, with the youngest being 26, I should be able to relax. I shouldn't have to be the one to hold them together."

"Is that what you think you do?"

"It's what I know I did. I shouldn't have to check up on anybody now."

"But when has that ever been the case in anybody's family? My mother is still flying back and forth to Arizona for my sister whenever she needs a shoulder to cry on."

"Okay! I'm going home, even though I don't know how I'm going to fix what I'm supposed to fix. I'll keep in mind that everybody's fami-

ly needs somebody like me, so it's no big deal. " Her voice quivered on
the last word.

"What's the matter with you? You want me to go with you?"

"No," she said quickly, and saw his expression change. Immediately
she leaned close to him and pressed his lips with hers. "I can handle this."

"You sure?"

"If I can't, I can call on you, can't I?"

He pulled her face to his and opened her mouth with his tongue,
which she welcomed, leaning her body into his. Her heart pounded as
she waited to see if she had convinced him she would be okay. Del was-
n't easy to put off, if he felt something wasn't right, and her voice had
betrayed her. She had to do this right.

She felt his hand move down, over her butt, then back up and across
her breasts. She knew she had put him off, at least for now. Her mind
was already on her calendar, booking the next train to Baltimore.

******

"Mom!"

Marietta yelled out to her mother the minute she walked into the
house the next evening at five. Mama's big white Buick LeSabre was in
the driveway, so she knew she was home.

"Mom!" she yelled again from the doorway.

A door upstairs opened, and her mother called back, "Marietta?"

"It's me. Can I come on up?"

Marietta ran up the steps and reached for her mother, who stepped
out of the bathroom in her blue terry robe, her mouth open in surprise.
Tears sprang to Marietta's eyes when she grabbed her mother in a hug
and felt her mother squeeze her back.

"What's the matter now? First, Bernadette come here without telling
me, now you. Is something going on?"

"I'm here because of Bernadette. I'll tell you all about it over dinner."

"Well, wait a minute. I got something in the refrigerator to warm up,
soon as I put on some clothes."

"Mama, I'm not here for you to feed me. Come on, let's go out to
eat and talk."

"You ain't got to spend money on me. I have plenty to eat downstairs."

"But I want to spend money on you. I want you to go out with me.

It won't be expensive. How about TGI Friday's?"

"I got to leave for work at eleven. I'm on the midnight to eight shift."

"That's fine. Throw on something casual and come on. My treat. I'll be downstairs waiting for you."

Marietta went into the basement to use the bathroom, wondering if she should first tell Mama why she was here, or just follow her gut feelings and take it from there.

She flushed the toilet, washed her hands and face, then repaired her make-up as she made her plans. Her first stop was in the kitchen where she picked up the lime green wall phone.

Flipping through her small red address book, she stopped at the tab marked 911—her most important phone numbers were all in here, all others behind. When Bernadette had given her Beatrice's new number, she put it under 911. No telling how long it would be important, but for now, it was paramount.

"Hello?"

"Hello, is this Beatrice?"

"Who's this?"

Marietta laughed. "I would give you a guess, but you would never imagine. It's Marietta! How are you, girl?"

There were a couple seconds of silence, then Beatrice said, "I'm doing fine."

Marietta hesitated, then said, "Well, I'd sure like to see you for myself. You know, the last time I saw you was a couple months after you had Toukie. It's been a while."

"That's because it was the last time you wanted to see me. Ain't nothing wrong with that."

"It's not that, Bea. If I lived closer, it would be a different story altogether. Look, I took the train down to spend a little time with Mama, and I was thinking, since I'm here, I'd like very much if you would join us."

"If you came here to spend time with Mama, then you should. Why call me?"

"Because I want to see you. I never see you unless it's an occasion, you have a baby, or somebody dies. I just want us to be together for no other reason."

"Well, that's nice of you, Marietta, and I appreciate it, but I can't do that tonight. My boyfriend is taking me out with some people we plan to go into business with, so this is not the night."

"It is awfully short notice, I realize, but I have to go back up to New York tomorrow. Do you think maybe we can get together after you come back from your date?"

"Not unless you tell me what you want to see?"

Marietta finally stopped trying. "Okay, Beatrice. I'm here because Bernadette told me about this letter she got, and she's so worried that one of us is going to die next, she asked me to figure out who sent it. I don't have a clue, and I was thinking that maybe, if we put our heads together, you would."

"Why would I?"

"If we could talk about who might possibly want to throw this at us, we might come up with a name. If you tried, don't you think you might come up with some idea where it may have come from?"

"No more than you. Why would I have a idea about this?"

"You may not. It's something all three of us are going to have to work out. I mean, unlike Bernadette, I don't think it's true. I think it's ridiculous, but somebody sent it to her, so that in itself means somebody thinks they know what buttons to push in this family. And you know that has Bernadette ready to go to war."

"I don't care about that poem, Marietta. If that's what you want me for, then you don't want me for nothing. I told Bernadette to get over it, it don't mean a thing, and I'm telling you."

"Well, it doesn't mean what it says, but it does mean something, Beatrice."

"Not to me."

"Why are you so evil about this? I'm not asking you for anything I didn't ask you for back when we swore ourselves to each other using that promise box. You promised, if I needed you, or Bernadette needed you, you'd be there. Why don't you go look at that box and see what you wrote to remind yourself. You promised us."

"Don't play that guilt game with me 'cause it won't work. Whatever I wrote in that box is what you told us to write, and it's not going to help you Marietta. Whatever you think you're going to come home and handle tonight, I wish you luck. 'Cause, it sure ain't going to be me."

"Well, if tonight is not good, maybe tomorrow. Do you think we can talk tomorrow?"

"To be honest, no. I'm really busy right now, and, we don't have to talk Marietta. Just tell Bernadette what you said, the letter is a joke, and move on. Stop trying to take over us; it just won't work no more."

When Beatrice hung up, Marietta sat with the phone to her ear, feeling tears fill her eyes. It just didn't make sense for anybody to be that rude. Beatrice was the worst news. The worst news. Anybody who knew her would probably end up hating her, and if they could send it in a poem, Marietta had no doubt, they would.

But that still didn't really help at this point. Beatrice wanted to see Daddy, and that couldn't happen. She would just ruin everything for everybody in the family, and why? There was no reason for it. Marietta would have to get through to Beatrice. She had to try again tomorrow.

******

Marietta had just placed the butter dish on the kitchen table when she heard the front door open, and the jingle of Mama's keys. She waited by the breakfast spread she had across the table to see Mama's face, hoping she could make her smile; make her happy.

Mama pushed open the French doors to her kitchen and stopped, looking down at the food, then at Marietta.

"Girl, what you in here doing now?"

"I didn't know if you ate before you left work in the morning, or if you ate after you got home, so I took a chance. I know you must be tired."

"But you didn't have to cook for me. I usually pick up a sandwich before I go to bed, and I did this morning. I bought some croissant sandwiches with me," Mama said holding up the Burger King bag.

"Well, now you have hot cream of wheat, scrambled eggs, Pillsbury buttermilk rolls, orange juice, and coffee. I wanted to do it."

Mama shook her head, but when Marietta smiled, she responded with one of her own. "Let me hang up my jacket."

When Marietta had Mama seated and eating, she put a dab of cream of wheat on her own plate with a big, fluffy roll, added a spoon of eggs, then said, "You know how we talked a lot about Beatrice last night at dinner? About how she doesn't want to be a part of this family?"

"Umhmm." Mama agreed, chewing steadily.

"I told you that Beatrice was interested in joining a business association that Daddy was in, but you kept using the word club. Like it was something small and local. I was thinking about that all morning. Is it really a club?"

"All I know is your father would go, from time to time, to this little social club with some of his friends. He wasn't in it himself. It was little, his mother had some of her friends in it, and I believe some professors at Howard was in it. I don't know about no business club or nothing like that, so I don't know what Beatrice is talking about."

A little club? Marietta took a swallow of orange juice, then took the ice tongs and picked up two cubes for her glass.

"You went in my China closet and took out my dishes?"

"Mama, you're supposed to use your dishes for yourself, not just for when you invite the President over. I love this set. I bought it for you."

"I mean to tell you, you set up a nice table and I thank you. But ain't no need to go to this much trouble for breakfast." Mama said, scooping another roll and slathering it in butter.

"Mama, I want to do this and more for you. You know, I was waiting for a better time to tell you this, but maybe now is the best. I'm pretty sure I'm going to marry the man I'm dating. We've been together for almost three years, and I really love him. He's dying to meet you, and the rest of my family."

Mama's eyebrows shot upward.

"Three years? And you never said a word about him to me? What kind of love is that if you can keep it to yourself that long?"

Marietta laughed.

"Because I wasn't sure about him. I mean, it's been going well for so long, I keep waiting for something to happen. You know my luck. I was still living in Flushing, he was in Manhattan, and we started off that way, just seeing each other when we could. He would end up staying with me, or I would stay with him, and it was so often, we got an apartment together. I know I led you to believe I'd moved by myself, but I thought I'd find out what he was really about then. But it's been nothing but good. I'm crazy about him."

"You sure Marietta? You ain't never picked nobody that treated you like anything."

"Have you heard me complain about anything in the last three years?"

Mama shook her head. "I can't say that I have."

"And Mama, sooner or later, we are all going to find somebody to love."

"Good. I'll be happy."

"Except for one problem." Marietta took in a spoon of eggs and chewed thoughtfully before saying, "I don't want Del, my boyfriend, to find out about what happened on that other side of the family."

"Why you think you got to tell him? Your father been gone for a long time. Just say that."

"Because if this is a little club that Beatrice is getting into, she will surely meet Daddy. And Daddy will tell her what she wants to know, about me. And you and him. Then, my life, as I know it, will be over."

Mama poured coffee in the china cup, then awkwardly lifted the saucer, stirring in sugar and cream.

"Marietta, your life is not going to be over. If Beatrice want to meet her father, it don't have to end your life."

"Just think, if Daddy tells Beatrice the whole story."

"Then Beatrice is going to know the whole story."

"Well, that would present a problem for me. Or have you forgotten?"

Mama put the cup down. "No, I haven't forgotten. But what I want to say is, we kept the girls safe. We did what we could do. Beatrice is a grown woman with two children. Bernadette is grown and taking care of herself. You got to go on with your life, and not let the past worry you."

"But Mama..."

"It's over. You don't have a choice, Marietta. If you happy with this boy, Del, you say you love him and I hope you also mean he loves you, then it's going to be okay. Everything is not perfect, and no, your life was not. But I told you, you can be a victim, and feel sorry for yourself forever, or you can take control over what you do from now on. Beatrice and Bernadette took control. They are already out there, so you need to stop worrying about them. Think about you."

"I can't forget what happened to me! I'm glad that my sisters are now grown, as you pointed out, and maybe I don't need to worry about them anymore, but I can't forget about me."

"You don't understand. You got to move on now, Marietta. You can't keep everybody else ignorant if they want to know Daddy. They might not ever know about you. You think that's something Daddy is proud of? That he would want to tell them? Just get yourself and Del together and live your life."

"I never thought I would hear you say that."

"Have I ever lied to you?"

"No."

"Haven't I always been there for you?"

"Yes"

"Then why you think I'm wrong now? You can't be a victim, Marietta. You been a strong little girl for a long time. You moved yourself along just fine. Now that you can be happy and enjoy your life, you scared that something in the family will come out. If Bea or Bernadette find out anything that happened with you, you think that's something they plan to go out and tell anybody? You think they plan to call Del?"

"No."

"Then what is your problem?"

"Mama, what if I just don't want them to know what happened to me? It's my life. It's my secret."

"It's still your life. It's going to be your life. Leave them alone."

"Well...there is one other thing. There's still Toukie. Bernadette thinks she may be in trouble around Bea's new boyfriend. She says he's scaring her. She wants me to see what I think by going there."

"What did Bea tell you last night? She don't want to see you."

"But why?" Marietta paused and when her eyes quickly filled with tears, she wiped them with her fingertips. "Why does she have to be so nasty to me? It's not just a mind-your-own-business-sis attitude. It's more like a I-hate-you-and-want-nothing-to-do-with-you attitude."

"She don't mean it. And she won't let that boy, that Witt, hurt Toukie."

"Well, I am here now, and I haven't seen her in a long time. Nor Toukie, so I will still go to see them."

"I can't say nothing more about it. It's your sister."

"And I hope you're right. I hope I don't have to worry about her finding out anything."

*six*

But after Mama went upstairs to sleep and Marietta cleaned up the kitchen putting Mama's china safely back in the china closet, she took out Bernadette's letter and noted  Bea's address. Mama did not understand how everything could affect her, so, it was still up to Marietta to take care of her own life. She hated Daddy, and it would kill her just to have Bea develop a relationship with that man. She had to get to Beatrice to stop her, and she would, even if Beatrice cursed her out for coming to her house. She had to do it. Marietta took Mama's car keys off the table, slipped out the house and into Mama's big Buick, and drove to Bea's, her heart pounding in her chest.

She didn't get there until 10:30, and when she pulled up in front of the house, she was scared to get out, so she just sat there. What was she going to actually say? How would she approach the questions about Witt and Toukie, especially since her sister had already told her not to come?

It was a dingy looking block of houses, Marietta thought as she noted all the trash lying on the streets, and nobody sweeping it up. Depressing actually. What made them choose to live here?

She sighed, turned on Mama's radio that was set on a gospel station, and turned the knob searching for jazz. There was something familiar on 96.3 FM, and she let it play, trying to decide how to approach Bea.

Just ring the bell and wing it, she thought to herself. What else?

She tried to think of something witty to say, decided nothing, and turned off the radio. Just as she popped the lock, the front door to Bea's house opened, and Marietta's eyes widened. Had they noticed her sitting out here?

She resisted the urge to duck down, or turn her face, watching mesmerized as a man, presumably Witt, came out and stood on the top steps looking around him. Nice looking man, Marietta thought as she watched him go down the steps and make his way to the Cavalier that Bernadette said was Bea's. He got in.

Marietta stuck her key in the ignition, and pushed the button to roll down the window of her car so she could stick her head out and watch him. He sat there, pulled out a cell phone and spoke for a minute or so. She saw him put it down, lean over the passenger's side rifling through something, then heard the car start. She eased lower in the seat, easing her head in the car until he pulled out and went up the street. Then she started her car and followed.

What am I doing? She asked herself when he hung a U-turn to go back down Broadway, and she pulled to the side a few seconds to let more cars in between them before she took a U. Then they rode.

Witt moved fast. He whipped through lights, causing her to speed with him. Then without a signal, he cut a left on Ashland. She saw that no other car behind him turned left. She would be in the next car right behind him. But maybe he hadn't noticed her car. She turned left. He turned up Ashland, went up a couple of blocks, then swung over into a parking spot. She had to drive past him, but as soon as she saw a space, she parked. It was at the end of the street, and she sat there wondering what good it would do if she couldn't see him. She wondered where he was going. This certainly wasn't working.

Marietta decided to turn the corner and circle the block, coming up behind him where she could keep her eye on his car. But when she turned the corner, there was a red light that she waited through. After she turned and went around the block, she saw that Witt was back in his car already. She glanced in her rearview mirror and looked for a spot to pull in and wait, but there was none. She had to continue driving to the corner, and he pulled up behind her.

"Crap!" she said aloud, hoping he hadn't discovered she was following him. When the light changed, she kept going straight down Ashland and noticed that he was following her. He must have seen her! She kept driving, looking at Witt through her rear view mirror. Was he looking straight at her? What if he was? She would just tell him who she was, and why she was here. Maybe she could find out more about the business he was going into, more about the club, and talk him out of joining. She could offer him some help through Del. Del worked as executive director of a lucrative public relations firm. He could give her the names of some business associations that Witt could join.

Suddenly she looked in the mirror and his car was gone. He had turned off! Marietta sighed and pulled over. He had to have just turned. She waited patiently for traffic to pass, then made a U and started back down Ashland. She looked up the side streets she passed, and on the second one, there was the red Cavalier, double-parked. So she turned.

She sat and waited. When Witt came back and started to zoom up the street, Marietta followed a safe distance behind. What were all these stops for? They drove through east Baltimore onto Hillen Road, a long stretch that led them from East to North Baltimore. Marietta then followed him in a turn onto Cold Spring Lane, then again on The Alameda. She noted when he started driving more slowly, and pulled over. Sure enough, he pulled into a driveway and cut the engine. She let him get out and bounce up the walkway. When he got to the door, she pulled out and slowly drove by.

As she passed the house, she saw him embrace a tall, thin woman with a head full of dark red ringlets. The door closed behind them.

Marietta stared at the address, and as soon as she got the chance she wrote it down. No wonder Beatrice was so evil. Her man was creeping on her, and she was stuck home with a baby, which was certainly not Beatrice's bag. Maybe now was the perfect time to go to Beatrice. She was probably vulnerable. Would welcome a comforting shoulder.

But she wouldn't do that to Bea. She would never tell her about Witt just to break her down to size. Soon enough, Bea would find out. And maybe she would be more receptive to her at that time. However, that made Bernadette's point more critical. What did Witt want with Beatrice? Why join Daddy's club? And more so, who really did write that poem? If they couldn't prove that Danny and Nita were killed, since no one had been able to so far, what did they really want from them?

Marietta wondered how the hell she ended up on The Alameda, now that she had to get back to Bea's. She made her way back to Hillen Road, it turned into Harford Road and she followed it to Broadway, and back to her sister's door.

This time, Marietta got out and rang the bell. All she wanted was to hug her, to ask about Toukie, and talk her out of finding Daddy. She didn't think it would be a problem if she offered Beatrice something in return. She had the names of several business associations that Witt could join, that would help him get started in a business. What she hoped was to take away any incentives he thought he had going after Daddy's club so hard. She didn't know if that would work, but she would try.

But nobody came to the door. She rang, and rang, even knocked a few times, and looked at her watch. She had a train to catch. Where was Beatrice? Had Witt dropped her off earlier?

Back at Mama's house, she tried to reach Beatrice by phone, but there was still no answer. She called to change her train reservations until the evening, so she could continue to call Bea. Nobody answered all day.

Mama dropped Marietta off at Penn Station at 7:00 p.m., so she could get herself to work by 8:00. As soon as Marietta went through the station doors, she pulled out her Nextel and called Beatrice. After one ring, someone answered.

"Hello?"

Marietta hesitated surprised. It was a young voice.

"Hello? Toukie?"

"Yes."

"Sweetheart, this is your Aunt Marietta. How are you?"

"Fine."

Marietta tried to picture Toukie as a hundred questions jumped in her mind. What are you doing? Where have you all been? Did you go to school today? She remembered Bernadette saying Witt kept her out. Is your mother home? Do you even know me? All the questions started bubbling in her brain at the same time, and she couldn't think of which one to ask first before she heard Toukie saying to someone, "Aunt Marietta."

The next thing Marietta heard was the click of the phone.

"Hello?" she said stupidly. After several surprised seconds, she jammed the END button and clicked redial, but the phone just rang and rang. Finally, she clicked off her phone and wrapped her hand in the strap of her suitcase so that it rolled behind her. She felt numb. At the train schedule board, she picked out her departure gate, and followed the signs to the track where her train was leaving. Through tears, she pushed her suitcase in the luggage compartment, and found a seat by the window. As the train pulled out promptly at 7:38, all she could see was a blur of colors through the tears that fell from her eyes. She was glad to be leaving.

\*\*\*\*\*\*

In the middle of November on a cold and gray Saturday, Marietta woke up shaking and sweaty. It wasn't quite six in the morning, and she was restless, staring down from their 20th floor apartment at the streets darkened with the glaze of rain. A light, steady rain fell, but the cars hardly broke speed as they zoomed up East 39th. She had not told Del much about her visit home except that her niece and sister were fine. She knew he was annoyed that she didn't want to say more.

How could he ever understand her family? She couldn't herself. It was scary that he asked if her family hated her. All her life she had thought they did. And Bea, with her rude, obnoxious self not only hated her, but was also teaching Toukie to do the same. What could she tell Del that he would understand about them? Not a thing. Yet, the more she thought about Bernadette's concerns, the more she knew that Bernadette would soon do something herself. If Bea felt so cold and indifferent about her, and then found out about Daddy, she would see no reason in the world to keep that to herself.

She had even written Bea. Asked about the baby, about Toukie and Witt. Wanted to know if she could have a picture of the children. Asked if she could invite them all to New York for a week-end of activities, or if she and Del could come to Baltimore and spend the afternoon or evening there. She had heard nothing.

Bernadette had written Marietta twice asking for progress. And Marietta hadn't written back because there was none. Telling Bernadette that she had found nothing would be like asking her to step in and take charge, and she had to shut Bernadette down. Now. The truth was, she was scared to death it would all come back.

She sat on the stool in her kitchen sipping hot lemon tea, ignoring the small Sony TV on the counter giving news, and staring at the rain streaked window as her mind swirled in thought. How did Witt know about Daddy's club? It wasn't common knowledge, so he had to have an in. Who was it? She shivered uncontrollably. What would happen if she called Bernadette and just told her the truth? Could she take it? Did they really need to bring all this out?

Marietta shuddered, feeling a tingling sensation course through her body.

She was still tender after the ardent lovemaking she and Del had shared the night before, which made her realize, with an even greater urgency that she couldn't afford to have Bernadette snooping around and ruining everything. Del knew her emotionally, sexually, intellectually— he was everything she could have dreamed of, hoped for, and it just wouldn't do for all that mess to come out about her family at this time.

It was so unfair! If only she could think of the right way to handle her sisters once again, that would keep them patient...and most important, quiet.

Marietta pulled the cup to her lips and sipped. The hot liquid worked its way down and warmed her chest. It was unusual for her to leave the bed so early on a Saturday morning, and leave Del under the goosedown comforter, naked and alone. Something was going to have to be done soon.

"Marietta?"

The hot liquid splashed over the side of the cup as she banged it down and turned startled.

"Del! What are you doing up this early?"

"Looking for you. You don't have to go the center today, do you?"

Marietta sometimes volunteered at several women's shelters in the Manhattan area, but not today. She wasn't even sure if she was supposed to be somewhere, but she knew she didn't feel up to it. It was a nasty, dreary morning.

"No, I just couldn't sleep."

Del yawned widely, then scratched his head. "C'mon, you've been saying that all week." Del went over to the coffee maker and turned it on. He reached up and pulled down his Yankees' mug, looked for a spoon, then said, "You want to talk about it?"

Marietta mopped up the mess she'd made on the counter with a paper towel, and made a face behind his back. She'd rather be shot with a million poison-tipped arrows.

"There isn't anything to talk about really. I may need to take another trip home. My mother may need me to help her with some family business." She was not sure why she said that. Why didn't she say her sister?

"What's wrong?"

"Nothing serious. I haven't been able to help her straighten out some daily living decisions, that's all."

Del didn't say anything to that. Marietta moved over to the refrigerator, wondering if he wanted anything to eat this early. Usually after a night like they'd had, he was famished.

"How about an omelet?" she offered.

"It's not even 6:00! How about you make up your mind to tell me what's going on or we go back to bed."

Marietta sighed, then bent over to search for milk. "What makes you think there's something going on?"

Del walked up behind her, pressing himself against her butt as he peered in the refrigerator over her head.

"What if I say because I know something about you after three years. You haven't been the same since the letter from Bernadette."

He had a point there. He did know her. She had met Delaney Peterson in a training session the Navy had set up for military representatives from all branches of the armed forces to boost recruiting in a time of war. Del worked for the second largest PR firm in New York City, *WPP Group USA, Inc. WPP* Group delivered, and to Marietta's surprise, they were chosen to educate them on things they could do for recruitment, which must have cost the government good money. This firm raked in the dollars, and everybody who worked there had minds like steel traps. She had been thrilled to attend, along with her boss and one other male representative. Though *WPP* was located on Park Avenue, the training site was actually at a Sheraton Hotel. Still, Marietta imagined herself strolling through those Park Avenue doors one day for the meetings she would hold there to create the kinds of spins they did for important clients. She would be great working for the White House, putting a good face on their voluminous military interventions throughout world, much like Martha Raddatz, the current National Security Correspondent.

The Navy was always working on new material to attract better talent, something that had been a serious lacking in recent years. It was serious enough that the Navy was willing to suspend some of their basic requirements—like a high school diploma-- in order to fill basic ranks. Better recruitment and advertising became a priority, and using a top New York ad agency to provide a series of training, Marietta had been sent.

She had no idea in that first meeting, in a room of military personnel from all branches, that one of the head executives, Mr. Del Peterson had been taken with her. It took several scheduled meetings before she noticed how much Del singled her out for questions and examples. After the third meeting, he'd invited her to a working lunch, and right after, to dinner.

Marietta handed him the carton of milk and closed the refrigerator, then moved to the table.

"Did I mention that I may have to make a week-long trip somewhere for this new recruitment brochure?"

"Before or after you stop in Baltimore to help your mother?"

She looked at him.

"You did say you were going through there, didn't you?"

"Yes, but why are you pushing me?"

"Am I? I guess I just don't get why you are so touchy about your family. I never get to hear about your family. You talk about your mother, but I have yet to meet her. So, why can't I ask? You've met my parents, and my brother Jim. My other brother and my sister know all about you, and they're looking forward to meeting you at Christmas when they fly in from Arizona. When am I going to meet anybody from your family?"

She'd never had to worry about her boyfriends meeting her family or even wanting to. She'd had few relationships. The few she had all involved military men whom she thought understood her and her career. In every situation, things hadn't worked out for one reason or another, and she hadn't been willing to settle for some inferior status, not like her mother had done for years. For some reason her boyfriends seemed to put her down, sometimes physically pushing her around. Her best girlfriend, Gloria, thought it was because she was so small, and smacking her to control her was easier than debating with her. Del dropped into her life when she had given up.

"Your parents live in Long Island, Del. It's easy for us to see them."

"And Baltimore is hard?"

"It's inconvenient."

"For whom? And why?"

"Del, I thought we'd gone over all this last year when we started seeing each other seriously. Remember? We talked about any problems we might have, and what we were going to do about it, and the first thing we said was be honest. I notice how this year, a lot of the people you were good friends with I've hardly seen. Either you meet them outside the home without me, or you aren't seeing them at all. And you haven't brought it up or said anything about losing friends."

"What are you talking about? What does this have to do with me seeing your family? I haven't been honest, so I can't meet your family?"

"No. What I'm saying is, we promised that we would discuss our problems. And your friends..."

"What friends are you talking about? I haven't lost any friends because of you. My friends all love you."

"Or they pretend to until they see this isn't a fad. And if you haven't noticed, it doesn't mean it isn't happening. So, I haven't brought my family into this yet, because I don't know how long we're going to last."

"What difference does it matter how long it lasts? I can't see them until we make it last for what? How long? What's the magic number?"

"It sounds stupid, but Del, if I see you losing friends, how long will it take for you to see it's because of me. And I don't think you'll give up your friends."

Del looked surprised.

"You're seeing things."

"I'm not willing to hide from them."

"So, if that is true, which I don't believe, but saying it is, what does that mean? We shouldn't be together because somebody else might find it offensive? I'm not blind to the fact that somebody will, but I'm also not polling for public acceptance. I love you Marietta, and I don't care if, as you say, my friends may not. The people I call my friends haven't changed one bit toward you, or me and even if they did, I still love you. This thing with your mother, if it's really important, should be taken care of. And if you want, I can go with you. I'm going to meet her sooner or later. You do know that, right?"

"That's not a problem. You don't understand; I love you, too. I want this to work out between us the way it has so far, and I don't want anything stupid to happen between us. We have to go slowly."

"Stupid? What do you mean? How much more slowly do we have to go? How much time do we have? It's almost like you're hiding something—me? From your family? Or vice versa. It's something."

She looked at him. What if he knew, really knew what was going on? What would he do? Would the trouble in her family keep him away from her? He was an executive in a powerful ad agency, constantly being groomed for top leadership. She loved him enough to spare him embarrassment.

"I hope you don't really think I am."

Del looked in her eyes.

"Why don't you tell me what's holding things up between us? What is it that I'm feeling that's holding us apart? What's keeping you awake at night?"

She moved closer to him.

"Del, if there was anything to worry about, I would tell you. I've just been thinking about my family a lot. That's all."

Del studied her a moment.

"How do you really feel about me, Mari?"

"How do you think I feel?" she asked, then sensing his hesitation, moved close enough to press herself against him until she knew he could feel her breasts and the outline of her naked body under the silk Victoria's Secret robe.

He reached his hands under the soft material, sliding his hands up her hips, over her rear, and pulling her stomach flat against him. He leaned down and opened his mouth on hers and they kissed deeply, his tongue carefully exploring her mouth, her tongue getting lost inside his. After letting him kiss her long and deeply, she felt Del push down her robe over her slim shoulders, untying her belt until it fell to the floor. Then he got on his knees, and pressed his lips in a lingering kiss against the area between her thighs. He reached to pull her down with him, then leaned over her, first her lips, then neck, then down over her chest, his mouth eagerly seeking her small breasts, sucking her rose colored nipples greedily as he gently squeezed her behind.

She moaned and blocked out every other thought as his tongue went to work on her. He left one breast and moved to the other, carefully licking around the nipples, then trailing a line down to her navel. He explored her there until he ended up between her gaping legs, his tongue working madly as they both stretched out on the floor. Del's tongue was magic as it snaked around inside her, titillating her until she felt she was riding a wave of pleasure. They were both hot and wet with perspiration as he held onto her perfect waistline. The rush ran from his tongue and into her groin making every nerve cell scream with excitement and causing her passion to climb. Waves of sensation began to bombard her, and as he felt the quiver, he slowly moved his mouth to the inside of her thighs, running his tongue up and down both sides, before moving squarely on top and thrusting himself into her.

She wrapped her legs around his back and buried her hands deep in his hair as she moved her hips to meet his thrusts. The sensations reached every core, every lining of her body, shot through her as the waves deepened and her only thought was on making this relationship work. He knew her body like they'd been together forever. As she arched her back, her loud moans echoing, she felt his release go through her. They held each other tightly as she felt her orgasm reverberate throughout her body.

No, she couldn't let Bernadette ruin this. No one made her feel as complete as Del. She was crazy about him. She couldn't let the past catch up with her now.

# *seven*

Click-click. Marietta, back straight against her ergonomically correct chair, ran her fingers over the keyboard of her office computer, and pulled up a long list of e-mails, trying hard to focus on work. What a weekend, she thought, stifling a big yawn behind her hand. It was not quite seven on Monday morning, and she couldn't have felt more hopeful. Even the crowded subway stations, late trains, and standing room only rides couldn't pop the bubble she felt inside. She'd spent the weekend, in and out of bed, getting some talking done in between. She loved listening to Del, and shared as much as she dared without telling him everything. Del made promises, gave her encouragement, and she could almost believe whatever she had to go through, he would go through it with her. Almost.

She would handle Bernadette today. She'd gone back and read through Bernadette's letter, trying to see exactly what she would have to say. She would simply tell Bernadette that she had talked to Beatrice, which was true, and that everything was okay with Witt, which may not be true. But who would know? She didn't have to give Bernadette details. Bernadette told her to handle it and she could say she did. Period. Everything would not come tumbling down the way she had thought when she first opened the mail.

Clicking the mouse button, she skimmed down, doing a rapid reading and organizing entries. The first thing she saw, a top priority nine a.m. meeting gave her a moment to pause. She felt her manic joy slowly ebb. Monday morning reality was sinking in.

She leaned over to buzz her secretary for a rundown of the agenda for this Monday meeting when her phone rang. This early?

She picked it up.

"Happy Monday!" It was her best friend Gloria Tilden.

"Hey Gloria, same to you!" Mari replied smiling into the phone. "What's going on?"

"On a Monday this early? Not a thing, girl." She paused then told Gloria she was worn out from the weekend. Gloria hooted when she told her briefly about how she'd spent the whole weekend in that pink satin robe with Del pulling it off every chance he got, and was surprised when Gloria told her how she'd never thought she'd hear herself say this, but Del seemed to have calmed down all Marietta's nervous jitters in every way.

"You know how jumpy you are Marietta, always popping pills to keep yourself calmed down. Del calms you naturally."

Marietta leaned back, saying, "You know, I haven't taken any kind of sedative in almost a year, Gloria. I guess that says something."

"I can tell. You are a different person with that man. Really. And I hope you don't let this stuff at home get you all worked up again, I'm serious. You've come a long way, and you know it."

She had called Gloria 's cell phone early last Saturday before Del woke up telling her she wanted to ask her opinion about a family problem, but after the weekend, she realized she didn't want to share much with Gloria. She could trust Gloria to keep some things, but this was taking friendship to another realm.

"It's like a miracle for me. Things have been going so well, I can't believe it."

"You finally stopped picking up all that riff-raff that washed up at your feet. You know some of your past boyfriends haven't been worth the time it took to speak to them."

"We all make mistakes."

"Oh, I agree! But you weren't learning from yours until now. Del is good for you and I don't want to see you blow it. By the way, what did you want to tell me about your sister in Baltimore? You said you had a family problem, so it must be Beatrice, right?"

"Not this time. It was actually my sister Bernadette, but it's okay. I got it under control, Gloria. I mean, I'm going to handle it."

Gloria paused. "You sure? You have a way of trying to ignore stuff…"

"Absolutely sure. Look, let me get back to you. I have a ton of e-mail to get through."

"Okay. Give me a call."

Marietta hung up wishing she'd never given Gloria a hint of anything. Gloria wouldn't forget, and she'd keep asking what was going on until Marietta convinced her it was over. Marietta shook her head and then moved back to her computer. She finished prioritizing her work, and thought in the back of her mind how important it was to pick up the tone of the written word. She noted one of her e-mail messages that caused a knot in her stomach. She hated when people demanded she do anything, and it was clear the deadline on her article about the Hall of Fame for female military officers at the Pentagon was being moved up for some reason and she had to get it out.

Her secretary, Clancy, came to get her for the meeting right before nine, and Marietta successfully shut out everything she'd been wrestling with all weekend and focused on the activities she had to get done this week. They spent all morning fleshing out the plans for the recruitment brochure, then by noon they let out to get started.

Marietta rushed back to her office telling Clancy that if she went to the cafeteria, she wanted a bowl of soup and a roll. Then she set up to work from her files on the Hall of Fame article. She almost missed the light tap on the door, but when it came a second time, she paused her hands over the keyboard.

"Come in!"

The office door opened, and in came Clancy with a huge colorful bouquet of flowers, struggling to make her way over to the desk.

"My goodness!" Marietta exclaimed jumping up to help.

"And you didn't have to carry it! Isn't it wonderful?" Clancy exclaimed. "It's just gorgeous—oh, if anybody would buy me a daisy every now and then, I'd be happy."

Marietta stepped back to admire the bouquet, an obvious autumn arrangement with lilies, hydrangeas, delphiniums and marigolds. Several stalks of Bird of Paradise were aesthetically placed with Japanese bamboo and river cane. The arrangement sat in a clear glass harborlight pitcher with green marbles at the bottom. It was breathtaking.

"Aren't you going to see who they're from?"

"I know who they'd better be from," Marietta said and she and Clancy laughed together.

Marietta found the small green envelope and pulled out the card, then felt her face flush. "Think about me unwrapping you every time you see these," the card read. With Del, you couldn't even leave the card open.

"That good, huh?"

"And it's from the right person," Marietta said. After a few seconds, she noticed more eyes from the doorway and she stepped forward to beckon inside other office mates who wanted to come in and admire her bouquet before she shooed them out to go back to work.

She sat back at her desk, her fingers poised over her computer and started to type, then changed her mind and called Del's office.

His secretary was brusque, telling her that he was busy, and not to be disturbed. She was sure that woman hated the fact that she was black and Del loved her, but she let it slide.

She hung up disappointed, tried to go back to work, and wondered what she could do to give him something surprising. He always knew the right thing to do for her.

She had barely gotten back into focusing on the article she had to finish when there was another knock at her door, and when she paused and yelled come in, this time it was Clancy with a large Federal Express envelope.

She had a hint of a smile on her face.

"What now?" Marietta asked.

"I don't know. I was just looking at the return address."

When Clancy left, Marietta shook her head and looked at the envelope. Altoona, Pennsylvania was supposed to mean something to her?

She opened up the envelope. Inside was a smaller envelope that she opened to find a booklet of questions with a little black bean-shaped figure and a bubble over his head.

On the cover was the first instruction: "If you're not afraid to find your love in all the right places, dive in. Remember, only the truth will lead you to him."

She smiled and opened the booklet.

"Your name will fit into the blocks on the bottom of this page if my love belongs to you."

She carefully printed her name in the blanks.

"Circle the number of times you had sex this weekend."

She giggled, thought about it and circled.

"The best part of fall is what?" Her choices were colored leaves, wood burning fireplace, warm mugs of cider.

She circled them all.

"Which of the following descriptions teases your fancy: Cove

Harbor, Roman Towers, Lakeside Chalet?"

Marietta circled Lakeside Chalet, then followed the instructions at the end which gave her an unrecognizable address where she was to bring the completed pamphlet and the larger white envelope with her at 7:30 p.m.

She paused, thinking warmly of Del before Clancy interrupted, bringing in a tray with a large bowl of soup and a piece of a French roll. Gulping down her lunch, she turned back to her computer to finish up her work.

Unable to hide her anticipation, she got through the remainder of the article by the end of the day and e-mailed it to her commanding officer, then, throwing her things together, she paused only to smell the bouquet before rushing out to the subway.

******

By 7:05, she got out of the yellow cab glancing at the address she'd been given. She had been unable to reach Del at work all day, and by now she was a little nervous. What if this white envelope wasn't from him? She'd had men try many things to get her attention, and this wouldn't have been a first.

She was dressed in winter white Merino wool, a long straight cardigan, sleeveless turtleneck, and pull-on matching pants. Large skinny gold hoops hung from her ears, and her cropped hair blew just slightly as she examined the club entrance, which had a board with the club acts listed outside. In her hand was a blue ticket with the address and name of the club, which was The B.B. King Blues Club & Grill on West 42nd Street. She was lucky to arrive just as a line of patrons was going through the front door. She went down the narrow steps and handed her ticket over to the man at the entrance who stared at it, smiled secretively, and led her to a table, near the stage set up for the live band.

She asked for a glass of Cristal and waited.

By 8:00, she started to worry. Del wouldn't do this to her. He knew how high strung she could be and he wouldn't want to upset her. Who could it be if it wasn't Del? Who might she be meeting?

The dreadlocked waitress had come by for her $10.00 minimum order, so she selected the special, and as the woman hurried away, Marietta looked around her nervously. It had to be Del, she told herself at last. Who else could it be? Del hadn't called or come home all day. He would have if he hadn't sent the flowers. It had to be him.

By the time she finished her drink, she pulled out her phone and dialed her apartment. There was still no answer. She thought about getting out of there, then paused.

The band was coming to set up. What if she held tight a little longer? It couldn't hurt.

She ordered another glass of champagne and watched the members of the band, and just as her attention was diverted, Del came up behind her dressed in a chocolate brown suit and crème colored shirt with a brown, navy and crème paisley tie. He leaned down and kissed the top of her head, startling her, then sat down beside her.

"You look absolutely beautiful," Del said, and she grinned.

"That bouquet was wonderful! How did you ever find anything like that?"

He grinned.

"Didn't you order me a drink?"

"I would have if I was sure it was you."

Marietta puckered her lips when Del gave her a questioning glance before calling the waitress over for a drink.

"I see you followed the directions so far," he said with a wink, and before she could ask about the questions and what they meant, the band started loudly tuning up so they watched them with curiosity. She had never heard of the Kent Bradley trio, but Del looked like he had, and when they started, she was pleased to say the music sounded great.

Del ordered a roast beef sandwich when the waitress brought Marietta her special of shrimp and angel hair pasta and they watched the musicians and moved with the music. By the time one set was done, Del's face was flushed from his few drinks and his smile was expansive.

"That's what I'm going to do when I get our first few millions under my belt. I'm going to learn to play just like that."

"Oh yeah?"

"Yeah, just like that."

"Which instrument?"

"Sax. What other instrument is there?"

They laughed.

"So, how do you like the evening so far?"

"It's great. We don't normally spend Mondays this way, you know."

"No." Del reached in his jacket pocket and looked over at Marietta. "Did you follow the rest of the instructions?" He put an envelope on the table, and slid something under his seat.

Marietta smiled, and reached into her purse.

"What are the chances we have the same answers to the questions?" he smiled at her.

"You answered my questions?"

"Let's see."

He opened his envelope as she followed his lead and opened hers.

"Did you get your name?"

She giggled when he asked her to spell it.

"How many times did we have sex this weekend?" he asked. She had circled 6. He'd circled 10.

"What?" she asked.

"Every time I put my mouth on you, anywhere I put my mouth on you, you count that."

Marietta dissolved in laughter.

"That would be about 100 times this weekend!"

"Well?"

"What about the leaves, or the fireplace or the cider? I circled them all. I mean, how can I choose leaves over the fireplace, or the fireplace over leaves, or warm cider?"

"That's cheating Mari. I said choose one."

"I can't."

"If you had to. Choose."

"Oooooh." Marietta pouted. "Fireplace."

"Good girl." He showed her he had chosen fireplace.

"Now, the most important one. Which description did you choose?"

"Easy. Lakeside Chalet."

Del smiled. He'd circled the same thing.

He then reached down and pulled up a large white envelope. "Open it," he instructed.

She pulled it over and tore it open. A big brochure describing the Poconos Mountains and the Lakeside Chalets was inside, and she looked over pictures of the heart-shaped pool, king-sized round bed, log burning fireplace, 60 inch color television, stocked kitchenette with winter drinks, such as chocolate and cider, and huge window views of the autumn countryside including horse rides through the woods.

There was a confirmation envelope inside. They had a three-day, two night package on the weekend.

"I can tell you need it. So do I."

They kissed like they were on their couch at home and only stayed to hear a couple numbers from the second set before they caught a cab home and she thanked him, the way she knew he liked best.

# eight

The weather was cold and icy, Marietta noted, pulling her full-length arctic coat around her as she opened the passenger door upon her arrival in the Poconos Mountains. They arrived late Friday evening, but as Del was quick to point out, there was no shortage of things to do indoors.

She immediately fell in love with the cozy little chalet they had reserved, and hurriedly unpacked for them. They changed and started with the all-you-can-eat buffet before they hurried back to their rooms to dress up for the Friday night club act, which they discovered would be Diana Ross and two of the lesser known Supremes. They shared a table with two other couples, and after ordering drinks, found that most of the audience was up and dancing.

When Diana Ross came on, she started with songs from way back, "Baby Love" and "Come See About Me" then on to "Stop in the Name of Love" and rolled right through her 60's hits. She was sure the way the club was set up, Miss Ross expected to be the center of attention with the audience seated around the stage to gaze at her, but not this audience. The people were on their feet moving to the music, and Del and Marietta were no exceptions. Diana was supposed to do 90 minutes of songs, but after an hour she left and didn't come back out.

The band played on however, and as they did, the audience danced and had fun. It was 1:30 a.m. and Marietta was bone tired by the time it was over and they went back to their chalet.

The following morning they got out just before noon, and she and Del scoured the countryside hiking in the fallen leaves along the trails for hours before they went to their cabin for snacks and a dip in the pool. It was near-ly 6:00 p.m. when Marietta woke up from her nap to an empty bed, and got back into the pool to swim around and relax. Relax she did, freeing her mind of everything. She felt incredible. In fact, she rarely felt this good.

Finally, her life was coming together in a way she had never imagined. She glanced around her at the cozy chalet, as she hung onto the side of the pool, the warm water covering her body. If only she would feel worthy of this…if only she believed Bernadette would not eventually destroy it all…her eyes filled with tears.

Gloria knew her, knew how comfortable she felt dating the men Gloria had called riff-raff. They weren't riff-raff any more than she was. They were men who thought by holding on tightly to her, they could make her theirs. She had been with so many men who tried to run and own her. In her few long-term relationships, her boyfriends had set up what she could and could not do. She had never felt like she shared an equal relationship. Gloria accused her of looking for men to take over her life. Maybe she was right. For years she dated MP's, SP's, AP's, all military enforcement occupations, men who exuded control.

It wasn't until her last relationship five years ago, that she knew she needed to change when her boyfriend at the time insisted on backhanding her at every opportunity. If she came in late, he backhanded her. If she answered him too slowly, he backhanded her. If she looked too good, he backhanded her. It got so good to him one time, he kept on until she was black and blue and had to call Mama.

It was the first and last time she'd ever called Mama out of fear of a man, because Mama almost killed him. She arrived at their apartment in the middle of the night. When she saw Marietta's face, there wasn't anything within reach that she didn't grab and throw at him until he left.

Then Mama moved Marietta out to stay with Gloria until the boyfriend had taken all of his things out of the apartment. Mama was the one who took her to the hospital and talked her into pressing military charges. Mama was the one who made her see that she could not expect more of her sisters if this was what she was willing to accept.

"You can't look for a father in these men! That ain't what they supposed to be with you for. You want a partner, Marietta, somebody to work with you. Not somebody to work ON you. If they don't treat you like a lady, like they worship the ground you walk on, you don't need them. You don't need them or anybody with them who let you suffer like that!" She could almost feel Mama's sorrow over Daddy when she spoke. Mama understood about suffering and seemed to know how much was enough.

A man like Del required a whole woman, without the baggage she had. What would he do when he found out that maybe she wasn't whole…that her background was clouded with doubt and suspicion and that Mama's sorrow had become hers. The promise box, as Bernadette so aptly called it, had helped her as much as it had Beatrice and Bernadette. How much riff-raff could she have married if she hadn't had it in mind not to fall prey to men who would easily find her attractive? That promise had saved her from truly destroying her life. Now that she'd struck gold, what was she to do about Bernadette? Could she trust Del enough to share what she would one day have to before Bernadette found out everything her own way?

An hour later, Del came in, sweaty and talkative. Marietta was stretched out on the bed. She had just willed herself to banish all the negative thoughts surrounding her when Del came in, loudly blowing her calm. He'd found somebody to play racquetball with and wanted to know if she wanted to try horseback riding before dinner, or wait and do skating or bowling after. Several other couples were getting together, and he thought they would be fun. Besides, one man seemed interested in talking business and Del wanted to capitalize.

She didn't really want to but she agreed to do the bowling, and after dinner they met up with the other two couples.

Even though she didn't really want to socialize, she had to admit, the bowling was fun. She was actually very good at it, beating the other women handily with a score of 192.

They went back late to the chalet to relax. Over wine, she read a bit of a best-seller she'd brought along with her while Del watched one of the cable channels until she heard him snore. She closed the book then went over to crawl into the king-sized bed and watch him close up. He looked so peaceful lying there, she bit her lip as she wondered what would become of them. He had put himself out there with her. She did know what he was, what he came from, what he wanted. She knew he wanted a full relationship. He wanted to know as much about her, and he deserved to. She felt tears well in her eyes as she watched him. What could she say? When the truth came out, what would he do?

She turned the light out and moved close to him. Almost automatically his arms wrapped her against him, and she fought hard against the tears that threatened her.

******

Their last morning, she opened her eyes and looked around surprised to find Del already up. Bacon was frying and coffee was brewing, and she slipped into her fuzzy slides and wandered into the bathroom to wash up, then into the kitchen.

"Hey," she said with a smile. "I'm surprised you have the energy to be up so early."

"Hey yourself," he said, and he met her halfway for a deep kiss.

"What time are we leaving?"

"I was thinking early rather than late. I left my laptop, and I…"

"Can't wait to see who needs you?"

"No, not that. But I should have brought it."

She opened the cabinets, filled with old mismatched dishes, then looked at the bag on the counter.

"You went out?"

"And you never heard a thing."

She pulled out the paper plates and cups he'd bought and poured the orange juice into two cups, to the rim.

"Ah, bacon," she said as Del lifted strips onto a paper towel and she bent over to steal one, burning her fingers.

"That's what you get. Look, make yourself really useful and find the pastries."

"Pastries! Oh, God, Del, I'm going to gain so much weight just from this weekend alone."

"Diet tomorrow. I got you an apple and raisin job. Put them all out on the plate."

Marietta sighed, grabbing a plate and taking the pastries out carefully and arranging them. She put the apple one on her plate and waited for the bacon and eggs. Finding a newspaper, she pulled it apart and gave him the sports section while she took the front page and settled herself.

Del fixed their plates, and she thanked him before they said grace.

She started on the eggs and bacon while Del looked for the rest of the paper, then quickly swapped with her, taking back the front page.

"Well give me the section with Dear Abby or something!"

"Eat your pastry."

"I don't need it. I can feel my hips jiggling already."

"You eat this pastry and you don't have to eat another thing."

"Why? Is it that good?"

She picked it up, the smell of cinnamon getting her taste buds going, but just before she opened her mouth to bite into it, she frowned, and pulled the pastry from her face.

"What?"

"Something's in my apple!"

She put it back on the plate and stuck a plastic fork in it. Peering, she dug around it and her mouth dropped open.

"What?"

"Oh, Del!" She reached in and pulled out a platinum marquis diamond ring, glimmering. Still sticky, she stuck her finger through it, and tears came to her eyes.

He got up and stood over her.

"Seemed like something you'd like."

"Del…"

"I figured if you liked it enough, you'd go ahead and make up your mind. I'd sure like to marry you."

She couldn't stop the tears. "I ab-so-lutely love it. Oh Del, how can you spring this on me?

"How do you think?"

Marietta stood up and grabbed him to her.

"I love you so much. You know I'll marry you. I'd be happy to marry you."

******

"I'm thinking sooner rather than later," Del had told her when they thought about the best time to tie the knot, so the Friday evening after Thanksgiving found Marietta and Gloria at the Hilton talking logistics. They agreed to meet in midtown Manhattan for a late lunch/early dinner and drinks. Del had been called to Denver at the last minute to pacify an unhappy client, leaving Marietta to spend the holiday weekend with her friend. They had made reservations to see the Christmas show at Radio City Music Hall, and then gone straight to the stores and shopped like crazy, putting a dent in their Christmas lists. They ended up near the Hilton, stopped for cocktails and stayed to eat.

Marietta could not remember feeling so relaxed as she had the last couple of months. Everything was coming together for her. And as the waiter brought their coffee, taking away the dinner dishes, Gloria leaned back in her seat and gave a big sigh.

"That's why I like coming here for dinner," Gloria praised. "They give you enough food to fill you up for the rest of the night, and most of tomorrow."

"It was delicious," Marietta said considering one more martini.

"This is way overdue," Gloria added, pulling her napkin up to her lips to belch. She motioned for the dessert menu. Marietta decided to order chocolate cake, and Gloria agreed, then as the waiter left, Gloria said, "Now that we got some foundation work done on your wedding plans, you never told me if you were able to help your sister Bernadette. You know, help her check up on the one in Baltimore with the boyfriend."

"Yes. The one in Baltimore is the one who needs the help." Marietta had a few drinks in her and felt about as free as she'd ever felt. "My sister Beatrice is living with some 'lunatic'- my sister Bernadette's word. Bernadette thinks he's hard on my niece and thinks it's affecting her health. She says my niece is bald, has bitten down nails, and shakes when he talks."

Gloria's forehead creased with concern. "My goodness, is it true?"

Marietta shrugged. "Hard to tell. When I went to Baltimore, my sister wouldn't talk to me."

Gloria swirled her drink in her glass. "That's strange, isn't it? Maybe this man is out of control. I mean, that would make me want to know even more about him; whether or not he is safe to be around."

"Maybe. If Beatrice was normal. Beatrice is not a normal girl." Marietta motioned the waiter over, deciding one more martini would be okay. "She dropped out of school before her senior year of high school, after my sister Juanita died. She started hanging in the streets. She did drugs and stayed in flop-houses and did nothing my mother asked. She didn't come home until she got pregnant with my niece, at 19 almost 20 years old. And my mother took care of her.

"She's a loose cannon with no rhyme nor reason. To top that, she's selfish, mean, hateful, and even though she has beautiful children, she doesn't know how to appreciate them. She's a horrible mother."

Gloria laughed. "Wow. I see you're really on her side."

"I'm speaking the truth."

"But what we don't understand is what's wrong. Have you talked to her, Marietta? Have you listened to her? If she is all those things you say, then something is terribly wrong."

Marietta took a long sip of her drink. "I'll say. What do you expect me to do?"

The waiter brought their desserts, and the women paused to be served before Gloria said, "You might need a family intervention. If one sister can't get herself together, everybody as a group can step in and get her attention. If her behavior is that bad, she's affecting her children."

"You don't rope Beatrice in. She doesn't mistreat her kids, I'd say she loves them. She just drags them around through all of her crazy friends and dangerous boyfriends."

"But that's enough to step in and do something."

"Let me tell you, my mother did everything in the world for her. You can't do much more than that."

Marietta turned her chocolate cake around, and cut a piece with her fork before putting it in her mouth.

Gloria stared at her friend.

"Mari, you know you are my good friend, and I love you dearly. But you've got to realize you can be judgmental. And maybe Bea does not need your judgment right now. Maybe she needs your love."

"I've tried."

"You have to try again. Let me go with you to talk to her. Sometimes another person can help."

"I won't have to worry about this in about another year. Del told me he has an opportunity to relocate for about a year to London where they're doing some recruitment, and he would like that. I would too. I would so definitely love to get away from here if I can."

Marietta was stuffing another bite of cake in her mouth and missed the look her friend gave her.

"Well, if you leave, what will happen with your sister?"

"Beatrice, just so you know, is a drop dead gorgeous girl. Beautiful hair, skin, body. She will always land on her feet."

For a minute neither woman said a thing, the only sounds being the distant conversations of other tables, and the clink of Marietta's fork hitting the plate. Then Gloria shrugged.

"So, you're going to leave me here while you go to Europe?"

"Only for a year. It probably won't happen until well after the wedding, which isn't for another year, and I'll be finishing up my 20th year the year after that, so I can retire from the military and move on. I can't wait."

"I'm jealous."

"Why? I'll have you and Cecilia imported as soon as I get settled, and you know I will," Marietta said referring to Gloria's 12-year-old daughter.

The women laughed. The rest of dessert was much lighter as they reminisced about their years of friendship, and by the time they departed in separate cabs, Marietta was feeling so sentimental, she actually thought about whether it was possible the three sisters could get together.

But then it hit her. There was still no answer to who wrote that poem. That troublemaker was still out there, and it was no telling what else they wanted to reveal about her family. If they sent Bernadette another letter, Marietta was sure Bernadette would go straight to Daddy to see what she could find. Unless there was some way Marietta could give her an answer about that poem. Could she just lie, and make up a person and a reason, or would Bernadette push on?

If she could stall Bernadette for a year, just a year, then it didn't matter. Once they relocated, she had no intention of returning.

******

"Excuse me, can you please call me when the doctor is ready? I'll be right outside in hall," Marietta said, then slipped outside the door and pushed the redial button on her cell phone.

"Mari?"

"Yes, Del, what is it?"

"I've been trying to reach you at work all morning. You didn't mention that you weren't going in."

"I was there, but left early. I had a doctor's appointment. It's nothing to worry about."

"Well good. I wanted to tell you they're moving up the date for my London trip. Instead of this summer, I may have to leave right after Christmas and be there for the New Year."

"Oh Del. I'll probably be off in San Diego doing that Navy brochure in January. The one you said you'd go on with me. I told you my sister Bernadette would be out there, and I plan to stop in and see her."

"I might not be able to get away to go. If I don't, you could always take Gloria. You told me she wanted to get involved."

"It's not the same, and I really don't want to do this alone," Marietta said feeling sweat break out on her forehead. Things were moving fast, too fast. She did not do well when things moved fast.

"I know how you feel, so we'll talk more about it when I get home."

"About what? You promised me you'd go."

"About everything, Mari. I don't think I'll be able to go."

"But Del…" the door to the doctor's office opened and Marietta looked up and nodded. "Okay. We'll talk later." She clicked him off.

Marietta wiped her sweaty palms and followed the nurse to the back of the doctor's suite.

"She wants to talk to you here first. She'll be back in a minute." The receptionist closed the door leaving Marietta to sit and grip the chair, her heart pounding so hard it felt as though it was shaking her whole body. Every time Del had to go on trips that took him far away, she panicked. She needed him. He was going to be there and help her get over this bridge, get married, have a family, cut the past loose. She just had to hang on.

Her stomach had really been cramping lately, pains she hadn't felt in years. It started with Bernadette's letter and hadn't let up. At first, she thought it was nerves, but she'd had these problems off and on in the past, and she knew these pains were more.

Also, she hadn't had any sightings of a period in two months. Although that wasn't unusual for her body, she worried when it was accompanied by such pain.

She hated doctors. The best thing she could do was to avoid the military physicians, who gave her no confidence, and find civilian physicians with the best reputations. Thus Dr. Bindu Noor.

Marietta crossed her legs, started when a serious cramp gripped her deep in her stomach, uncrossed her legs, and placed her palms flat on her abdomen. The door to the office opened, and the doctor breezed in, closing the door and smiling over at Marietta. Marietta returned the smile the best she could as she watched the doctor go around the desk, sit and open her file, glancing down a minute. When Dr. Noor looked back up, Marietta's lips twitched.

"Ms. Windsor. So, how're you doing? Don't look at me like that. We go through this every time, and I haven't done anything to you yet, have I?"

"You've also never given me good news, yet."

"Oh, come on now. Look, in my field, when I don't walk in and pull up the chair on your side of the desk and take both of your hands in mine, that is good news. I have to deliver so much bad news, believe me, your news is good. It may not be exactly what you are looking to hear, but you're going to live and have a long, happy life."

Marietta clasped her hands.

"The tests look good?"

"I'm not saying that it's all normal. In fact, we need to discuss some of these results. However, I'm saying that, with the right kind of care, you may be able to do everything you've always hoped to once you were married. Ah! Let me see that stunning ring."

Marietta wiped her palm again across her pants, then extended her hand while the doctor's face registered something close to surprised respect at the size of the marquis diamond.

"And, he wants children?"

"Yes. We both do."

"Mmmmm. And what did you tell him?"

"I didn't know what to tell him."

"Mmhmm. We have some work to do, lady. We have some work."

Dr. Noor stared at a page before her, flipped it over, and said, "Now, first thing. You're here to listen to the results of the tests I had you give blood for. Very interesting, actually. It's like a puzzle, your condition of amenorrhea, or the lack of a period. It's caused by many conditions. I was interested in proving to you what I believed was the cause of your condition, that you're just so thin Ms. Windsor. You need body fat to produce enough estrogen to get this thing moving for you every month.

"But, as I said in the examination, I noticed that your female organs have some distinct abnormal formations. Appears congenital by all indications, but it appears that this abnormal shaping affects function, which surprised me."

"I'm extremely afraid of surgery, if that's what you're saying. I just couldn't bear going under the knife, and--"

"While we have some options to try here, surgery isn't one. We have a variety of medications we can try to regulate your reproductive cycle."

"Good. Then, maybe we can work on something."

"Of course we can. I believe we are going to make a baby. Eventually."

Marietta looked at her.

"But I have to start at the root to figure out what we have to do for you. Root causes are the best start for solving problems. So I had a lot of your blood work sent to a genetics lab. There were some things I was seeing... that I wanted to understand more. The types of physical abnormalities I see in you are rare. Extremely, so I had to find out what I could about recessive genes. You understand the concept behind recessive genes?"

Marietta stared, and carefully answered, "Just that when they come out, you're screwed."

"In so many words, you could say that. What I wanted to check into, was the probability that, if you did have children, what other types of problems would your children likely see in their progeny. So, the findings that I've uncovered show, in all probability your physical deformities are caused by recessive genes. And, to find out anything more specific, I would need to send in samples from your parents. By the way, how much do you know about the blood lines of your parents?"

"Not that much. My mother and father were married and had six normal kids."

"Well, I have reason to believe that some of your problems are caused by consanguinity, or more clearly, the mixture of close blood lines at some point in your family tree. Things that happened far back can end up trickling down to you."

"So, somewhere in either one of my parents ancestry, close relatives had sex."

"And even worse, had children. Now, what that means to you is, if we can also get a profile of your mother and father, I could give you a much clearer picture genetically of what you could expect."

"Well, that's out of the question. I am not in touch at all with my father's side of the family."

"But, can you be?"

"No."

"Well, we can work on you. We have drugs to stimulate the proper amounts of hormones that are necessary for periods. We can probably get you fertile enough to reproduce. But the question for you is, are you willing to take a chance on the line of recessive genes you have continuing?"

"Will my children run a greater risk of congenital disease? If I have children?

"If these results are accurate. By getting the blood samples from your parents, you could get the genetic counseling you may want to have, before you have children."

Dr. Noor studied Marietta, whose lips had begun to tremble. It took only seconds for tears to fall. Marietta accepted the tissues from the doctor and wiped her eyes, and when she finished, she sat quietly.

"Ms. Windsor, your knowledge of your parentage may be helpful in treating you, but not completely necessary. You do know your father?"

"What I know is my mother was told as I got older, that I would probably outgrow the painful menstrual cycles I had. All pain and next to no blood. They thought it was something that would correct itself. Gave me every brand of birth control pills out here. Nothing really worked. And I always feared I would have a problem when I wanted children. They told my mother that I probably would. But that's all I know."

Dr. Noor waited, watching Marietta struggle with the news. She leaned forward and said, "You do realize, I did not say that you have 60 days to live. I did not say that you have a painful, incurable disease. I did not say that life, as you know it, will never be the same. I did say we have options that would probably make you fertile, or in any event, raise your potential to conceive. It's just a fact that you may face birth defects in your children, or children's children. Then again, you may not."

"And of course, you think I should share this with my fiance?"

"I think that anyone, man or woman, who makes it known up front that children are important, should know that this may or may not happen. Often, this is not news that will stop a marriage. Not when two people love and want each other more than anything else. I think you should tell him."

Marietta's tears started again.

"Ms. Windsor, this is a serious matter, but this is not life or death. You need time to digest this news, and to talk to your mother about what I've told you. Maybe she can shed some light on your father's side. Then, if you're willing, we can help you conceive, okay?"

Marietta watched the doctor's lips move, felt hers move in response, and even heard herself saying, "Okay. I'll talk to my fiance and get back to you on what I want to do." Dr. Noor said something else, her lips moving and smiling. At what, Marietta had no clue. Then Marietta got up. What made her think she would ever lead a normal life? What made her think she was better than the riff-raff Gloria said she loved to pick up? What made her think she could escape what Daddy and his family had done to her? Had done to them all?

She could not get away from the past. It was here. And there was someone who knew about them, out there sending notes to warn them that it was not over. She could bow out now, and save Del a lot of pain and agony. Or she could move forward and live her life until it all came crashing down.

She hailed a cab, and as soon as she settled inside, pulled out her phone and punched in numbers.

# Beatrice

## nine

*"Deck the halls with boughs of holly*
*Fa la la la la, la la la la"*

Bea sang out loudly, pushing her face into the baby's. She tugged the mint green sleeper over the baby's protruding stomach, watching his arms and legs flail wildly like he was trying to fly off the table.

*"We'll be rich, and we'll be jolly*
*Fa la la la la, la la la la"*

Bea giggled. Witt had a partner to pony up the rest of the money! They were going to sign papers tonight. He was going to be in touch with the club secretary tomorrow, and by the end of December, Witt said he'd be interviewed. And he'd be in.

She felt like laughing. She would start the New Year off knowing her father and together they would stand up to Mama. Never mind that poem, she had a few things to say. Yes, Nita was dead, and she was going to prove to her family what had really happened. She drew up a deep breath, inhaling the baby's scent, rubbing his soft skin against hers. He smelled like Johnson & Johnson baby gel, cottony sweet and clean. Just as she was about to lift her head, he grabbed a handful of her hair and made her laugh out loud as she took his soft, smooth, fleshy hands and opened his little fingers enough to move her head away. She was just about to lift him up to fit him in her arm and feed him his evening bottle when Witt's voice rang out loudly. She jumped, and the baby stopped moving, his eyes watching her face closely as Witt's words rained down from the room above.

"Toukie, what you still doing laying around in the bathtub this time of night? Why aren't you in the bed and out the way?!"

His voice was directly overhead which meant he was standing in the bathroom with Toukie in the tub. Again. She had already told him not to do that anymore, Toukie was getting too old for it. Her body was changing; she was getting a little hair and Toukie didn't want anybody looking at her. Toukie was furious that he burst in on her whenever he wanted to, and had told her mother about it. She definitely didn't want Toukie telling Bernadette, and she had a feeling if Witt didn't stop, that's what would happen.

With the baby in one arm and the bottle gripped in her hand, she hurried up the steps and was halfway down the hall when Witt stepped out of the bathroom.

"What you yelling at her like that for?"

"Did you see the time? It's after nine and she's still in the bathroom laying in bubble bath like she's the Queen of Sheba. I told her what time I wanted her in the bed, and she's not in there yet."

"She's going, you give her a chance."

"That's what's wrong. I got someplace to be and you want to give her a chance. You always want to give her a chance. When she's wrong, she's wrong, and you got to show her she's wrong or she's never going to learn to follow directions! I expect her to show the baby how to follow rules, and she can't follow them herself cause YOU never showed her how."

"She don't give me no trouble and never have, so I don't know why you got to complain about every little thing."

"'Cause if I don't show her, who will? She doesn't have to do one chore around here and that's just fine with you! Every time I see her, she's got on something new, walking around here like she's in charge of something, wearing more new outfits than any of us. I don't appreciate it. I told you to tell your sister to stop sending money here for her, or I was going to tell her. We don't need Bernadette's money, we don't need Bernadette, and it's not helping Toukie to give her something for nothing. If she wants money, she needs to work for it, but I guess your sister don't know anything about that huh?"

"Witt, she give her money for her hair! You think Toukie's hair grew back like that? Bernadette send me money to take her to the hairdressers to braid her hair up in that ponytail until her hair grow back. That's all it is."

"Hairdresser? That's a bigger waste of money than all those clothes. She has hair. All she needs to do is to learn how to take care of it. I'm telling you Trice, she's getting spoiled, and you don't want that."

"She ain't no more spoiled than this boy, and you know it."

"She's not supposed to be. He's got to go out here and be a man in the United States of America. There's not a damn person who's going to give him a thing, and the only way he's going to know what he's about is if we show him here what it's like to be a man. It's about breeding and discipline. Toukie's not going to be a man, and she can't get it through her head where her place is supposed to be."

"Why don't you get off her back? She always do what you say, everything you say, and she still good in school, so what if she don't do it all perfect. She is a nine-year-old child, Witt. Not a woman. Remember, she is not a woman."

"I know what she is, and I know I want her out of that tub in five minutes," Witt said and stalked off down the hall.

Bea stood and looked after him, the baby bumping her chin with his big head. Witt could blow the high after a lottery win. Anybody else would be kicking their heels with joy if they found out that they had a partner to go into business with, but not him. He hadn't been the same since Bernadette's visit two months ago. Boy did she get him riled up when she wouldn't touch the baby. Then Toukie's teacher's call right after Bernadette left didn't help, telling them what she thought they should do to help Toukie. Witt was so scared to give Toukie any special attention, like if he did, it would mean he wasn't paying attention to the baby. It wasn't true. He didn't want to give Toukie an inch.

Bea stood undecided. Should she go into the bathroom and check up on Toukie? Witt was pretty hard on her and she was probably in there crying. Or should she go to the bedroom to calm Witt. If Witt messed up this meeting tonight, she would kill him herself. She looked toward the bathroom, then back in the direction of the bedroom where Witt had gone. She always felt torn between her man and her child, and if she didn't know better, she would swear Witt wanted her to choose. She hugged the baby to her and started toward the bedroom. Witt was the one she had to worry about now.

He didn't mean Toukie no harm. These business meetings got him worried. She rubbed the baby's back and followed Witt into their room where he stood before the closet, his navy suit hanging up on the door and a white button down shirt in his hand that he held up against it. He hung it beside the suit, then went to the dresser and started looking through his socks, tossing out a pair beside his clean underwear. She stared at his back and broad, sturdy shoulders.

When Witt found out that Freddie Caldwell, a young engineer at the Westinghouse plant where Witt worked the docks, had a father already in several small local businesses, he made Freddie his choice and set out to get him as partner. Freddie's father had all the money they needed, so his search for a partner was over. All Witt needed was their money and their silence. He would make the business decisions and take care of operations. He would get in the club; Freddie and his father would reap the benefits. What he had to do tonight, according to Freddie, was show the old man a business proposal he liked, and it was done. Freddie was taking Witt to meet with the father and they would lock up a deal tonight.

Beatrice was holding her breath. When Witt discovered Freddie's father's success, all he could concentrate on was impressing him. He spent money that they didn't have taking Freddie and his girlfriend over to DC to Wizard games, and out to dinner in the Harbor, and down to Annapolis to the Ramshead where they grooved to jazz groups. Sometimes, he just had them over in the basement, Witt's den, where Witt cooked them full three course meals. He was an excellent cook having learned it in the Marines. They'd spend all night talking, Witt spinning stories in between planning and talking numbers.

"If it don't work out tonight, Witt, just leave. We can get a new partner."

Witt turned around to look at her standing in the doorway.

"I think I can handle this."

" I know you can. But I just can't help but think, what if it don't work? I'm just saying, don't let nothing stop you if he don't want to buy in."

Each time Freddie had come to talk business, his girlfriend Cynthia was glued to his side. And Bea couldn't help but notice how she hung onto Witt's every word, much more than Freddie. She'd already warned Witt. The girl took notes, writing down Witt's figures as though she were the one being asked in the business agreement. And she always brought a calculator and talked about the bottom line.

"I majored in business at Morgan," Cynthia would say, "And if it sounds good enough, Freddie, Jr. might be jumping into this even if his father doesn't. Sometimes Mr. Fred is slow to make a move, but Freddie can get that money up."

Real estate is where Witt wanted to start, where he said he would make his money, and when that took off, he'd find a little hole to work on carving his wooden pieces and selling those. Mr. Fred also had real estate holdings, and the most Witt wanted with the son was an in to the father. So he ignored Cynthia and her probing questions.

"I don't think I'll have a problem. I understand Freddie doesn't seem as interested in the business, but his father might. Especially when I tell him about the club backing me. Freddie, Jr. is still young, just out of Villanova; he has time to get where I am. Right now, he's all about Cynthia, and she knows a meal ticket when she sees one. He thinks he loves her, and while that's going on, I'm walking in and taking the father. He's all I need."

"Yeah, but you want Freddie to talk you up to his father, and maybe he ain't ready to. Maybe this ain't the right time for a meeting, you know? If Freddie don't care, his father probably won't."

Witt sighed.

"I can handle this one, Trice. Okay? When it comes to business, I can make the decisions. You want to do something? Go and get your daughter in the bed and out of my way. Go sit in her room and rock your son to sleep. That's what I need you to do right now."

Beatrice glowered. Sometimes he made her so mad she could slap him. She didn't know that much about business, she didn't know anything about it, but she knew how much $22,000 was worth, and she didn't see throwing it at people who didn't really want it. Especially since all the money to her name—her retirement fund she cashed in and the cash from the furniture she sold-- was involved in that sum.

She came quietly into the bedroom and sat in the rocker, holding the bottle to the baby's mouth. She rocked him gently while Witt pulled out different shirts. The baby's eyes were already closing, the way they always did after his bath every night. She hugged him tightly in her arms, and watched Witt critically. Beads of sweat were dotting his forehead and that thick vein just over his temple had popped up. He was too wound up. Even if he got to talk to the man, he was bound to mess up. He was bossy when he got nervous, and people did not like that.

Determined to calm him down, she wet her lips and said, in a low patient voice, "If you just go there and be yourself, not begging but just laying it out like you do to me, real business-like, he'll do it. He can see how serious you are, and he'll do it. But you got to stay calm, Witt." *My life savings are riding on this.*

Witt's eyebrows rose, she could see even at this angle but she noticed how his shoulders suddenly relaxed as he turned to face her.

"He's going to say yes, Witt. I feel it. And then, how long before you get in the club?"

"I can be at the next monthly meeting in January. I could be making good money…in probably as soon as one year."

"Then what? We get to move from here when?"

"As soon as the business grabs hold. It won't take me long. We have to finish with this house, get it all fixed up and sell it. Then we can move on. Get a nicer one."

"And a truck. I want a big truck, a Ford Expedition. I love them."

"We can do it in a year. Promise."

"All right, Witt. If you talk to him just like you talking to me, I know we can do it. Don't let him get you mad. If he say no, then just take it. You can find somebody else. You got money he can use, and if he don't see that, walk away. Don't be getting all mad and up in his face."

"Don't you believe in me?" he asked shortly.

"I'm here with you, ain't I? I wouldn't be if I didn't."

"Then let me do it. It's going to happen for me, baby. I deserve it, and I've been working for it all of my life!" Witt's eyes sparkled brightly, and he came over to where she sat in the rocking chair. Slowly, he leaned down to Bea's face, where he could press her lips with his. He moved down to one knee and put his arms around her, holding her close to him and hugging the baby between them as well.

She didn't even realize how tense he was until he kissed her, and as he pressed her lips harder, kissing her deeply, she felt his tension easing away. Every time she moved the baby to protect him from Witt's crushing embrace, he held her steady. Suddenly his kisses were yearning, his tongue seeking until finally he stopped to move the sleeping baby from her arms and into the play pen beside the bed. Then he pulled Beatrice up from the chair and over to the bed. He quickly undressed her, keeping his lips glued to hers before he jumped up suddenly to close the door. When he came back, she moved against the pillows as he dropped his pants, his eyes intent on hers as he climbed over her, strong thighs inside hers. She helped him inside her and tried to move with him but he held her tightly, almost rigidly pounding into her so hard it hurt before he slowed down enough to lift both her heavy breasts and run his tongue over her fat nipples, slowly, back and forth, holding her breasts together. He gently sucked at her, so gently she felt her herself wrapping around his manhood. She closed her eyes as he stayed fitted tightly inside. He slowly rotated his hips, and she began to respond, almost whimpering. He was good at this. If nothing else, this man could make her cry when he was in her.

Biting hard on her bottom lip to keep from making noise, she knew he felt her spasms. Picking up his strokes, it wasn't long before he answered them.

"Witt," she whispered wiping the perspiration that dripped from his forehead onto her face. "Just be cool about it." She kissed him quickly, and he looked down at her and smiled.

"I always am."

\*\*\*\*\*\*

She must have dozed. She woke up surprised the lights in the bedroom were still on, and reached over to touch the empty spot of bed beside her. Then she sat up and looked at the clock. One a.m. Why wasn't Witt back? She looked over and saw his suit was off the door and his dirty clothes were in a heap by the bed. Then she remembered calming him down and smiled.

She glanced over to the playpen where the baby was still asleep on his stomach, then closed her eyes, lying back down. She felt hopeful.

She was finally going to see her Daddy after all these years. He was going to tell her how everything happened, because she needed to know. She needed to understand how...

*Thursdays. Juanita and Beatrice went with Daddy after school on Thursday, because that was their day they got to spend with him. Mama had Bernadette, and she would pick up Marietta then rush them downtown to Marietta's modern dance class at the Y. The boys had school events that kept them busy. Daddy belonged only to her and Nita on Thursdays, two little girls' dream.*

*He left it up to them to pick where they wanted to go each Thursday. They went to eat different places, they went to concerts, arcades, Disney shows on ice, skating, movies and then they'd drag home late. Daddy would let them decide on an activity, and go along with it, even if it kept them out late. Anything after 11:00 p.m. would start Mama hollering when they came in, but Daddy made it okay. He always made everything okay.*

*Saturdays were for Daddy and the boys. And because he couldn't get Bernadette on Thursdays, he often took her with the boys. He sometimes took them to sporting events, but just as easily, he took them to business events and to as many cultural affairs as he thought they could stand. He'd often switch up, and take the girls to see professional basketball, and the boys out to dinner or a concert. Then there were times Daddy would rent a van and take them and their friends someplace. No matter what Daddy came up with, the boys were always ready to go with him. Daddy was always fun, even when he was punishing them for something, he made them laugh. He liked to laugh.*

*Funny thing was, Daddy never took Marietta on any day. There was never a day just for her.*

*That last Thursday Daddy was not himself. He didn't ask them where they wanted to go. He picked the restaurant, a Japanese place called Nichi Bei Kai in Dulaney Valley, and while she and Nita giggled about taking off their shoes and sitting on the floor pillows, Daddy said nothing.*

*He kept ordering sake. They ate. When they turned and asked him questions, he answered, but he was quiet otherwise until it was time to go. Then Daddy told them, some things were going to change.*

*"Your mother is very angry, and I don't know...I don't know what will happen. But I promise you, whatever it is, if you need, no matter what it is, I will come."*

*Beatrice saw his eyes. Red as they were, they glistened. And she was scared.*

*"What Daddy?" Nita asked. "What is going to happen?"*

*"I don't know. Just remember, I'll be there."*

*But Beatrice was only seven, and she could see his eyes. She cried all the way home, while Nita stayed quiet. He'd made them feel so special. No matter what, when he was happy or mad, he made them feel special.*

*And then he was gone.*

Mama threatened them with things she would do if she found out they had talked to him. She told them, they would be gone. And if she found he ever talked to them, she told them she would kill him.

But Bea had tried to find him when Nita was sick. Where was Daddy? Daddy should have come. He could have saved her. He loved them, and always had. Had he called them back, and Mama found out?

Mama hated her and blamed her for Nita's death. But Daddy could have helped, if Mama let him. Bea was sure it was Mama who stopped Daddy from helping, and then blamed her.

If she could find Daddy, she could prove it--if she could only get to him.

And Witt was going to help her do it all.

*ten*

Bea screamed. Her eyes flew open and she jerked her leg up to her chest in pain. When she heard the baby holler out, she sat up and saw him lying on his stomach beside her leg, eyes glistening with tears, spit drooling. She rubbed her shin, and as the sleep cleared away, she saw Toukie standing down at the foot of her bed, her little arms folded across her chest, lips poked out, eyes glaring. Had she dropped that baby on her?

"I got to go to school. Poohbah was crying, so I changed him and gave him his milk. Now can I have some lunch money so I can go?"

Bea stared in surprise at her daughter.

"Are you crazy? Why you drop him down like that on my leg? You know how bad that hurt? You could really hurt the baby."

Toukie reached down and pulled up the rolling telephone, a block of wood on wheels that had been in Toukie's hand and had actually hit her mother's leg.

"I didn't drop him."

Bea snatched her head around and looked at the clock. She frowned. It was way past time for Toukie to go to school. What happened to the night?

"Where's Witt?"

Toukie's little eyes narrowed. "I ain't seen him, and I sure ain't looking for him." She glared at her mother.

"What you mean? He ain't been here this morning?" Bea's voice rose in shocked surprise.

"I guess not. Can I have my lunch money please so I can go to school?" Toukie repeated.

Bea looked at Toukie's face. What was her problem?

Almost as though she could read her mother's thoughts, Toukie said,

"I heard you in here last night. I heard what Witt said about me getting out the bathtub, and I ain't hear you say nothing to help me. I hate him. He keep coming in the bathroom with me when I take a bath and yelling at me. He keep fussing about everything. He don't let me do nothing. He don't let me go down the basement with his stereo and stuff but he let Poobah go. He let you and he let Freddie and all them people he do business with go and touch his stuff. He hates me, and I hate him. I wish you would leave and let him just stay here."

"Toukie! Stop saying that. That ain't nothing to say about Witt. He trying to do what he can."

"Then how come I'm the only one he fuss at? How come I got the dirty bedroom? How come I got the little bedroom? How come he always tell me I got to follow Poobah, when Poobah gets big?"

"He already told you he want to do your room over when he do the downstairs. He mean it when he say it."

"He don't like me and he don't like my Aunt Bernadette and we don't like him either. She ain't scared of him or nobody, and she told me I don't have to be either."

"Toukie!"

"And he ain't getting my money. He don't want me to get money from Aunt Bern so he can have it, but he ain't getting my money."

"He don't want your money. He just don't want Bernadette to do too much."

"Why? He do too much for Poobah and not for me!"

"Toukie, that ain't true."

"It is true, and I need some money so I can go to school." Toukie sighed loudly, then walked over to her mother's dresser and stared down looking for some rolled up dollar bills that usually lay on top.

"It should be some money up there," Beatrice said as she finally pulled the baby up on the pillow next to her. She watched her daughter primp in the mirror turning her head left then right. Toukie moved aside the beer bottles, cookie box, and picked up two hairpins that she pushed under two braids, pulling her hair back from her narrow face.

"I don't see no money," Toukie said at last, turning around.

Beatrice frowned, then shook her head. "I don't understand. Witt left here last night to go to a meeting and never came back home? He should have been back home, and you talking about some stupid lunch money?"

"I don't care," Toukie answered simply.

Beatrice sat up straight and stared at her daughter.

"If I don't go to school, my teacher is going to call here to find out what happened to me. She told me she would. Did Witt take my money?"

Beatrice looked at Toukie. She must really hate him. She could care less that he wasn't home. She glanced over at the dresser, then back at her daughter who stood defiantly before her.

"Look under that glass wheel on the dresser. Take what I have there."

Toukie obeyed, counting the bills. She looked at her mother.

"I know how much Aunt Bern sends to me. She told me in her letter, and you don't give me all my money. It ain't right, Ma. That's what I say."

Beatrice watched Toukie's back as she retreated from the room, and sat there until minutes later, she heard her close the door as she left the house.

Where was Witt? Look like he would call and tell her they got in.

Beatrice took the baby with her into the bathroom and cleaned him up in the tub with her. She dressed him quickly, then herself and went downstairs to feed him. Toukie had left her cereal bowl on the table, the box open and the milk out. Beatrice reached for the Gerber Rice cereal for the baby and warmed up some milk. He would be screaming for food in 15 minutes if he didn't get some. She cleaned up the table and washed the dishes, wondering about Witt. What had happened? He should have been back.

That meant things had not gone well. If they had, Witt would have been home celebrating. She was only too scared to find out what had gone wrong.

******

It was just after six in the evening, the children had eaten and Toukie had the baby upstairs with her, leaving Beatrice in the kitchen watching Judge Judy on the small television. She heard the lock on the front door click open.

In a second Beatrice was up, running around the table through the dining room to the hall. She stopped and stared at Witt waiting to see his face. Maybe he did get Freddie's father to sign, and they'd stayed out together celebrating. But what she saw were his wrinkled clothes and that his hair hadn't been combed all day. His eyes were crusty like he just woke up and he didn't look at her or in any way acknowledge her.

"What the hell happened to you?"

She'd called his job and knew he wasn't at work all day, and neither was Freddie because she had called for him too.

"We didn't make the deal. Simple as that."

Bea felt so weak she leaned against the wall.

"Why not?"

He paused for so long she thought he wasn't going to answer. He slowly shrugged off his suit jacket and went to hang it in the hall closet. Then, in a quiet tone, he said one word, "Cynthia." He paused, and said, "She was supposed to meet us over Freddie's, then go with us to his father's, but she never showed up. So we waited.

"Freddie went out to look for her, and left me at his apartment. He stayed all night. His father didn't call or show up at Freddie, Jr.'s. So, that would have been that. But, while I was sitting there, thinking how do I get this back on track, I was looking through one of those little photo albums, and it was one that had pictures of Cynthia, like when she was little and in high school and college. Cynthia's had a picture where she was at her prom or something, and she was standing there with one of my old buddies from way back. And I remembered that girl. When I saw her in that picture, I remembered a whole lot about her. Stuff she wouldn't want Freddie to know."

Bea looked down as Witt reached in his pocket, pulled out a couple Polaroids and gave them to her. She squinted, seeing a young woman with shoulder length hair topless and on her knees in front of a tall, skinny guy performing an oral sex act. Was it Cynthia? She looked at a second shot, and saw more of the girl's face. It was Cynthia, and from the look on her face, she loved it.

"Oh, Witt," Beatrice said, turning her eyes. "Don't do that. That's his girlfriend, he don't want to see that. If you mad at her, don't hurt Freddie, 'cause if you do that, you can forget Freddie Sr. helping you. That's crazy."

"I'm not going to do it, if she stops interfering in my business. But I know she's going to freak when she knows I have these."

"Witt, I'm begging you. Don't play with people like that."

"No. People don't play with me like that, that's what I'm saying. I've done nothing but give them respect. That shit last night was unnecessary, and I need to make sure it doesn't happen again."

Beatrice noticed that large vein was standing out on his forehead.

"So you went and found your buddy from way back? That's what you did all night and all day?"

"Well, I stayed at Freddie's house most of the night waiting, then after I found the prom picture, I went out to get some insurance that I won't have any more trouble out of that girl."

"You never saw Freddie again? I mean, did you go back to the house?"

"No. I left trying to figure out what I wanted to do…and I finally made up my mind to do what Freddie was afraid to do. Find a way to put her ass in her place."

Beatrice frowned, giving him a long look.

"You showed her them pictures? What if this backfires on you, Witt? Ain't it more important to get the money and your business than to show her anything?"

He didn't answer right away. He looked down at the floor contemplating, his hands working to loosen his shirt from his pants, then to unbutton it. Again she thought he wasn't going to answer, then he sighed.

"I didn't show her these—yet. I found out what I needed to know about Cynthia. I figure, that my being there alone was no accident. So I have to do what I have to do. Remember, this is a man's business club. It's men in business together, not women. So, if Freddie can't get her under control, I will. And if I have to, I may just have to look for another partner after all."

With that, he pulled off his shirt, folded it over his arm, then turned toward the staircase. Beatrice watched him wordlessly. He never looked back at her, and she was left to wonder.

What was he planning?

******

She couldn't figure it out. Witt stayed in the basement sleeping all the next day, and as soon as the sun went down, he showered, dressed and went out. All night.

She went into the basement to wake him for work the next morning, but she couldn't budge him. She waited for Toukie to go to school before she went down to even try. And every time she pushed him hard, he turned, keeping his eyes closed.

Finally he raised his head, his red eyes and liquor breath hitting her hard.

"I know when I have to work, and if I don't get up, I must not be going. You understand?"

She stood there with her hands on her waist watching as he turned his back. And stayed there. So she didn't bother him again.

Later that night when Beatrice had the children in bed, Witt got up and went into the shower, dressed and hit the streets. He said nothing to her.

When he came back, it was in the morning, right before Toukie left for school. He found his way back to the basement and crashed on the couch.

He did this the rest of the week, saying nothing to Beatrice. She said nothing more to him. She thought of calling Freddie, Jr. to see if he knew what was going on, but thought better of it. Witt couldn't keep this up forever. Something had to give.

After a week of this, as Beatrice sat at the kitchen table with Toukie, about to dig into a Philly style hoagie she'd made herself and filled with thick fried onions, and thin sliced steaks dripping cheese, the door bell rang. Toukie jumped up.

"I got it!" she said sprinting away. Beatrice glanced after her but settled the baby with a bottle in his playpen. She had added a pitcher of juice to the table when Toukie came back followed by Freddie's girl Cynthia, wrapped in an ankle length, form fitting black trench coat, collar turned up, teeth flashing.

"Surprise!" she said with a full pretty smile, and Bea paused to stare. There was something refreshing about Cynthia, her picture-perfect homecoming queen look topped by sexy short hair perfectly cut and coiffed, golden fried chicken brown skin smoothly flawless, and shapely arched brows.

"It sure is, and Witt ain't here."

"I know. That's why I am." Cynthia raised an eyebrow for emphasis. "I was wondering if we could talk for a minute, without the men. The men take over when they're here, and I wanted this to be a woman's thing."

Bea wiped a ring of juice off the table with the dishcloth and told Cynthia to take a seat.

"We have Philly subs, Ms. Cynthia!" Toukie offered, and Cynthia, sliding her coat over her shoulders closed her eyes and sniffed dramatically. "I could smell them out on the steps!"

"Want one?" Bea asked, and Cynthia shook her head. "Every bite would stick right to these," she said hitting her curvaceous hips. "Besides, I just ate at McDonald's. I won't take long, but Bea, I guess you're wondering about the money and what happened."

Bea's eyes narrowed.

"You know Freddie's father talked to Witt, but he didn't sign to be his partner. He told Witt he could do better for his money if he didn't go to Fells Point to try to buy a building for an apartment house."

Bea looked at Cynthia. Witt never told her anything Freddie's father said. Why did Cynthia know all this shit? She wondered what Cynthia was really after. She wasn't after Freddie, not the way she jerked his ass all over. But she had her foot on Witt's neck, pulling the men away just as Witt was about to get the money. Why? What was it really about? What was going to happen when she found out about those pictures? Beatrice guessed she didn't know about those yet. She bit into her sandwich.

"Mr. Fred doesn't really want to go in business with Witt—for a lot of reasons. He doesn't need Witt, and my Freddie doesn't like the idea of real estate. But I want you to know, I told Freddie he and I should. I think Witt has good ideas and Freddie can get the money to help back him, even if his father doesn't want to."

Oh, so that's it. Cynthia wanted to be a partner.

Bea chewed with no comment.

"And Witt is ready to roll, he's got papers all drawn up to start a partnership. I made Freddie go ahead and open up the business account with Witt, you know. I had them do it at my bank. My manager opened the commercial account for him, so he and Freddie have taken the first step. But Freddie is holding off on some of the money, because he wants to look at something other than real estate. I want this opportunity for Freddie so bad, but if he doesn't want it, I was thinking, I do. Witt has really thought this thing through. I think I can get up the rest of the money he still needs so he can get it going."

Bea drank her juice listening.

"I told Freddie I'd take Witt up on his offer, but he said Witt wouldn't work with me, not even as a silent partner. So, to make a long story short, Witt ended up, when I asked him directly if I could contribute, saying a lot of crazy things about women…and business…and their place in the world."

Toukie snickered. Bea frowned at Toukie, then looked at Cynthia, waiting.

"And I'm thinking, surely he's just giving me a hard time because it's me. I know you don't stand for that! That me-Tarzan-you-Jane shit."

Bea lifted her brow.

"And I feel like…okay, if Witt doesn't get Mr. Fred, and Freddie can't make up his mind, you and I could use some of that money and get together to do our own business. We could raise money for him. It wouldn't be as big as Witt's ideas, but I've dreamed of opening my own business…" she paused, then said with a smile, "all I want is just one little place to open my own little shop." Cynthia pulled over the black leather bag that Beatrice thought was her pocketbook. She reached inside and pulled out two boldly colored garments of beautiful African print and the head wrap.

"I make these dresses or robes myself, and I guarantee, the money from these pay my livelihood. My teller job pays my incidentals."

"Oooooooo," Toukie exclaimed and got up to run her fingers across the shiny material.

"I have children's outfits too," Cynthia said. "I mean it's well and good to have talented men, but frankly I see no reason why we can't get a piece of this and do our thing. I'm here because I had to literally cuss Witt out and tell him to get away from me telling me how I shouldn't be looking into a business for me but for Freddie, if I were a true black woman. What the hell is he talking about?"

Bea said nothing for a moment, but when Cynthia continued to stare, she finally said, "Witt's business is his business. I ain't running it and I ain't got nothing to do with it. I don't want a business. If he want to work with Freddie and his father, fine. If they don't want to work with him, fine. I ain't got nothing to do with it. Neither do you."

"Wait a minute. Don't tell me you believe in all that black man mumbo jumbo with black woman standing behind?"

"I'm telling you Cynthia, you don't want to mess with Witt and this business. Leave it to Freddie. If he said he was going to open the account and get the money up, he is. Or Witt can take his money out and look for somebody else. You don't want to do business with Witt."

Cynthia looked surprised, then leaned back and looked at her under half lids.

"I know all that money in the bank isn't just his because you said in the beginning some was yours, but he wants to act like it is all his and you have nothing to say. He tells me that's how I should be with Freddie, Jr., but he's crazy! Why should I give Freddie my money and have no say over it?"

"Is Freddie complaining about Witt?"

"Yes, he is. Freddie has told Witt, in so many words, that he's not putting in the kind of money Witt is asking for real estate, but he'll give some. And I will too if he'll accept it and some of my suggestions. For some reason, Witt has it in his head that it has to be Freddie or his father. Here I am trying to give him an alternative, if he takes me. I can get him more money from Freddie. But he's telling ME how I should be getting behind Freddie to work with him, like I don't exist."

"That's because it's a business club Witt want to get into and it's only men. He can't go in with you."

"But you can. I refuse to get more money for Witt if I can't make suggestions. So, what if we took some of your money and started our own business. It would work. Then maybe you could earn money for Witt…"

"I don't want to open up a business. I trust Witt to do it."

"Well, don't get me wrong. It's great to have a black man who is out here trying to be about something. I have two brothers, and I swear, I love them both, but their home is the revolving door of the penitentiary. They never got on the right foot, and when you have a man who's trying, I'm all for it. But Witt is not using his head about this."

"If Freddie don't want to be bothered, can't Freddie be man enough to just tell Witt? You got to come over here to tell me to tell my man to back off Freddie?"

Cynthia set her large cinnamon outlined lips in a firm line.

"What I came here for was to tell you that Mr. Fred isn't biting, but I thought there was a way Witt could still get some money for his ideas. It'd take a little longer, but you would be more involved. I can see now that that black man bull Witt talks has gone straight to your head. You do let him run your show, don't you?"

"It ain't that. Witt don't want to do business with you 'cause he want a man for a partner. That's what he got to have. Why you want to force him to do business with you?"

"Because he needs me for business, and I need him. If he does business with me, he can get Freddie eventually, then maybe even Freddie's father. I'm the one who influences Freddie, not Witt, and I don't appreciate him trying to get Freddie to turn on me. Did he tell you how he

told Freddie I was bad news? That he didn't think I was the one he wanted to end up with? That Freddie needed someone special in his life, and
if he thought I was, he was mistaken. I told Freddie if he didn't keep Witt
away from me, I would kick his ass, then Witt's. If Witt wants a shot at
his dream, he'd better think about how I can help him get there."

Cynthia stuffed her work back in her leather pouch and shot up in a
huff.

"I thought if I came to you woman to woman, we could come to an
agreement to help our men get together. There's always more than one
way to do something, but I see Witt wasn't lying one bit about you. He
has you trained and under his thumb."

"We talking two different things. What Witt want to do, and what
you want. This ain't about you."

Cynthia rolled her eyes and pulled on her trench coat.

"What I'm trying to get you to see Beatrice, is it's not about you
either."

Beatrice threw up her hands. "Toukie, take her out of here," she said
turning away to a small plate of mashed potatoes which she was about to
feed the baby. Beatrice felt her blood running hot. Cynthia didn't know
who she was messing with. She had no idea what Witt could do to her
and her relationship with Freddie. She had no clue.

"Don't worry, I can find my way to the front door!" Cynthia
snapped, but Toukie stood anyway, and walked with her. As they moved
from the kitchen, Bea heard her say to Toukie, "Sweetheart, you'd better
be real careful. Real careful around here."

Bea turned her head and watched her walk up the hall, wondering
why she would say that to Toukie.

## eleven

Then, as Cynthia warned, things got worse.

Beatrice, surprised at the loud ring of the phone during the baby's nap-time, grabbed it up and barely said hello before an unfamiliar voice demanded to speak to Witt. Before she could respond, the voice identified himself as Witt's supervisor, and said he understood Witt was still sick.

Beatrice hugged the phone to her ear tightly, and felt her knees weaken.

"Yes, he had a friend drive him to the doctor this morning, I'm on my way there now," she lied quickly. She rolled her eyes to the ceiling, and listened closely. "We don't know what it is yet. He'll call back today though. He actually couldn't even talk, that's why you haven't heard anything. I know that, and yes sir, I will sure deliver this message to Witt."

Beatrice hung up hard, then slumped down against the refrigerator. What the hell was Witt doing? She knew he wasn't going to work last week; he stayed out all night, and slept in all day. But this week, he was leaving in the morning like he was going to work every day…only his supervisor had not seen him in two weeks.

Bea stared blankly, worried as Bob Barker's voice droned on, "My beauties are bringing out the next prizes for you to bid on, so if you look to your left, the beautiful Daisy and Tanya will show you the next prizes up for bid…"

She paused to glance at the screen, then back to the bags of groceries she had to unpack. She glanced over at the baby in the playpen, lying on his back sleeping, then stared at the frozen tubes of sugar cookies and boxes of cake mix she'd just bought.

All these cookies and cakes, they would be eating sweets until Easter, she thought, then turned to the ham she had on the table for their Christmas dinner. She might as well get started on that, it was already December 23rd, her birthday.

"Happy birthday, Bea," she said to herself as the phone rang again.

Bea looked at it, willing it to stop. When it didn't, she snatched it up.

"Hello?" She held her breath, then let it out in a second.

"Oh, hello Kenyatta? This is Beatrice. Right. Okay, that's been straightened out; you don't have to worry about your lights or anything getting shut down. That was a mistake."

Beatrice stared over at the baby who had rolled on his stomach and lifted his face up. There went her break. She hated when she had to straighten out the mess Witt's finances made with their tenants, and she was at her end. That was happening more and more these days.

They didn't have enough money to do anything but work on getting Witt's new business partners, giving dinners and shit. He just told her this morning, before he left for what she thought was work that he was giving her the last money he had to pay the electric bill before Christmas. There was nothing left to get Toukie or the baby anything two days before Christmas.

"Okay, right, we took care of the utilities, so all you have to worry about is paying the rent by the fifth of January, and having a good holiday. All right? Merry Christmas." Beatrice hung up, went over to the refrigerator and took out a can of Miller Lite, then sat at the table, opened it, and took a long, hard swig. Her eyes fell on the application she had photocopied and put in today at the gas and electric company. It was crazy she just did that, but there she was, paying bills with the last money they had, and standing before a job announcement board.

It was barely 20 degrees outside, neither she nor the baby was in a hurry to go back out, so she sat in the lobby and filled in an application to become a customer service representative. Whatever that was. Something that required a high school diploma she didn't have. But she lied. They weren't going to answer her anyway.

She sighed and drank from the beer can. Something was not going right with Witt and she needed to find Daddy. It was taking too long…

*Daddy was taking too long to come. It had been almost five weeks since Nita had hooked school without her, and spent the day with Otis Dent, one of Dunbar's star basketball players. She told her sister she hadn't had a period, and she was scared.*

*Mama had already put their brother Daniel out. At 19, after one year when he failed to get a scholarship to college, or a job, she made good on her promise, and put out a suitcase with his clothes. And he was gone.*

*Mama promised to do the same to the girls when they turned 18. Have a job, or have the means to get one. And, Mama said to them as often and clearly as she could, don't even think about bringing a baby in her house. You would be out, right along with Daniel.*

*Bea and Nita were too scared to think about abortions. It didn't seem like the right thing to do, and they couldn't think about being on the streets. Bea had written her father immediately for help.*

*When she couldn't wait much longer, after a whole week, Bea promised Nita she would get Daddy. She was so sure her father would move heaven and earth to save one of his own, she rode the buses, it took three, to get to Ms. Odessa's, her father's mother's house, to tell him. That's when she had first begun to understand where Daddy had come from...something Bernadette would have to find out.*

*Once she got off the bus that day and walked along the multi-lane, high-way to look for her father's street, she had been in shock. These were not hous-es, they were mansions! Right before the Baltimore National Pike, there were huge brick homes with sprawling lawns and circular driveways, and as she turned off Edmondson Avenue onto Winans Way, downhill she came to one of the largest, the home of Ms. Odessa. She had never been "Grandmother" to them, always making them call her Ms. Odessa, on the rare opportunity they spoke to her. They had never been invited to her house. She had never been to theirs. They had heard her voice only when she'd called their house and asked for Daddy, which was all she ever did. Those were the times when Mama and Daddy would fight the hardest. Mama had told them they were blessed each and every day they didn't have to see Ms. Odessa.*

*And seeing those houses for the first time had started Beatrice to wonder why. Why had Daddy kept them from all this. Why did they have to do with-out if Ms. Odessa was rich?*

*She had been more determined than ever to see her father then. Nita would definitely be saved. She'd rung the bell and waited, rung and waited, and when she could wait no longer, she'd started to beat the glass in the door and bang. No one answered.*

*Disappointed and in tears, she'd slipped the letter for her father in the mail slot, and started back for the bustop when a car horn got her attention. Beatrice remembered pausing as a friendly face smiled out at her and asked if she were applying for the job there at Ms. Odessa's.*

*A job? She was told every house on the block had a young school girl to do the cooking or cleaning or both.*

*The girl was a housekeeper working several houses down the block, and she knew Ms. Odessa was looking for another girl. She'd wanted Bea to know that Ms. Odessa was off on her Mediterranean cruise, and if Beatrice was interested, she could leave the information with her.*

*The girl gave Bea a ride back to her side of town where all she needed to catch was one bus home and that was when Beatrice learned...there was a whole different life going on inside her family that she knew nothing about. Their father was rich.*

*She'd waited, and waited for Daddy to come and help Nita once he read the letter. He would know he had to hurry. He was rich! He could take them with him, since Mama would not forgive them. It was going to be better than ever for them, she knew it, so she waited.*

*And waited. And waited. Though she never saw Daddy, or heard from him, she remembered how he cried when he told them he was leaving. He told them they could call him, no matter what, and he would come. She knew how he loved them. Why didn't he come? He had to have called Mama, and what had she done? She didn't tell them. She let them suffer, waiting.*

*By the time they gave up, by the time they faced the truth, he wasn't coming, Nita was four months pregnant. They knew they had to act. The abortion worked, but Nita got sick from infections and bleeding. Then when she got pneumonia, Mama was not nice. She took her to the hospital, then when Nita was released, she took her home and set her up in the bedroom, putting iced water in thermos bottles, and food that Nita could sit up and get to in her room, Mama worked everyday, leaving Nita alone. Leaving her in that room to die.*

*But she wanted to blame me, Beatrice thought. Mama killed Nita. No, she didn't shoot her, or stab her. But she got mad, and she took away her love. She got mad because they had called Daddy. And she did not treat them the same after that. Mama hated Daddy, and they couldn't be loved, couldn't be her children if they didn't hate him too. But Bea did not. She could not. It was Mama, she believed it was Mama who really let Nita die, and she was going to prove to the family that it was Mama...*

A movement in front of Beatrice snapped her from her reverie. The window of her back door was filled with a familiar face—that of her next door neighbor. Bea went over and opened the door.

"Hey, Ms. Jones."

"Hi, baby. Here is a letter for your boyfriend come in my mail."

"Thank you, Ms. Jones. I don't know how the mailman got Jones out of Coleman."

"These damn mailmen can't read. Anytime you can't read numbers, you can't read."

They laughed, and when Bea closed the door, she looked at the handwriting and knew it was from a woman. Who was writing Witt? She felt the thickness of the envelope, and wondered what the hell it was. Then she opened it.

Cynthia's four pictures, in her kneeling positions with her old boyfriend fell out. Who in the world took these shots, Beatrice wondered, surprised they were back in her face. There was nothing else in the envelope. No note, no return address. Nothing. Who had Witt sent them to?

Oh Witt? Had he gone to Cynthia and left them with a threat? What the hell did it mean that somebody had returned them to him? Well, she knew what it meant to their business. Forget about getting a partner. Forget it. Witt wasn't getting into Daddy's club. He'd once said they had about a third of what they needed. They had $22,000 from her pension, and they had Witt's portion. He never did tell her what he was adding to it, but she assumed it would at least match hers. So that was about $44,000, which Bea had rounded to $50,000. They must have needed a cool $150,000. And it was not easy to find people who had that kind of money on the side. She sighed and threw the pictures on the table.

Witt wouldn't listen to her. He just wouldn't. She needed to get somebody to talk to him about what he was doing. He couldn't just go out here treating people like shit. She was getting tired of telling him that, especially when it came to Toukie. He talked to her like she was nothing. Sure, he knew a lot. He was going to be rich, she knew he was capable. But he needed someone to control him just a bit.

Bea paced, and the baby, seeing her walk close to the playpen started to whine. She glanced down at him, then picked him up and left the kitchen hurrying for the steps.

His uncle! His uncle cared enough to tell him about the club. He would help. He would have to. She balanced the baby awkwardly, and opened Witt's side of the dresser, feeling like a thief for going through his paper drawer. Bills. Lots of envelops of bills. She looked for some personal papers, some telephone book, something with a link to Witt's past. Something that linked him to somebody other than her. There was nothing.

She put the baby on the bed, then pulled out the drawers and took them to the bed. She searched. All she could find was paper work and bills from their time together. The baby started to whine from the bed and she stopped to lift him on her lap.

In the bottom drawer was a black leather portfolio. She unzipped it and found his military papers. Well, finally something from his previous life. There was his formal portrait taken of Witt after boot camp. His induction papers, discharge papers which Bea scanned. He had received a dishonorable discharge? No wonder he had problems finding a decent job. He never told her that.

Then there were papers of a court martial. She looked through them, frowning, wondering what the hell that meant? It was some legal proceeding, she gathered, from the time he was in the Marines. When she found the paper listing the actual charge, she stopped. Attempted murder?

She zipped all the paperwork back up, and looked around her. Maybe there was more about Witt that she needed to know. What the hell was this? She decided to look in the basement. Witt took over the basement as though it were his private apartment. Surely he had something useful there. She laid the baby down and he immediately started to wail as she put Witt's papers back in the position in the drawers that she'd found them. Then she picked the screaming child up in her arms and went into the basement.

Nothing was locked. In a briefcase, she found the papers he had on her father's club. There was no club title, or address or phone, or even website, but there was a directory of names, and she looked at several pages of names and saw that there were years listed at the top. On a very old list, she was able to find Daddy's name: Daniel J. Windsor. And on the most recent list, there was his name. Now, where were the Coleman's?

She scanned the pages, which were listed in alphabetical order. From the oldest list, to the newest, there was no Coleman listed. Witt had said his uncle was a Coleman. Then why was there no listing of a Coleman ever in the member directory?

Bea felt sweaty, and a headache beginning. What the fuck was Witt doing? What was he doing with all that money? What was he doing not going in to his job? Was he even trying to get in the club, like he said? Bea didn't know what to think.

If nothing else, she had to get through Christmas. She had to have one for Toukie. The baby wouldn't know whether it was Christmas Day or Flag Day, but Toukie had already given Bea a list. She had to go to the bank and get some of that business money out. Hell, they weren't going to get a partner before Christmas, so they could put it back later.

She changed the baby, bundled him up, put back on her coat and called a sedan service. She had to get to the bank before they closed.

******

The bank lines were wrapped around the floor when she stepped inside. She untied the baby's hat, unzipped his snowsuit, and gave him a teething biscuit as she pushed his stroller to the back of the line. She might as well splurge, she thought as she tried to figure out how much to take out. She winced at the thought of the sedan fare, as the car sat waiting to take her to the mall, but she had to get started and needed to do some serious shopping. They needed a tree and she would just get an artificial one for now, since she didn't know when Witt would get a real one. Christmas was in two days and they hadn't started anything.

She should have made the decision to get out money a long time ago. What was she thinking? That they needed enough to stroke Freddie's and his girlfriends's ego forever? After all, she did put her foot down when Witt wanted to put everything they had in the account for business only. She made him take out a couple thousand for the house, for things they might need. But she'd never touched it.

The lines were moving fast. People kept touching the baby and telling her how handsome he was, but she barely acknowledged them, her mind caught up on Witt and what he was doing. Those pictures of Cynthia bothered her. Did he have the nerve to send them to her? Or did he, more than likely, send them to Freddie? Did he want to prove to Freddie that Cynthia was no saint? And then what did he think would happen?

When she finally wheeled the baby up to the counter and pulled out her little reference card, she was glad she had the cashier in the pink sweater. She seemed to be getting customers up and out in record time.

Beatrice filled out a withdrawal slip for $500.00 from the small account giving over her license and waited.

The girl was young and pleasant. She smiled at Bea as she took her forms and turned to the computer. She punched in numbers while Bea struggled to turn the stroller away from the line where an old man was coughing full force and not covering his mouth sending spit and germs everywhere. Everybody seemed to be coughing around this time of the year.

She admired the colored tin balls hanging from the ceiling of the bank, the colorful garlands and the big stuffed Santa on top of one of the vaults behind the steel bars. It reminded her of when she did hold a job, and how much fun they had at Christmas parties, decorating the office and swapping gifts. After her eyes had taken in everything on the walls, she turned and looked at the teller who was still studying the screen. Feeling Bea's eyes, she got up and left her station, going down the row of tellers to the end where she talked with an older lady for a minute. Bea saw them both turn their heads and look at her, and in a minute, the older lady came back with the young teller and looked at the screen.

"Okay, Ms. Windsor…it shows here that your account was emptied nearly three weeks ago. That account is closed."

Bea frowned. Had she picked the wrong card? She asked for her card back and pulled her pocketbook in front of her, searching her wallet for the other account number. She looked at the numbers and saw that she had put in the numbers for the smaller account. Did Witt decide to use the savings account to treat Freddie and Cynthia instead of the one with most of their savings in it?

She asked for a new withdrawal slip and put in the other number. She handed it over and waited, this time watching both their faces.

The girl punched in the numbers murmuring something to the lady beside her. They both paused, and in a minute, the lady turned to her.

"This account was also depleted the same day. It was withdrawn by the co-signer on the account, Mr. DeWitt Coleman."

"What?" Beatrice could barely get the word out of her shocked mouth.

"You do know Mr. DeWitt Coleman?"

She couldn't speak.

"He presented proper identification and withdrew the money from the accounts within our guidelines. He received a cashier's check for the entire amount…"

"That's impossible. I need to speak to the manager. I need to speak to somebody right now!"

Even in the manager's office, behind the closed door, things got no better. They explained their policy for joint accounts, that both parties are free to use the funds as they wish without requiring two signatures or any notification from the bank and when she asked what could she do to track the cashier's check, to see who got her money because most of that money was hers and hers alone, they told her she could prosecute Witt for taking the money. That was the only thing she could do. She couldn't stop the wailing in her head. It was like a rush of blood and sound and she had to get out of there. She had to run!

******

The yelling woke her up.

Witt's voice was so loud the walls were shaking. She stumbled up from the chair in the living room, trying to clear her head. What the hell was going on? What time of the night was it? Was he losing his mind?

She struggled up the steps wondering why he was yelling loud enough to wake the dead. What was he thinking?

"Witt! Witt!" she hollered when she found him and Toukie in the baby's room. Toukie was in tears and he was towering over her slumped body.

"What you yelling at her like that for? What's wrong?"

To her surprise, Toukie jumped up when her mother came in and started to yell back.

"He up here talking about I let Poobah get dirty and didn't change him and I did! I was getting ready to go to school, I already gave him some milk and he pooped all over the place and it came out of his diaper and everywhere in the crib and Witt up there saying I didn't do my chores but I did!"

Beatrice's head swung around to see the daylight streaming in around the curtains. It was Christmas Eve! She'd slept through the whole night. Then her nose picked up the stinging odor of fresh baby poop and she grabbed Toukie's shoulder.

"Go get your book bag and go on to school," Bea said, pushing her out the room. "Go 'head! Now!"

"Mama?"

"Don't Mama me!"

"But I didn't do nothing!"

"Just go! If you need money ask Ms. Alston to loan you some, hear? Tell her I'll pay her back later. Just get out of here, now."

Toukie heard the panic in her mother's voice and hesitated. She glared over at Witt before she obeyed and ran out, leaving her family together in the room.

Witt looked at Beatrice.

Beatrice glared back at him.

The baby was in the crib yelling. He didn't like the smell any more than they did.

"Didn't you see me talking to Toukie?" Witt asked, his voice dropping. " It didn't have anything to do with you. I was dealing with her, and I wasn't finished dealing with her."

"Yeah. You finished with her. Now, it's me you got to deal with."

Witt's expression didn't change. He kept his eyes on Beatrice's face. Bea hoped Toukie would hurry up and leave, but she closed the door to the room quietly to keep her words in the room. She faced Witt.

"What right you got to yell at my baby like that?"

Witt didn't answer.

"I went to the bank yesterday. It was two days before Christmas and I wanted some money to get some presents and decorations. We can't stop having Christmas just because you want money for a business. And they told me what you did. You took all the money. All MY money out of both accounts. Where is my money?"

Witt closed his eyes, and that's when a crushing pain moved across Bea's chest. Something flipped in her stomach. It wasn't going to happen. She had hoped he would tell her it was a mistake, that he still had the money somewhere in a new account, but she could look in his eyes and tell.

It took a long moment, but then Witt shrugged and gave in.

"Freddie's girlfriend took all that money and disappeared. I don't know how she did it. And I don't know exactly how I'm going to get it back, but I will."

For a minute, Beatrice looked at him, confused.

When she could speak, she sputtered, "Girlfriend? How in the world did Cynthia get my money? Her name wasn't on that account with you and me? I'm talking about our personal savings account, not the money you had with Freddie."

For a minute, Witt said nothing. Then, "I took the money out of our account to add to the business account. I wanted to have even more to impress Freddie's father."

"So, what you telling me? She got the business account with our personal money, and Freddie's money too? "

"Yeah. He matched mine, and she took it all."

"How? Her name was not on that account, Witt. Was it?"

"Hell no."

"So how did Cynthia get it?"

Witt looked down a moment, then back at her. "I talked to the bank. They told me a man came in saying he worked for me and Freddie, with a letter, that had Freddie's authorization, and it authorized a withdrawal of all but $1,000. The bank called Freddie's number to verify, and they said he okayed it. The check from the bank was made to Freddie, in Freddie's name. They said they handle commercial accounts this way all the time, and there wasn't anything different. Freddie would have to sign it, or it can't be cashed. Often business owners send assistants to take care of business…"

"To withdraw the whole damn account balance?"

"Well, it was supposed to be within their guidelines. They said to cash a check like that, the person would have to come up with solid identification."

"Well, Freddie is in on it then. He got to be, you said yourself that Cynthia ran him."

"No, he wasn't. Not with what we been through at work, I'm sure of it. I'm sure she took his money too, based on what he told me. That's why I haven't been at work for a while, we got into a physical scuffle at work, and we both got suspended. I just extended my time off with sick leave."

"What is Freddie doing about his money then?"

"We've been to the police. His father hired some investigators. We feel pretty sure she won't get to cash it, it's just going to take time."

"Going to take time?!" Bea started to pace, her heart feeling like it was beating out of her chest. "That money is every single damn cent I had to my name, all my furniture, my retirement, my life, everything for me and Toukie, I gave to you."

"I KNOW that shit! Don't you think I know it? What you think I've been trying to do every day since I found out? They suspended me from work because I got into a fight with Freddie about it. I've put the word out on the street that I'll give a reward for her whereabouts, and she knows I'm on her ass."

"I just don't believe this, Witt. You said yourself…"

"I know what I said, and I am going to get it back. Trice, I promise you--"

"No! Don't promise me. You can't promise me nothing, Witt, not one damn thing. What am I going to do now? I'm 30-years-old, Witt. I have no money. I have no job. I have no house. I have…what? A old, used up car. And that's it. That's it!"

"You got me. I'm not going anywhere."

"You don't understand what's wrong, do you? I believed in you, Witt. I gave everything to you to get me to a better place. Now, I'm sick of you! Sick of you and your lying, and your screaming at my daughter like she don't mean nothing to you when it comes to your son. She don't know what you screaming at her for! You scream at her when she come in: she walk too hard. When she go in the bathroom: she take a bath too long. When she wake up: it's too late. When she go to bed, when she eat, when she breathe, when she do anything! What you got to be screaming at her for? At least she got enough sense to keep her money in her pocket instead of giving it to strangers. I'm sick of you! Sick! Do you hear me?"

"Sick of me? Where the hell were you headed? What the hell did you have?"

"What did I have? What did you have? I must have had $22,000, you sure as shit gave it to your friends. What did you have? I keep hearing about this uncle. This man was going to get you in the big time. Get you big backing. Get you big business. But where the hell is your uncle? I looked in every one of those papers you got, and I don't see no sign nowhere of your uncle. I don't even see one Coleman, in the past, or now. So, what do you have?"

Witt's nostrils flared and his fists balled tightly.

"You went looking through my things?"

"That's right!" she said, barely, before Witt had her by the arms. She struggled to pull away, but when she couldn't, she swung her leg up and kicked him as hard as she could on his shin. He let go momentarily to grab his ankle, and she reached up and slapped him as hard as she could, to her own astonishment.

Witt grabbed her by her wrist so tight it hurt, and swung her around hard. She felt herself turning, her feet leaving the floor until she was flying through the air off balance, landing with a crash into the doorframe, banging the side of her face. She screamed out as she hit, then slid down on the floor. Before she could react, she watched in terror as Witt's steel-plated work boots came rushing at her. She covered her head with both arms.

He was going to kill her! He really was crazy, and she could only hope Toukie had gotten out the house by now and had gone straight to school, to Ms. Alston like she'd told her.

The boots stopped at her face, and Witt leaned down.

"Get up off the floor! Beatrice! Get up!"

She continued to cover her face. She was going to die.

"Are you crazy? Are you really crazy?" he screamed when she didn't move. "You going to beat me up? Me? I'm giving you everything I have, and you're going to raise your hand to slap me across my face? I'm getting out of here. You get yourself up and clean this shit up in this room and get yourself together. When I come back, we're going to sit down and talk. Get a hold of yourself. This is not the end. It's money. Just money. Can't you tell how bad I felt about it? I didn't even know how to tell you or what to tell you because I knew you would think about the dollars, but we have more than that, Trice. I'm not stopping now. I still have my other houses, and I'm going to get this all straightened out. I'll be back."

He stormed out.

After she heard the door open and slam behind him, Beatrice stirred. The baby was wailing at the top of his lungs until his face was totally pink. Her face felt like it was cracked where it hit the wall, and her head was pounding.

She had to get out! She had to find someplace to go, or there would be blood when he came back. She would kill him. She lifted the baby from the bed and took him into the bathroom to clean him up from head to toe. When he was clean and fed, she took him into the bedroom and pulled out her suitcase.

Tears flew from her eyes as she flung her things inside. After the few outfits she would need, she paused and looked around. She had to go somewhere fast and safe right away. She could come back later and get stuff she needed.

She decided she would call her girlfriend, Mae Jefferson. Mae used to be her street buddy when she was single, before she met Witt. They had hit all the nightspots together, went to every show that came anywhere near the Baltimore/DC area, racked up conquests and kept getting up. Mae was fun, she was independent, but most of all she was always a friend. Even though she hardly called Mae once she'd met Witt-- Witt hated her and asked Beatrice to keep Mae out his house-- whenever she called, Mae was glad to hear from her. They could talk like the old friends they were and if she ever needed anything, Mae was there.

She packed for Little D in a second suitcase, then Toukie in a third. Toukie was going to be so happy. She had been begging her to leave Witt forever. Mae would take her to pick up Toukie from school, which would be a surprise. Mae hated Witt, and right now, so did Beatrice. If she could kill him, she would.

She called Mae at work and gave her a brief version of events asking Mae where did she think she could go. Mae told her to go nowhere. She would come and get her, and Beatrice could stay with her.

Beatrice checked her wallet. It's a good thing Bernadette was sending checks for Toukie, or she'd be flat broke. She had about $28.00. If she went to one of Witt's houses he rented, she would see if she could collect the rent. Of course it wasn't January 5th, and she didn't know if they would pay her early. Still, she hoped she could get them to pay so she could get started on Christmas shopping. And if she got Mae over here, she could go to social services to see if she could get some kind of emergency check. She had to get the hell out of here.

It was a damn shame to be on the streets at Christmas time, but hell, it was life. She knew what that was all about.

# Bernadette

## *twelve*

Bernadette turned her wrist to check the time, then looked back at the bank statements where she stared in amazement. Could this be right? She had hoped to get her Toyota Rav 4 by the spring. As of last October, she had saved up almost $2,700 toward the $3,000 down payment she needed, providing they gave her the trade-in they promised on her old Grand Prix. Now it was January 3, and she was down to $1,500. All because she was sending Toukie what she knew she needed.

There was the $500 she sent last fall to Toukie for clothes, then $200 Bea said Toukie needed to see a doctor about her hair falling out. Medicaid would not give a referral to a dermatologist. Then, Toukie asked for $300 for an African braided hair-style, which would last her for at least 3 months. Then there were the $50 checks Toukie needed to get her braids washed and the loose ones tightened up every two weeks. Then last Christmas she'd sent Bea $400, telling her Toukie could probably use a new wool coat, and some boots, remembering how pathetic Toukie had looked in the school office.

That was it. Beatrice didn't even send a thank you. At least Toukie did, so she knew the girl got the money. She was sorry she had to stop sending checks, but she still had to live, in the meantime. She hadn't gotten that promotion to captain just yet, though she was told to give it another six months.

Twisting to move her jacket to the side, she frowned up her nose at the aroma of that Lava soap she'd showered with. On Thursdays, she played volleyball on base, unit rivalries. Not having time to go home to shower, she'd used their industrial soap, and regretted it.

"Sorry I'm late," Nancy said, rushing up to the bar where Bernadette sat. She dropped hard onto the stool beside her.

"Hey, slow poke, what's new about that?" Bernadette greeted, and she met Nancy's warm smile. Her roommate was short and full bosomed with small brown eyes and a head full of shoulder length black hair. She was sexy, smart, high energy, and Bernadette thought, in perfect sync with her.

"Just you wait," Nancy said. "You're going to scream when I tell you everything I found on those two."

Bernadette's attention turned to the waitress who, menus in the air, signaled them to follow her to their booth. No sooner had they settled in than Nancy ordered a Pepsi with a twist of lemon, and opened her brown suede jacket, revealing a black T-shirt with white letters that read, "I'm What Willis Was Talkin' Bout."  She'd changed out of uniform already. She pulled over her matching Nine West Hobo bag, found her daily planner, and then cleared her throat.

"Have I got some news for you—where do you want me to begin? With Witt, or your Dad?"

Bernadette's phone trilled, and she held up her finger as she flipped it open and muttered a few quick yeses, and one emphatic "of course!" before snapping her cell phone closed. "I have to meet Colonel Chisholm in ninety minutes."

"That was him?"

"No, Private Sugar. The one you like to call Martha Stewart. I asked her to pick up his specs so I can run them tomorrow, but she says she can't."

"He doesn't give it a break," Nancy remarked. As Bernadette stuffed her bank statements into her pocketbook and sat back, she wondered why Nancy's eyes were glowing. She acted as though she had good news, but what could be good?

"Let's start with my father."

"Good choice," Nancy said, flipping a page. "The weird thing first, your father is living his life wide open, no evidence that he is in hiding from anyone. His phone is listed in the Howard County phone book, he owns credit cards and property, and he has a clear paper trail that's been easy to follow all along."

"So why didn't he contact us?"

"Not sure. But check this:  After I found his address, I found out he was a registered voter, so public records were very easy. I didn't get information on the divorce, because I know that's personal and easily available if you want to read it, but I found he is remarried and has a wife and two step-daughters."

There was a pang in Bernadette's chest when she heard he lived with other daughters. Her 27th birthday was coming up in two weeks, and she wondered if her father would even know. But he would know the birthdays of these other daughters.

"He works as a freelance journalist, and does quite of bit of writing for both domestic and international publications. And I have a list of them all."

Bernadette crossed her legs and cocked her head to the side.

"How did you get all of that information with just his name and date of birth?"

"Okay, I had some help. I have a co-worker, another social worker, also from Baltimore, who could get this information easily, and he did."

"It couldn't have been that quick, so he must have been trying to impress you."

"Not really. He knew it was important to me, but he doesn't know who it was for."

Bernadette hesitated.

"He gave me some other really interesting news. He found out about the neighborhood your father lives in, the average cost of homes in the area."

"No way."

"They range from $850,000 to $1.5 million."

"Not bad..." Bernadette murmured, her eyes glazing over.

"And he has always lived well. Your grandparents are quite well off, Bernadette, and are known for their philanthropy. This kind of news begs as many questions as it answers, doesn't it?"

"Yes, like why weren't we well off."

"Exactly." Nancy turned a couple of pages. "How does he leave his family to struggle while he's doing very well? Why didn't your mother ever tell you about your father's legacy? Evidently, these people were pretty influential. You should have known about that." Nancy stopped flipping pages and paused.

"Now, our friend Witt. I should say DeWitt Myles Coleman. He's a lot more slippery to follow."

"I'll bet."

"If you didn't remember Toukie saying he attended Gilman, that private school in Baltimore, I may not have gotten anything on him. Witt doesn't vote, doesn't appear to be a registered driver, but surprisingly, he owns property."

Bernadette sipped her drink.

"He owns three houses, the one on Broadway, one on Ashland and one on Wolfe Street, all three are low-property-value homes, but the area has recently been targeted as a blighted area, and the city wants to buy back the homes in the area to tear down and expand Johns Hopkins Hospital," Nancy paused. "Goodness, Johns Hopkins Hospital is in the ghetto?"

"Close. A block in any direction and you're right in the heart."

"And Witt stands to get some nice bucks for those three homes, in a short period."

"Anything about his background? Who are his parents? Does he come from money? Where did he get his start? Gilman is a very expensive school."

"Before he attended Gilman, could not find anything on him in Maryland. Nothing at all. But through the Military Locator Service, I did confirm he was a Marine."

"Of course." Bernadette stretched back in the booth and stared at the stained glass and dark wooden beams of TGIF. She was surer than ever Witt knew her father, knew he had money, and the connection to Bea was money. He was trying to get to Daddy's money. Were Daddy's children dying to save his money?

"So, now you can contact your father about that poem and see what he knows."

Bernadette inhaled deeply, then after a few seconds, blew the air out from her cheeks. She craved a cigarette.

"I want to contact Witt. I just don't know how to get the truth out of him yet, but Witt knows something."

"Then wait until you know more. Don't let him figure you out."

"I won't. Just like, I haven't told a soul about finding that baby Windsor at the cemetery. My oldest brother, Michael Windsor. I didn't know there were actually seven siblings, but something tells me Marietta knows all about this. Since it's been a secret from me, I'll continue to keep it until I have to show my hand."

"You know, I don't think Witt wrote that poem," Nancy said slowly. "I think somebody who knows what Witt is up to with your family wrote it as a warning. But I can't see how it helps him to kill all of you. He's not a Windsor—he can't inherit."

"We don't know Daddy's side of things. It's about him. Maybe he's being blackmailed. Maybe Witt worked himself into our family to find out how to blackmail him. Whatever, it's about Daddy."

"You can ask him. Bernadette, I'll bet he'd be more than helpful to you in figuring this out. I mean, there's nothing bad about him I could find," Nancy said, then paused. "You know, there is always the possibility that your mother knows about this poem."

"I doubt it."

"Well, don't. There is something we run across quite a bit in my line of work with single mothers. Remember, I've been around a little longer than you," she said referring to their three years age difference, "and I have knowledge of social work. Sometimes, if a woman is in love with a man who has a problem with her children, she'll put her children in harm's way, intentionally or unintentionally."

Bernadette frowned. "My father had no problems with us."

"Usually these men are not up front with how they feel. For example, if a boyfriend, or a husband, comes to a woman and says, 'I'm jealous of your children' or 'You spend more time with them,' the woman would probably curse him out and tell him to grow up. But if the boyfriend starts to pull away from her, stays late at work, flirts in front of her, jeopardizes the family in some way, sometimes these mothers, intentionally or not, get the children out the way."

"That's ridiculous."

"Oh, it's true enough. You'd be surprised at what they'd do. Sometimes it's simple neglect. We have reports where women will leave their children alone, sometimes very young children are left for days to be with their man. That's intentional. But then there's allowing the man to punish the children and turning a blind eye. Sometimes the contact may be sexual, and the mother doesn't see it because she doesn't want to see it. Children will be sent away to live with a relative. Then there are times when children are killed. And mothers do kill their children, or let their men do it."

Bernadette's mouth dropped open.

"Well, not mine! She was a real mother to us. When my father left, she stepped up."

"I know, but I was a little concerned about how easily your mother put you all out when she felt she needed to."

"But not until we were old enough and able to care for ourselves. What good would it do to kill us as adults?"

"Well, think about it. Your mother came from a very poor background. She had nothing. Your father, on the other hand, came from money. He had everything to lose. Your mother had everything to gain. Their union couldn't have been easy. And who knows?"

"I do. She wouldn't have done anything to harm us. She couldn't have caused my brother Daniel's death. He died at the military base. She was hard but not crazy."

"I know, Bernadette. That's why I let that go. Your mother was there with you guys, always, throughout everything. But I just couldn't find a motive for your father—unless you found something in those articles he wrote you were looking up."

"That *Crisis* magazine? Well, there was something. My father stopped writing for *The Crisis* the year he left us, so I looked up what types of things he worked on at that time, and it was just one subject, a series of reports on this one rich Black family, the Limonses."

"You ever hear of them?"

"Never. They were a large, quiet, hard-working family of Louisiana African-Americans, non-typical because they were all doctors and lawyers who stuck together, sending each other to school to make sure everybody had his own. They were investigated when a series of childhood deaths plagued the family. The kids were born with fatal organ deformities and other medical problems, yet with all that money, they couldn't be saved. No foul play was ever found.

"Then the family was accused of interbreeding. The complexions in this family went from Michael Jackson brown to Michael Jackson white over the years, and, it got to be such a prevalent rumor, that they started losing much of their clientele. People thought they were weird. It got so bad, much of the clan moved to the Midwest. Their professions continued to suffer, and soon they disappeared."

"And that was that?"

"The Limonses' articles were the last Daddy did for The *Crisis*."

"There may be something there, seeing he stopped writing for *The Crisis* altogether after doing a series on the family. There may really be something there." Nancy closed the folders, and pulled out several pages from her daily planner, handing them to Bernadette."

"These are the dossiers on both Witt and your Dad. I think it says a lot, so I know you'll follow up."

"Wow. I can't thank you enough," Bernadette said, and Nancy made room on the table for her Pepsi as the waitress dropped off another glass.

Bernadette ordered another gin and tonic and started skimming through the pages Nancy gave her as Nancy said, "It's been a great year, hasn't it?"

"It will be when I get my Captain's bars," Bernadette said absently. "Then I can relax. I've been busy as hell with this detail work, and trying to keep up with my own regular duties, and then homework. But it will all be worth it. I just know."

She and Nancy started their comfortable chatter, and easily polished off a double order of coconut shrimp. Bernadette finished two more gin and tonics to Nancy's one Pepsi.

Then they called for the check. Bernadette asked for a tall glass of iced water while Nancy pulled out her compact and relined her lips.

"What's with all these gin and tonics, girl? I don't know if I can let you drive home."

"Ice water knocks my high right out," Bernadette said. "You know I like to drink. And smoke, in case you hadn't noticed that either."

Bernadette drained the iced water when it came, and threw in an ice cube to crunch as they went over the check.

"Water doesn't flush liquor out, who are you kidding?"

"I'm telling you, it clears my head."

"Well, get pulled over and blow a 1.0, and we'll see what water does," Nancy said frowning. She continued to wag her finger at Bernadette as she said, "that's why I got you all that information on Witt and your father. I've never seen you so stressed. I mean all you do is talk about your work for Colonel Chisholm, or Witt and your niece. You haven't been able to do anything for fun, you don't even have sex anymore. And it doesn't seem to even bug you. That's major."

Bernadette laughed.

"I guess it's getting really serious then, huh?"

"Very."

"I can handle this drought. If it's not with what or who I want, I can wait."

"Oh yes, that was a nasty surprise, wasn't it?" Nancy said, referring to Reggie, Bernadette's heartthrob. "Who would have thought he was an enlisted Marine, playing sax in the Marine Field Band, no less. He didn't have that dog-tag look."

Bernadette became silent, remembering how disappointed she felt when Lonnie passed Reggie's phone number to her, and it was a number to base housing. Officers and enlisted could not date.

"He had strong possibilities," Bernadette said wistfully.

"Just as well, Bernadette. I'm pretty sure little Ms. L.A. has had her hooks in him." When Bernadette frowned, Nancy continued, "I mean Shelley, the vocalist in Lonnie's band. She's from L.A. so I always call her that, and she's awfully possessive of him."

"Well, this drought won't be forever. How long can this one detail go on? It's like Colonel Chisholm knows, with this detail, and the late hours we put in, all we can do is work and sleep."

Nancy pursed her lips in a 'what –have-I –been- saying" expression, then said, "I'm sure that's what he's hoping for you."

"Well, I can handle it."

"Then there's one more thing I hope you handle as well."

Bernadette looked at her friend. Once again, Nancy looked like she had just hit a jackpot, her eyes brightly lit, her wide smile back on.

"My discharge date is at the end of this month, January 31. I'm pregnant. And Lonnie wants to get married as soon as possible."

Bernadette's eyes widened.

"You've got to be kidding me. Are you sure? But why? If you marry him, why do you have to get out?"

"I don't have to, but I think it's best for us. Lonnie isn't going to work in La Jolla forever, and he isn't going to follow me to different military bases, so I think I'll set up home near my parents in the Bay area, and start a new chapter of my life there."

"I'll be honest. I could kick Lonnie's little narrow, scheming behind for this."

Nancy giggled. "You'd have to kick mine, too. I'm so happy, Berni. It happened while I was on the shot, so it was meant to happen. And I won't raise a military brat like I was."

Her mother had followed her father from base to base until they ended in California, and stayed.

Bernadette drank a second glass of ice water as Nancy finished her Pepsi.

"So, that's what's with the lemon Pepsi. And that ridiculous glow all over your face."

Nancy laughed.

"I was hoping you weren't that happy about Witt or my father."

The two of them laughed out loud.

"Well, in a way, I was. Now you can move on that poem, Berni. Go to your father and get this over with."

"Don't worry. I'll figure out what to do. I just want to tell you, I've never seen you happier. And I want you to know, I'm furious you're leaving me, but I'm so happy for you, girl."

They hugged tightly, Bernadette's mind spinning. She had to get home, now that she knew about her father's money. She would worry about Nancy and life without her later. For now, she had to fly back out, and find her father.

## thirteen

However, Bernadette's leave to go home was promptly denied. "We need you," Major Whitaker explained, seeing Bernadette's disappointed expression. "You are my ace in the hole when it comes to getting these reports out, and we haven't met our goals for the first quarter yet."

"One week isn't going to make a big difference, ma'am," Bernadette dared to insist, holding her breath. Major Whitaker leaned down and pulled out a drawer, then slapped a file in the middle of her desk. "Meet my prospectus for this quarter," she said, then went on to explain the one-year work plan, and how instrumental Bernadette's skills were in helping her meet the goals.

"And Colonel Chisholm is counting on you a hell of a lot more. His detail is almost over and he sings your praises every chance he gets. You have a big fish in your corner," she reminded Bernadette, "and I wouldn't jeopardize that unless it was a dire emergency." Somehow Bernadette knew Major Whitaker did not believe looking for a father who had been missing 22 years qualified as an emergency. So that ended that.

Then there was the hoopla of Nancy's small, intimate wedding, that continued to balloon all over the place until it squeezed out any time Bernadette had to work on her own family. Nancy's planning committee had taken on eight other friends, crammed into their apartment each evening, so it was all Bernadette could do to make it to her bedroom for some peace and solitude. She let them take over the living room and kitchen at the front to hold their boisterous, marathon sessions. Often she fell asleep fully clothed, trying to work on debugging the programs she'd written for Colonel Chisholm's project.

Finally, there were the stacks of invitations that she helped Nancy stamp and mail out. Like a dream, February 12 finally came, and Nancy's wedding date had arrived.

February 12 turned out to be a beautiful, balmy Saturday. The sun was brilliant against the stained glass windows of the small, picturesque church, but the monotone voice of the preacher, and the heat from what had to be at least 200 anxious bodies combined to make Bernadette nauseous. She felt like she would puke any second all over her overpriced black knit Anne Klein dress, and it wasn't even halfway through Nancy's wedding. All that planning and Nancy ended up standing at the altar with just her sister as matron of honor, and Lonnie with just his brother. Or was it his cousin? She didn't remember; she was too hung over, and unspeakably tired.

Four months since she'd been to Baltimore, she had not heard from Beatrice, and since Christmas, had not been able to reach her or Toukie. Marietta had even stopped writing. What were they doing over there? Something was obviously wrong. Still, she could not get approved leave.

And now, Nancy was officially leaving the comfortable arrangement they had, and leaving her financially bereft. She didn't want to live with anybody else. Bernadette was past disappointment. Her $2100 a month gross salary was barely enough to cover the rent and utilities in her bayside apartment, let alone car payments, telephone, gas, and food? She needed help and fast.

The two girls that Bernadette rode over to the church with were supposed to be possible replacements Nancy had said. Nancy worked with them, and thought either girl, both second lieutenants would be reliable and good company. But in the first five minutes of the car ride, Bernadette had crossed them both off. Too flighty and silly, giggling over everything they said.

Bernadette felt antsy. Despite the fact that she'd interviewed Nancy before letting her move into her apartment and gotten promises of how much it meant to Nancy to stick out the military for a full career, here they were. Her Lonnie was going to be the next Lionel Hampton; she was going to be there to support him, and nothing else was important to Nancy after that.

The best thing about Nancy and Lonnie as a couple, that Bernadette could see, was their relationship with Reggie. Reggie loved music as much as Lonnie, and spent a lot of time with the band working on different pieces and helping Lonnie put tunes together. Nancy would drop tidbits about Reggie's habits, how much Mountain Dew he could drink, and his habit of a daily bag of Pork Rinds, how he could make up a song over the stupidest little thing, and crack everybody up, and how he loved competitive bike riding. It's what he did whenever he wasn't hanging with the band.

Of course, the moment her black satin, strapped sandal hit the walkway, the first person she spotted, out of the huge crowd gathered in front of the church, was Reggie. It was like he had a magnet in him that drew her eyes, caused her heart to pound, sweat to gather on her forehead, under her armpits, and in some other private places. She couldn't control how her body responded.

Especially since she had not had sex- or any other fun- for quite a while. Her whole existence had morphed into a surreal experience where she was barely alive, at work or at home. She kept reminding herself when they got the program written and debugged the way the Colonel wanted, it would be over, and as one of two project leaders, she would get kudos. It would pay off when she became captain. But she felt like her life was bleeding in the mean time. She couldn't do anything else.

No one understood how good the Colonel was for her. He did his job, but always taught her as he worked. He was like a father, asking how things were going, and directing her path clear of problems. It was his connections that got her the apartment on the bay she was about to lose. "How big can you dream?" he'd asked her, and made her believe that she could have it all. He made her feel important, and that relationship she couldn't explain to Nancy or anybody. She could see how proud he was of her, and she knew her hard work made him look good. So even though he called on her everyday, she knew in the end it would pay off. That was his promise.

But as she sat waiting for the preacher to wrap it up, Bernadette's instincts were humming. Nothing in her life was working according to plan. Nancy, who advised her to get out of the Colonel's detail and cut her losses, thought his evening phone calls were over the limit and did not realize that she had gotten a certain level of clearance to work on this project of classified material. Nancy wasn't aware of the US efforts to track the Middle Easterners serving in the US military and coding these tracking programs was top priority. It was a time of war, and she had to complete what they needed her to do.

Bernadette looked down her pew, and then closed her eyes when her stomach started to flip. The bachelorette party two nights ago was huge. She hadn't been sober since then. One of Nancy's friends had rented a furnished bungalow for the festivities in Oceanside and rolled in four of the tightest looking male exotic dancers you'd ever want to see. The women were screaming at the top of their lungs, and some of the stuff that went on in those rooms…well, looked like a free for all. Bernadette made good use of the liquor, trying to stay clear of all the bumping and grinding and God knows what else. It certainly wouldn't do for her to be caught there but the thought of all that sexual playing had heated her up, and there was nothing she could do about it.

Most women were crazy for wanting the whole nine yards--marriage, monogamy and babies-- when it was the rare man who was worth it. And she wasn't about to make any mistakes with her life. That had to be what Mama meant when she asked had Bernadette fallen in love yet. Love for a woman was a mistake. It meant relinquishing your power, losing your control, dealing with emotions, and trusting. How could you trust a man?

She crossed her legs, her smooth Hanes Absolutely Sheer hose rubbing together, and squirmed against the wooden pew. Her eyes skimmed over the fat faced, sweaty preacher, staring critically at him, then at Lonnie and the way Nancy stared up at him. Love. Ha! She turned her head suddenly and her eyes caught Reggie's gaze. He met her look and gave her a slow, easy smile. She quickly looked away flustered. It didn't help that Reggie Taylor was sitting just across the aisle from her and looking sexy as ever in a black, double-breasted suit. Reggie, the sax player. One thing Bernadette realized without a doubt was that if she wasn't careful, she could be in trouble with him. Every time she got a moment to think about a man, his picture came to mind. And they hadn't spoken a word beyond hello.

Just on sight, he revved her motor. He wasn't what she would call handsome. He was just cute. He was tall, a good six feet, lean, maybe even lanky, and he had a devastating, drop-dead smile. In fact it was his smile that made him. He would flash it in a heartbeat to make his case, showing even white pretty teeth. He kept his hair cut close and even, showing off a perfectly shaped head, not like a lot of men with lumpy, shapeless domes. And the way he carried himself would cause any woman to look twice, whether she liked him or not. He exuded confidence, maybe too much of it.

She sighed, not realizing the disapproving looks she drew for doing so loudly. Were all weddings this long? Bernadette's mind began to wander when she finally heard the pastor reading some words Nancy had written for her and Lonnie. Nancy repeated them faithfully, then Lonnie. In a matter of minutes, the pastor asked, "Do you take this woman…." And Lonnie, loudly, answered, "I do, sir!" The audience snickered as the pastor gave him a long look, then turned and asked Nancy who, smiled widely, and quietly responded "I do." The pastor pronounced them man and wife and instructed Lonnie to kiss the bride. He did, with a long, drawn out delivery, and Bernadette turned her eyes impatiently. They landed on Reggie who sat staring at the couple with interest. She noticed how he sat, with his fingers intertwined. A solid gold chain link bracelet hung on his wrist over his watch. When she glanced back up, she found his eyes had turned on her, and she looked away embarrassed to be caught.

He wouldn't be easy to avoid at the reception but she intended to try.

Lonnie must have been friends with everybody, and every one of them had shown up at the reception hall to party. Nancy's married brother plied her with a French martini and tried to corner her, but as soon as she could, she gave him the slip for a group of familiar faces from the base. It all seemed so different with everyone dressed as civilians.

She dumped the martini and settled on merlot, and after several glasses, in a mellowed state of mind, she got out on the dance floor with the first man who asked her. She was actually surprised at all the second and third looks she attracted in the short black evening dress she had chosen to wear. It was probably the spiked, black leather heels and sheer black hose with the thin black seam that punctuated her long shapely legs.

She felt the dangling rhinestone earrings she'd bought for the occasion hit against her neck each time she moved her head back and forth, which was plenty because she didn't keep up with the latest dances. She figured, if you just moved your head and shoulders to the beat, the rest would follow. It always did. And she knew her hair looked good! She had paid $70.00 for this perm and expert shag cut, and every silky strand of her hair was in place and perfect.

She spent as much time as she could on the dance floor, trying to make herself feel better about losing Nancy to Lonnie, and what this meant to her financially and socially. To be honest, she was hurt, and just under the hurt, she was scared. Scared for herself, not being able to afford the apartment alone, even though Nancy would continue the rent through the end of the lease. Scared because Nancy was her family in San Diego. Now what she was going to do? It was a hell of a way to start the New Year.

Even on the dance floor, she couldn't stop her worries, especially about Toukie. Her instincts told her Toukie was still in trouble with Witt, and she wasn't in a position to do a damn thing about it. Would Toukie be intact by the time she got leave to see her?

When Nancy stepped out on the dance floor with her new husband, everyone cleared and let her and Lonnie have their first dance together to Gladys Knight's *You're Number One in My Book*. Nancy looked absolutely flushed from all the attention, and from the happiness and joy of being a bride. She looked wonderful. Bernadette watched Nancy's family make over her, and felt herself choke with envy.

Her eyes welled with tears. She was losing her roommate and best friend, she was no longer tight with her sister Beatrice, her niece was in trouble, and she believed something terrible was happening to her family, but couldn't find what. And her work! It was mounting, no matter how many hours she spent. She had a feeling it was a test, that the Colonel was pushing her to do more and more, but why? She was spending 16 hours a day to stay afloat.

She grabbed another glass of merlot and enjoyed the numbness after she gulped it down. She closed her eyes and paused, waiting for the alcohol to work its magic. With her eyes closed, she could hear Nancy's voice: *"Are you going to be all right when I'm gone? You know you've been drinking an awful lot lately, Berni, and I don't want to see anything throw you off track. I know you'll make it to the top. I hate to see you so upset about your niece."* She was going to be better than all right. She was going to be absolutely fine. If she ever found somebody that could make her look at him the way Nancy looked at Lonnie, she would just throw in the towel. It must be the most wonderful feeling in the world to be able to love like that…to feel that open. Just as she let herself imagine, she nearly jumped out of her skin from a light squeeze on her shoulder.

His warm breath on the side of her face started her heart before he spoke a word.

"Would it be okay to save a dance for me, Lieutenant?"

Bernadette turned to see Reggie's face. He only managed to say "hi" at church; this was the first sentence he'd been able to speak. She had dodged him nicely till now.

His eyes gave her the most intense feeling as he returned her gaze, and when she dropped her eyes to his lips, she felt her insides quiver. He had full, smooth, kissable lips that opened to reveal his beautiful teeth. This man was just plain delicious.

"I think I may be able to do that."

"I'd appreciate it. It's not every day I can get this opportunity to catch you without a bodyguard."

She frowned, her eyes sweeping upward to look into his. "Excuse me?"

"Your bodyguard. Whenever I see Nancy and ask about you, she tells me you're off with the bodyguard. Or you're working for the bodyguard. I understand I'm not an officer, but you spend a lot of free time with your bodyguard. I can't believe he let you out alone, and here as a civie. Patience pays off."

"Are you referring to Colonel Chisholm?"

"That would be the one."

Bernadette laughed. Why did people assume anything more about their alliance? They were soldiers and assigned a special task. Besides that, Colonel Chisholm was not young. Bernadette didn't know his age, but he had racked up a good 30 years in the military, plus he had a wife and children. Granted, they lived in Oregon, but he was still married. He'd never talked about his family to her, and discouraged her to talk about hers. He was an absolute gentleman. And he may as well have been, because he did nothing sexually for her.

"He's not my bodyguard."

"Don't be so sure."

"It's about work. He's very particular about what he has to do, and what he turns out."

"Maybe. You should know that the word out about you two is… there's more."

"Oh, Reggie, haven't you ever heard? Believe half of what you see, and NONE of what you hear. It'll make your life miserable."

Reggie smiled. "Haven't YOU heard? There are none so blind as those who will not see."

Bernadette paused, frowning. "And that means?"

"It's suicidal to walk around with your eyes closed."

"Are you saying I'm in danger?"

"You are if you don't know he's your bodyguard."

Bernadette smiled. "I find that a most interesting statement, Reggie.

You should know there's only one person responsible for me, and I look out for myself very well. That's why when you gave Lonnie your phone number to give to me and I found out you were enlisted, I let things go. You present more of a danger for me than any bodyguard you can think of."

Reggie shifted his stance. "Well, I didn't want to threaten you. I thought if you enjoyed music, and I'd seen you at the club with Nancy before, that it didn't have to be more than listening to some nice sounds."

"As friends? That's fraternizing."

"I understand. So, I guess that's that."

"Yes, it is."

"But, I hope you don't mind if I tell you, you're the most beautiful officer I've ever seen. "

She closed her eyes and laughed. "Flattery, soldier?"

"Sincerity."

Their eyes met and they smiled together.

By this time the crowd was moving in around the bridal couple as R. Kelly's 'Love Slide' started up. Reggie reached out his hand, and she accepted, joining him on the floor. She was pleased to see Reggie could move so well.

When Marvin Gaye's 'Distant Lover' came on, slowing everybody down, Reggie pulled her into his arms without asking. They moved together slowly, and Bernadette closed her eyes, feeling the power of a perfect moment as his long arms wrapped her close but not flush against him. She could pick up the scent of something soft and fragrant. She swayed against his chest. Not every moment could be this way, but immediately she felt her fatigue ebb as she leaned into Reggie. She wished she could do this all night long.

"We're still not crossing the line, are we Lieutenant?"

"You seem to know where to stop."

"So what's the difference with this, and you coming up to hear the band play sometimes? Your girlfriend will be there all the time, and you can enjoy the music with her. I get to play with them, every now and then."

"Really? Maybe I'll make it my business to attend when you play."

"I wish you would. Even an officer can sit back and enjoy good sounds."

"You're absolutely right. I'll try to find a free night."

"I have a perfect song that I'd like to play for you. And you can trust me, it won't go any further."

"Oh, Reggie," Bernadette said, almost in a drowsy tone. "I know you'd keep it perfectly decent. And if you didn't, I would. You can trust me on that."

"I'll trust you on that if you'll trust me on something."

"I don't know, should I?" Bernadette teased.

"You should."

"Well, what?"

"He likes you, Bernadette."

"Who?"

"Your Colonel."

Not again. Bernadette snickered. "Ridiculous."

"Okay. I'll leave it at that."

"Please do."

He said no more to her until the end of the song, then he thanked her politely and moved away. She moved in the opposite direction, feeling her whole body on fire. His fragrance surrounded her. She went to find some cold water. Instead she found a waiter who offered her a glass of ice, and she took it, and started toward a seat at a table. Then, glancing about on second thought, she could see out the side door of the reception hall and onto the patio where she moved. She paused to look at the large circular stone landing.

Plenty of people had already migrated to the outdoors because of the heat inside. Clear plastic glasses, half-filled with drinks were dotting the walls and the grounds as were balled up napkins. People in small groups were laughing, whispering. Further down a group seemed to be dancing together. On one end of the patio, a quartet of guys had gotten together to sing 'End of the Road' a capella, and they sounded so good, the whispering stopped until they finished and everyone applauded.

Bernadette smiled, then dragged herself to an empty lounge chair and dropped her body into it. When Reggie's voice started in her mind, she blocked it out. She didn't have time for that. She had to go to square one. She had to find another roommate. She had so much work to do...too much.

She leaned her head back and shut her eyes tightly. She had to get back to Baltimore. Three of them were dead, three more were to go. Colonel Chisholm would have gone home if something threatened his family. She was sure he was pressuring the major to keep her there. When she mentioned to the colonel himself that she was having family problems, he told her she was a soldier first. Period. Like she could ignore them.

She let the depression sink in. She could hear the gaiety all around her, and that was enough. After awhile, the mood began to creep down her back, into her spine. She began to relax. She wasn't sure how long she sat there. In fact she must have dozed because when she opened her eyes, she was looking up into Nancy's brother's face. The married one. His hand was on her bare arms, rubbing her goose bumps.

"It's cold out here," he announced with concern.

She blinked a couple times, unable to believe his audacity.

"You shouldn't be asleep out here. I could drop you off and come back." His eyes traveled down her body, then back up to her face. What the hell was wrong with him? Why did Nancy think it was okay to offer their apartment to her two brothers and sister, even for one night? This was crazy. She could not sleep near this lunatic.

She sat up, snatched her arm out of his hands and looked about, somewhat disoriented. There were still people outside, how long had she been out?

"It's not over," she said slowly, her mind thick from the wine.

"But if you want to sleep…"

"I don't. I'm okay," she said and then a voice from the doorway interrupted them.

"Bernadette! I've been looking all over for you. Ready?"

It was Reggie. In several quick strides he was beside her chair and helping her up.

"I was about to leave and I know you're on my way."

"Yes, I am," she said quickly. She had promised herself to be nice to Nancy's family no matter what, but she could see it wouldn't be possible for much longer. Nancy and Lonnie were leaving for Mexico tonight, and she had no reason to stick around longer. She excused herself from the disappointed glare of the brother and quickly followed Reggie inside.

She found her purse that she had left at a table, and went to extend best wishes to her friend and Lonnie.

As she hugged Nancy, she whispered in her ear," I don't know when I'll ever forgive you for this."

Lonnie gave her a short kiss, and Reggie kissed Nancy, then he pulled Bernadette behind him into the night.

Reggie walked her to his black Camaro. The windows were darkly tinted and the car was so buffed and shined she could see her reflection in the door of the passenger side from the light of the street lamp. A black leather cover stretched across his front headlights and a spoiler rose up on the trunk giving his car a sporty look. Her eyes followed the leather covering around to the front where she had to step over to peer, wondering curiously why anyone would put a leather cup on their car. That's when she noticed his license plate. Piccolo.

Piccolo? Who called him Piccolo? And why?

He pushed his alarm button, which flashed the lights, then opened the door for Bernadette. She slid into the passenger seat easily and felt the cool leather under her butt and against her legs. Her eyes skimmed across his dashboard noting his steering wheel had a woven leather cover, and a lone solid gold chain hung from his rearview mirror. She wondered whose it was. The inside was impeccably clean.

As soon as he slipped into the driver's seat, he glanced over at her.

"Straight home?" he asked.

"I was thinking," she said slowly. "I saw a Marriott not far from here. You can just drop me off there." She had a lot on her mind, and home was the last place she could think. "I'll find my way home tomorrow."

"Marriott? Don't you want to go home?"

She sighed and turned her eyes on him. "My home is filled with Nancy's out-of-town relatives. I think the Marriott would be best."

Reggie stared. "That dude from the reception a relative?"

"Her brother."

"Seems like you would put him out into a hotel. It's your place." He started the car, his engine jumping to life as he sat for a moment listening. Suddenly he clicked on the ceiling light and reached into his ashtray pulling out a business card. Reggie read it, flipped it over and pulled a pen from the small shelf under his CD player. He wrote on the back, handed the card to her and then pulled off into the night.

Bernadette started to look, but as he flipped off the light, she laid her head back into the cool leather seat gripping the card. She closed her eyes.

Reggie pushed in a CD, and in seconds, Gladys Knight's 'If I Were Your Woman' purred through the speakers. He had Gladys? Reggie drove on without conversation, while Bernadette enjoyed the feeling being next to him. Without doing anything—just by "being," this man could excite her. Or was it residue from four strippers at Nancy's bachelorette party?

Whatever, every fiber of her being tingled warmly as she sat and listened to the sound of Gladys' rich deep voice soothe her. Every boom-boom in the song vibrated throughout her entire body as her husky sound filled the car.

They arrived at the hotel, and Reggie surprised her by not just dropping her off at the lobby door, but parking and walking her inside.

"I'm really okay," she said as she glanced down at the card in her hand and noted his name and a phone number. She stuffed it into her pocketbook watching him shrug and stick his hands in his pocket.

"You know, it's pretty late. I'm tired. You're tired. Why don't we just get one room together and sleep over? It won't be more than sleep. I know you have a bodyguard, whether you do or not."

"If you're really concerned about that, you'd get your own room."

Bernadette turned as the clerk asked to help her. Reggie laughed.

She asked for two standard rooms and was told there were none left. She asked what was vacant, and while the clerk read off rooms that sounded outrageously expensive, Reggie asked her why didn't they just get a suite and split the cost. She wasn't sure that's what she wanted, but at the moment, it sounded like the quickest way to get out of her shoes and lay down in peace and quiet.

They got a room together.

As soon as they were inside, Reggie pulled off his jacket and unloosened his tie and shirt. Bernadette walked through the suite noting the huge living room area, big desk, big television, huge bedroom and bath area.

I could live here, she thought as she quickly came out of her heels and walked over to the large window and stared out over the sea of lights below. As she looked out, she heard music come in from the living room area, and she looked over her shoulder thoughtfully. He wanted to be with her.

She smiled to herself as she rubbed her foot through her hose then went over where the ice bucket and glasses were sitting. She picked up the bucket, and went into the other room. The way her head was swimming, she needed some ice to put against it.

"Be right back," she said to him as he leaned over the box that looked like a CD player, studying the dials.

When she returned, he was stretched out on the couch with the television muted, jazz playing in the background. He had on his pants and an undershirt and a 10-ounce coke sat on the table near him. She peered over and saw that his eyes were closed, then went into the bedroom and put down the bucket.

Now what? Should she take off her eye makeup and lipstick? Should she slip on the robe in the closet? Should she go back to the couch and sit with him?

She put several cubes into a washcloth and went over to the bed, putting it on her forehead. He should come and ask her to join him. If she went out there, it would be like inviting him for something. She was here to rest, nothing more. Like, what was with giving her his phone number? Did he expect her to use it? They couldn't date. And, if he wanted to talk to her, he knew how to contact Nancy. She wasn't about to trip up into something with this man, no matter what.

She stretched across the bed marveling at having him so near. Even if she could never tell another soul, her mind was always going to Reggie. His lips, his mouth, his walk. His movements. Just picturing him thrilled her.

She sat up. This was her chance to find out what he was about. She couldn't deny, she was attracted to him. And she was sure he knew it. Fraternization was only a crime if you were caught…or if you used it against a subordinate. She knew it couldn't be a relationship, it would end their military careers. It wasn't like these things never happened, especially if it was only for one night. Had she hoped she would get a chance to be with him? Why else had she pulled out her lingerie drawer and selected her black satin bra and panties from Victoria's Secret.

She wanted him. Now how much sense did it make to do anything about that? Maybe it would make plenty sense if she made it clear it would just be for one night. If she could just abandon herself to him for one night, he had no idea how good it would be. She could be happy for the rest of her career just remembering. So could he. Was he thinking about how to come to her as much as she was thinking about how to go to him? She laid waiting.

Then she stood. She should just go out to the front room now to him. What did she have to lose? Reggie wouldn't turn her down. Neither of them was married, and she knew for a fact, Nancy would call her crazy for letting this opportunity go. She just hated to make the first move. Yes, it was wrong, but still, she was the officer. He should give her the chance to turn him down, shouldn't he? She sat back down.

After a little while, she felt her lids grow heavy. Before she knew it, she dozed off.

When she woke up, the light was still on in her room and she realized she was still fully dressed. In fact, one side of her dress was yanked up around her waist and badly wrinkled. She could still hear the music from the radio outside her room. She pulled herself up, blinked several times and looked over at the clock. It was 0200 hours. Where was he?

She climbed off the bed and went to find him. When she walked into the living room area, she headed over to the couch and there she paused.

He was stretched out, stripped down to his underwear, a pair of gold silk boxers, and snoring. One arm was stretched out and one was curved above his head. He snored softly, leaving no doubt. He was out like a light.

Bernadette stared down at him. What the hell did this mean? She wanted him. She wanted him badly. How could he not feel the same? She reached her hand out for his shoulder, and then stopped.

All she needed was tonight. That was all. And if tomorrow, he didn't want to acknowledge her…

It would kill her. It would kill her because she would care. She did care. With Reggie, it could never be for one night. It would never be like the others…she stared down at him. Why hadn't he come to her? He hadn't even TRIED anything. Didn't wake her…ask her to listen to the music, or have a coke. He acted just like he said, like he really just wanted to zonk out.

She was tempted to wake him. To grab him, slap his eyes open and ask him what he was doing laying there sleeping on her. She wanted to put him out the room. What was the point in being here with her if all he wanted to do was just sleep? He could have gone home!

Then she looked at him closely. His cinnamon colored body seemed to glow in the dim light, and her eyes were drawn to his broad shoulders, which tapered to narrow hips and muscular thighs. There was a furring of fine, baby hair over his tummy which dwindled to a thin line that traced down, down, and disappeared into his shorts. He was truly a beautiful specimen, so much more real than the dancing sexpots at Nancy's party. She had to wonder what it must feel like to be against that body, to have those incredible lips kiss her. Really kiss her.

She turned suddenly, aware of the confusion that gripped her. She marched back to her room and slammed the door so hard, it had to make him stir. She almost tore the black dress off her body and jumped under the covers alone.

He would pay for this.

******

But when? Reggie never called her, and one day stretched into another in an endless seam of weeks, finding her at her computer day in, day out, still thinking about that night. Three weeks later, she still wondered how she could have made things different. Even with no sex, Reggie was adorable. She loved just looking at him, let alone anything else.

Bernadette sat hunched over her desk, well after six in the evening, crossing the completed errands off her to-do list. Marketing was left, she needed food and badly but she had no money. Then she had added "call Dina????" That gave her pause. Dina, her best friend from Baltimore, had called this morning, this morning, and asked her to be the maid-of-honor in her wedding, scheduled for next week. When Bernadette told her she couldn't possibly do it, Dina had gotten irate. Her mother wouldn't pay up unless Bernadette was there, Dina said, and she sounded crazy mad when Bernadette was firm. Why did the world have to go crazy all at one time? Like Colonel Chisholm and this work.

The Colonel had e-mailed her a long piece on changes he needed her to do, and she had to rub her eyes. He wanted all this new information to be worked into the programs now, telling her she had to make the programs more selective. Lately, any reports that gave back more information than requested, he bounced back to her as unacceptable. In order to get this right, she needed about a week to work on this project alone, and it wasn't supposed to be this involved. He'd even pulled back on the help he was giving her. And she hadn't talked to him personally in weeks.

He was starting to act funky, and though she knew they were about to finish up this detail, it couldn't end soon enough. She intended to get every bit of credit she deserved for the months of extra work she'd put in. If she could only get some help right now.

Speaking of help, her mind switched to Beatrice. If only she could be sure her sister was safe. She ached to dial Beatrice's phone number again, but now Witt didn't even answer. Had their business taken off? Or had Bea met Daddy? It had to mean something that she could never reach anybody on the phone.

Bernadette brushed her hands over the pages of computer printout, frowning, then looked up and out over the computer floor. She could still see Lance Corporal Weeks, one of her subordinates, at his desk working. He was redoing a large report he had run incorrectly, and was furious with her for having to redo it. He was the one ass in her unit she could not control. A loudmouth jerk, he half did the work he was capable of doing, and enjoyed the challenge to her authority. She had no time for this now—right when she needed everything to go right, everything was going wrong.

Weeks should have finished that report by now, but making her baby-sit him undoubtedly brought him joy. Of course, she was missing her Thursday volleyball game, which thoroughly pissed her off. It was the only release she got these days. If he got up to leave before that report was finished, she vowed she would spend the night in this seat writing him up from a to z. She sat wondering just how long she'd have to wait, when her phone rang. Stupidly, she thought of Reggie, and picked it up.

"Good evening, this is Lieutenant Windsor speaking?"

"Berni?"

Bernadette sat up straight as an arrow. "Marietta?"

"Hi Berni! I'm glad I caught you."

Glad? What a lie, Bernadette thought. Ordinarily, she would never be at her desk this late. Marietta had left a couple messages on her work phone in response to letters from Bernadette, after hours, which meant she had to wait until after nine or ten east coast time to call her. She did not expect to hear me, Bernadette thought, wanting to laugh.

"I'm glad you caught me too. What's up?"

"I wanted to call you about Bea. Your letter scared me," Marietta said, and Bernadette turned anxiously in her seat, pushing the phone tighter to her ear and waited.

"You were saying you couldn't reach her, and you were concerned something had happened. Well, I called Mama and asked her to go over to Witt's to see if he knew where she was."

"Good. I was actually hoping you would drive down to Baltimore and check yourself. You know how Mama is, but if she checked, that's great."

"Well, you're right. She didn't want to check. Didn't want me to bother Beatrice, but I told her how often you'd called and couldn't get Bea at home."

"And she found her?"

"No. But she called the police, because she thought it was odd that you could not contact her. The police went there late in the evening and Witt was there. He said Beatrice had left him. Then Mama said that one of Bea's next-door neighbors told the police she hadn't seen Bea or the children, but the little girl attended the school down the street.

"So the police went there the next day, and they found Toukie had been transferred to a school in another district by her mother. Since they believe Bea and her children are okay, they don't consider her missing."

"This is too weird, Marietta. Don't you think?"

"Well, not for Bea. No, I don't."

"I wonder if she found Daddy, and just went off to stay with him."

There was silence. Bernadette pulled the phone from her ear to look at it and then put it back saying, "Hello?"

"Is she still trying to get into that club with him?"

"As far as I know."

"I don't understand why she would insist…"

"That's neither here nor there at this point. Where is my sister? I don't see how anybody can be calm when I have a letter threatening that something like this would happen to one of us and now one is missing. And don't tell me that Daniel died of a simple car accident, or that Nita died of simple pneumonia. We were not in North Carolina at Fort Bragg. We don't know for sure--"

"Daniel didn't die at Fort Bragg," Marietta said then. He died in Baltimore, on his first leave after boot camp. I thought you knew."

"In Baltimore? Really?" Suddenly that old fear gripped her heart. "Was he in the car alone?"

"No, he wasn't. A friend from Baltimore was with him. I believe it was a school buddy, but he survived the crash."

"Do you know who?"

"I don't remember his name, but Mama may know. He was a good friend of Dan's from high school, and they'd just left her house when it happened.

"What kind of accident was it?"

"A tree. Dan ran into a tree. He had been drinking, and I think they said he had something else in him, one of those party drugs. Mescaline or something."

Drugs. *He had died home in Baltimore after being with Mama.*

"That's interesting. Let me ask you this, was Daniel happy in the Army?"

"Dan? You must be kidding. He wasn't happy after he left home at all. He hated it."

"Do you think he might have gone to Daddy because he was looking for something better?"

"Daddy? No, I absolutely doubt it. Dan wouldn't go against Mama to find Daddy."

"Why would it be going against Mama? Why couldn't he just want to talk to Daddy, and it have nothing to do with Mama?"

"Because, Mama made it clear that Daddy was off limits."

"Why? I'm sure if Dan needed him, he should have been free to see him. What did Mama think would happen?"

"Bernadette, it was a long time ago, and honestly, it was between Daddy and Mama, and it's what they both decided, as you can see."

"I can't see anything. Do you, or do you not know what the deal was with them?"

"That's something that you should ask Mama."

"Or Daddy. I'd rather ask him."

Marietta said nothing to that.

"I'll do my best to follow up on Beatrice, and I'll let you know. I can tell you now, she's okay. She's doing what she wants to do, what she always does. She's living her life in the streets."

"I hope you mean that you'll go to Baltimore to look for her. I'm just sorry you feel it's okay that she's living in the streets with a 9-year old and an infant. I don't understand you, Marietta."

"That's because I know Beatrice better than you do. But I'll be back in touch."

Bernadette hung up thinking. What was it that Marietta and Mama were hiding? Would somebody please make it clear to me? Bernadette fumed and jumped up.

She had to get out. She had to find somebody to bounce this off. Nancy was gone, but Colonel Chisholm had a mind like hers. Maybe he would still be in his office. Maybe she could ask him for some help, and he'd see the stress she was under and release her from the project. He'd stopped calling, maybe he knew it was all becoming too much. Why hadn't she heard his voice?

Bernadette secured her area, noting the evening personnel had come in. She thought about calling the Colonel's office first, but figured he would be conveniently busy, or not in, so she decided to take her chances.

Gripping her keys, and the file on her father, she rushed out to the lot. Hell, she could live with Reggie's indifference if she had to. After all, he was off limits to her anyway. But Colonel Chisholm? She'd rather not. If she hurried, she could catch him.

# fourteen

There was Mrs. Mabrey, the colonel's long time secretary, at her big desk with the fancy computer. She smiled widely at Bernadette before she seemed to catch herself and cut it off.

"Hi, Mrs. Mabrey!" Bernadette greeted brightly. "Is the Colonel still in?"

"Yes he is, but he's pretty busy."

Bernadette stared at the woman. She could tell the way Mrs. Mabrey's bright gray-blue eyes avoided her eyes that something was up. What was the matter? She frowned.

"I'll wait. It's really important. Please, just tell him I'm here."

She faltered. "I…I don't think he'd want you to wait right now. Can he call you?"

"He could but lately he hasn't, and I'd rather wait here. Can you buzz him?"

Mrs. Mabrey touched the gray bun in the back of her head and looked clearly uncomfortable. She got up and walked the few feet over to the office door and knocked once then slipped inside. What the hell? Bernadette thought.

He had to come out eventually.

When she came back, she said he'd see Bernadette, but it might be quite a while. Still, Bernadette assured Mrs. Mabrey she'd wait.

After 45 minutes, and Mrs. Mabrey's constant glancing as she went through her ritual, of organizing her desk for the night, she finally said to Bernadette, "I think it's ridiculous. You know?"

Bernadette looked at her. "What?"

Mrs. Mabrey clucked her tongue loudly. "How they get away with these things." She shook her head, convincing Bernadette something was terribly wrong, and though she looked like she wanted to say more, she

glanced at the closed door, and continued to cluck her tongue. In minutes, after at least an hour's wait, Colonel Chisholm finally opened the
door. He looked over at her and told her she could come in.

By the time she got up and went through the door, he was already
back behind his desk, clicking his computer keys noisily as his hands ran
over the keyboard, eyes glued to the screen.

She stood expectantly, waiting for him to look at her to acknowledge
her salute. Certain that Mrs. Mabrey would have gone but for the alter-
cation she must have suspected she would hear, Bernadette closed the
door firmly before she stood at attention. When he didn't acknowledge
her, she blurted out, "What's the matter, Colonel? What in the world is
wrong?"

He swiveled around in his seat.

"You find a problem?" His close cut gray and black hair was brushed
down neatly, not a strand sticking up. His tone was formal.

"Request permission to sit down, sir?"

He never returned her salute, and she sat herself down, looking at him.

"I left several messages this week. Is something wrong? I was beginning to think you were sick, but then I knew Mrs. Mabrey would have
mentioned it."

"What is it, Lieutenant?"

He actually sounded annoyed.

"Have I done something to you, sir?"

He looked at her over his eyeglasses.

"Have you?"

She blinked surprised.

"You're angry at me. Why?"

Finally he let his eyes meet and hold her gaze. He examined her face.

"I'm not angry. I just don't appreciate wasting my time. My time is
very important to me, Lieutenant, and I resent it when I find it's been
wasted. I never thought you were a waste, as you know, but even I can be
wrong."

"What do you mean?" He was beginning to scare her.

"I mean, I thought you were serious about things, about your job,
about your life. I thought you were trying to do everything you could to
build a career that any officer would respect."

"Nothing has changed, sir."

"Really? Are you saying that is still what you want? That your career here is still the most important thing to you?"

Another trick question. Did he mean, more than family?

"It's still what I want, sir."

"That comes as a surprise to me." He tented his fingers and stared in her eyes. "You remember, we had this discussion about women soldiers who get sworn in only to find every reason in the book to avoid their full obligation. We talked about using family, and ill preparation as the most common excuse. We talked about the things that held women soldiers back, and you agreed then that it was unfortunate. But that you would have none of those problems."

"I don't understand sir, you're not being very clear. I am still here for the long haul. I have no intentions of leaving until I've met every goal I discussed with you. Things have not changed."

"Maybe this will make it clearer. Did you attend the wedding ceremony of your good friend and former roommate on February 12?"

She paused. "Yes."

"And then what? Did you go to the reception?"

Bernadette looked at him, the surprise slowly finding it's way across her face. This is what it's about? She could see where it was leading. Someone had told him about the bachelorette party. It was raunchy, and a whole lot was going on, but she wasn't doing it. Then she frowned. He didn't say bachelorette party. He said reception. Everybody was at the reception.

"I did go."

"And did you go home following the reception? Or let's put it this way, to whose home did you go?"

Amazing, she thought then, staring at him. It was about leaving the reception with Reggie. Someone had tipped him off that she left with him. Did they know she'd ended up with him at the Marriott? He was acting like he knew she had spent the night there. She could quickly tell him what happened. Not a damn thing! She got a room and nothing happened, even though Reggie was there and she wanted it to. But why should she tell him anything? How would he know?

"I stayed at a nearby hotel. Sir, what is this about?"

"Don't make me ask about him, Lieutenant. Just tell me."

"With all due respect sir, nothing happened when I left the reception. And I'm not sure why you would want me to give an account of the people I encountered there? If I'm not mistaken, I was off duty, and I was with friends. To speak frankly sir, I would never jeopardize my career."

Unable to stay behind the desk, Colonel Chisholm got up and started to the door as though he were going to leave. He opened it and said something to Mrs. Mabrey, then he closed the door and Bernadette distinctly heard the lock click. He walked back to her, then pausing a moment, continued past her and around his desk. He stopped, standing in front of the computer.

"I'd like to show you something I was working on when you came in," he said, and waved his hand toward the screen. Bernadette got up forgetting her file on the chair, and went around his desk to look. It appeared to be some type of log sheet, with her name and other names she recognized from the detail. She could see that he'd listed the reports requested beside the names of the personnel responsible. Now he was going to let her have it. Tell her how her work had slipped. That she wasn't what he thought. She looked at the names and waited. Then she felt him move close behind her.

"What do you see?" his tone was a whisper and his breath blew on her neck. She stood frozen, her mind screaming, I-don't-believe-this-shit.

"I...see a list of names." She didn't dare turn her face around. Then she felt him move closer until his pelvis was against her.

"And what do you see beside your name?" As he ended his question, she felt his body push up against her butt.

"I see the reports you requested." Oh please, she screamed silently, not moving. She had the strong urge to spin around, but knew that would be the end.

"The ones that I haven't gotten back from you yet. Because you've done them all incorrectly."

"I wanted to talk to you about them, sir. That's why I'm here."

He pressed harder.

"Then talk. You've never been afraid to talk before."

Not while you're rocking against my butt, blowing air on my neck and in my ear. What are you doing? she asked silently. Then swallowed.

"I...request permission to sit down, sir."

"In a minute." She felt him doing something. Moving something on himself, his hand touching her behind as he did. She closed her eyes, wondering if she should run. Bolt across the desk and out the door. Then decided, why? He wouldn't dare try to rape her, would he? He had to know that action would get him hurt, and he would have to explain why the office was wrecked and he was stemming the flow of blood from wherever she could land a blow with that wooden in-box which she was eyeing.

He touched her hand that hung limply at her side, and the next thing she knew, he had put himself into her palm, wrapping his hand around hers.

"I like you, Bernadette. And I don't like people easily. I want to help you, and I don't want to help people very often. You make me happy to see you, to see your work, to see how you think. You're smart; you're fast. And I don't like to feel that you are a waste of my time. You haven't wasted my time, have you?"

He was hard in her hand, but still rather small and skinny. And it jerked as he spoke. Quickly, Bernadette snatched her hand from around him and turned to face him, her mouth opened in shock, but he took advantage and plunged his tongue down her throat.

That's when she grabbed the front of his uniform, material, buttons, medals, all balled in both fists and pushed away with all her might, twisting her head nearly backward to get his mouth off of hers.

He stumbled back awkwardly, banging his hand on the side of his in-box which broke his spin and dislodged the box. Papers flew across the floor.

"Excuse me, sir," Bernadette spat, her feet moving her as fast as they could back around his desk. "Excuse me, sir," she repeated, her knees almost buckling as she grabbed the desk to face him. He straightened himself up, immediately righting his uniform, adjusting his pants, zipping up, taking both palms and brushing down his hair. Then he waited, as though he wanted to let his actions sink in before asking, "Do you understand what trash is?"

She stared at him, waiting for an apology. Waiting for him to tell her to get out. Waiting for him to acknowledge what he had just done.

"You know, there's black trash and white trash. Same thing. People who have no redeeming qualities. People who don't know anything and who don't want to know anything, and want to make a life out of their ignorance. That's trash. And to my surprise, I've found that may be what you are, nothing but trash."

Bernadette's eyes narrowed immediately.

"How dare you call me trash? Because if I am, what does that make you? You went for me."

"Don't get cute. It doesn't become you."

"I'm dead serious."

He looked at her, an expression she couldn't read.

"I'm very disappointed in you, Bernadette. I held you on a pedestal and would have bet my life that you were way above the majority of the women and the men who come into the military. Bet my life that you were going after that top rung. You always walked the straight and narrow, seemed to understand what it would take to get you there. Then, I find out I'm wrong. To find out you have an interest in a...horn player. An enlisted horn player, of all things. And that this is what your career will come down to."

"My career?" Her face was hot and her stomach was jumping but the adrenaline was pumping through her. "I have done nothing *wrong*, sir. I don't know what you heard, or think you found out, but I've done nothing to tarnish my oath to the Marines. What makes you think you know so much about me?" Bernadette demanded. "What do you have, spies? Whatever this is, I didn't expect it of you! I thought so much more of you."

"Would you have spent the night with me, Lieutenant?"

"Sir? Of COURSE not, sir! What do you mean? You're married."

"Tell me, Bernadette, what has HE done for you? What can he do for you?"

"Who?"

"Don't play with me. If this is what you want, let's just lay it out and look at it. If it's not what you want, if you can admit it's not, then tell me. Maybe I'm wrong. I don't like to waste my time. So, is this what you want? Are you satisfied with what he can do for you?"

"I don't believe you! You don't know what you're talking about, and for you to behave this way. Talk about behavior that's beneath you, I can't believe you!"

"I'm not totally stupid, Lieutenant. You may think I am, but I'm not. My time is valuable to me, and if you just want to waste it, let me assure you, you've wasted enough. I have no more to give you."

"Then why didn't you pick up the phone and say it! Why would you send me thousands of notes that the reports are not according to your specifications, and you've made no particular specifications other than what I've been running? If this is the way you want it, fine by me. But let's not play games. You may be surprised, Colonel. When I said I would make it to the top, I certainly didn't have my hopes pinned on anybody but me. I thought you were my mentor. I'm..." she stared at his unblinking glare, biting back the words, "sorry it didn't work."

She grabbed her father's file off the chair, shot him a parting glance, then turned on her heels and hurried out his office, making a big show of loudly unlocking the door, in case Mrs. Mabrey was there and hadn't heard him click it on.

Bernadette slammed out the office door and shot past Mrs. Mabrey's empty desk. So, he had made her leave. Tears blinded her. How could she have been so stupid?

*fifteen*

Outrageous! Bernadette went through the rest of the week incensed over the colonel's behavior. Incensed because who could she tell? Getting a colonel reprimanded based on her word alone was not going to happen. Yes, reports would be taken, and then she would be made to look like a fool for opening her mouth. She would never tell, but she had to find a way to let him know, she would not be used that way again.

Smoothing out the comforter over her fresh rose-colored sheets, Bernadette puffed up her pillows and stood in the doorway. She had changed around her bedroom, moving her head away from the window where it got a little cool. Her CD player was blasting Stevie Wonder's '*Do I Do'* and every step she took was in time to the beat. Every now and then, she stopped to do a little hip shake. It made her feel better as she worked.

The television was on in the living room, going over the March Madness lineups for this evening's NCAA final four college basketball games. Nancy and Lonnie were having a party, but she wasn't driving all the way there to watch the UCLA Bruins' game. It was clear the Maryland Terps were going to take it, and if she wanted to see it, there were a million bars closer where she could go and watch in the company of many.

She ran back to check out the toilet bowl she was bleaching clean. The smell of Clorox made everything seem antiseptic. She hadn't given the house a good cleaning since Nancy pulled her things out, and Lord knows, it needed it.

She thought back to the wedding. She should have listened to what Reggie told her about the colonel's feelings. She should have been prepared. Now, the colonel had lobbed the ball back in her court, waiting to see what she would do. His position seemed to be: 'If you fucked him, you're going to fuck me, or I'll ruin your career.' Would it help, she wondered, if she told him she hadn't done anything? Probably not. He'd made his move, now he wanted something in return.

But, he didn't understand her, obviously. She wasn't going down, it was simply not an option. He wasn't forcing her off the task force, nor would he force her into bed. Yes, he'd stuck another wedge in her plans, but what he failed to realize was the more scared she felt, the harder she fought. If she went down, he was going too.

That must have been the reason she hadn't heard from Reggie. Didn't he understand that they just couldn't date? They could talk. Was she afraid that she would hurt his career? Maybe someone had warned him away from her. After all, he was in the band, and it would take hard work and good luck to get far in the band. Crossing officers was not the way to get ahead.

She was very anxious about that. She was still banking on becoming captain this year. She had finished her Applications class at UCSD last month, in her personal effort to keep up with the software manufacturers' changes. That class would help her stand out on the best-qualified list. Still, she wasn't fooling herself. It wouldn't be so easy now. Colonel Chisholm knew what she wanted and how badly, and as easily as he had been directing her moves, he would surely step in and put an end to her ascent.

How ironic that Colonel Chisholm happened to be called in on a programming problem and she was the head applications programmer on duty at the time and helped him turn the problem around in an afternoon. She was dead on accurate in her abstract reasoning, and he was amazed. He suggested she contact him for some pointers on running programs in general and from there, she had confided her goals, and he had volunteered to give her guidance when she needed it. Now, she'd have to do it all on her own.

Maybe the thing to do was call Reggie to see if he knew anything. How was the colonel going to get back at her? Sometimes everybody else on base knew what was going on before the person involved.

She pulled out the card with his telephone number from the bottom of her jewelry box where she had buried it the morning after the wedding. She dialed him from the kitchen, leaning across her plate of leftover scrambled eggs she'd eaten for breakfast. She had to find the colonel's snitch, and decide what action she would take, if any. She couldn't get the

Colonel, but she had a chance against the person who had told on her.

To her surprise, Reggie answered after two rings.

"Hello, Reggie, how are you? It's Bernadette."

"Hey. I'd know your voice anywhere. You found a minute to say hi?"

"Actually, I found a few. I'd really like to talk to you, if you could you stop over?"

She directed him to her home address, and then hung up breathless. Was she crazy? Her heart pounded wildly. She could hardly believe he was on his way.

******

She'd gone through the apartment like a hurricane, finishing her cleaning. She picked up, straightened up, and paused to try to look at her apartment through impartial eyes. Since Nancy left, she hadn't gotten used to it. It looked strangely empty without Nancy's tons of junk. She had gotten used to all the ceramic figures that Nancy collected, jungles of houseplants, walls of prints and fleet of lamps. Nancy had a thing about lighting, and she bought a lamp for every type of luminance she desired. Many were hanging lanterns that had left holes in the ceilings and walls now that she was gone.

Still, the absence of her junk was a good deal. Bernadette had missed the simplicity she used to enjoy before Nancy's invasion. Maybe she wouldn't get another roommate after all. Maybe she'd get a part-time job. Roommates never seemed to know what it took to stick it out in the military. Everyone heard of the travel, visiting other countries, living allowances and thought "great deal," but everybody wasn't suited for the kind of mental stamina being in the military took. The reason many women dropped out of the military was men. Getting pregnant and sexual harassment ranked near the top, but men complicated everything. Fear of losing them, fear of leaving them, fear of working with them, it was the male problems that sent them packing. The mental ability to play the game, if Bernadette had to guess, was what some women lacked. And she was determined not to fail.

She cleaned up her little kitchen table, and after staring in her empty refrigerator, decided to serve Reggie the foot long submarine sandwich she'd bought for herself to eat as she watched the Maryland game. She cut it into quarters and put them on a plate.

She ran back to the bathroom and finished cleaning the toilet bowl, and just as she stuck her head down to check everything, felt her earring hit her shoulder on its way into the toilet bowl.

"I can't believe this is happening." She could not see past the sudsy, bleach water.

Tears came to her eyes. She liked those silver hoops. She had so few pieces of jewelry and these were a favorite that would now change colors because of the bleach. When things went wrong, everything went wrong, like she had money to buy more. She sighed, and reached her hand in the dirty water, touching the bottom until she felt it, then pulled it up.

Did she have ice cubes? She kept sodas in the kitchen; she could chill a few cans before Reggie arrived. Too bad none were Mountain Dew, Reggie's favorite. She ran back into the kitchen and put two six packs in the freezer, and checked for ice.

Then back in the living room, she paused to straighten the Persian rug under the coffee table and hurried to the bathroom to check out her reflection. Her lips looked a little chap, so she wet them, then ran a comb through her thick hair. She smiled at herself, liking what she saw, as the buzzer sounded. Bernadette went into the living room to buzz Reggie in, then waited until she heard him on her landing before she peered through the peephole and opened the door.

When she opened the door, her eyes locked on his as she smiled widely.

"Well hi! Please, come in and join me," she motioned expansively and he smiled at her.

"Thanks for the invitation." He handed her a small package, wrapped in brown paper.

"For me? You are full of surprises," she said smiling.

"Think you'll enjoy it," he said, glancing around. She hung up his jacket, package tucked under her arm, and directed him to join her in the kitchen, the brightest and safest room in the apartment.

"Wow! You cooked all this for me?" He pointed to the Subway sandwiches.

She laughed. "I'm a master of many talents! I also have drinks--orange, cream, grape, ginger ale and the best, Pepsi sodas in the fridge."

Reggie rubbed his hands together. "Give me the best—Pepsi."

While she got glasses, he picked up two of the sandwiches and put them on a plate, then leaned over the tray of Toll House Chocolate Chip cookies and took several.

"The little homemaker, huh?"

"I could be."

She opened the package, tearing the taped ends and flipped over a CD with the letters SOS on the front.

"SOS band, " he said when she looked puzzled. "Not a band you hear about everyday, but they have some great songs on that CD. Remember in school when you had to read those dry, pointless books for literature?"

Bernadette looked at him. "I usually didn't. I'm a movie girl."

"Yeah, but remember your teacher asking you the theme? What's it about? Not until I heard this CD did I ever understand theme. You're the one this whole CD was written for. I only wish I'd written it."

Bernadette smiled.

"I hope it's not stepping over the line, Lieutenant. If it is, I apologize."

"No, I'm sure it's okay. I can't wait."

She joined him at the table where they dug in, both eating heartily. They talked easily with each other, which was a relief to Bernadette since she remembered how quiet he was with her the night of the wedding. Reggie talked about the newlyweds, what Lonnie was going through the first few weeks as a husband, and Bernadette told him how much Nancy was enjoying it. She missed her roommate immensely, and had gone to visit her a few times. When Reggie started about Lonnie's bachelor party, she shared some tidbits of Nancy's party with him, and disclosed that she really wasn't sold on the idea of having one herself when her time came.

After they had eaten their sandwiches and nibbled on cookies, Bernadette told Reggie that she had something on her mind and that she needed his help.

Reggie leaned forward, elbows on knees, long forearms dangling between his long legs as he stared intently at her.

"Remember when we were at the reception and you kept telling me Colonel Chisholm was my bodyguard? What made you say that?"

Reggie smiled easily.

"Thought about things, didn't you?"

"Yes, you could say that."

"Word gets around, you know. I mention your name, and the dudes tell me the deal, your hook-up is Colonel Chisholm. I know he takes up a lot of your time, like when Nancy is with Lonnie at the club, she says you're on base working with him. And everybody knows he protects you. That he's got you on his radar. Everybody but you."

"Protects me?"

"When people are 'protected,' they don't get messed over by anybody."

"Why would I be protected? I have no special relationship with the colonel. Nothing more than any other Marine?"

"Don't believe it. Why fight it? It won't hurt you and damn, if it's no sweat off you, so to speak, why change it?"

Bernadette felt anger course through her.

"Because nothing has been automatic for me. Where is all this special treatment? I'm working my ass off for everything I get, and I don't belong to anybody but myself. I owe nothing to anybody but me. I don't like to find that somebody is manipulating my life and I don't even know it! What does that do for my credibility? Everybody will think I made it with help, and that's not what I'm about."

Reggie shrugged and that angered her more.

"It doesn't matter what you believe. I was just wondering if maybe you felt afraid to speak to me because of the rumors about the colonel's attention?"

He looked at her and smiled.

"I'm here, right? And I'm here on the Final Four basketball weekend. No, you don't have to worry about me being afraid. I think if he wants you that bad, all's fair in love and war. In the end, neither one of us is eligible to see you. He's married, and I'm enlisted. So, it doesn't matter what he thinks of me."

"Do you realize you may be watched for being with me?"

"I'm off the base. I doubt that anybody is that nosy."

"I'm telling you. I believe he is that nosy."

She watched his expression change to questioning.

"You two had words about me or something?"

"Well. Let's say, he knows we were both at the wedding."

Reggie smiled, that beautiful smile that tugged his lip to one side.

"Oh," he said in a laugh. "I see he's on the job."

"Yes, as in bodyguard. That WAS your term, and I think it was most accurate. I'd like to know, who told you that I was in protective status?"

"Told me? It's general knowledge. I mean, there is no one person that I could name. I didn't know he'd actually have people out doing the job for him after duty hours. When I said bodyguard, I was talking about the colonel himself."

Bernadette scooted her chair over and leaned closer to him. Her foot touched his accidentally and she felt electricity shoot up her leg, through her whole body. "Somebody reported us to Colonel Chisholm the night of the wedding. Probably the fact that we left together and maybe even said that we went to the Marriott."

Reggie laughed again. "Well! You're more important than you knew, aren't you? And just think, I'm the one who first told you."

"Reggie, who's telling you to watch your step with me? I'd really like to know who I'm up against."

"Nobody in particular. I'm being honest."

Bernadette paused.

"Okay. Then why haven't you called me since the wedding, if you say you're not afraid."

"Not because of him. I do have to remember who you are."

She knew he meant respecting her rank, and she sat back straight and shook her head in agreement.

"Well, that's understood. I meant, why haven't you called, as a friend. That's why I have you here now. As a friend of a friend. I can certainly prove that."

"Is that why I'm here?"

She looked in his eyes.

"What did you think?"

"Well, I can tell you I'm here right now because you're a beautiful woman who called and said, 'I want to see you.' And even though it's the Bruin's big day, I've wanted to hear you say that to me since the night I saw you at the club last year. And when you called me, it was exactly what I wanted to do."

"Really? To be honest, I'm glad. I've been looking forward to talking to you again too."

Reggie looked her over.

"Sometimes I think we're speaking the same language, but saying two different things."

"I think we understand each other perfectly," she responded.

He gave her his slow, sexy smile. "At least you're more honest today than you were the night of the wedding. Maybe because you know I saved you twice. I saved you from that dude in the green suit, and now, from a man you didn't even know had you in his sights. I guess you realize you owe me."

Bernadette laughed.

"I can't think of anybody I'd rather be in debt to."

Reggie let his eyes rest on her.

"I haven't told you how I'd like my pay." He looked intently at her.

"If I can, I'll accommodate your request. What do you want?"

"To stay here for a while."

"Oh, I wasn't asking you to leave yet. I like your company."

"But do you like me?"

Bernadette cocked her head. "Of course, Reggie. I wouldn't have called you if I didn't."

"I mean, do you *like* me. I know the night of the wedding, you got mad because I didn't come in that room with you. You wanted me to come in there and sneak it from you. Get you to say yes while you were feeling good. Make you feel like you didn't have a chance to think about what you were doing. But I didn't want that. No games. I want you to know that you want me. Cause that's how I want you."

Bernadette's eyes opened wide. She wasn't high, if that's what he meant by feeling good. He was going in the wrong direction now, and she had to stop him firmly. She opened her mouth to lay down the law, and heard herself say instead, "You're wrong. I didn't want you to sneak up on me."

"That night you did. You weren't sure about me. But, the way I look at it, we're off base. Nobody lives here but you. Nobody has to know. I'm here, and I want you as bad as I did the night of the wedding. You're the one, Bernadette. You have more to lose. As long as you want me, I'm here."

She watched his lips, and something strange happened. Everything around them seemed to fade, and all she was aware of was him. First, his lips. When they stopped, his eyes, which stayed fixed on her.

He reached his hand out to her, and she reached out to place hers in his, thinking once again, now was her chance. She could take his hand and pull him into the living room to safely watch the game. But when he stood, he pulled her up from the seat and into his arms. His eyes never left hers as he bent his head down and she moved her face to meet his. He pressed her lips gently in a long, sweet kiss. Feeling those tender, full, succulent lips cover hers sent her heart racing madly. He pulled back a moment to look at her, then pulled her tighter and kissed her again as her arms wrapped automatically around his neck. He ran his long fingers through her thick hair and she pressed herself to him until their bodies molded together. They kissed again and again and the last traces of uncertainty gave way to raw hunger as Reggie awakened something in her she had never felt.

He rubbed his face in her hair, holding her tightly against him as they caught their breaths. Then he let his arms drop to her small waist. He held her in both his large hands as he looked in her eyes.

"I want you, Bernadette. I want to get to know you, I've been trying to get to know you, and I want you to know me. I want you to give me a try."

Bernadette, longing for his lips on hers couldn't even remember what she murmured, but it got them into the bedroom, and she started to undress, regretting she had on her plain white jockeys from JC Penney. Suddenly Reggie stopped her. He continued to undress her himself, and instead of wanting to go through the floor, she felt herself heating up at the way his breath came out harder, and quicker as he looked at her. He bent his head to her, and this time when their lips touched, he let his tongue meet hers, causing her insides to quiver.

When he paused to undress himself, she laughed at how quickly he moved. Then she jumped under the comforter. In a minute, he joined her, and they came together again, the flames igniting in her as he kissed her intently. Reggie kissed her neck, her eyes, her nose, her lips, her breasts, stopping to knead them gently, then moved his hands slowly down the curves of her body stroking the roundness of her buttocks, and her long shapely legs, before they came back to stroke her stomach.

His tongue in her mouth was like a torch, setting her ablaze. When he licked her slowly and sensuously starting from her lips, he went down her neck, tantalizingly slow over her chest, stopping to rest on each breast and then very gently to touch them with the tip of his tongue before moving in circles over each one. She moaned deep in her throat. He nipped them lightly between his teeth, as his magic fingers lit her body everywhere he touched. Everywhere his hand and mouth roamed on her body set her on fire until she heard herself moaning out loud, almost shaking by the time he took his mouth off her.

The pleasure was exquisite.

"Your body is so beautiful," he whispered. "You don't know how hard it was for me to stay away from you the night of the wedding. But guess what? No matter when you said yes, I was going to be here."

She sighed her response and heard the announcer on the TV in the living room build up the seconds before tip-off. The clouds outside the window looked ominous, she thought fleetingly, as she pressed her lips together and then slowly opened them when he bent his head to give her another kiss.

When their lips slowly parted, he held up one finger, and leaned down to his pants on the floor beside the bed. She watched him slip on a condom, then smiled back at his lust- filled eyes as he moved her under him and pressed his body down on hers moving slowly. He continued to look directly into her eyes as he pushed his way slowly, gently into her softness, bending down to her face and running his tongue across her lips, which, along with everything else, quivered in passion. He rotated his hips slowly to help ease his way inside, and she realized the man was huge.

She dug her nails in his back, biting her bottom lip as he lifted her buttocks slightly and completed the merging of their bodies, then he paused to kiss her passionately.

"Relax," he whispered as his body began to move.

What in the world, she thought as he started slowly inside her, and wave after wave of pure pleasure rocketed through her body with each of his movements. What was she thinking to have waited so long? Everything fled her mind but this moment, and being here with him. His firm belly met her softness, and she could hear him suck in air as his movements began to pick up rhythm. She had never experienced this level of pleasure before, it was just plain delicious. His slow, easy strokes rocked her gently, building the tension inside her ever so slowly. "I could stay like this forever," she thought as she hugged him tightly around his shoulders.

Then his movements picked up speed, became faster and faster, and she felt the tightness moving deep inside her and building. She knew she had to be careful. This man had her number.

She squeezed her eyes tightly as she felt her juices flow and spastic release sweep down over her. Wave after wave of pleasure hit, and when she felt his back stiffen under her hands, and felt his beautiful lips press into her neck, his sweat dripping onto her face, she held him tightly looking up at the ceiling and giving up a silent prayer. She stared transfixed on the little Japanese lantern Nancy had left her, the one that gave off the faintest glow at night when she couldn't sleep. She would never let that lantern go, no matter where she went from this moment on. It would always remind her of Reggie. He was a missing piece of her existence that she didn't even know should have been there. He was better than wonderful. She couldn't have guessed he would be this good. And she closed her eyes and felt herself falling…

******

For the next few weeks as March flew into April, she couldn't believe this was her life. She knew she had to be circumspect about everything, but the reward was well worth it. It wasn't like their duties caused them to cross paths on the base. And she made sure when their paths crossed, they were well away from everybody and everything. Even her apartment wasn't far enough. It wasn't as often as they wanted, but she made herself be patient for those opportunities when he could take her on that trip to ecstasy. And although she fought hard, although she tried to hold onto her emotions and let her body respond, it didn't take long before she felt herself falling hard, and loving him with everything she had.

She hadn't forgotten her family. There was no word from Bea, and nothing more from Marietta. She was honestly too afraid to put together any more pieces to this puzzle, too much was unclear about Mama, and the file on Daddy fell further and further down on her list of to-do's. Thinking of calling Daddy now felt harder. What if Beatrice was right, and Daddy was the good guy. She was still worried, still uncertain about what would happen to them, but it started to seem like a distant problem, like it would not affect her life. It seemed like nothing would, as long as there was Reggie.

She had never felt this way about a man. She lived for the weekends when they drove up, sometimes as far as Los Angeles to enjoy themselves with each other. There was so much to do in LA and the traffic was so dense, but Reggie could navigate that town like he was born there. Reggie opened up another dimension to her life she could not have imagined.

The e-mails for the task force meetings and progress reports stopped coming to her. She made a disk of all her work, labeled it and decided to hold on to it to cover her ass, even duplicating a copy of her completed work for her commanding officer. Just in case Colonel Chisholm called for the files when she wasn't around, she'd explained. She'd asked Major Whitaker if she heard anything about the task force disbanding since the Colonel had not called her back, and the major had adamantly informed her that everything was still in progress.

She had met two of Reggie's good friends, Flynn and Marcus, who sometimes showed up at the clubs they went to out of the area. She and Reggie found fairs, parks, and beaches to browse. They went to movies and ate huge buckets of popcorn. His favorites were action-adventures, hers were anything that scared her or made her cry. Reggie talked her into getting a navel ring, he said she had the sexiest stomach and waistline he'd ever seen, and often made her tie up her blouses to show it off.

She found out just how passionate he was about cycling when she realized how often he talked about it. He raced a sleek Schwinn and told her he usually spent at least one day of the weekend on his bike. He wanted her to get used to it, and if she wanted to, learn to ride with him.

She didn't think so, and was preparing herself to just get used to his absence one day a weekend when he surprised her by presenting her with a used Diamondback Sports bike.

By the end of April, when she realized just how serious he was about getting her to ride, she decided to get herself in shape. She was already athletic, and became eager to learn, not knowing a thing about cycling for sport. She was determined to show him how good an athlete she was. She knew she had to get herself in physical condition so she could endure hours on that little seat if she wanted to spend bike-riding time with him. It didn't take long before she was as familiar with the terminology bikers used and could understand when others rattled off terms like berms, catching air, holeshot, pimp, snap, stylin', honking which referred to different movements riders made with their bike.

Reggie first taught her to ride in the more comfortable top bar position, because of her straight handlebar mountain bike, and because he said she would be doing more casual riding than racing, but soon she was learning the drop position that had her down and distributing her weight over the bar for greater pedaling power. She was quickly able to cruise the hills and other terrain right along with him.

He had participated in several bike rides on behalf of the Marines, and he got Bernadette involved where he could. As a Marine, company against company, it was legitimate. They did short runs for breast cancer, cystic fibrosis and AIDS. She was becoming more than eager to join him in his four day run from LA to San Francisco for AIDS. It was exciting just to meet with the groups and plan for the stint. Reggie was totally consuming her.

She was beginning to understand why Beatrice had lost her mind over Witt and had another baby, and why Nancy had given up on her oath to the country and left to be with Lonnie. She was beginning to wonder if she understood enough to now hear Mama's side of the story.

One spring weekend after she and Reggie had mailed in their lists of people who pledged to sponsor them in a summer bike ride for breast cancer, they drove all the way up to Santa Barbara to relax together.

It was evening, and they bought food to eat in the room, then celebrated four months together by making love long into the night. Reggie was excited about the summer bike ride, and kept telling Bernadette things she would have to do to keep up with him over the four-day trip. She said nothing, picturing herself riding alongside him, even though that was highly unlikely. He was always at the head of the pack, her personal Lance Armstrong, and she was always well behind, but that was okay. They couldn't be together in this, and her skills made sure they wouldn't be. Still, he was concerned that this was pushing her more quickly than he should.

Suddenly, as she imagined herself coasting along beside him, in the wind, she sat up in the bed. That's when it hit her.

She flipped on the lamp and leaned over him.

"It's from Peter and the Wolf, isn't it?"

Reggie had fallen into a light doze when her question woke him.

"What are you talking about?"

"Piccolo. They call you Piccolo because of that sound your bike makes when you're going really fast downhill. It might be those things in your spokes, but it's just like the instrument from the story. I knew I remembered that sound when we were riding. You make your bike sing that beautiful, high-pitched sound like the piccolo in the story."

Reggie leaned over her to turn off the lamp, and threw his leg over her thigh.

"Bingo Bango. You know what you get for coming up with that one, don't you?"

She laughed as he nuzzled her neck, then closed her eyes.

"Bernadette?" he whispered, and she slowly opened her eyes. She could hear it then, the raindrops hitting hard against the windows. It hadn't even looked cloudy today.

"Tell me one thing. Something I've been wondering," he continued.

"What?" she asked.

"Tell me something personal about you. Something you don't tell everybody. I don't care what. Take your pick."

"Like what?"

"Like something about how you feel. I tell you things about how I feel. You never tell me how you feel about anything. You just do things."

"You never tell me personal things. You've never told me you love me, if that's what you mean." She pulled away from him.

"I mean tell me something you really feel. Don't make it up. You can tell me with no problem when you want to go to bed. You can tell me what you want me to do in bed. You say everything, but never I like you, or I want you, or I need you."

"That's what you want to hear?"

"The truth, Bernadette. I want to hear what I mean to you. I talk about personal stuff, my family, my brothers, my mother, you. I tell you how I like you, but you don't do that."

"Don't you feel it? Some things you can feel. You don't have to say."

"Don't you trust me?"

She lay silently. He pulled himself on top of her, and whispered in her ear, "Baby, you know how much I trust you. I put the fate of my whole career in your hands."

"Then why do I have to say it? You know I trust you as much as I can."

"It's like a crust of cold around you. It's frozen so hard, it's going to take years to crack it to get to you. I can be with you, but I can't get to you."

"Reggie, I'm not cold."

"Then let me hear you. Tell me something personal from your heart to me. Say it."

He kissed her, ran his tongue down her neck and back up, kissed her again. "I'm waiting."

"I'm not cold," she repeated. "But, if you think it's true, then you're just the man to get through to me. That I promise."

He sighed, falling off her onto the bed. He left one arm around her waist. She lay silently, closing her eyes tightly, feeling her heart pound. She couldn't give him more, didn't he realize? She was giving him all she could.

******

That Monday morning, exhausted from her long, unsettling weekend, she sat at her desk, a business envelope in front of her with Reggie's
handwriting on the front. When she returned from their trip to Santa
Barbara, she found it propped up on the back of her toilet, so he must
have left it before they went up. She immediately freaked out. It had to
be either a marriage proposal, which she doubted, or a Dear John letter,
which scared her. She'd spent an hour fuming at the unopened letter in
hand, wondering why couldn't he have just told her whatever was in here.
Finally, she got up the nerve to open it and found a single page of white
legal paper with Reggie's printing on which he had written:

> *Pieces of My Dream*
> *There was nothing, it would seem, in all the years I tried*
> *Nothing good had crossed my path, until I saw your eyes*
> *Nothing that would make me sing, until I saw the hips you swing*
> *Nothing that would make me look, until your smile, my breath you took*
> *When I turned and saw your lips, I think you know, my heart did flips*
> *There was nothing it would seem, 'til I met you and found my dream*
>
> *You are my heart, the biggest, secret part of me I share*
> *You are my soul, the other half that makes me warm and care*
> *I see in you, my whole life through, it's like we are a team*
> *When I met you, I knew I'd found the pieces of my dream*

She was surprised, that he had actually sat down and wrote about her.
The whole weekend was one of those funny times when she felt some-
thing else was going on. Like the air around them had a different charge.
Reggie had been fun, but he seemed quieter, and a lot more thoughtful.
She had the feeling he was trying to tell her something.

Bernadette had decided to contact Nancy after work to talk it over,
but first she had to get her day in some kind of order. It wouldn't be easy.
She had come on to the floor amidst rumblings that there would be
emergency assignments. Major Whitaker was sent away on detail at 29
Palms, but there was an e-mail for an 0800 hours meeting with her XO,
so she knew someone from her unit would be affected.

The meeting was fast. After some official preamble, her XO, a tall,
skinny, Anthony Perkins look-alike handed her papers, which she

clutched in stunned surprise. She stared unable to believe that her tour of duty had been changed that suddenly. Her next stop:  Saudi Arabia. Why? Why now? And she had to wait until Major Whitaker's emergency detail ended to find out what it was about.

****** 

"She'll be with you in just a minute, Lieutenant," the young private said and she smiled at Bernadette, who was so upset she barely acknowledged her. She'd had to wait two days for her commanding officer to return from duty in 29 Palms before she could schedule this meeting. And she was boiling. Her stomach felt like it was literally about to overflow, with painful churnings and rumblings that Bernadette knew were probably the result of the pint of gin she had consumed in her apartment alone last night. She played with the peppermint candy she'd pushed out from under her tongue to hide the smell of liquor on her breath.

Two soldiers were at the end of the hall standing in front of the soda machine talking. Bernadette got up, wondering if a Pepsi would settle her stomach. She was in turmoil, and knew she couldn't keep going to the bathroom, like she felt she needed.

She studied the tiles on the floor, wondering what her commander would say when she asked to get out of this. She was pretty sure she knew why she was going, but she wanted to make sure her suspicions were concrete--and she wanted something to be done!

"Congratulations, Lieutenant," two lance corporals from the computer section where she worked strolled by and greeted. She didn't salute, barely nodding at them.

Congratulations? Did they think it was an honor to go to the Persian Gulf? Well, maybe some people did.

"The major will see you now," the same private informed her when she came back, and Bernadette got up and followed her in the office. She walked through to the back, where Major Whitaker was waiting in her glassed in area.

She saluted and was invited to sit.

"What brings you in to see me this early in the morning. Good news I hope?"

Bernadette sat stiffly, keeping her face straight and willing her heart to slow down. She'd swallowed the mint whole and was now forced to talk with the candy lump stuck in her throat.

"Well ma'am, I had a question or two. I got my orders the other day for my new assignment to the Persian Gulf, and I just wondered…"

"Oh, did you? Great, I hadn't had a chance to go through my in-box yet. Well, where is it, Kuwait?"

Bernadette looked at her a second quickly realizing this may not go as she'd hoped.

"Saudi Arabia," she responded. When her commander said, "Well!" she waited.

"Well," she finally said repeating her commander's last word, "what I want to know is how did I draw such an honor as the Gulf?"

Major Whitaker gave her a surprised look. She was a big woman. Her stature alone made her imposing, but her brusque manner and no-non-sense tone kept most people at bay. For some reason, Bernadette gravi-tated to her type of leadership and had always liked and respected her. She was straightforward, something fool hearty or indecisive leaders had a tough time being. Bernadette appreciated her because when she made a decision she stuck to it, even when there was hell to pay for making the wrong move. She called the shots and stood firm. She had heard others say they had trouble relating to her, had even seen Major Whitaker ream out a whole room of males without blinking an eye. If they deserved it, they got it, and the fact that she was a woman meant not a thing. She could only recall one time when she had gotten chewed out unfairly, but that was the major's call.

"Let me tell you what they want," Major Whitaker said clasping her hands together, excitement on her face. "We're looking to send good per-sonnel over to Saudi Arabia, Lieutenant, to set some things up. You know that spot's getting hotter all the time. Frankly, after looking over your records, seeing how you've handled your assignments and your staff, I can't think of many who would beat you out of this assignment."

"But I didn't put in for it! I didn't volunteer."

"Then they looked beyond their volunteers and decided to open the pool to get some qualified candidates. They want you badly, evidently."

"I don't think that's it," Bernadette said then, shifting uncomfortably. Her eyes stole a glance at the major's walls where she had plaques and pic-tures of herself receiving various awards and commendations. Under a big plaque was a small one on which was etched, "Women who seek to be equal to men lack ambition."

"My concern, if I may be personal is, well, did Colonel Chisholm have anything to do with this sudden assignment? I mean, it's out of the blue! I was hoping to finish the spring semester at school and tie up some other loose ends at home and personal charity work."

Major Whitaker's expression flickered a tad. Her eyebrow raised, and she watched Bernadette's face.

"If you'd like to be personal Lieutenant, go ahead, speak freely. Why are you asking about Colonel Chisholm?"

She didn't want to get that personal. It was just that, if she were a betting woman, she'd bet all she had that Colonel Chisholm was responsible for this sudden change. He was ignoring her. After she'd had a moment to think, she tried to be the bigger person and call him for a one-on-one. He refused her calls.

When she saw him on base and greeted him, he walked past her like she didn't exist. She had been with a group from her unit, and his behavior had caused the most embarrassing moment. Her subordinates' eyes had cut to her, expressions had registered the slight, but nothing was said about it. Not to her, but she knew word was getting around. She was no longer protected.

Not only that, when she had submitted her monthly reports on her personnel, statistical information basically, they had bounced back twice, something that never happened to her, for the most minor oversights. Colonel Chisholm knew people and he could say things and influence opinions. It was one thing to need him to get ahead, and she'd decided she didn't, but it was another thing to live with his manipulations making her life hell. And why should she take it?

She looked at her commander's face and saw her discerning scrutiny. She opened her mouth then paused. What would happen to all her work on the task force? She understood the look she was getting. She couldn't make waves. In a man's world, you didn't whine. You rose above it. She knew she could complain about a lack of attention, but it would never work in her favor. In the end, he had the power, and that was all there was to it.

"I'm relieved I got the assignment through the luck of the draw," she started knowing she was being studied, "but I think that there is something else going on here."

"You mentioned Colonel Chisholm. If there's a problem, Lieutenant, you have every right to file a charge through the proper channels. Harassment of any kind of anyone in MY units will not be tolerated in the least. I don't care who's doing the harassing."

"Oh, no!" Bernadette quickly said. She wasn't opening that can of worms.

"Then you are not listening to me. This is a special tour. We need good people over there who can keep track of the numbers, of personnel and ordnance and keep the stats accurate and timely. We need the right programmers, so we can get the right numbers and send out the right people over there NOW. You aren't the only one being pulled to set this up and you won't be the last. We need it done fast and we need it done right and from this unit, you fit that bill."

Bernadette wanted to tell her she WAS listening. She wanted to know what to do about an asshole who was also a colonel, but she couldn't say it. Maybe she could find a way to stop this on her own. She'd always been good at watching her own back.

"You understand me, Lieutenant?" Major Whitaker's voice came out in a bark.

"Yes ma'am," Bernadette responded sharply.

There was silence while Bernadette and the major eyed each other. She believed she could see, in the woman's eyes that she understood her as well. Then Major Whitaker leaned forward.

"Now," she said in a quieter tone. "I suggest that if there is a problem between you and Colonel Chisholm, you get it cleared up and you get it cleared up fast. You don't want anything nasty getting between you and your career at this stage of the game. Let me assure you."

"Yes ma'am!"

"You're dismissed."

Bernadette walked from the office with her chest out and her shoulders rolled back. She would deal with it, that's all. She had two weeks of training before she was shipped out, so she'd take care of the loose ends, writing Mama, Marietta, Bea and Toukie. She would have to do what she hated, send her file of information about Daddy to Marietta to finish. Then she'd wait and see what Marietta uncovered.

And she would have to tell Reggie. Just as everything was shifting to a new level between them, she would have to put it all on hold. After all, she was a Marine first.

# Beatrice

## *sixteen*

Rock bottom. There was no way to describe how Beatrice felt, sitting on one end of Mae's filthy living room couch, with Toukie on the other end popping gum and reading *Little House on the Prairie* with the same enthusiasm she had for her favorite teen magazine, *Sister to Sister*. Her girlfriend, Mae, was the one person who had her back, no matter what, and had for years, but she kept the craziest house you'd ever want to visit.

It was dirty, roach-infested and had a fair amount of mice scurrying through, but every evening, filled with people, it ran like a fair. People were drawn to Mae like moths to a flame. Card parties, sports parties, and sometimes, just fish-fry parties, Mae hosted big gatherings and everybody had a good time.

She didn't hesitate to open her house to Beatrice and her two children, even though Mae's own girls, 13- year old Keyona, and 12-year-old Christina, whom Toukie nick-named Lil' Kim and Foxy Brown respectively, were quite vocal against their mother taking them in. The girls had to double up in one bedroom to give Bea and her family the third one. And they put up a shouting, cursing fit about it until Mae grabbed Christina by her tight, flimsy jersey top, pulled it around her neck and threatened her. That shut them both up, but they were careful to freeze Toukie out.

It wasn't long before they noticed how much Toukie read and wrote, and they started coming to her for help with homework. At first Toukie tried to help them, not able to understand why it took them so long to do their homework until she realized they couldn't read. Then she refused them.

Now six months into their stay, she and Toukie were running their

Monday routine. Beatrice had to defog her bedroom for bugs every other week, and Clorox all the corners and drawers, throwing out old roach traps for new ones to make it livable for her children. And they did not see bugs in their room, even though armies of them freely roamed the rest of the house. In fact, to say Mae had roaches was like saying Morton's had salt. They came with the territory.

After cleaning and debugging, Beatrice and Toukie would make the two-block trip to the laundromat where they washed and dried their clothes. Mae did have a washer in the basement, but when Beatrice had ventured down there the first week, there were some awfully big, fast, four-legged shadows fleeing from the lights, knocking over things in their efforts to hide. She let them have the basement. Toukie stayed home to help her clean and wash because she hated the new school where she had been transferred. Everybody was dumb, Toukie reported, and nobody did homework. True enough, the school didn't seem to care whether she attended or not.

Beatrice had spent most of these last six months living in a daze. She swore this was temporary, but it was like taking 10 steps back from where she was when she first met Witt. When she called her caseworker at the Department of Social Services last December, the woman was not at all helpful. She needed immediate shelter, she'd said, reporting she had lost her rental unit in Witt's house. "There's a list," the caseworker snapped, and she would have to wait until her name came up, which would not be for at least two years, at the earliest. "We might get you in a shelter in 24 hours, because of the children, but if not, we might have to separate you and them until we can find something for everybody together." The kids could go in temporary foster care, and they felt Beatrice could find a place with family or friends.

To top it off, since she had to ask for an increase in the amount of her check, she was forced into the welfare-to-work program, which required her to get into a training program in order to qualify for the higher amount. She could get the maximum benefit, but she was going to be tapered off after she finished the program. So, three days a week, she took the baby to a babysitter that welfare paid, and she went off to work at a plant nursery where she was supposed to be learning computer basics. The program was a screaming joke. Santana Nurseries got money from the state for 'training' welfare mothers to use all the Microsoft Office software, but all they did was use them to transfer their inventory from files to computers, basic data entry work.

They did not learn the programs that had been promised. Moreover, there were fights because the black girls did more time in the basement files putting the paperwork together in order for the trainees on the computer, who seemed to be mostly white girls, to key in. Beatrice spent all her time working the computers, because she knew more about data entry than anybody there, including the supervisor, having done similar work for the Social Security Administration years ago, and she was fast and very quiet. The only girl she talked to, Durelle Williams, caught the same bus she did, so they fell into a pattern of waiting for each other, and taking breaks together.

"Ma!"

Beatrice looked up.

"You said we could go to the movies when you finished spraying roaches."

Beatrice got up, and went over to the stack of mail she had taken from her old house on Broadway to pull out her check. She hesitated and then pulled out a piece of mail addressed to Toukie. She was going to save it for later but Toukie had been a lot of help today. She would be overjoyed to get this. She found a way to get over to her old house every day after Witt left for work so she could take her mail before he came back. He did not know where Mae lived, and had no idea where she had gone. Beatrice planned to keep it that way.

She expected to take a few dollars from the welfare check today to treat herself and Toukie. Truthfully, she was going crazy. It was nice of Mae to put them up, but she could not stand it. The noise, the filth, the neighborhood were all too much. She did not give up everything she had to live like this. She was going to have to come up with a plan, because she could not live off welfare and all the shit that came with these checks.

"Here. Look what I found in the mail." Bea tossed the second envelope to her daughter.

Toukie paused, looking at the address, then jumped up. "Aunt Bernadette wrote me? From waaaaay over there!" Bernadette had sent Beatrice several letters from overseas, asking her to write back, but she wasn't about to as long as she was living like this. Toukie grinned, tearing into her envelope quickly. "I'll read it to you, Ma."

Bea came and stood beside Toukie, looking over her shoulder. Still, Toukie cleared her throat as though she had a large audience, and read aloud:

*May 28*

*Dear Toukie:*

*I promised myself I would write down everything that happened to me over here in Saudi Arabia, and mail it to you, so you'll know whether you ever want to be a Marine, like you said. I think you should know exactly what it's like to be here. Plus, I may stand a chance getting a letter back from you. I tried contacting your mother before I left California, but she never called or wrote back. I wrote her when I first got here, and she never answered. So, I've decided to keep in touch with you. Here goes:*

*So far, the main story here is the heat. It is so hot. No matter how much you wash, you stay sweaty if you go outside for more than two minutes. My hair frizzes up so bad I look like a clown. I have to keep wetting it and pulling it back into a ponytail. No wonder most of the women here keep their heads covered.*

*Speaking of the women, here they have to do what the men say, or they can get in big trouble. If a woman doesn't keep her head covered, the people in the town will spit on her for being so forward. They spit on me once, when I went into town and forgot to cover my head, and somebody almost got hurt.*

*The men can stand around and talk all day in coffee shops, but the women are not supposed to be out in public socializing. Even in places like McDonald's. The men go in and get the food and bring it out to the women. I know you wouldn't like that.*

*Here they drink a lot of coffee, like it's a national past time. They are not supposed to drink beer or whiskey. Their coffee is so strong. They roast the beans themselves, and pound them into a fine powder, then add sugar and water and all kinds of spices. I make myself drink it to have something different to drink but it has a strong, bitter, weird taste.*

*Water is scarce. They have to keep it pumping in from underground wells. It's a good thing this country is rich with the oil that the rest of the world needs, or they couldn't afford their expensive water system.*

*They don't ride camels in deserts the way I thought they did. They have nice cities with beautiful buildings and everything is air-conditioned. Their churches, called mosques, are just beautiful. I got the chance to go to the Al-Haram, their grand mosque in Mecca. It was fabulous.*

*I'm stationed in Dhahran in a logistical unit. It's like a computer center, and there we keep track of all the people and equipment and other informa-*

*tion we need to run an operation here in Saudi. It's not bad.*

*I got to travel to Riyadh, the capital of Saudi Arabia. I went there with my friends from here. We saw a basketball game and a soccer game. They have a really nice sports arena in Riyadh. But the funniest sport I've seen is the camel race. They're popular here, and they have little boys for jockeys. You would love it.*

*I'm sending you a picture of my boyfriend Reggie. You would really like him. When I come back to the states, we're coming to visit you. I may ask your mother if you can come visit me for a while. Would you like to? Remember, if there is anything you want to tell me, or if anything goes wrong, you write me and you call grandma. Okay?*

*Gotta go. Love you much.*

*Aunt Bern*

"Can I write her back now, Mom?"

Beatrice had moved over to the couch and sat back, listening to Toukie's words as she read. Imagine living somewhere so different, doing something so different. She definitely didn't want Toukie writing Bernadette, telling her how they were living now. Definitely not, she thought as she looked at the mail stack again, searching for the check.

"Where did this come from?" Beatrice said, her hand pausing over an envelope from the Baltimore Gas and Electric Company. Why would they send her a bill? Everything was in Witt's name.

She tore open the letter, looked at it, then slowly made her way back over to Toukie.

"What's wrong?" Toukie asked, getting up.

"Read this for me, Toukie."

Toukie took it, frowning. "What did you do now?" she asked her mother, but when Bea sat quietly staring at her daughter, Toukie turned her attention to the words. After a couple of minutes, Toukie was still quiet, looking at the letter.

"Girl, you planning to say something or not?"

Toukie hesitated, looked over at her mother. Then, as instructed, she read aloud:

*Dear Ms. Windsor:*

*We are interviewing for the position of customer service representative with the Baltimore Gas and Electric Company. The starting salary for this* *position is $25,000 per annum. You would also be entitled to health and life insurance coverage.*

*If you are still interested, you must report for an interview on Friday, June 15th, 10:00 a.m. at the Charles Plaza branch. If you cannot attend or are no longer interested, please contact Ms. Julia Goldberg at (410) 955-9090.*

*We look forward to seeing you.*

*Sincerely,*

*L. T. Drummond*

*Regional Director*

Beatrice, biting her lip, looked at Toukie, whose mouth was open. "This means you got the job, Ma."

Beatrice sighed. "It means I got to interview. And if I do good there, I got the job." Beatrice looked away, her eyes drawn to the living room window where there was a group of teen-age children running up the sidewalk yelling loudly. They should be in school, she thought absently.

"We can get out of here?"

"If I get the job."

"And we don't have to go back to Witt?"

Beatrice looked at Toukie. "No, no more Witt."

Toukie leaped in the air and let out a loud whoop, causing the baby to stir in his infant seat.

"I got to pass the interview first, Toukie. It ain't just me getting this letter."

"You can pass. What they do in the interview?"

Bea picked up the baby and rocked him on her shoulder as she told Toukie what an interview was.

"You got to look pretty, don't you?"

"That'll help."

"Come on Ma, let's go find what you going to wear!"

They spent the afternoon, going through clothes until they found a simple black dress that covered her, but when Toukie tried the zipper, it would not go up.

"You are so fat!" Toukie complained, sweating from pushing in her mother's skin around the waist and pulling the zipper.

"I can wear a girdle. This is it. I'll borrow a blazer from Mae, and wear this."

"We getting out of here," Toukie declared.

Beatrice didn't tell Toukie, but she didn't see how. She had lied on that application. She never finished high school, the first thing they asked. But, maybe they wouldn't know.

Still, she worried. The day of the interview, Mae took off to drive her. Mae had done Beatrice's hair in an upsweep, like her own, and loaned her a tweed blazer, which set off her black dress nicely. With Beatrice's natural beauty, she was stunning, full-bodied or slim. She could see, in the eyes of the two men who sat on the panel, they liked her. She couldn't tell about the woman.

She had been interviewed in the past, and she had worked ten years with the Social Security Administration, which looked good. She answered their questions carefully, and when she left, she felt good. They told her they would get back to her in two weeks. There were others to interview, but she knew she had done her best.

And in a week, they called her and told her the job was hers. Just like that.

She packed up to move the day after Toukie's school year ended. Mae got several male friends to help move her, and she waited until Witt was at work to go back to her old home for the children's bedroom furniture, televisions, and to take his bedroom, praying he didn't come home. Her new townhouse was in a development called Morningside Heights, in Owings Mills, a largely upper end section of Baltimore County where, by law, they had sections for low and middle-income families.

When the movers had gone, Toukie ran around calling all her friends, going over everything she was discovering in their new home. Beatrice sat on the bed and pulled out the papers from Witt's drawer in the basement that she had taken with her. She'd had $22,000 in her name in the bank. Now she had nothing. She'd loved Witt, believed every word he'd breathed on her for the last two years. What was $22,000 when he could take that and double it or triple it? Then he would get them set up in something that would pay them a whole lot more for the rest of their lives. And on top of that, what was $22,000 when she would be near her father? She would have given up that amount and more if she believed it would be worth it for herself and her family. She didn't understand what the hell had gone wrong. She had taken a big, stupid risk and now she was back to square one, with no definite opportunity to see her father.

That was still her goal. She had all the names of the club members.

She was going to find her father. And she would start by tracking down Witt's family, and finding out what she needed to know.

******

Armed with Witt's military papers and the folder naming all the club members, Beatrice twisted in the car seat and screamed out, "Right here, Mae!"

Mae slowed down, then turned up the driveway as Beatrice directed. "You sure?"

"That's the home address Witt got down here. This ain't a bad looking spot."

"Yeah, Northeast Baltimore is good. I used to date a man lived in Morgan Park. That's just up the street near Morgan State University, you know." Mae pushed aside her Suzanne Somers' bleached blonde bangs that framed her Whoopi Goldberg chocolate face as she spoke.

"I should have called," Bea said hesitating. "Probably. But you know how people act. You call them, they might want to act funny, and not let me in."

They got out of Mae's blue Malibu, staring around them, impressed at the flower-beds and neat landscaping around the house. Bea went up and rang the bell. She waited, looking over at the new olive Volvo sitting in the driveway.

The door opened, and when Beatrice introduced herself and asked for Witt's mother, the woman let them in. She was cordial, but stared skeptically.

"I'm Witt's mother," the woman said. Beatrice was surprised. This tall, slender, youthful looking woman with a head full of auburn ringlets was dressed in a black lounge dress, her face lightly made up. "I'm Charlene."

"I'm Beatrice, a friend of Witt. This is my friend Mae." Charlene still had a look of uncertainty, but she let Beatrice and Mae sit down in the dining room where she appeared to be in the process of hand sewing a large garment in a seat by the window. Sitting opposite them, she patiently listened to Beatrice explain who she was to Witt, that they had a baby together, and that she had come to track down members in the business club.

"I mean, I been with Witt two years, and I didn't know your name or where you lived. I just saw it on his military papers, and was hoping you still lived here," she said in response to Charlene's long stare.

"Witt isn't much for sharing information," the woman finally said with a small laugh. "He isn't that happy with me. We were very close, in the past, but things happened, and Witt has a way of putting the blame on others. He had a promising future, but, when we fell on some rough times, he threw it all away. He just got so rebellious, always in trouble with the law, I didn't know what to do with him."

Bea paused. "He never told me that. All he ever talked about was his uncle and how good he did. He never mentioned his mother or father."

"I never married Witt's father. I only knew him briefly before he moved back to Minnesota where he was from. Witt lived there with him summers, and again when he dropped out of school and got into trouble. He thinks a lot of his father; I'm surprised he never mentioned him."

"He must get along better with his uncle."

"His uncle? I'm not aware that he was around an uncle. I don't have any brothers, but Witt's father had a half-brother. As far as I know, they aren't close."

"Well, somebody is in this business club that Witt wanted to get in." Bea pulled out the folder and showed it to Charlene.

She frowned, looking down the list of names.

"His uncle's name is supposed to be on that list. And I know Witt got a ring from him, a club ring that he wears on his neck all the time."

"Oh, you mean THAT ring." Charlene laughed. "You got it wrong. He got that ring from a lady I used to work for when he was little. Her name was Ms. Odessa Windsor. She was my best customer, buying quilts I used to sew, faster than I could make them. I make exclusive quilts, special designs, using material that people want. I use clothes of loved ones, whatever customers want me to use in making special quilts.

"Ms. Odessa got so many customers for me, she decided that in exchange for working exclusively for her and her society friends, she would take care of Witt's future. She had a lot of money and she told me she could give him the best. She got him into an excellent boarding school in Massachusetts. Witt was kicked out for fighting in a year. He didn't fit in with those snobby children and he knew it."

"Well, did he want to go there?"

"He did after talking to Ms. Odessa. That woman could talk and make you want things you didn't know you wanted. Witt ended up at

Gilman, and was doing okay there, but just as he was making strides, Ms. Odessa had some big family trouble, some kind of scandal that I never did find out what it was, and she just went undercover."

"Couldn't you just ask her what it was? Wouldn't she tell you?"

"Not Ms. O. She was really funny about people. Black people, white people, it didn't matter. Everybody, to her, had a place. She put you in it, that's where you belonged. And, she didn't let you in her circle. She stopped her money for Witt's schooling when he was 15. He was able to get on scholarship for awhile, but it didn't work out.

"Anyway, that ring was something Ms. Odessa actually had made for him. She had one made for her son, and she used to tell Witt that he would be a very rich businessman one day, like her son, and deserved distinctive jewelry. That ring was just his beginning, she told him.

"Witt didn't adjust when we lost contact with Ms. Odessa. He missed that attention. He missed hanging with the rich, privileged kids, and continued to get into trouble. I sent him to Minnesota, and he hated me for it. Next thing I know, he's off in the Marines. And when he got there, he got into bigger trouble."

"I know he got a dishonorable discharge. He was court-martialed."

Charlene's eyes widened. "He told you that?"

"Well, no. I found it in these papers."

She said nothing for several seconds, then excused herself and left the room. Mae and Beatrice exchanged looks. Mae got up to peep out in the direction Charlene had gone.

"I don't know," Mae laughed, then walked over to peruse the pictures on the wall, and those set up on a small desk in a corner of the room. Bea sat looking around her for signs that Witt had lived there. In moments Charlene returned with a tray, a liter of ginger ale, and three glasses of ice.

"So, he didn't tell you about the court-martial," Charlene said pouring the soda, and handing Beatrice a glass. "I'm not surprised, considering it was for attempted murder. That must be hard to just bring up to your girlfriend."

"I guess that's what he thought, too. He didn't tell me."

Mae came back to the table and thanked Charlene for her glass, immediately lit a cigarette and sat back, riveted.

Charlene wrinkled her nose and went to her server, pulling out an ashtray.

"Did Witt really try to kill somebody?" Beatrice asked.

Charlene crossed her legs under her lounge dress, straightening the material. "Well, Witt was going with a girl when he was stationed in Georgia, and there was an argument. She was also a Marine, and I guess when she told him to leave her apartment after the argument, and he didn't, she thought she could threaten him with a knife. He said he was trying to take it from her, and she said otherwise, but, whichever way it went, she ended up getting stabbed. And he got arrested."

"Did he stab her?" Bea asked again.

"Not intentionally. Even the girl later recanted the events of the fight so that it could not be considered deliberate. Because there was a fight, and she had bruises, he still got in trouble for that, and kicked out of the Marines."

"Where is this girl now?"

"All in the past. Still in Georgia, far as I know. Witt came home and still couldn't get in gear. He has three older sisters, all college graduates, married and doing well. Witt is still out here, doing God knows what. Well, you say he's now a father. He never even told me that. I just don't understand what happened to him."

Beatrice barely took a sip from her glass. She hesitated, staring at the woman. Could this lady really not know she was a Windsor? The granddaughter of Ms. Odessa, the woman she'd made quilts for? Didn't Ms. Odessa ever mention them at all? Did Witt really not know, or had Bernadette read him from the very first minute? Was there no resemblance? Beatrice thought about telling this woman who she was and stood up.

"Maybe it wasn't easy for Witt, living with people who thought they was better than him. Maybe he got mad at you for making him."

"Are you kidding? Witt loved it. At first, he was out of place at the boarding school in Massachusetts because it was far away, but when he got to Gilman, Witt loved playing rich. He used to tell me I was stupid for working around people with so much money and not taking advantage of it. With Ms. O's money, he could do no wrong. And then she pulled it all away. Every dime. That boy never got over that." Charlene paused.

"Sometimes I wish I never let Ms. O get involved with him, but when you're a mother, you do the best you can. You don't ask your children what they think if you know what's best. I'm sure you'll do the same for your son; it's what makes you a mother. By the way, do you have a picture of the baby?" Charlene stood also.

Beatrice nodded and snapped open her purse, pulling out the baby's most recent shot and handing it over.

Charlene's face softened as she stared. Mae finished up her cigarette, crushing it out and standing with a sigh. She drained her glass.

"This baby is Witt, all over again," Charlene said quietly, then went over to her china closet and pulled out a photo album, turning right to the first page and showing Beatrice. Witt and the baby looked like twins.

"You can keep this," Bea said when Charlene tried to hand the picture back.

"Well, thank you. Aren't you sweet?" Charlene paused, staring at the picture. "I love my son, God knows I do. But he has a mind of his own. He plays by his own rules, wants everybody he's around to play by his rules, and doesn't expect anyone to ever disappoint him. He's hard to handle when he's disappointed. He can be hard…and that boy never forgives."

"Believe me, I think I know him. I just don't understand why he told me about an uncle, if he isn't real."

Charlene considered it. "Maybe he really wanted to impress you. Maybe he knew talking about the club was the way to win your attention. I can tell you, he must have wanted you, and he must trust you. Witt would never have a baby with just anyone."

Beatrice smiled. "Well, thank you. Thanks a lot for your time." Her stomach jumped as she walked through the door, imagining Witt living here, coming here and never mentioning them. Witt had consumed her physically, mentally and emotionally. He knew far more about her than she knew about him. He knew her grandmother, and didn't ever tell her. Was it possible he didn't know? She doubted it. And that worried her.

She sighed as she climbed in Mae's car and they drove away with Mae ranting about how crazy Witt was.

"I don't know what you think, but I think that's one crazy motherfucker. You don't need to know no more than that. Just let him go."

Bea pushed the car seat back and looked out the window. She needed to know more. There was no uncle, so what did he want from her? What did he need? She narrowed her eyes. Her money? Was that all it was?

She crossed her arms. As long as he owed her money, it was not over.

She was not finished with him yet. Just like he had plans for her, she had some for him. And they were not through until she was finished.

# Bernadette
## *seventeen*

Bernadette breathed deeply, her face against the window of the plane as it flew low over the Potomac. She could scarcely believe it was over. It had taken her 18 months instead of the six-month tour they had promised. She was surprised she had lasted that long in Dhahran, Saudi Arabia, and now, it was finally over. For once, she felt as though she had missed home. Instead of the hate she'd always felt flying into Andrews, the pit of her stomach actually jumped with joy. She wasn't the same person.

It wasn't just the life she'd been forced to endure, like the abayas, long black habits from head to toe she had been forced to wear for her security when she was in public in Saudi Arabia, or the periodic ambushes of civilian buildings that housed Americans. Nor was it the put downs, the blatant prejudice against females in that country, both on and off base. Women were considered the source of all seduction and evil in the world, according to the Saudis, and therefore made to live as though they were only shadows instead of humans. But that wasn't the reason she was not the same.

Nor could it be because she'd lived in fear. Truth be told, she had often dressed herself as a male and hung out with the male soldiers for recreation whenever she could, pushing the limit. So she knew it was not fear that changed her. What she found was how much her old beliefs about power and life could not be true. The bars and medals she craved so badly meant nothing when it came to life or death. It was indeed a fact that she had absolutely no power over there, yet she survived with the protection of her fellow male soldiers and had relied heavily on them to make it back whole and sane. It took more than any power she had to get her back home intact. Colonel Chisholm knew Saudi Arabia would feel as close to a prison as anything she could imagine. She had definitely changed, but not the way he thought.

The roar of cheering soldiers on the plane made her stomach jump more. They were happy to come home, probably had things to look forward to, some catching up that they were eager to start, to make up for the last year or two of their lives. She clutched a fashion magazine she'd been handed by a flight attendant, and wondered what she was going to find in Baltimore.

Life in San Diego last week had been no treat. She'd gone home first to check on her apartment and car and catch up what she could. After paying the garage fee for the storage of her Grand Prix, and keeping up with her bills for 18 months, Bernadette had $75.00 in the bank. She kept her face against the window. What the hell could she do with $75.00 and no new roommate?

As the wing dipped left and the plane broke through clouds, Bernadette stared dully at the grounds below. No one in her family would be at Andrews to greet her. But they never had. So Bernadette focused on the good news; no one had died in the time she was gone. It had taken her nearly the entire 18 months to realize that no one would. No one would die until she came home because she was the one they wanted. She had to be. She was sure only she had gotten that letter because only she was the target. No one else.

Beatrice, who hated to write, sent Bernadette a rambling letter after Berni's sixth month in Saudi Arabia, saying she'd left Witt, found a job, got a new townhouse, and had placed Toukie in a school where she was doing well. The only reason she'd given for leaving Witt was that he hadn't been truthful about his business. Beatrice's second letter was a huge surprise Bernadette had gotten just days before she was to leave the Middle East. Bernadette had the letter in her pocket, not sure what to think. She'd wanted to ponder the words on the flight to digest the news. Thinking about Bea now, Bernadette pulled out the letter, and slowly read:

*Dear Berni,*

*I'm sorry I didn't write you all this time, but I've been so busy. My new job in customer service sent me to some training classes for diction, speech and grammar, and I've been practicing everyday with Toukie's help. I have tapes, and I have a book, and I'm doing much better, but this stuff is HARD. I have to do this if I want to move up in my job, my supervisor said.*

*You were right about Witt's sorry ass. Witt wasn't good for Toukie, the baby, or me. I didn't tell you he lost my $22,000 retirement fund with his business partner, and they can't even catch the girl who stole it. You were right. Witt wasn't as smart as he thought, so I started thinking. You also said Witt knows Daddy. I think you were right.*

*One thing I can't get over is why Daddy left, and never came back, not even for Nita's funeral. To this day, I want to know, so when Witt came to my new place and begged me to come back to him, I did for one reason. To meet my father.*

*Believe me, it's a whole new day around here. And I have a surprise for you when you come home. Toukie told me you wrote her that you were coming back in February, so I'm holding off my birthday party until you are here. I put an invitation in this envelope, and I'm inviting everybody to be there that night. You have to be there for this. (My teacher did check my grammar, but I almost had it all right)*

*I'll be so glad to see you Bernadette.*

*Love you always,*

*Bea*

Bea sounded like a whole different person. Even Toukie's mail, which had come in bunches the way mail did in Saudi Arabia, sounded more like she was a new person. But how could Bea go back to that damn Witt? Didn't she see he was phony?

Bernadette wrote Marietta with news of Bea's party, but just like every other letter she'd sent to Marietta after being deployed, she'd heard nothing. So she was worried about what she would find coming home, and what she would have to do.

The address of the party was something else Bernadette couldn't understand. It was at the old house on Broadway. Why were they still living in Witt's old house? Bernadette was too hyped to think what all this meant exactly. She'd just have to wait.

One way or another, her questions about her family were going to be answered in this visit. That much she knew. So feeling numb, as her plane landed at Andrews, she gathered her luggage, jostled and pushed her way to the nearest exit, then remembered Preston, the soldier on the flight who had tried to make her talk the whole time she sat quiet in thought. He'd promised her a ride to Pimlico. She rushed back in time to meet up with him and his brother and catch a lift into town.

And at the Pimlico racetrack, they dropped her off. It wasn't until she started her trudge up Northern Parkway, that she realized just how far she still had to walk. And it was a bitter cold February day, even though she wore a hat and gloves with thermal lining she wasn't warm.

Bernadette trudged up the road struggling with her duffel bag thrown over one shoulder, and her small black suitcase rolling loudly behind her, her body buffeted by a strong, icy wind. It was so cold, she could hardly breathe. Her face started to hurt after five minutes, and she knew she had at least another 25 minutes of walking to go.

But it was time for Bernadette to plan. A whole slice had been taken from her life during those 18 months in the Middle East, and from her career. She doubted the Saudi Arabian tour would help her get her double bars. It hadn't so far. Saudi Arabia was not Iraq, where soldiers were coming back with purple hearts, and bronze medals just for being near areas that were bombed. She hadn't saved anybody and was damn near invisible with all the other invisible females in that country. There would be nothing special in her file for this service.

Bernadette sniffled, wiping the tears that the frigid air pulled from her eyes, as well as the others that came pouring out uncontrollably. She could not stop crying. She felt like she was starting her military career all over again.

Before she left, she had a stellar career, everything falling in place for her at work and in her personal life. Now, she wasn't sure what she had. Bit by bit, her career had been taken apart while she was in the Gulf. Colonel Chisholm had waited until her deployment to orchestrate everything. And he had succeeded.

The innocuous letter, buried with all her other mail surfaced her first night home in San Diego last week. It was in Major Whitaker's writing, and Bernadette wondered why wouldn't she have sent it overseas. It was very brief: "Know you're about to go home on leave. Need to see you or speak to you ASAP upon arrival."

They'd met off base, a trendy bistro in the Gaslamp District and ordered beers. Major Whitaker was glad to see her, and Bernadette, on edge about the off-base meeting, answered her questions perfunctorily about her overseas duty. It was successful, by all accounts. She had worked very hard, she had worked long hours, she had been sharp, and she had been given the opportunity to extend her tour after her month of leave, which she had declined.

Still, Bernadette was almost giddy with expectation. When a boss wants to see you right away, it's either very good, or very bad. She had done nothing but good and, therefore had no idea how bad it would be.

Major Whitaker laid things out in her typical straightforward way. The colonel had gone to her superiors and charged Bernadette with fraternization. In addition, her favorite employee, Lance Corporal Weeks, had also filed a claim of sexual discrimination.

Bernadette had done nothing but stare, her bottle of Rolling Rock non-alcoholic beer beside her opened and untouched.

"He'll have to prove it," Major Whitaker said confidently. "And unless you tell me now that I'm wrong, I'm not worried. I have nothing but excellent reports about your overseas duty. So, let him prove it."

Could he prove it, Bernadette had wondered, but gratefully, the meeting had ended there. Now, Bernadette wanted nothing so much as to go straight over Bea's house to curl up with her and Toukie and decompress. She longed to see them, to hug them and be with them. She missed them so very much. She had so many gifts for Toukie and the baby, so many pictures and things to show them.

It seemed to take forever to get to her mother's house, with the cold and the wind, and lanes of traffic speeding dangerously near as she walked up the Parkway with tear-filled eyes. But at last she was able to turn onto Narcissus Ave. and walk down two houses to her mother's. She sighed when she didn't see her mother's LeSabre, and groped in her duffel bag for the keys. She had hoped, so badly, her mother would be home waiting for her, but as she opened the door and called out to an empty house, she knew she'd have to calm down her jitters alone. It would have been nice to have a big pot of Navy beans warming, with smoked turkey necks for seasoning. And a couple of pans of Mama's homemade cornbread to sop up the gravy and coat her stomach. It would have been nice to have her mother at home to see her after 18 months overseas. Didn't her mother love her?

Exhaustion overwhelmed her and she felt tears of loneliness spring in her eyes as she closed the door to an empty house. She couldn't remember the last time she had been in such a funk, and going to this party alone tonight wasn't going to make it better. In all the time she had been gone, what had she gotten from Mama? Several boxes of Gushers, Pop-Tarts, Smart Start cereal, and Pepperidge Farm cookies of all kinds. No letters. Nothing more than her usual note saying, "I'm praying for you." Was that love?

Her brother Corey sent her cards of encouragement every week, and comics he cut from the New Yorker magazine on the war. Nancy wrote letters the length of books. The one person she had hoped would clear up the information she had pulled on Daddy was Marietta, but the more she wrote her, the more obvious it was that Marietta wasn't going to answer. Even her e-mails were deleted.

That still was not the most surprising. What did surprise her most was that Reggie had never written her one letter. Not one single letter. Oh, he sent her some postcards, it seemed, from various engagements off-base, but no letters. No matter what she wrote, no matter how she poured her heart out, nothing.

How in the world did that happen? Had someone reported them to his commanding officer? Still, he could have written something. She missed him so much she felt as though the very core of her was broken. How could he go so long without talking to her? Hadn't he missed her? Was she crazy for having risked her career for him?

She wanted to know if she had totally misread him? In fact, her first week back in the states, she sat waiting to see him. What she found was that he had been sent to the East Coast for a string of performances, and his return date was not certain. The only other stop she'd made before flying home to the party in Baltimore was a stopover to visit Nancy in San Francisco, who swore she'd help her figure out the best way to handle Colonel Chisholm and the whole fiasco.

She'd told Nancy about Reggie, and Nancy was also perplexed. She seemed to listen thoughtfully, but Bernadette couldn't help notice, when she mentioned calling Reggie from overseas and hearing from his roommate that he was up in LA for a week, Nancy looked away from her quickly. "He said he wrote to you," Nancy assured Bernadette. Bernadette knew Reggie meant those damn postcards, which said nothing. Too hurt to go on, she'd left her mother's address and phone number with Nancy, in case anything came up while she was away from home.

Now, up in her old bedroom, Bernadette pulled out the little black dress that Reggie had liked so much at the wedding and hung it up. She stared at it and remembered the good time she'd had with him while wearing it. Then her common sense kicked in...Reggie drove through

Los Angeles like he lived there… "I don't know why, Bernadette, but he took a week of leave to spend in LA," his roommate Marcus had said…"Just as well Bernadette," Nancy had told her…"I think little Ms. LA has had her hooks in him…Shelley, the lead singer in the band…she's very possessive of Reggie…"A sudden dizziness gripped her, and she quickly sat on her bed and held her hands over her face. It was clear if she were willing to see. Reggie had moved on.

Bernadette licked her lips. This level of sobriety was totally new. She hadn't had a drop of liquor nor a cigarette since she touched down at the Ali Al Salem Air Base in Kuwait, before final deployment in Saudi Arabia. Liquor was banned, and women weren't supposed to smoke. Sure, women on base could smoke, but Bernadette hadn't seen anybody touch anything that resembled liquor. All they did was pray. She had been forced to discipline herself, and hadn't touched anything for the whole period. Not even the daily doses of 500 mg Tylenol that she once lived off. She felt weird, but much cleaner.

Now, she could clearly think. Bernadette tried to check the tears that threatened to roll down her cheeks, but unwillingly they fell and continued to stream down her face. Her eyes were going to swell to the size of plums. She went back and plopped across her bed to think about what she wanted to do about Colonel Chisholm, but kept thinking of Reggie. Could she decide, push come to shove, she would not see Reggie again? She quickly realized that these tears that wouldn't stop were not the result of any scenario she imagined with the colonel. Or leaving the Marines. It was every time she thought about being back in the States without Reggie in her life. She felt a pain that was almost physical.

She couldn't imagine what she would do, not seeing him. Nothing seemed real, and before she knew it, she crashed.

******

The voices downstairs woke her. Bernadette sat up and clicked on the Care Bear lamp by the bed and listened. She glanced across the room and stared at the Louis Vuitton suitcases now sitting beside her bags. Then a burst of laughter rang out. Who else had come home?

She threw off the purple and black Ravens throw someone had covered her with and sniffed. The smell of fried fish was overwhelming. She hadn't seen any of her family in so long…so very long…she sat there listening. This was it. This was finally it.

In seconds she had freshened up in the bathroom, then sailed down the stairs barefoot. Just as suddenly, her feet stopped moving when she spotted Marietta's profile over the French doors as she stood by the kitchen sink talking to Mama.

That wench! An overwhelming urge to rush in and strangle Marietta almost overtook Bernadette. Not a letter, not a phone call, not a peep in the 18 months she was away, and now here she was. Talking to Mama like everything was normal. Marietta and Mama had always gotten along effortlessly. She was Mama's right hand, Mama's confidante, whatever happened, Mama shared with Marietta. Bernadette could hear her telling Mama now about her job and how she had helped put together a series of articles on a famous five-star general, who had called to compliment her on the article.

Unable to stand another moment, Bernadette burst through the doors.

"Marietta!"

Marietta turned startled.

"OH MY GOD! Is this 'little' Bernadette?"

"Marietta!" Bernadette squealed again, and pushing aside her anger at her sister, she ran over to her and they clasped arms around each other hugging, long and hard.

When Marietta's arms dropped from Bernadette's shoulders, Bernadette felt something sharp scratch across her skin.

"Did I get you?" Marietta asked, grabbing her sister's arm.

"What is this?" Bernadette said, taking Marietta's hand and pulling the platinum marquis diamond closer. She studied it, then looked at her sister.

"Didn't I tell you I was engaged? Berni, I have so much to tell you! I can't wait for you to meet Del. He's going to love you."

Bernadette couldn't stop staring at the size of the rock on her sister's hand. No wonder Marietta wouldn't answer her letters. She was too busy working on this man.

"I see why you don't have time for me or Bea. Where is he?"

"He was delayed for a meeting he couldn't miss, but I assure you, he will not miss this party."

"I didn't even think you were coming," Bernadette said, to which Marietta responded, "Berni, I couldn't have missed this if I wanted to!"

They paused to stare at each other. Marietta looked damn good.

Shorter than Bernadette remembered, and thin as a pole, her sandy brown hair cut into a feathery cap, she had a pixie look. Had she always looked like this? There was hardly any brown in her skin, which made Bernadette recall in a flash from childhood how they teased Marietta by calling her albino girl. She hadn't known what that meant until she got older.

"Look at her, Mama!" Marietta beamed. "Isn't Bernadette beautiful? All shaped up so tall and pretty!"

"That won't save you today," Bernadette countered, crossing her arms and pursing her lips. "You're lucky Mama's standing here, cause I have some choice words for you, hussy! I wrote you a million times and you have never answered." Bernadette wiped at her eyes quickly, wondering why she felt like she wanted to boo-hoo all over again.

"Berni, you are not going to believe me, but I had every intention of answering your letters. I was fearful for you everyday, thanking God that you weren't stationed in Iraq. It's just, every time I sat down to write you, I just couldn't. I kept thinking, if I write, is it going to be enough? We haven't been together or spoken in years, and I kept thinking it would be better to talk in person. So, I decided to wait to see you."

Bernadette shook her head.

"It's been nearly two years, Marietta. I needed to know what was going on, and I sent you everything I had on that man. How long were you willing to wait to tell me?"

Marietta rolled her eyes in Mama's direction, and locked her eyes on Bernadette's as a signal.

"Well, not forever. I knew we would come together sooner or later, and I just thought it would be better if we could talk face to face."

"Face to face? I don't understand you, girl. The way you made us promise to have each other's backs, and then when I write you with a problem, you don't respond. You are the eldest, what's that about?"

Marietta reddened slightly.

"Whether you knew it or not, I did have your back. I kept in contact with Mom, so I knew what was going on with everybody. I never ignored what you said."

"Well, keeping in touch with Mama may work for you, but not for me. I'm talking about checking on us personally, acting like we really are family, you know?"

"Okay, Bernadette! You want direct contact, I got you," Marietta said, a bit too sharply.

Mama stepped forward, facing Bernadette.

"Would you let that go? This is not the time for that kind of foolishness, especially from you Bernadette. I'm worried about you, child. You looked like a rack of bones laying in that bed. You ain't never been that skinny in your life."

Bernadette felt a quivering smile cross her lips as she acknowledged her mother for the first time since coming home, opening her arms wide when her mother came to her, hands still full of flour from kneading dough. She hugged Bernadette hard, sending white powder flying everywhere.

"You were knocked out across that bed when I looked in," she said patting Bernadette's hair and leaving traces of flour that she tried to wipe out with the sleeve of her shirt.

"I was so tired."

"You need to rest, and you need to eat. I'm trying to get the food ready now," Mama said, turning away as she went over to her cabinet under the sink, rattling pans until she found the one of her choice.

Bernadette glanced around. She'd finish with Marietta later.

"Just the three of us are going tonight? "

"I'm not going nowhere," Mama corrected, standing with a large rectangular pan in her hand.

"Why not?"

"'Cause I wasn't invited."

"Oh, Ma! It's Bea's birthday party, and you know she wouldn't want you to miss that. Besides, I've been dreaming of everybody being together again this time to have fun."

"I don't care about your dreams. If she wanted me there, she would have asked me."

"Marietta, talk some sense into Mama."

"I can't. You know how Mama and Beatrice are, both stubborn as the devil, especially with each other."

"I treat Bea just like I treat every other child I had. She was the one who had it easier than anybody, and always want to be mad about everything. Well, she can stay mad for all I care. I did the best I could."

For a few seconds, no one said anything. Then Marietta lifted one of her finely arched brows and looked at Bernadette.

"But you and Beatrice can't keep on this way," Bernadette said. "She wasn't always out of control. I know she changed after Nita died, but Mama, she's still your daughter."

"People don't change, Bernadette. When something happens to push them, you get to see what you got. Beatrice was hateful before Nita died and been hateful since. She's just as ornery and evil as ever."

Shocked at her mother's tone, Bernadette stared. Beatrice did change when Nita died, and maybe Mama was hurt by it. But couldn't Mama see Bea's hurt too?

"But, you do love her, don't you?"

"Of course, I love her," Mama said simply. "I love all my children."

But did she? How could Mama be so cold in discussing Beatrice? And why didn't Marietta tell Mama it was wrong? Bernadette looked at her sister, who had a little smile on her face. Were Mama and Marietta together against all of them? Something was not right with Marietta.

"You know, Bernadette, you seem to expect a lot from Mama when it comes to Beatrice. Have you looked at things from Mama's point of view?"

"Mama's point of view? What exactly do you mean?" Bernadette asked slowly, trying to understand what was happening, when the doorbell rang.

No one moved.

"Bernadette," Mama said quietly. "I want you to calm down and let that stuff go. You ain't off fighting a war now. Don't come home acting that way. Just let it go."

Mama set her mouth in a straight line and turned her stout hips around the table nearly knocking over a glass as she started for the front door.

"I'll get it, you stay here," Bernadette said, her frustration nearly choking her. "It must be Corey and Alaina by now."

"Berni, they came in a while ago, and went downstairs to rest up before the party," Marietta said.

"Oh?" Bernadette said, her feet moving her through the swinging French doors and away from the kitchen. Silently she started repeating, "I've got to do this. I've got to get through this tonight."

She snapped the lock hard and swung open the front door.

Then stared.

It was Reggie. Not only was it Reggie, but it was Reggie looking better than she could ever remember him looking, with the same sexy smile pulling at the corner of his lips. Standing on her mother's brick porch, in Baltimore.

"Baby," he grinned and opened his arms. Without thinking, Bernadette stepped into them. The cold wind slammed the door closed behind her, but she didn't even notice.

Reggie's lips crushed against hers in a bruising kiss. She had forgotten just how tall he was, or just how good he smelled. The soft fragrance of his cologne floated around him and she tried to melt into his delicious body. All she could think as her arm tightened around his neck was that it was a miracle he was here now, and that was all that mattered. He pulled her tightly against him and moved his hands up and down then across the back of her USMC gray tee shirt slowly.

"Feels like it was just yesterday," he whispered, smiling down at her. For a moment she closed her eyes and savored his touch. Then, just as suddenly, she opened them and pushed him away slightly, looking up into his face.

"I shouldn't be doing this! You didn't write me, Reggie, not even once in a whole year and a half."

"Bernadette, I did write you. There was something wrong with the APO you gave me, and my letters to you came back to me for some reason. If it wasn't for Nancy telling me about this party…"

"I just left California yesterday. Nancy knew where you were?"

"I asked her to let me surprise you. I thought I would surprise you at home, but she got to me and told me you came here, so I followed you."

"That little sneak! She knew I was looking for you, she could have eased my mind."

"Isn't this better than having her tell you I was coming?"

"I don't know." Bernadette looked at him and laughed, the hawk blowing her hair and causing goose bumps to rise over her arms. She grabbed him to her again and pressed her lips against his until he wrapped her in his arms. When they finished, Bernadette tried the door.

"Oh, shit." She shivered violently. "I think I locked us out." She tried the knob unsuccessfully.

"What'd they do to you over there?" He grabbed her waist with both hands. "You are skin and bones, girl. Did they put sand in the food or something?"

"Hard work and fear. That's all it took."

Just as they burst out laughing, the front door opened and Marietta peered out curiously.

"I'm okay, the wind closed the door on me," Bernadette explained, as Marietta stared past her. She moved inside and said, "Marietta, this is my friend, Reggie. Reggie, this is my sister. The old one."

"No kidding," he said laughing and holding out his hand.

"Oh, we do better than that around here," Marietta said, and she took his hand to pull him inside and hug him. "Come on in out of the cold, Reggie. Bernadette will keep you outside all to herself."

Just as he stepped in, Bernadette heard more voices coming from the kitchen. Her feet picked up speed, and as she burst through the doors, she stopped and let out a squeal.

"Corey Windsor!" She yelled and leaped into her brother's arms as Corey laughed, catching her easily.

"Hey, baby girl!" He kissed her cheek hard and hugged her to him tightly. It took a moment for Bernadette to see the woman behind him, and she leaned over his shoulder to speak.

"Hey, Alaina, you have to excuse me. I haven't seen my brother in years!" When Reggie and Marietta stepped through, there were more hugs, kisses and introductions while everybody started talking at once in Mama's little kitchen. Bernadette noted how mature her brother now looked-- tall, fit and handsome as ever. His eyes still had that look of mischief, that sparkle that let you know Corey was always thinking, but his voice was new. It was so deep and modulated. He could have been on TV or the radio instead of designing computer games in Winston-Salem.

Then she turned her attention to Reggie, who was being grilled by Marietta. Mama pushed everybody out of her kitchen. She directed the women to take out the place mats and set the table, the food was about ready. As Alaina and Marietta went to the china closet, Bernadette grabbed Reggie.

She led him downstairs to show him where to put his bag and to give him a towel to wash up, but Reggie had more immediate plans.

As soon as their feet hit the basement floor, he turned her around and pulled her against him as his lips opened hungrily, meeting hers in a deep long kiss. Her heart pounded wildly against his chest.

"How long do I have to wait before I can get me some?" he whispered.

She smiled.

"At least until after the party tonight."

"Do we have to stay for the whole party, Bernadette? I haven't seen you in over a year."

"Well, maybe not the whole party. I mean, we need to put in an appearance, and I want you to meet my niece and everybody."

"I stopped by the Sheraton downtown and got us a room."

"You've been scheming, huh?"

"Baby, I'm sure those people at your sister's house been with their women this past year. I haven't." He rubbed his hands gently across her breasts as their eyes met, then over her small waist to her hips. Cupping her buttocks with both hands, he pulled her tightly against him and kissed her again, opening his mouth to her. She felt him growing hard against her.

"Reggie, not now."

"You sure?"

She laughed and caught his roving hand.

"I promise, it'll be worth it to wait."

"I've flown miles just to be with you, you know that? You know how bad I want you?" His voice was husky and deep. Bernadette smiled at him as he bent his head to trace her lips with his tongue. "The least you could do is give me some private time."

"All right. First we'll go to Bea's for a little while."

"Just a little while," he agreed.

"Then we'll slip out. According to my sister, there'll be a lot of folks there. After a couple dances, we'll go off to your room at the Sheraton. Okay?"

"Promise?"

"Yeah." She tried to kiss him quickly then run upstairs before her mother came down, but he held her to him and kissed her again long and slow. The heat had started in her stomach. As their lips slowly parted he whispered, "I got so much to tell you, baby. I have to tell you personally."

"Well, hurry up. Mama cooked, and everything is home made."

When she came up, she hoped everyone couldn't see Reggie had been sucking on her lips. They felt swollen, and she could feel how taut her breasts had gotten in her tee shirt. Mama was carrying pans of food to the table, and Corey pulled enough chairs to circle the table. Everyone found a seat, and the conversation flowed as if they all knew and saw each other everyday.

When the talk turned to Beatrice, everybody agreed they were eager to see her and the children, and Corey started up with some old Beatrice stories, which made everybody laugh. Then, the doorbell interrupted.

Bernadette frowned, looking around.

"Who now?" she murmured as she jumped up saying, "I got it, Mama."

She was surprised to see a tall, nice looking white man in a short brown bomber jacket shivering before her.

"Hello."

"Hi," Bernadette said. "Can I help you?"

"I hope so. I'm looking for Marietta Windsor. Is this the right place?"

"Depends. Your name is…?"

"I thought she'd have told you. I'm Delaney Peterson."

Del? Was a white man? And Marietta never said?

"Oh, Del! Come on in, and forgive me. I know it's cold as the dickens out there."

He stepped inside fast, rubbing his hands together. His ears were the color of sangria from the cold.

They shook hands. "I'm Bernadette. Good to meet you! Come on in the house so I can introduce you."

Bernadette closed the front door, then led him inside where she took him around the table and everybody greeted Del and shook his hand, then she took him to wash up in the kitchen and fixed him a plate. When she left Del at the table to eat and talk to the others, she went back in the kitchen and her mother followed.

They exchanged looks.

"You're a pretty cool customer, Ma."

"Why? Cause that boy is white?"

"Well, you probably knew."

"Don't matter to me. I'm not living with him."

"How do you think he'll be at a party on Broadway?"

"Just fine! He may not see no more white people over that way, but he must have known. Marietta knew and she brought him, so they can deal with it."

Bernadette agreed and sighed.

"You got a full house tonight."

"Yeah and that reminds me. You and Mari can take the middle bedroom and Corey and Alaina the back. The men can sleep downstairs."

Bernadette frowned.

"Ain't nobody married but Corey and Alaina, and ain't no sleeping together under my roof unless you married."

"Ma, Marietta is 38-years-old and engaged."

"And still not married. So what?"

Bernadette laughed. "You are a trip, but okay."

She kissed her mother and ran upstairs. It gave her a few minutes alone to absorb the evening so far. She still felt a gnawing fear.

Why did Mama and Marietta team up against Beatrice? What did they know that she didn't?

One thing for sure, it would all come out tonight at the party.

# eighteen

They arrived at the party late, what with all the playing at Mama's house. There was Marietta, pulling out Mama's basket of family photographs and catching them up in picture gazing and reminiscing. Then Bernadette announced the time, and herded everybody from the table to get dressed.

It reminded Bernadette of Christmas as they wrapped birthday gifts for Beatrice. Marietta, dressed in an Eileen Fisher mid-calf mauve wrap dress and knee length brown suede Jimmy Choo boots with three inch spike heels looked fashionably beautiful as she pulled out her gift, a bottle of Dior, to show to Bernadette. She paused and examined the gold bracelet Bernadette had fallen in love with in Saudi Arabia, with Arabic etchings and matching gold hoops. When Bernadette commented on Marietta's expert makeup, Marietta sat her down and pulled out her bag of tricks for Bernadette.

Bernadette felt more than cute when she saw how Reggie's eyes widened when he saw her. The glint of raw desire reflected there reminded her of the night he had planned for them. She admired his handsomeness, dressed in all black, pants, turtleneck, and his black leather jacket. She couldn't wait to get to him.

When they stepped out Mama's car on Broadway, Reggie had almost talked her into just leaving the present with Beatrice then going straight to the room at the Sheraton. Almost. But Bernadette remembered there would be a surprise. She was sure she didn't want to miss this for anything, not after two years, so she got Reggie to hold out for at least one dance. Then they would go.

They'd parked around the corner because there were cars lined up and down Broadway on both sides of the street. There must be over 100 people or more packed inside, Bernadette mused. They put Mama's club on the steering wheel and activated her alarm. There were a lot of people just milling about the street. As they turned the corner, they could hear the bass of a tune vibrating clear out into the neighborhood.

"I hear muuuusssic," Reggie crooned, and Bernadette moved her feet in time to the tune. "He got the Isley Brothers on? I know we're here to party."

Two people loitering on the front steps looked up when they got there, and Bernadette paused to look around for the other family members who were coming in Corey's van, which she did not see.

"Excuse us," Reggie said, and slipped his arm around her waist nudging her up the steps. The couple on the steps moved to let them by, and the girl quickly asked, "Is there a party in there?"

Bernadette noticed they were quite young, teenagers looking for a good time.

"Sorry, private party," Reggie answered ringing the bell.

The door opened almost right away.

"We're looking for Beatrice?" Bernadette asked the woman swinging on the doorknob, staring at her long, blonde weave that contrasted the deep mahogany skin.

"Straight in the back. I'm Mae Jefferson, friend of Beatrice."

"Hi, I'm Bernadette, Beatrice's sister. This is my friend, Reggie."

"So you're Bernadette, how you been?" Mae closed the door and beckoned them to follow. "I believe they're about to sing "Happy Birthday" now."

Bernadette grabbed Reggie's hand and pulled him behind her, as she followed Mae. She glanced around her, mouth open, unbelieving. It was astounding. Was this the same house she had turned her nose up at a year ago? She had to pause as she passed the living room. Gone were the old cracked black vinyl couch and seedy looking arm chairs. Her eyes took in the new furniture, the bricked in wall with hanging prints on most of the available space, wall papered hallways, mirrors everywhere, oriental carpeting and soft hanging lamps.

As she stepped into the dining room, the huge, crystal chandelier caught her attention. She stared up for a few dazed seconds, then when she looked down, she turned her head to view the entire room, amazed at all the people who were here to wish her sister happy birthday. Beatrice had so many friends, it surprised her. People loved Beatrice, just as they had Nita. There were all strange faces, laughing and talking in a huge circle around the dining room table. Bernadette pushed her way in, until she could see the head of the table, then grinned.

"Beatrice!" she yelled when she saw her sister staring mesmerized at the cake full of lighted candles. Beatrice looked up.

"Berni! Oh, my God, girl!" Bea hollered back reaching out her arms. Mae, however, was closest to her and pulled them back.

"We all came, Bea" Bernadette yelled, and tried to push closer, but it was impossible.

"Okay now, gotdammit," Mae called out, standing on a chair behind Beatrice. "We are going to sing "Happy Birthday" together this time, y'all don't know Happy Birthday or something? Come on! Take it from the top"—

Everybody started to sing the Stevie Wonder version, clapping to the tune. Bernadette sang out with them, then looked back for Reggie. He was standing well behind her in the crowd, clapping in time, and staring about curiously. She smiled and made her way back to him, grabbing his hand. She still couldn't believe her good fortune that he was here with her. She felt a sudden tug on her dress and turned. There was Toukie, smiling up at her.

"Toukie! Baby!" Bernadette screamed out, grabbing her niece to her. Toukie had changed again. This time, she looked very grown up. Her hair was in small braids and pulled up high on her head. She had on a dress with a black velvet top and sleeves that puffed up at the shoulders. The bottom was black and gold taffeta. She had on black tights and black suede pumps with low heels.

Bernadette pulled Toukie against her as they finished singing Happy Birthday and watched Bea make a wish and blow out the candles.

"Where's Witt?" Bernadette asked.

"Downstairs playing the music," Toukie said. Beatrice's loud laughter made them both turn to look. "I know y'all thought I couldn't blow out all 32 candles, but I fooled your asses, didn't I?" she said loudly, as everybody laughed with her.

There was clapping, loud talking, people grabbing at Beatrice, kissing and hugging.

"My mother got a lot of presents," Toukie announced.

"Well, she's getting some more. Look, Toukie, I want you-"

"Give me your presents and your coats now, Aunt Bern. I'm in charge of taking those upstairs."

Before Bernadette could get out of her coat completely, Toukie had snatched it, and the present from Reggie and dashed away.

When Toukie left, Bernadette turned to Reggie. He was already engaged in a conversation with a guy standing next to him. She reached over and pulled on his hand.

"Excuse me. Listen, we need a game plan," she said. He leaned closer. "You are going to dance with me downstairs, then I'm going to introduce you to my sister, then Toukie, then Witt, so we can go."

She pulled him down the stairs to the basement where Toukie said Witt was, and was immediately sorry. Some serious booty-shaking music was going on and the floor was packed full of people moving steadily to the beat of a Janet Jackson song. Bernadette noticed that several men at the bottom of the steps were checking her out. She pulled Reggie closer, her small hand holding tightly to his large one, as they edged onto the floor. In a tiny space they started to dance.

The truth was, she loved to hear music played through a good sound system and Witt's sounded like one of the best. With the music thumping like they were at a club, she closed her eyes and moved her body to the beat, feeling like another person in another day and time. People bumped into her, the floor was so crowded, but she kept her eyes closed and pumped it. She was back in the world, away from all that craziness across the globe, and she was so damn happy she couldn't stand it. At some point, she became aware of the song ending and a second one beginning. Just as she was twirling around to let loose, she felt two hands on her shoulders. Her eyes flew open.

"It's just me," Beatrice laughed. "Listen, I need you to come upstairs for a minute." She looked over. "You, too," she said to Reggie. "You all can dance later."

Bernadette followed her sister, wiping her forehead with the back of her hand. It was smoking hot down in the basement with all those writhing bodies on top of one another. She welcomed the cool air hitting her full in the face when her feet touched the first floor. Pausing slightly, Beatrice linked her arm in Bernadette's, and pulled her along.

"You didn't tell me about Marietta and boyfriend."

"I just found out tonight! Are they finally here?"

"In the living room," Beatrice said, and then Bernadette pulled Bea close. "What are you doing back in this house, Beatrice? What did you find?"

"What did I tell you? What's the only reason I would come back here?"

"Daddy?"

"That's the only reason."

"Just tell me. Where did this money come from? You didn't tell me about you and Witt hitting the lottery. This house looks amazing!"

"Oh, that's a long story I'll tell you about later, and no, we didn't hardly hit the lottery. But I'm glad you like it," Beatrice answered, and Bernadette noticed how much her speech had changed. Suddenly, noticing Bea's eyes looking past her and at Reggie, Bernadette paused.

"Well, excuse my sister's manners. I'm Bernadette's sister, Beatrice," Bea said, and gave Reggie a seductive smile.

"And Bea," Bernadette said smoothly, "I want you to meet my boyfriend, Reggie." Reggie reached out for Bea's hand while Bernadette watched him proudly. She didn't understand why Beatrice was giving Reggie such a long, careful look, but Reggie smiled confidently keeping one hand on Bernadette's waistline squeezing her.

Beatrice then looked at Bernadette.

"What?" Bernadette asked her.

"I'm proud of you. This man is something to be very proud of," she said. Then she turned to Reggie. "And this woman is my heart. If you don't love her, step out now."

Reggie put a protective arm around Bernadette.

"You don't have to worry about her."

"Good. I don't want to, ever."

Bernadette looked Beatrice over, seeing for the first time the complete change in her. Not only her speech, but her body, too. She was stunning in a straight purple dress that clung to her figure flatteringly. It had a plunging neckline with just a hint of cleavage pushed up. She must have lost 30 pounds since she'd last seen her.

"My God, what did you do to yourself, Beatrice? You look great."

Beatrice winked.

"I've been taking care of a lot of business I should have long time ago. Wait till I tell you."

Bernadette stared at her sister's back puzzling over her comment as they followed her lead to where Marietta, Del, Corey and Alaina were seated. They were all in the living room, talking in a corner when Bernadette and Reggie squeezed in. Beatrice stepped back from the group and smiled widely. The conversations fell off as they all looked at her expectantly.

Toukie came down the stairs at that second and over to her mother and whispered in her ear. Beatrice held a hand up to her in a wait a minute motion, then looked back at her assembled family.

"I guess you all want to know why I made sure I invited everybody in my family to my party this year," Beatrice began. "I never have before."

Bernadette held her breath. The surprise was coming. She looked around expectantly. Was Daddy here?

Beatrice paused, then took a deep breath, blowing out a gust of air and glancing up at the ceiling as though fighting tears. Bernadette felt a catch in her chest.

"There's only one thing wrong here, one thing missing for me tonight."

Beatrice looked down at her fingers, and Bernadette scooted to the edge of the sofa. Beatrice looked fabulous in purple. Radiant, with an air of confidence and happiness, she faced them.

"I never thought I could get my family together for something positive. And believe me this party tonight is for something positive."

Bernadette could feel the others looking at Beatrice, waiting and wondering. What was she talking about? What was she going to spring on them?

"I'll bet she found him," Bernadette whispered to herself.

Marietta, sitting the closest to Bernadette, snapped her head around to look at her.

"Who?"

Beatrice continued her speech. "This party tonight is my birthday party, but it's in honor of my sister, Juanita. Because of her, I understand what she had to learn about this family, and tonight I want to tell you."

"Ma!" Toukie suddenly screamed out and stamped her foot. "You got to come upstairs right now!"

Beatrice turned her attention to Toukie and frowned. She then turned back to the group. "I'm sorry, but I'll be right back." She sighed and quickly left them, with Toukie following behind.

"What was that all about?" Alaina asked.

Bernadette looked at Marietta.

"She's going to do something tonight. Can't you tell? She's going to surprise us," Bernadette said, waiting for Marietta to respond.

"Surprise us how?" Marietta asked in a small voice, her body twitching.

"How do you think?" Bernadette dropped her voice to a whisper. "I'll bet she found Daddy."

Bernadette watched Marietta's face turn chalky.

"Why?"

"Why not? I'm sure you could see how happy she was. What else would she gather us to say? And, if you had done what I asked you months ago, Beatrice would probably not be springing this surprise on us all like this."

"Why are you blaming me? Oh God! I hope she didn't do that."

"Why not? What's so bad about having him here?"

"Believe me, Bernadette, there are some things better left alone."

"What's going on?" Alaina interrupted the whispering. "What do you think happened with Toukie upstairs? "

"Well," Reggie shifted his body and raised himself off the sofa. "I don't know about you, but I'm hot sitting up close and personal like this. I'm going to find me a cold brew."

He straightened his pants legs until they fell over his shoes just so.

"Sounds like a plan to me," Corey said getting up with him. They walked out together.

"What are you two whispering about?" Del moved over near Marietta.

"Believe me, you wouldn't want to know," Bernadette answered, and she got up. She suddenly felt the urge to get a drink, something she knew she didn't want to start up. She paused, letting her eyes follow the sanded staircase that was now dressed in a brick red runner with black trimming, all the way to the next landing. Who was upstairs?

She started to move toward the stairs when she heard her name.

"Aunt Bern!"

She turned surprised. Toukie was back downstairs.

"Where are you going?" Toukie asked, panting when she reached her.

"Why? Where do you want me?"

"We can go dance downstairs, or we can go in there and eat some cake."

Bernadette hesitated, glancing up at the stairs before giving Toukie her hand, and letting herself be lead away. But after several steps, she stopped and leaned down.

"What did you call your mother away for?"

"My Mommy told me to. She said if Mr. Derrick came, I had to take him upstairs and call her right away. Before Witt comes up."

"Mr. Derrick?"

"Yeah. He was our friend when we moved from Witt. My mother said he's still her friend, even with Witt." Toukie looked down.

"Even with Witt? How can that be? Doesn't she still like Witt? Don't you?"

"I like him okay. When he's nice. My mother said everybody's father is mean sometimes."

Bernadette stared hard at Toukie.

"Well, I don't know why your mother would ever have left him, Toukie. If he was like everybody's father."

"Because she likes Mr. Derrick. She just lives with Witt."

"What?"

"My mother is going to move away from Witt again, but it's a secret. Mr. Derrick is going to help us. My mother said he promised."

"Wow, that's a lot of information for such a little girl."

Toukie swished her hand in the air. "I'm 11. I know all kinds of stuff."

Bernadette glanced up toward the second floor. Mr. Derrick? Was that Bea's surprise announcement that Toukie interrupted? No, it couldn't be. Bea said it was about family.

"Come with me, Toukie. I think our first stop should be the kitchen."

And Toukie followed, slipping her hand in Bernadette's.

"Heeeeey!!"

Corey greeted them as they walked in the kitchen, turning from his conversation with Reggie to put his bottle on the kitchen table and lift Toukie in his arms for a kiss.

"I don't believe I met this beautiful young lady," Reggie said moving closer to them. "And who are you?"

"Oh, Toukie. This is Reggie, my boyfriend. Reggie, this is my niece."

Toukie's mouth dropped open as she stared. "Hi Reggie," she said quietly.

"You want to go downstairs and dance with me?" Reggie asked Toukie, and she turned to look at Bernadette.

"Go ahead! I must warn you, Toukie. The man can dance," Bernadette said waving a finger.

Corey put Toukie down and she grabbed Reggie's hand and headed for the basement. Bernadette waited until they were out of the kitchen, and then started over to Corey to tell him what Toukie said about Beatrice when her name rang out.

"Aunt Bern, come on downstairs with me!"

She agreed and reluctantly picked her way behind them. She soon found herself crushed against the basement wall again. More people had come into the basement. She couldn't see anyone in the dimly lit space at first, just felt the bumps of moving bodies as she realized she wasn't on the wall alone.

"Want to dance?" A guy standing next to her asked. Before she knew it, she was pulled into the mass. After two long records, she begged off and made her way to a spot on the wall to rest. She looked around for Reggie as another record came on, and found him dancing with, of all people, Alaina. She tried to find Witt among the men around the music table and thought she picked him out of the four men who stood by talking. There was a stream of people moving up and down the steps, light fixtures on the edges reflected constant traffic, and she was surprised to see Del was one, threading his way through. Holding a cup in his hand, no less.

She noticed how several people turned to give him a hard look, like he must have been lost or something. He did appear to be searching, and she stuck her hand up, hoping he could spot her. When his eyes found hers, they locked onto her until he made his way over.

"If you came down here, you must be ready to boogie, Del."

Del was game, and Bernadette liked that. She took his cup, put it on a shelf, and pulled him into the mass. Once on the floor, he let loose, doing his own thing, right in time with the music. Del was cool. He absolutely moved in his own groove not giving a damn about anybody else. Bernadette had fun doing her own thing with him. When one record ended and another began right in the same beat, Del begged off.

"I'm too old for this," he said, and Bernadette laughed. "But," he continued, " I wondered if I could talk to you a moment?"

Bernadette leaned her ears close and he pointed to the front of the basement, away from the speakers. They moved as far as they could, and once again, against the wall, Del thanked her.

"I've been wanting to talk to you since I got here and couldn't imagine when or how. But I guess this will have to be it."

"Sure," Bernadette said. With the strobe lighting, everybody appeared to be in a black and white movie, an eerie background as they huddled together.

"You know, I love your sister."

She smiled. "That's a good feeling to have for someone you're going to marry."

Del continued. "But as much as I love her, I know there's something she's keeping from me and I don't understand why."

"Something like what?"

"I don't know what it is, but something has her scared."

"Like how? What is she doing?"

"She hides. She lies. She pretends. And what I see is a brave woman. A stubborn, but brave woman. I just don't know why. All I know is that every time she gets a letter from you, each and every time, she gets upset. She's jumpy. She gets moody. She closes up. And I want to know why. I've asked her. She says I'm imagining things. I didn't imagine that she came to Baltimore last spring and stayed about three weeks. She said she came to stay with your mother, because your mother needed surgery. But I found she came here to be hospitalized herself. For what, I don't know. It's all a big secret."

Bernadette's eyes were fixed on Del's lips, but her mind was miles away. Del spoke quite clearly, carefully choosing his words. "Some bright person from the hospital accounting department called Marietta at home. They needed to validate her health insurance. I followed up on the call, and couldn't find out why she was there. Only that she was there, for a week. When she came back to New York, she said she had just been visiting your mother. When I told her about the call, she said I was mistaken. She said she had taken your mother to the hospital. I know when something isn't what it seems. Marietta is lying, and she's pretending about things. But I don't know why."

Bernadette didn't know either. In fact, Del's news was a shock. Why was Marietta so deceptive, even with the man she loved?

"You aren't telling me anything," Del said.

"There's nothing for me to tell you," she answered him slowly. "Do you think I would tell you a secret my sister had if she didn't want you to know?"

Del didn't say anything for a few seconds before he answered, "I guess not. Maybe what I want from you is a feel for how serious this secret is that she's hiding and will she ever be able to tell me?"

"You know what, Del? If I were engaged to somebody whom I was sure was hiding something from me, I'd wait until I knew what was going on before I married him. That's really all I can tell you."

"And I was hoping that you would help, Bernadette," he insisted. "You're the one who gets her crazy, and I'm here to help her, but I can't if I don't know what's going on."

"Me?" She was surprised. "Marietta has never paid me any attention, and I don't believe I'm causing her actions."

"Can't you see? It's probably what you know that's making her crazy."

"What I know?" Bernadette repeated. Then her mind went back to her thoughts earlier that evening. Mama and Marietta were afraid she'd find Daddy. Then what? It's what she thinks I might find out about Daddy that's driving her crazy. Del was way off. Marietta was afraid of what Bea knew. A picture of Marietta's bloodless face came back to her when she thought Bea had found Daddy.

"I hate to disappoint you, Del. I don't know what's wrong with Marietta, but from what I've seen, I'm pretty sure she loves you. If she can't tell you now, I think if you make it clear you know something is wrong and give her time, she will tell you, but I can't help you."

"She's really stubborn, but I see she's not the only stubborn one in this family."

Bernadette laughed. "The good thing is you know beforehand what you're getting."

"Ah, well, maybe tomorrow," Del said. He touched Bernadette's shoulder in parting before she stopped him and pulled him through the people until she found Witt. He was still at the table with a stack of cassettes and CD's all around. She found him squinting at the labels.

"Excuse me, Private, but you do have an officer in your presence."

Witt looked up and seeing her before him slowly smiled.

"Lieutenant, how's it going? And, that's Private First Class to you."

They laughed. "I want you to meet my sister Marietta's fiance, Delaney Peterson. Del, this is Bea's friend, Witt."

They shook hands and exchanged a few words of greeting. Del then told Bernadette he was going to find Marietta, and Bernadette turned her full attention to Witt.

"So, what's been happening?" She moved closer to him to be able to hear.

"Working hard, day and night, on the job and off. We went on and re-did our house, and your sister, soon as the last nail was in, told me she was having a celebration party. Turned out to be her birthday party. I didn't have a choice."

He actually laughed again, she with him.

"You did a hell of a job on the house."

"I've been working at it. Did most of it myself."

"You did well. Really well."

"Thanks. You want to take this one Bernadette?" He indicated he wanted to dance and quickly she agreed.

Witt handed off a CD to one of his friends standing nearby as he guided her by arm to the edge of the crowd. He slid his arms around her and she felt how thick they were, especially compared to Reggie's long, lanky build. She wondered if it were possible to become friends with this man. After all, she had hated him upon first sight, but now she had to admit, Bea was happy. But then, if Toukie was right, it was now because of a man named Derrick. Or maybe Daddy? Maybe Witt did take her to Daddy, and she had just what she wanted. She no longer needed Witt.

Then Bernadette wondered. Just what did Witt know?

# nineteen

Just as she was about to find out, Witt cleared his throat.

"Did you get a chance to check out the kitchen?"

"Of course. It looks amazing. How did you get so much done so fast?"

She could hear the smile in his voice. "When I want something done, I get it done. I always find a way. And, as you can see, Bernadette, I always win. Always."

For a minute, the song they had been dancing to, Will Downing's "Cool Water" faded out, and she was conscious only that he had just said something weird about winning.

"What?"

"I mean, regardless of all the checks and letters you sent to my house, regardless of all the things you said and did against my wishes, I'm still here. I'm going to be here. And there isn't a woman alive who can win against me. "

Maybe she hadn't been wrong about Witt. Maybe he still had a part to play, but what? It felt more like he was still trying to prove something, but what did he still need to show?

"You thought I did things against you?"

"I know how we first began. It was clear what you thought about me."

"I don't think so. I didn't know what to think. The thing about you Witt, that bothered me then, and that bothers me now, is that I think you knew Beatrice, long before you formally met her. I felt it then, and I think I'm right. Am I?" She held her breath.

Witt leaned his head back to look in her face. "Where did that come from?"

"Am I right?"

He hesitated. "Not really."

"Of course you did. And then you made it your business to get next to her."

"What do you mean?"

"How did you just happen to meet Bea?"

"I met her in a club."

"You can be honest now, Witt. It wasn't a chance meeting."

Witt laughed.

"Let me ask you," he said then. "You never liked me and never trusted me. What do you think I'm after?"

Whatever my father wants, she thought, but kept to herself. She simply said, "My sister came back to you. As long as she's happy, what can I say about you?"

"You can start by paying me some respect. You could say 'Witt is actually a smart businessman, and if I remember my place, and keep my sister and my niece in theirs, they will end up very rich.'"

This time Bernadette leaned back. "Now that's what I don't like about you. You have this superior attitude."

"I could say the same for you."

"But mine will never hurt anyone. I think yours already has."

"I see you still don't trust me."

"I don't think I can until I understand exactly what you're about. Like, that ring you wear around your neck."

Witt paused, then said with a hint of surprise, "My ring?"

"Yes. Where did it come from?"

"That's a long story."

"Then just answer this: Did my father give it to you?'

This time Witt laughed louder.

"Let's just say, some things are better left between me and your sister. It's better that way."

"Fair enough," Bernadette said as the record was ending. It was only a matter of time before she would know. "But," she said before they parted. "I will tell you, I don't think we need to resent each other anymore, Witt."

"We won't. As long as you remember who I am, you won't have to worry."

Bernadette rolled her eyes, saying, "As if I could forget," before turning on her heels and walking away from him. Her anger was boiling as she flew up the steps in search of Reggie. She needed to get out of here, before Witt said one more stupid thing and forced her to forget herself.

She rushed through the dining room, her eyes searching the throngs of people hanging onto each other with drinks and cigarettes and plates of food in her way. She couldn't find anybody in here, not even Beatrice, who seemed to have disappeared.

And there was no Daddy here; that much Bernadette had searched out and confirmed. So, what the hell was the surprise? Things had changed for Beatrice, but there was no chance to find out anymore from her tonight. Bernadette was more than ready to go.

"Where's Beatrice?" she asked the first woman she met in the kitchen doorway, who sat balancing a plate of food on her lap. Bernadette wanted to wish her sister the best for the evening and not waste another minute in Witt's house. The man was a lunatic, and there was no reason to stay longer.

"Did you try the third floor? She took some people up there."

People had started to clear out, leaving singles, people sitting alone and eating, and several couples, drinking and laughing together. Bernadette headed straight for the steps. The more she saw of the house, the more astounded she was. Her eyes devoured the black art pieces, both the prints on the walls and the wooden sculptures on the mantel. The thick oriental carpeting with fine details and fine furniture belonged in Architectural Digest.

As she stopped in the living room, she found herself staring up at the light fixtures Witt had between pictures. Why did he put that kind of money in a house in this neighborhood?

She paused at the bottom of the tall staircase. She needed to let Beatrice know she was leaving, but her feet in these heels did not want to move. She was exhausted. All she wanted was to find Reggie and leave. Maybe she could warn Bea about Witt later, after all, he was a lunatic and that wouldn't change in one night. What a crazy fool!

Bernadette sank into the thick cushion of the nearest chair and let out a long grateful sigh. She immediately pulled her feet out of her heels, and rubbed them slowly, pulling the hose from between her cramped toes. After a second, she left her feet alone and leaned back in the seat. These new chairs Beatrice had were not only pretty, but also very comfortable. She ran her hand over the cushions, thinking again of Witt.

In seconds, Toukie slid into the seat next to her and let her head fall on Bernadette's shoulder. She was winding down.

"Hey," Bernadette said reaching down and rubbing the child's face. "Having fun?"

Toukie grinned from ear to ear as Bernadette touched her neat, stylish braids.

"The best. I wish Poobah was here. Guess where he is? Didn't you miss him? He's next door with Ms. Jones."

"Well, that's good. He'd never be able to sleep in here."

Toukie sat with her, smoothing out her aunt's dress as she talked about her brother and all the things he could do now. As she rattled on, Bernadette watched the confident tilt of Toukie's head and the clarity of her speech, she realized that Toukie was different. She could see Toukie felt better about herself. She could see something in Toukie that hadn't been there before.

She felt good. She felt very good. She put both arms around Toukie.

"Look, Aunt Bern," Toukie said raising her head from her aunt's shoulder. "People are coming in the door with no invitations. My mother said she wanted somebody to stay at the door cause she didn't want no trouble tonight."

"What kind of trouble?"

"I don't know, but my mother said…"

"Oh, don't worry so much, girl! You worry too much to be a little girl, you know that? If Witt or your mother was worried, they'd be on the door themselves. See? They're somewhere having a good time. So, chill out, would you?"

Toukie set her mouth and leaned back. A frown was still on her face.

"You look so pretty tonight. You really look more and more like your mother everyday. Know that? Real pretty." Bernadette tried to get her to smile.

Toukie looked at her without any expression.

"Look, I'm going upstairs to the bathroom. Do me a favor?" She looked at her watch, wondering what happened to the game plan she had with Reggie for one dance and then for them to split. "Go downstairs and get Reggie up here right away, please? Thanks."

Bernadette left her shoes under the chair and went upstairs. Reggie was the one all eager to come here for just a minute, and then leave. And now where was he? She padded quietly down the hall, her ears perking up. Where was the party she thought was going on up here?

Suddenly, giggles started and Bernadette glanced through the open doorway of Toukie's old bedroom. She heard voices. Well, maybe there was a party going on inside.

She hurried by, and in the second she looked over her shoulder into the room, she saw Beatrice, her face only inches away from the face of a strange man. Bernadette's feet stopped moving, and the voices stopped. She backed up, and looked in the room. Beatrice looked back unfazed.

Bernadette stared. "Everything okay?" Her eyes sought out her sister's.

"Just fine, no problem," Beatrice said. She stood and motioned Bernadette in. Bernadette hesitated in the doorway.

"This is my sister, Bernadette. The one stationed in Iraq the whole time I've known you."

"I was in Saudi Arabia, Bea. Not Iraq."

"And this is Derrick. I met him my first week at the Baltimore Gas and Electric Company. He's an attorney there, and he's helped me a lot."

"Oh? Is this the surprise you were about to show us downstairs?"

"Derrick?"

Both of them laughed, easily with each other. There was obvious familiarity. What the hell was Beatrice doing? Bernadette frowned.

"Not at all. My surprise was something for my family, and I still have to do that."

"Well, Reggie and I are planning to split. I tried to wait, but I haven't seen him in almost two years."

"What do you mean?"

"He just came into town, right before your party."

"You haven't seen him in all the time you've been overseas, and you still came to my party first?" Beatrice reached out and pulled her sister in a tight hug, then turned to Derrick.

"Do you see? Berni is my girl, always has been, always will be."

"You look so much alike. The same facial structure. The same smile. And you said there's three more of you?"

"Two more. But one sister is dead."

"Bea? I think you may need to go down and check on the party. Your daughter is spending a lot of time worrying about the people still coming in, and…"Bernadette stopped there. Surely Bea hadn't forgotten she had a boyfriend in the basement.

"Was I gone long?" she asked, giving Derrick an impish smile.

"I'll go down first," he offered, and surprised Bernadette by leaning forward and pressing Beatrice's lips with his.

"Let me go first and check on my daughter," Bea said. She winked at Bernadette and walked out of the room, leaving them. Bernadette continued to look at Derrick. He gave her an uncertain smile as he glanced at his watch. He told her he'd see her downstairs.

Bernadette stared after them. What the hell? What if it had been Witt who had come up on them? What was Beatrice trying to do? Get herself killed at her own party?

Bernadette jumped up. She stared down at the bed, wondering what might have happened if she had not come upstairs when she did. Then, she squinted and leaned closer. The quilt. There was a picture of Venus and Serena Williams, in tennis gear, woven into the fabric. She flipped it over, searching until she found it. Charlene Coleman, stitched carefully just as it was on Nita's quilt in Mama's trunk. Just how deep was Witt's connection?

Bernadette quickly went to the bathroom, then back downstairs. Should she confront Beatrice? Obviously, if Witt had come up there instead of her, and found her with Derrick, it'd have been all over with. She went looking for Beatrice.

Toukie, still sitting on the same spot on the couch, looked at Bernadette with a frown on her face.

"Did you get Reggie for me?" Bernadette glanced at her. "Tell him I'm ready to go," she added, then hurried toward the kitchen hoping to catch up with Beatrice.

"No! Don't just open that door!" Bernadette heard Toukie yell out loudly. She was still trying to oversee the rules of the party, as if anybody still cared. Where the hell was her stupid sister? Bea said she was coming down to check on Toukie.

Bernadette saw Toukie run over to the front door, then heard her yell out, "Ms. Cynthia!" Watching the woman hug Toukie, Bernadette turned and walked quickly into the dining room heading toward the kitchen where she thought Beatrice was.

"Somebody up here looking for me?" she heard Reggie ask loudly behind her. She started to stop and tell him to wait for her so they could leave, but it was more important to get Bea away from that man. Why was she flirting with fire? She couldn't do that again.

"Is it that motherfucker?" A voice at the door yelled, loud enough that Bernadette heard from the dining room. That stopped her, and she turned. She saw Reggie walk into the living room.

"Him?" The same voice yelled again. Bernadette's reaction slowed. She thought first about Toukie, still in the living room with some fool yelling. She didn't know exactly where Toukie was, and in that second she knew she should.

She pushed her way back through the people who stood in the way talking, some voices pausing as there seemed to be more commotion at the door.

She could see Reggie's back as he moved ahead of her toward the voices. Where was he going? She couldn't get through the people fast enough. They all seemed to be rooted to one spot, staring toward the foyer at the sound of the loud voices.

"I'll handle it," she said loudly, pushing people aside, trying to get a better view of the front door. When she did, she saw a short guy in black jeans with a long leather coat hanging open like a cape. He looked past her.

"Hey, Cynthia, where he at? " his voice boomed.

"Can I help you?" Bernadette asked in her best let-me-take-charge-of-this-situation voice as she approached him. She had even pushed her way past Reggie.

Toukie made a frantic sound.

"Get the fuck out the way," the guy said, stepping around her.

"Who the hell are you?" Bernadette started, but felt herself jerked back roughly as Reggie stepped in front of her.

"What's going on?" he asked and just as he did, they both heard the pop, pop sound of a gun going off and everybody on the first floor of the house started to scream and run. Bernadette turned instinctively to grab Toukie and in one fluid motion her bare feet hit the center of the couch and then she leaped over, pulling Toukie with her as they hit the floor hard. She reached up, to pull the sofa down on them, but she couldn't. Instead, she covered Toukie's body with her own and squeezed her eyes shut tightly.

"I got him," she heard the man say, before another voice asked, "You sure?"

"Let's get the fuck outta here, man. He ain't going after nobody else."

Bernadette heard the sounds of scuffling feet, more screaming. People from the basement spilled into the dining and living rooms. The front door banged as people rushed out. Hollering erupted from the streets. When she peeped up, she saw people standing in a circle in the middle of the living room, some kneeling, someone sobbing. She heard the squeal of car wheels and the noise of cars banging together.

"Shit, he's running into somebody's car out front!"

"Call 911!" Someone yelled. "Someone's been shot!"

Bernadette jumped up. She looked down, but all she saw were people's legs. Where was Reggie?

She moved in closer, pushing them aside. The next thing she heard was a long piercing scream. She didn't know it came from her until it stopped when she hit the floor.

# twenty

Marietta sagged against the hard plastic seat, her head back and eyes staring up at the bright fluorescent lights in the hospital waiting room. "What now?" she wondered. Lord, she hoped that man didn't die. It was a mistake to have come. Bernadette had turned out to be a beautiful young woman with the tenacity of a tiger. As far as Marietta could tell, she was much the same as she had been as a young girl, ready to take on the world if she had to in order to find out what she needed. And if it were true that Beatrice was about to announce finding their father, Bernadette would not let it go. That's all Marietta needed.

All she wanted was the same love and respect of her sisters and brothers she'd always had. It almost looked like everything was going to go okay. She had made it through the hard part, getting Bernadette over the fact that she hadn't written. Having Reggie here had helped a lot. Bernadette was a big ball of mush around that man, then he goes and gets shot. It would make them all think of the last time they were together for Juanita's funeral. And questions would start.

Now what?

Del and Corey had been the picture of cool, getting the ambulance there quickly and Reggie down to University Hospital's Shock Trauma. After about an hour, a doctor had come out and told them Reggie was going to be fine. His wound was to the neck, but the direction the bullet had taken allowed it to exit without apparent critical damage. There would be stitches and bandages, but according to the doctor, it appeared he would live. Please God.

She'd never gotten the chance to talk privately with Berni and Beatrice. She still needed to give them a reason not to pull Daddy into their lives. The investigative file Bernadette handed to her had made it easy. She knew Bernadette was definitely on the right track. The only thing she hoped was when Bernadette got the chance to ask her those same questions directly, she would accept the lies Marietta planned to tell. Somehow, she didn't see it working out. She had no idea what was going to happen when and if everything came out.

The thing she wanted most was to just get herself and Del out of Baltimore as fast as she could, the sooner, the better.

Marietta looked over where Bernadette was walking outside of the hospital, on the slope by the window where white flakes were aimlessly floating ever so often. She was wrapped up in Reggie's big leather jacket, plucking away cigarette after cigarette. Marietta wanted to go out to her, but something kept her in the seat.

Alaina was beside her on her cell phone checking on her husband and the status of things at the house, the fifth grade teacher triggered into action. She clicked off just as Bernadette came inside and walked over to them, reeking of tobacco.

"What's taking them so long if he's all right?" Bernadette asked.

"Come and sit down," Marietta said grabbing Bernadette and pulling her in the seat beside her.

"Things could have been so much worse," she told her sister and slipped her arm around Berni's shoulder, squeezing her.

"It's not that I'm unhappy about that fool being a bad shot, it's just the whole idea. I mean, I can't get over this shit. Anybody sitting in that living room could have died over nothing," Bernadette said, shaking her head.

Alaina got up and sat on the other side of Bernadette.

"It's unbelievable," she agreed, squeezing Bernadette's hand. The three of them looked up when Del came over with two styrofoam cups of vending machine coffee and handed Bernadette one.

"You want one, Mari?" he asked, and Marietta shook her head no, as did Alaina when he asked her. "What was the shooting about? Alaina, did anyone tell you more?"

"Yes, I was just talking to Corey, and he said the man who shot Reggie was there after Witt. Some girl who had just walked in the door--Toukie knew her--was supposed to go in and point Witt out or get him to step outside. But somebody got trigger happy, so when Reggie came in asking who was looking for him, they thought he was Witt."

"Why did someone want to kill Witt?" Del asked.

"Yes, what is he into?" Bernadette said.

"Nobody seemed to know," Alaina answered with a shrug. "Yet."

"They're still with the police, aren't they?" Marietta turned to Alaina. "I guess when Corey and Witt leave the police station we can find out what it's all about." She shifted in the hard plastic seat stifling a yawn. It was nearly 9:00 a.m. and she was beat. The make-up still on her face felt caked and crusty. She needed a bath.

"Is Toukie with them?" Bernadette asked. "I didn't see her after Reggie got shot. I jumped up and left her behind the couch."

"She's probably with Beatrice. You know Bea didn't go to the station." Alaina answered, and Marietta suddenly said, "When I called Mama to tell her where we were, she said she wants us all to come back there with her today. She said we could have stayed and partied right in her house."

They all laughed, Bernadette saying emphatically, "For real."

Then Marietta rubbed her face and said, "I am so ready to go home." A big yawn followed, then she ran her fingers through her cropped hair, sighing loudly.

A nerve pricked in Bernadette.

"Why are you always so ready to go home? Do we actually bore you that much?"

Marietta looked at her, surprised.

"It's just been a long week," she said. She felt her face flush.

"So what? What makes you think our week was any shorter? My boyfriend's just been shot, some people are trying to kill Beatrice's boyfriend, and you're worried about getting some rest?"

"It's just the stress of the situation, Bernadette, that's all," Del said quickly.

Bernadette shot him a glare.

"Okay, he was shot, and that's why I'm here. We know now, it's not like he's going to die," Marietta said. She glared back at her sister.

"Yeah, you're right. Maybe it's not like he's going to die, and it is like you don't give a hoot about anything that you can't wrap around your body or hang from your ears or arms, so yes, maybe you should go home. It's not like you've been much of anything to anybody in this family anyway since Nita died, so you should leave. Why don't you just get up and go the fuck on home!"

"Bernadette!" Alaina said shocked.

"That is not true, Bernadette!" Marietta said then, and Del said to her, "She's under stress too, Mari. Let's not carry this on."

"Not true?" Bernadette repeated. "What have you done for us, Marietta. Made us fill out pieces of paper pledging that we would always be there for each other, promising all we would do to make Nita proud, and what have you done? Run and never looked back to Baltimore the minute you got away, like we don't mean a thing to you! Well, if we don't, stop pretending. I'm doing fine. I will make it with or without help from you, and as long as there is breath in my body, Beatrice and Toukie will make it. Whatever they need, they know they can depend on me. Who can depend on you? Just like your father when the going gets rough, you get out and don't look back. So please, don't let what happened to my boyfriend stop you from getting your almighty rest!"

Marietta's fatigue disappeared and her head popped up like she'd been slapped. She felt the tears welling.

"I've been much more to this family than you'll ever be," she shot back. "I took care of everybody while Mama earned the money, that's including you when you were a little snot nosed brat. So, don't tell me I didn't do my part!"

"If you did your part so well," Bernadette said, her voice strained with emotion, "then why is my sister dead? You were taking care of us? How did she end up in a grave, and Beatrice end up in the streets? Why weren't you there when Nita needed you?"

Marietta shot upward, the pain was so acute. She blinked, and the tears rolled down her cheeks.

"Bernadette, come on now," Alaina said, her tone disapproving, but Marietta stood over Bernadette.

"I was AWAY in the Navy. I wasn't even here when she died!"

"Yes, and how convenient for you! You weren't there for Juanita, you were never there for me, and even though I asked you to help Beatrice and especially Toukie while I was overseas, you weren't there for them either. So, what's there to defend? You don't give a damn, you want to go home, GO!"

Marietta whipped around and grabbed her purse from the chair, then her coat. She felt Del's arm around her shoulder, pulling at her, but she leaned over Bernadette and pointed, her finger stabbing the air, "You'll never know what I had to go through in that house to protect you and everybody. Never! And I hope you never do!" She turned abruptly and marched ahead toward the exit.

"Come on, Del, it's time for us to go!" she hollered over her shoulder.

Marietta was marching blindly, her eyes so full of water, she couldn't see but she had an idea where the door was. As she got closer there was a blinding flurry of white flakes swimming outside of the glass doors. She heard Del behind her, and in the distance, Bernadette was still saying something but she didn't want to know what. At the door Del caught up and so did Alaina.

"Please, Marietta! I'm sure she didn't mean those things. You know how it is when families get emotionally charged."

"You don't have to worry about me, Alaina. "

"I do. I don't like what's going on in this family, and I know less than anybody because Corey doesn't know what goes on between the sisters, but it shouldn't be this way. This is about more than Reggie getting shot. Can't you see that Bernadette is hurting?"

"If all you can see is Bernadette hurting, I don't think we can have this conversation. I need to get away." Marietta pushed through the door, and Del called out to her. Alaina followed.

"Marietta, you're obviously hurting too. I see it, but it all stems from years ago. Maybe the day your sister died. What happened? Why don't you and Bernadette resolve to get to the bottom of it? She's angry. You're hurt. What hurts you so? What is it that's going on inside you?"

Marietta paused to glare at her. "Thank you, Dr. Joyce Brothers, but I'm not ready for your analysis."

She reached for Del's arm and left Alaina standing there.

******

Marietta ignored Del slamming the bedroom door behind them, rattling Bernadette's pom-poms and wall hangings. She marched over to the closet, yanked out her suitcase, and threw it on the bed. Then she sat down on the edge. Del hadn't said a good two words to her in the cab, so she knew she was in for it now.

He walked over, stopped in front of her and in a surprisingly calm voice said, "Okay, Mari. Come out with it. Now's the time."

"With what?" she said, her eyes still red from crying all the way from the hospital.

"Whatever you're hiding. You've been trying too long, and it's not working. If something bad happened to you here, just tell me. You left, and never told anybody how you suffered, but it's time. You may not want anybody to know things were not normal for you here, but let me tell you, I think they know. We all may not know what happened, but we know something happened to you, and it involved your father and maybe your dead sister. Just tell me, why are you hiding it? Because your mother wants you to? I don't know, but it's time to come clean."

"Nobody knows anything because nothing happened. I can't believe that Bernadette! I never deserted any one of them! I came home and brought this family together after it threatened to fall completely apart when Juanita died. I made the arrangements, I was the peacemaker when my father wanted to attend Nita's funeral and my mother didn't want to see him. I was the one that made my sisters sit their fast asses down and make Nita proud. I got them all to get a grip, and not one of them has any idea of the stress I was under while doing it."

"I'm not talking about Bernadette. I'm talking about you. What did your father do to you? He left years before Nita died, but why? Tell me."

"Nothing! He did nothing to me." She looked over at the window.

"I think you need to stop pretending. It's not okay. Whatever you may have done to make it through the years helped you this far, but you don't need to anymore. I love you Mari. I love you, and I know you're hiding something from me. Bernadette knows it. Probably your sister who had the party knows it. They know you. They don't understand that you're not running from them because you don't care. It's because you do. And you need to face it now, whatever it is. I'm going to be here for you after you tell me."

Marietta covered her face surprised that more tears were falling.

Del sat beside her and pulled her in his arms.

"Sweetheart, was it rape?"

"My father would never do something like that."

Del said nothing, holding his arms around her.

"Okay, so what did he do?"

"Del, if I could just talk about it, I would have. If it were as simple as just telling someone, I could have. But it isn't. I made promises to my mother. I have to do it this way."

"Do what? There's nothing so great about being a martyr if it's killing you in the process. Look at everybody else, your brother Corey is doing fine with his family. He's not carrying on the weight of the world. Your sister Bernadette is doing fine, and she's going to do fine, no matter what. She's not carrying on the weight of the world and she wouldn't. Your sister Beatrice seems to be doing quite well, so who are you protecting? Juanita is dead. What has you so scared?"

"It's two different things, what happened to Juanita and what happened before." Marietta looked down at her hands together in her lap, her head leaned against Del's shoulder.

"You meet somebody, you fall in love with them and you never think about how what happened in your life is going to hurt them," Marietta whispered.

"Hurt me? Sweetheart, you can't hurt me."

"Del, don't sound so stupid. If I didn't know what I was saying, it wouldn't be hard for me." Marietta pushed away from him and stood up in the cramped little bedroom. Del watched her.

"Mama and Daddy broke up because of me. No, he didn't rape me, but it was a situation that I promised Mama I would not tell out of respect for her. Nobody else knew. The thing with Juanita came later, and did it's own damage.

When Juanita got pregnant, naturally my sisters were really scared. My mother was very tough on us and threatened that if we were ever grown enough to lay down with boys and get pregnant, she would pack us up to stay with them, and we believed her. So, when Nita got pregnant, they didn't tell her.

"They wrote me, but I had been in the Navy for only two years and I just couldn't leave at that particular time. I told them that Mama wouldn't throw anybody out if they told her. The next letter said they handled it, and I thought abortion. Okay. But then, a couple months later I get the news Nita was dead."

"Beatrice must have blamed me for not coming home soon enough, and hated me ever since. I didn't want any more problems. I did what I could to make Berni and Beatrice promise to do what they had to do to take care of themselves, and they did. And that other thing…they don't even know why Mama and Daddy broke up, and it's just as well."

"You can't expect to hold on to something that happened between them, especially if it's tearing you apart! Does your mother know how it bothers you? Well, I do! And you can't do it anymore, Marietta. Why did you have to go to Johns Hopkins Hospital? Is it related to all this?"

"I told you that call was a mistake. It wasn't for me, it was for Mama."

"You can't keep lying to me, Marietta. Whatever it is, I'm going to find out sooner or later."

"It's not a lie. What I'm doing, I do it for Mama."

"Then why did you say something about the past hurting me?"

"Because the skeletons of the past are shifting. I don't know which ones will rattle loose and destroy everything. And," she added quietly, "There are some pretty big ones."

"Well, I'm not going to marry you until I understand what's haunting you. If you can hold it for years, why can't I help you? You say it's not rape, then what can be worse? I need you to trust me so that I'm in it with you, Mari. I love you."

"And I'm not ready, Del."

"Okay. Then I'll tell you what. I'm going to call a shuttle to the airport and I'm going home. You stay here and you get with your mother and you make her understand that you can't keep this up any longer because you can't. If I stay here, I'm going to tell her. It's killing you Mari, and for what? Your mother can handle herself and anything else just fine. And if you want to know the truth, your sisters are all grown up, and the truth, whatever it is will be something they can handle just fine. You have to believe it, and until you do, everything is on hold."

Marietta watched him walk out the room and stomp down the steps. In seconds, she could hear him on the phone with Baltimore Washington Airport scheduling a flight. She fell across the bed and closed her eyes.

He'd never understand, she knew he wouldn't. As much as she loved him, she could see marriage to him would never work. It just would not work.

******

The quiet in Mama's house that evening was unsettling as they assembled in the dining room to eat. Mama hustled back and forth bringing bowls of steaming hot food to place before them. She had fixed another veritable feast: smoked turkey, cabbage, corn pudding, yams, potato salad, rolls, and sweet potato pie.

Reggie seemed none the worse for the wear. He was quieter, his eyes were red and thick-lidded, which let Bernadette know his experience wasn't completely painless, but he cracked jokes whenever Corey mentioned the shot he took in the neck, and did everything for himself with one hand since they'd immobilized his right arm.

The surprise was that Del "had to leave in a hurry," as Marietta explained. Bernadette was disappointed because she liked him, a lot.

Marietta could have done worse. She tried to read Marietta's face, but it was absolutely expressionless. There must have been a fight between them, Bernadette reasoned, staring at her sister's red eyes. Or was she still mad over their argument in the hospital?

She sipped the strong, sweet lemon tea her mother had made as the conversation slowly wound its way to Witt.

"Who tried to kill him?" Alaina asked. Bernadette stayed quiet.

"Bad business deal, " Corey said. "He had money in a business account with someone whose girlfriend stole it, and they said Witt put out a reward for information on her. Her brothers took it as a contract on her, and came to take care of him."

"To kill him?" Marietta asked, horrified.

"Guess it depends on who you do business with," Corey said, taking a heaping forkful of cabbage into his mouth. "He talked about a lot of business ventures he wants to get into. He has some big plans."

"He must be doing something right. Their house looked wonderful," Alaina said.

"He made some deals selling houses back to the city," Corey said.

"He's pretty good with music, too. He really has a nice collection," Reggie said. I appreciated it."

"He seems like a nice guy. And an awfully proud father. All he talked about was his son," Alaina remarked.

"Oh, definitely," both Corey and Reggie agreed.

"He talked about that boy like he was the next Muhammad Ali, Michael Jordan, Tiger Woods or somebody. He's only a year old, isn't he?" Alaina asked.

"Two, by now," Bernadette answered. "And he is really cute, but Witt is over the top when it comes to him, and most other things."

When no one said anything to her comment, Bernadette sighed.

"Is everybody going to tell me they didn't pick up anything unusual about Witt?"

When they faltered, Marietta said, "I think I know what you mean, Bernadette. I got the impression that, although Witt was there at the party, he didn't really approve. The way he dressed down, the way he stayed in the basement out of the way. I mean, it was Beatrice's birthday and everybody was giving her congratulations and when they sang happy birthday, and she opened the presents, everybody was there but Witt."

"He was playing the music! He was doing his part," Reggie said.

"And he probably had wished her happy birthday before the party," Corey added, and they all laughed.

"No, Witt makes a statement," Marietta said. "And I get the impression he's pretty strict. Like, he likes things a certain way, and that's it. I made a comment to him about keeping such a stylish house up with two children living there, and he said something about them knowing where they belong and staying there."

"There you go," Bernadette said, slapping the table. "He puts everybody in a place."

"What's new about that?" Corey asked. "You do have to let children know boundaries."

"But it's not just children," Bernadette said. "Let a woman talk to him, and you'll find that out."

"Everybody started to talk at once until Corey's point broke through, "I think the thing is, Witt is taking care of his family and he's taking care of business. He adores Beatrice, and he obsesses over the children. He's a family man."

"He obsesses, Corey," Bernadette said, "and he obsesses over one of the children. The picture of Witt is full of holes. Doesn't anybody else see that? He isn't what he seems."

The men started talking at her at once, defending Witt, and Bernadette thought seriously about bringing up what he said during their dance, but before she could, Alaina broke in.

"Well, until Reggie got shot, I thought it was a great party. Good company, good food, good music. And the only thing I still don't understand is what Beatrice wanted so desperately to tell us about something she discovered. I wished she had finished explaining what it was she wanted to say."

"Oh, yeah," they chorused in agreement. All except Marietta.

The talk turned once again to the magnitude of the work Witt had done on the house, designing the renovations and his other personal handy work.

As they cleaned up after dinner, Bernadette noticed how much snow had fallen. She went to stand by the kitchen window, the warm air from the floor vent blowing heat around her ankles. It looked like something from a Christmas card the way the snow now covered everything, coming down quite heavily and sticking. She felt a nervous churn in her stomach as she looked out the window thinking of Beatrice. Beatrice should be here with them. She needed to tell her what she knew and find out what Bea wanted them to know. She had called Beatrice right before their dinner to invite her and Witt over, but no one answered the phone. Something was not right, no matter what her family thought.

She jumped when she felt a tickle on her neck, and tried to turn, but Reggie's body pushed her up against the door. She felt his luscious lips on the back of her neck as his arm wrapped around her. Awkwardly, he pulled her around to face him.

"What are you thinking?"

"It's snowing kind of hard."

Reggie looked out and frowned. "It's deep, too, isn't it? And you know what? I'm going to be leaving tonight."

Bernadette turned quickly. "Not tonight, Reggie! Give yourself a chance to heal a little. Besides, the weather is too bad."

"Yep, tonight. I told my mother I was over this way, and she made me promise to come home before I went back west. I told her all about you. She knows I had to see you first."

Bernadette looked him in the eye.

"Reggie, this doesn't have anything to do with what happened at Bea's does it? I mean, you have every right to be, but you aren't mad at me, are you?"

He laughed.

"Of course not. My mother got everybody waiting down there to see me. You know I told you how big my family is."

He had five brothers and four sisters.

"They're all waiting for you?"

"Not at one time, but they're down there. You know I can't disappoint Rachel Delores Taylor. You got to meet my mother to understand."

"Looking forward to it," Bernadette said seriously. She slid her arms around his waist.

"I called a cab. They said they're still running trains south, so I got to get myself to Amtrak in the next hour or so."

"You made reservations and everything without telling me?"

"I wanted to tell you. I wanted to tell you so many things last night, Bernadette. I wanted to tell you why I took some leave for myself to go up to LA. How I handed over some songs I wrote, that I thought were good, and think I might have a sale on two. How I've been working real hard to get myself out after my four years, so you and I can stop running and looking over our shoulders when I want to see you."

Bernadette studied his eyes closely.

"Are you for real?"

"Why would I lie?"

"And you let me sit around since yesterday, not knowing that things are about to take off for you, while you had all this good stuff going on?"

"Baby, we have so much catching up to do. "

"Reggie! You should have told me this sooner. What songs? I didn't know you wrote songs. Can I see them? Any of them about me?"

"Well, look. This is what I was thinking about. How long you plan to hang around in here anyway? The party is over."

She thought a second. "I have a whole month's leave. I don't have to stay here the whole time."

"Good, come home with me tonight. Just grab a little bag and come on. You can come back."

"Home with you?" She looked at him like he was speaking Greek.

"Yeah, to Marion, South Carolina. Come meet my family."

She stared at him. She wanted to. Oh God, she wanted to. She wanted to leave this craziness, to let Bea take care of Witt herself, to meet Daddy later after things had all calmed down. She wanted to figure out if they were all safe now. She wanted to tell him what Colonel Chisholm had done, she wanted Reggie's love, and needed his support. She wanted them to straighten out their thing together, to figure out their options, to hear him some more. To feel him some more. She had been waiting for this. But she knew, she had to act on her family's behalf now. With all her family here, she had to lay her suspicions to rest now. She could never do it once they all went back home. And she had wanted to do this, for a long time.

"You know you promised me something when I first came here, and you still haven't delivered."

"You got shot, fool!" she laughed and pretended to punch him.

"That's okay. That had nothing to do with where I was shot."

They laughed together.

"No really, Berni-- I like the way Marietta calls you that-- why don't you spend some time with me? I know you're worrying about your sister, and your niece and everybody, but aside from Toukie, these people are grown, Bernadette. Beatrice is your big sister, she's older than you are, and she can handle herself, baby. She got her family and everybody got their family, and I need you. I haven't seen you or been with you in a long time."

"I know, Reggie. Believe me I do, but it's just not that simple." People just don't go in a house and shoot at the owners for no reason. The answers were about to come now, and she had to be there. It was her job to understand why Nita had died, why Danny had died, and just what the hell was still going on with her father. That's why when things happened in families, everybody wanted to point fingers at everybody else because no one picked up on the signs. What if something happened, after all the clues she now had?

"I'm asking just for a couple of days. It's been over a year, Bernadette."

"Sweetheart, I know that." She pulled away. "I'm so sorry about this, Reggie. I get you here and Beatrice and Witt get you shot…"

"It wasn't her fault."

"I feel so bad."

"Then come home with me."

"Reggie, don't pressure me. I can't go now. I know we need to talk, but baby, we waited a year. I'm sure if you really wanted to contact me during that time I was away, you could have at least called one time. I tried calling you. I'm back, you're back, and we still like each other. Let's not act like this visit to your mother is now or never."

He looked surprised. "Whoa. How many times did you call me? If talking to me really mattered to you?"

"At least I did call. You never called me back. The letters were returned. Okay, but you just decided to sit back and wait for me. Now, I'm telling you my family is going through a crisis, and I'm only asking you to wait just a little longer."

"And I'm asking you why I have to? Why can't they wait? Why can't you come with me now, and come back to them later?"

"Because I don't know if I will be able to do anything if I wait."

"Like what? What's going on here?"

"I'll tell you, Reggie. I promise, I'll tell you. But I can't now."

"Nothing changes with you. The crust of cold is still there, keeping everybody away. You say you want me, you want us to take off, enjoy life together. But that's not how you act and it never has been. So, just tell me. Do you want me, Bernadette, or not?"

Bernadette looked at him. "Of course! I'm saying not right now, not no Reggie--"

"Okay, cool. I understand. I think I really do." He took a step back, turned away and went downstairs.

Bernadette started after him, but stopped. Why was he so pissed? What else could she do? Reggie didn't know everything, and she couldn't tell him yet, but she would. She wanted him to understand, to see why she had to sacrifice her own happiness. When she told him, she hoped he would. She heard him downstairs moving around and considered going down to say more, but what? She wasn't prepared to start from the beginning and talk about her father and the kind of life they had. She wanted to go down and try, but she kept thinking 'what will I say?'

Soon he was back with his bag in hand and looking at her. She went over and reached for his free arm.

"Reggie, this doesn't mean no. If it wasn't so personal, and if I wasn't in the middle of it…"

"Well, do me a favor, Bernadette. Why don't you call me when I get as important to you as Toukie and Beatrice and everybody else, okay?"

He pulled away and she watched incredulously as he banged through the French doors and away from her. She heard him in the living room thanking Mama and bidding everybody goodbye. She went in the living room with him, and stood quietly until in minutes it seemed, the doorbell rang and there was the yellow cab, ready to get Reggie to Amtrak on time.

Then Reggie was gone.

## twenty-one

Bernadette sat quietly in her bedroom asking herself what happened. What had she done wrong? She loved Reggie, it wasn't supposed to end. But she couldn't stop going after the secret, not when she was so close.

Why did Reggie take it so hard? Sure she'd wanted to go to the Sheraton last night as much as he did, but he got shot! Sure she would love to meet his family, if things were different. But they weren't.

Suddenly, Bernadette sat up straighter. She thought back to her meeting with Major Whitaker, when she mentioned having sent Bernadette a short note about Colonel Chisholm's charges. She said the letter was returned to her. Just as Reggie had said the letters he sent were returned to him.

Their letters were sent from the base. Could this mail foul up have been deliberate? Would that be something Colonel Chisholm had a hand in, along with everything else? How did he manage to thwart her mail? And if he did, how could she prove it?

The hard raps on her door disrupted her thoughts.

"Come in!"

Alaina stepped in, a little smile on her face that Bernadette noticed without acknowledging. She laid back down on the pillows on her bed waiting. She had been upstairs in her bedroom since Reggie left, trying to hide her pain. She wasn't in the mood for Alaina, or any of them, at least not sober.

"I know somebody is feeling a little blue. I overheard just a teensy bit when you were going at it in the kitchen and I wanted you to know, things aren't as bad as they seem. He'll get over it because it's clear he adores you."

Bernadette frowned, wishing Alaina would disappear.

"Thanks, but you don't understand what's going on in my life, so let's just leave it at that."

"I understand more than you think. I know you were worried about Toukie, so I did contact them at home. Everyone there is fine. As well as can be expected."

Bernadette sat up. "Really? Bea's okay then? Where was she?"

"She said she took her children and stayed with a girlfriend until Witt came home from the police station."

Bernadette sighed with relief.

"And, Bernadette," Alaina picked her words carefully moving further inside the bedroom. " I have more good news for you." Alaina's face was all aglow, beaming with pride. Bernadette immediately grew suspicious.

"Guess who just called me?"

Bernadette waited, looking at her. Who on earth did she know that Alaina knew?

"I haven't the slightest."

"Your father!" She could barely contain her excitement, clasping her hands together.

There was a pause. "Called you where?"

"Here."

"Here?" Bernadette's voice rose. "At my mother's house? He called for you here? You gave him my mother's phone number?"

"No! Call forwarding. He actually called my number, and it was forwarded here. He doesn't have your mother's number at all."

"What did he call for?"

"Because I asked him to! He is your father. Just because he and your mother didn't make it as a married couple doesn't mean he shouldn't know what's going on in your lives. It doesn't mean he shouldn't know his grandchildren."

"Don't you think if he really wanted to know about us, Alaina, he would?"

Alaina hardly missed a beat. "To be truthful, yes. But I think it's more important that you talk about it with him. He needs to know what it meant to your family that he wasn't with you. I think as a group you should all tell him, and stop just hating him and each other because he wasn't there."

Bernadette felt the tiny hairs on the back of her neck rise.

"Who asked you what you think?" Bernadette snapped. She rose up from the bed and glared at Alaina. What did she think she was doing?

Daddy was hers to find. It was her decision what to do after she found him. She didn't want Alaina in the middle of something so important, running interference.

"Right now you guys are hurting," Alaina answered. "You can't be objective about this, but I can. I just wanted to open the door in case anybody wanted to go through. I think it's time to grow up and put this all behind you." She passed Bernadette a small card with a phone number and no name.

"If you're curious, you'll use it. If not, you won't." Alaina turned and left the room leaving Bernadette so angry, she was nearly shaking.

Did Alaina actually think she could waltz in, say something like that and walk away? Bernadette shot out the room behind her, hot on Alaina's heels. When Alaina got downstairs and stepped into the kitchen, Bernadette was a step behind. Alaina actually jumped, then backed away when she saw Bernadette's face. Bernadette was breathing hard just thinking of Alaina's nerve.

Corey and Marietta's voices fell away as they looked up at the two women.

"Where's Mama?" Bernadette asked first, and it was Marietta who quietly said she had gone to bed. Then Bernadette started, pointing to Alaina's chest.

"Do you know what she did?" Before either could answer, she continued. "She got in touch with Daddy!"

Marietta drew in a shocked breath, while Corey looked at Bernadette, then Alaina.

"Did you know about this, Corey? Did you know she found Daddy without asking us, and had him call here?" Bernadette demanded.

Corey threw both hands up in a defensive gesture. "No, I didn't."

"Well, that's what she just told me! And she gave me his phone number." Bernadette slammed the card on the table. Alaina stood by the counter, her proud shoulders back, chin up.

"Yes, that's what I did," she said in response to their shocked faces.

"But who asked you to, Alaina?" Bernadette nearly screamed.

"No one. I watched you and your sister going at each other in the hospital and it was quite evident that both of you are fighting each other instead of dealing with the cause of your anger."

"What do you know about what happened to us?" Marietta asked suddenly, her expression frozen. "If it was easy enough for you to find him, don't you think, if we wanted to, we would have?"

Before Alaina could respond, Corey got up and stood beside his wife. "Wait a minute. Let's not get bent completely out of shape."

"Why not?" Bernadette fired back. "It's not her father and nobody asked her to do a thing! If Marietta and I want to fight over stuff that happened years ago, we have every right to do it without somebody deciding we have to handle it their way!"

"Absolutely," Marietta said then, her eyes boring holes through Alaina. " If you really wanted to be helpful, why didn't you ask us if that was something we wanted to do?  We're not your 5th grade class, and if you must know, where my father is now is not news to me. I've had that information for some time and haven't acted on it. I haven't wanted to, and I think it's presumptuous of you to step in and take over something that you have no emotional investment in. You don't know what can of worms you may be opening."

"Well, wait for a second ladies, please!"  Corey's voice was loud enough to stop them  and they all paused to look at him. "Let's get this in perspective. What's done is done, and if you stop and think about it, maybe Alaina has a point. She just gave you the number; she didn't say anything about setting you up with him. We haven't seen Daddy in years. We don't know him. We don't even know why we don't know him. It may be time to see why he isn't a part of our lives."

"Why Corey?" Marietta asked. "Does that really make sense to you? Did he come searching for you?  There are some things that aren't worth pursuing. You know that. You pick your battles, and is this one worth it? Why introduce something that Mama obviously decided years ago we should leave alone. It was her decision."

"Battle? I'm not finding him to fight about anything. I was just wondering if maybe we're wrong."

"What if we're not?" Marietta asked. "Suppose you feel worse after you contact him?  What if you find out Mama had a point in cutting him out, and you hate him for something he did?  She wouldn't have put him out and raised us alone if she had no reason. It couldn't have been easy working 12 hours a day and putting up with us. She did it, she did her best, and she did it out of love. If it wasn't easy, and she chose to go that route, what makes you think she didn't have a damn good reason?" Marietta demanded.

Bernadette had quietly watched the exchange between Marietta and her brother. Whew! She was surprised that Marietta had that much fire in her about Daddy.

"And I'm sure Mama did have a damn good reason," Corey answered. "But that was her fight. I respect her for it, but now, I'm thinking that maybe it's time to see if it's our fight, too. Maybe it isn't. Who knows?"

"Well, before you decide, I can answer some questions. Maybe it'll be all you need to know," Marietta said, and looked him in the eye.

Corey paused, as did Bernadette.

"Like what?" he asked.

"Well, when Bernadette wrote me to check up on Beatrice a while ago, she said that Witt was interested in joining an influential business club that Daddy also belonged to, and I did check into it, and there is no way that Witt will even smell the air that surrounds the building where they meet. It's all money, and yes, the members are all black, but they're not likely to cross our paths. Witt wants to believe he has enough money, and maybe he does have some. But it's nothing like what he's going to need.

"So, I didn't ignore you, Berni. I never would. And using what you gave me, I found out all the other facts about the man that you should know."

Marietta crossed her arms very deliberately and turned her eyes from Corey to Alaina.

"He lives in Columbia, Maryland and has a wife who has two kids of her own, girls, over 20, and living on their own. Daddy comes right here in town. He's a freelance journalist and does a bit for the Afro-American on Charles Street, but his work can be found in many major publications, national and international, and he's doing quite well in his career. Even with all his success, he hasn't looked any of us up, so I can't imagine why we should go looking for him."

"Because it's time, Marietta. It just may be our time," Corey said, and looked at Bernadette. "Think about it, Bernadette. What do you have to lose? You can find out what's going on with him now, and maybe we can put it behind us."

Bernadette, her back against the refrigerator door, listened closely to her sister's words. Her anger had changed into something that tingled in her chest and in her hands and feet. She stood still thinking about Corey's words.

"It's kind of funny," she answered him, after a couple of seconds. "I'm surprised to even consider this, but all I know is I want to hate that man. I'm mad with him, and I'm not so sure why I shouldn't be. I don't remember seeing him at any of the funerals, or ever hearing from him. He never sent me a birthday card or a graduation card. He never saw me cry the night before I left for the Marines. Never saw my tears. He acted like I wasn't here, so I feel I have a right to be mad about that, but then, why did he do it? You know Mama wouldn't let me ask her anything; she never wanted to talk about it. And I don't know why."

"Are you two crazy?" Marietta asked standing up. "I think you two are heading right into trouble. Trouble Mama didn't want you involved in. I respect Mama, and I don't want to get involved. I know you're making a mistake if you do. But I can see it'll be hard to convince you two of it."

Bernadette frowned. Marietta's face was as red as the sweater she had on. She was trembling from head to foot. With what? Fear? Anger?

"So, before you do this," Marietta continued in a quivering voice, "think about how many years it took Mama to keep the split and what you may be uncovering if you seek him out! Think about what you're doing!" Marietta spun around and left them.

They heard her run up the steps before anybody spoke, and this time it was Alaina.

"She's right, I am just a fifth grade teacher, but it doesn't take a mastermind to see that something is really wrong here. Just look at Marietta. Why can't Corey contact his father if he wants to? I don't see what's the big deal. If she gives him a chance and finds she never wants to speak to him again, she doesn't have to."

"Does that mean you'll call him, Corey?" Bernadette asked.

Corey's face was full of concern, and he slipped his hands in his pockets.

"Damndest thing, I never thought of just doing it, but...now that I know he doesn't mind...I will. I'll talk to him."

"He really wants to talk to you," Alaina said.

"Why don't we all go see him?" Corey eyed Bernadette. "You, me, Beatrice. I don't think we'll change Marietta's mind. Let the three of us find out everything together."

"When?"

"I'll find out. I'll call him tonight and if he can see us tomorrow, then we'll get together, if you want to."

Bernadette nodded dumbly. The fight wasn't just between Mama and

Daddy. It was Marietta and Daddy. Of that she was sure. She wouldn't miss this meeting for the world.

******

Larry's Café was brightly lit, and crowded, with a post-Meyerhoff concert crowd. Judging from the state of dress, Bernadette guessed it had been an opera or a symphony of some sort, and she felt ill at ease as she sat rigidly across from Corey, waiting for their father, who was already 10 minutes late. Things had moved fast. Corey called him, and right away he agreed to meet them--not the next day, not the next week, not a minute more, but the same evening, with a good five or six inches of snow on the ground. He came up with the coffee shop idea, which they had agreed to. But getting the others to go with them had not been easy.

Beatrice turned them down flat, sounding very fatigued. She said as much as she wanted to be there, she had something else very important to take care of. Bernadette scoffed at that when Corey told her. Meeting Daddy was the only thing Beatrice ever talked about, how she needed to see him again. But she left it alone. No surprise, it was down to her and Corey.

They'd been quietly waiting but now Bernadette was beginning to twitch with nerves. Corey had a cup of black coffee sitting in front of him that he sipped while intermittently staring at the black, green and white tiles covering the floor and the walls. Bernadette watched him and noticed the many pictures of entertainers that lined the walls all around them. She had hot tea and a slice of apple pie before her that she couldn't touch. She couldn't digest anything. She was actually feeling sick to her stomach, the kind of sick she'd felt all during Marine boot camp. It was the kind of sick that she felt when something bad was happening that she couldn't avoid.

"I can't believe we're doing this either," Corey said, looking at her with amusement.

"Oh, I can believe it. That's the trouble," she said, and he reached over and put his hand on hers.

Corey seemed happily excited, like he was about to go on a trip or something. His emotions were not as mixed as hers. Bernadette felt scared and started to chastise Corey for showing his obvious joy, but decided to leave it alone. It was enough that he kept Ms. Busybody Alaina, who had wanted to come, home.

"Got it all under control, don't you, Core?"

He gave her his adorable, full press smile.

"You know me. You ever seen 007 sweat?"

She laughed with him, and then, much too quickly, she looked up and saw a man heading toward them. Her eyes locked on him. As Corey turned his head, following Bernadette's eyes, he rose slowly. Bernadette couldn't believe it. Her father's face was as familiar as if she had been seeing him everyday.

"Corey?" he asked cautiously, and suddenly the two men were hugging warmly, faces all smiles as he patted Corey's shoulder several times. Bernadette stared at the hand that patted Corey, and noticed all he wore was a silver and diamond wedding band. It was eye-catching in an understated way, and clearly matched his silver and diamond Rolex. What could this man say to make it all okay?

"Bernadette?" he said after several minutes of greetings with Corey.

She stuck out her hand and he shook it, looking intensely at her.

"My God!" he exclaimed still standing. "You turned out to be a gorgeous young woman."

"Please have a seat, Daddy," she said somewhat coolly. She didn't need to hear a bunch of compliments that, coming from him at this late date, meant little. She had too much hurt and too many questions.

Her father took off his hat and a shearling jacket. He slid down into the narrow iron seat between Corey on the left, and Bernadette on the right, then turned to stare at his son. Bernadette turned to stare at him.

"You look like me," he remarked to Corey with a sense of pride. "Like I turned back the clock and looked in the mirror. Your mother did a fine job with you children—just look at you."

"It's good to see you, Dad," Corey said, his piercing eyes examining his father closely. "I didn't expect to ever be able to say that to you."

Bernadette glanced away from her father a minute, feeling her heartbeat quicken. She was glad to see him. Why didn't she feel mad? It was hard to believe she had him right here. She could ask him anything. She could find out everything.

"This meeting is way overdue," her father said, and paused to look at his daughter. He produced a handkerchief that he used to mop at the sweat that had popped up all over his face and head. Nervous, was he, Bernadette thought watching. He had no idea how nervous he was going to get.

"So, how have you been doing?" Corey asked, and Bernadette cut her eyes to Corey. Who gave a shit? The question was, WHERE had he been? she thought.

"It's funny you ask," he answered and gave a slight laugh. "You've all been on my mind a lot lately."

Bernadette stopped looking at him to stare at the fork beside her plate of pie. She pursed her lips at his words. Lately?

"I've been doing all right, Corey, better at some times than others. But I want to know about you two. Tell me, what have you been doing? Fill me in."

The waiter, a tall man with a swishy walk who kept staring at Corey came by to see if Daddy wanted anything. Corey asked his father to take a cup of coffee, which he did.

"Well, it's been a long road," Corey answered. "I guess you could figure that much--what it must have been like for the family without you."

"If you cared to think," Bernadette interjected. "Or even bothered to look behind you once you left us. I'm surprised you feel the need to know now."

"Then you don't know me very well."

"How could I? You left when I was four."

"And believe me, it wasn't because I wanted to go," he said staring directly at Bernadette. "I didn't want to, and when I had to, I missed every one of you something terrible. I'm so amazed that you called me now. I didn't think any of you would ever come to me, or that I would ever see you like this again."

"Why? Did you ever try to contact us?" Bernadette asked and watched her father squirm.

After a moment, he said, "Things can get out of control so fast. You end up doing something you never wanted or planned to do. Right now, you're still so young. You can't imagine anything stepping in and turning your life upside down, but it can happen. I certainly never planned to leave you. In fact, if it were up to me, I wouldn't have. I left because I dug myself into a hole and at that time, there was no other way."

"Wait, Dad," Corey said, giving Bernadette a sharp look before she could say anything. "I know things happen, things you don't plan for. I have four kids myself, and I know how things pop up and turn you around. But I can tell you, no matter what happens, I'm going to be there for them. No matter what happens between Alaina and me, those kids are still going to know me. Nothing would make me change that. We were yours. We would have appreciated hearing a word from you sometime. Look at us now. We're all grown. Bernadette is the baby, and she's got to be pushing thirty."

"I just turned 29, thank you," she said.

"And the rest of us, we're all getting old, Dad. We spent a lot of years without you."

"It was never my idea. I gave in to everything at the time because I thought it would be better for everybody. I did whatever your mother asked, but I never should have! I made my mistakes, but, in hindsight, I wouldn't have left."

"Why do you say that?" Bernadette asked sharply. He was plucking her last nerve with the pity act. He'd made a whole life without them, and he knew he did. What was this act for?

"Nobody put a gun to your head to keep you away," she continued. "Even if Mama told you not to come near us, I can't believe you wouldn't show up at all. Like birthdays, and weddings, graduations and funerals. Those are things you just don't decide not to attend."

"Bernadette, I was at the funerals."

"Oh, I forgot, you had to have your own ceremony apart from us."

Her father said nothing.

"I have to know," Bernadette said then, throwing up her hands and shaking her head. "I just have to know, is there a ring that you used to wear years ago, that represented a business club you were in?"

Her father met her eyes.

"No."

"You don't have a ring made like a thick, gold rope with three diamonds in it?"

He squinted. She remembered that expression, and it gave her a warm feeling in her stomach to see it again. "I used to wear a ring like that. But it was years ago."

"What happened to it?"

"I don't know. The last time I had it was over my mother's house. I believe she asked me for it."

"So, do you know a man by the name of Witt? I believe his full name is Witt Coleman. He wears that ring now."

"No. That name doesn't ring a bell. Why would you think he has my ring?"

"I wouldn't, except he all but admitted knowing you. And he's been trying to join a club that you belong to, for black businessmen."

"Well, I never heard of him, number one. Number two, I'm not a member of a business club. So I don't know what he's telling you, but it isn't true."

Bernadette hesitated. "But I'm sure he knows you…what about the last name Coleman. Does that ring a bell?" She paused for a moment, and then added, "Charlene? What about a Charlene Coleman?"

Her father paused, his eyes staring off. "Charlene…Charlene…You know, there was a Charlene Coleman who worked for my mother, years ago. Yes, she had a sewing business, and could make anything. She did a lot of detailed work for my mother and her circle of friends for years, a lot of quilts. Yes, I do know a Charlene Coleman. And you think Witt has something to do with her?"

"What are you talking about?" Corey asked, and Bernadette held up a hand to silence him.

"Did you know this Charlene personally?"

"Charlene? No."

"And what about your mother. You said she worked with her. Did their working relationship end badly?"

Her father paused. "I don't know. Why? Why would you think that?"

"Well, about two years ago, I got a letter from somebody telling me my brother and sister did not just die, but were murdered. And that one of us, the surviving children, would be next."

"Somebody threatened you in writing? And you think I know something about it?"

"They knew some things about us that let me know it wasn't just a joke."

"I know nothing about anyone who would threaten you. You're saying you were actually threatened? And you went to the police?"

"I didn't. The letter was in the form of a riddle. It wasn't a clear threat, so I thought it would be hard to prove to the police my life was in danger."

"I'd like to see this letter," her father said, and Corey grunted and leaned forward. "You didn't even tell me?" he said. "I thought you were telling me everything."

"I have, now. I'm sorry, Corey. I shared this with Marietta and Beatrice because I thought it could be handled between us, but it never was."

"Well, where is the letter?"

"At Mama's house. And I'll gladly show it."

"Someone sent that to you only?" Corey asked.

"It seems."

"That's ridiculous," her father said, looking surprised. "Nobody was killed. It's just not true.

"I'm not so sure about that."

Her brother and father looked at her.

"What happened to little Michael Windsor, Daddy? What happened to the little baby, Michael Robert Windsor, that you and Mama had?"

Her father's lips parted wordlessly.

"I think I know more than you may believe. So, please be honest."

"He was stillborn. My first son was born dead."

Corey sat speechless.

"And no one ever mentioned him? How can you and Mama have a baby that died, and never tell us about him? There were seven of us? We were always told we were six."

"Well, it was the first year we were married. And your mother decided just as well that you all didn't know."

"I know nothing about my family that far back, but what I do know is three of us are dead, like the letter said, and three more will go. Until the letter, I didn't know three were dead. So, why shouldn't I believe the rest of the letter, that they were killed?"

"Because it's preposterous. No one would have reason to."

"How do you know that? It's like we came in this world against somebody's will, and that somebody still doesn't want us around."

"You were very much wanted. You know, Bernadette, the thing about life is this: it's all a surprise. You don't know what's in store, but you go for it with everything you have. You don't know what will hit you when you go around the corner, but you aren't afraid of turning corners all the same. You go out in the world, and you find love, you find hate, you find happiness, you find sorrow, and you don't know which one you'll find first. I loved your mother right off the bat, and it was something that just hit me. We couldn't have been more different, but I knew I wanted her to be mine. I just didn't realize how hard it would be for her."

"You left her," Bernadette reminded him. "You made it hard."

"She put me out. I spent my marriage to her building up everything for us. We came together at a time when it was good to be black. We'd been invisible for so long, then in the 70's, we were out front. Blacks everywhere were doing things, not just the few privileged with money."

He hesitated, and then went on. "Back then, it became vogue to get black reporters to share their own perspectives about their people in mainstream publications. Articles about black education, black middle class, black politicians and black corporations. Black life was in. And I started digging up stories. People were interested in how we got to be where we were, and I could tell them. Things escalated for us so fast, I lost control."

"So you did more writing than teaching?" Corey asked.

"I did a lot of both. I could ferret out anything, find all kinds of angles and facts. I dug and dug until I dug myself in a hole. Then it all backfired."

Bernadette sat expectantly beside Corey, who was on the edge of his seat, waiting. The silence stretched.

"What backfired?" She finally burst. "How did the digging and writing end the love you had for Mama and us?"

Her father shook his head, and took out a handkerchief, pressing carefully around his hairline.

"Well, you know, when that happened, it was impossible for me to walk in the circles where I had once been accepted, and do the same work. It was the greatest irony, because I was the one who opened that box."

Bernadette exchanged a look of confusion with Corey.

"You're losing me, Dad. What did happen?" Corey asked.

Their father looked at Corey, his eyes squinting. "Of course you know why your mother and I split up."

Corey stared blankly at him, as did Bernadette.

"Between your mother and me…she did tell you what happened?"

"Nobody ever did." Bernadette said, and studied him as he mopped at his head again. He shifted uncomfortably, very much like he was on a hot plate. He frowned, made a humph sound once, twice, then shook his head.

"All this time. You mean, you didn't know why I was even gone? This is a surprise."

"Why? Why did you think she would tell us? If it was so bad, why didn't you?"

"Because she said she wanted to. She said it would be better coming from her." Her father slumped in his seat.

"I agreed to go along with her, pretty much because of what I did. I didn't have a lot of say against anything she wanted. I willingly allowed your mother to handle the split as she saw fit, since she insisted any other way would traumatize you."

"What was it, Dad?" Corey shrugged, and Bernadette felt a grip of fear as she whispered, "Yes, what did you do?"

"It's…uh…one of those things that's hard to explain. When it happens, you're caught up in it, but afterward, there are no words to explain."

"Like another woman?" Bernadette asked.

"A little more to it than that. You were too young to understand, and I'm not sure you would now."

"I'd like to try."

"I'd like to tell you but it's something I probably couldn't explain if I tried."

Bernadette leaned back, feeling herself heat up with anger. After all this time they deserved an explanation, and it shouldn't even be an option. Then she thought of something.

"Would it be better if I asked Marietta to explain it?"

His reaction was immediate. His head jerked around, his eyes cutting over to her quickly, and she saw the color drain completely from his face.

"You okay?" Corey asked reaching for him. He handed him one of the glasses of water on the table, and her father took it and drank it all down. There were a couple seconds of silence after which her father cleared his throat. He mopped at his face again and avoided their eyes.

"Look," Corey moved his seat over to his father. He reached across to squeeze Bernadette's hand hard. "I didn't call you here to beat up on you, or to threaten you or try to make you feel bad. I can respect that you and Mom were different and had problems. But we want to help. I want to know what do you want to do with your family now? You still got us here, four of us anyway, and you got six grandchildren, four from me, two from Beatrice. What do you want to do, Dad?"

"I want to do what I always wanted. I want to be a part of my family."

"But, that's not true!" Bernadette interrupted. "We were right here, all the time, and you never tried to be a part. You stayed somewhere, rich, fat and happy. You got married again, and you let Mama struggle and raise us with no help, no money, no nothing from you."

"Bernadette, I don't know what you've been told, but you have it wrong about me. I put money into an account for each of you until you all turned 18. I never left your mother financially."

Bernadette looked at her brother, her mouth open.

"What happened to it?" Corey asked.

"Nothing. It's still there, as far as I know. Is this something else your mother never mentioned?"

Bernadette grew quiet when Corey took over then, saying how little they knew about everything, and how they had to start to make it up. Corey suddenly pulled out a card and said, "This is just a start, Dad, and I think we all need to go slow." He looked a little shaken as he spoke, his brows furrowed. Dad agreed to stop for now, and they made arrangements for the very next day. Bernadette bit back her words.

When she looked at her father, there was little doubt, he looked about as sorrowful as you could look, and she didn't miss how his eyes held hers in a pleading way. Why couldn't she be like Corey? Why couldn't she just give him the hug that she really wanted to feel? This nastiness wasn't making her feel better. Why couldn't she go ahead and cry, hug him and get it over with? She wiped at her eyes quickly when she realized to her horror what her dilemma was. She did love this man. This man she wanted to hate and had been told to hate. She loved every memory she had of him. But he had done a bad thing. A very bad thing, and though she didn't know what it was, she knew it was bad enough that he didn't want to say.

She was more than glad when it was time to go. Their half- filled cups sat cold on the table as they rose and put their coats and hats on. Bernadette laced her boots for the snow piles still on the ground and they left the café together. They said their goodbyes on the sidewalk and Bernadette watched her Dad walk down the street a little ways picking his steps over the tricky sidewalk in his neat little leather loafers. He climbed into a navy blue Lexus.

They got into Corey's Windstar Minivan and sat tight while Corey warmed it up.

At first neither of them spoke to each other until they saw the headlights of their father's car pull out and move past. Then Bernadette gave a loud, long sigh and said, "What on earth made you stop and let him leave? There is something really wrong here. A big, fat, secret, and we were so close. Didn't you feel it?"

Corey looked at her incredulously. "What do you expect, Bernadette? A theme song to start and a cue from Oprah to kiss, hug and confess? I don't know about you, girl, but I look at it like this: The past was between him and Mama. As far as I'm concerned, it's over, and whatever it was, let it go. It's not helping now."

"But you don't know what the past was. Remember when he left Mama, he left us too! I'm so sorry I'm not with that, 'Oh, it's so good to have my father back' bullshit if I don't know what he did. What's good about it if he did something wrong enough to have to leave? There must be a reason Mama didn't want him to have anything to do with us. Marietta seems to think so. Evidently, you think your own mother and sister are crazy and have hated him all this time for no reason at all."

"I didn't know they hated him. I didn't know Witt or this Charlene Coleman had anything to do with this. I didn't know anything. Okay?"

"Well, I don't know how, but I know that Witt has known us for some time. I think he has a lot to do with the poem I mentioned, and with what it means. Witt also has Daddy's ring, and I want to understand why. What is it about?"

When Corey frowned, Bernadette told him what the poem said, and caught him up on what she'd found out about Witt and Daddy. Then she mentioned how Marietta refused to help.

When she finished, Corey laughed, a mirthless sound, than rubbed his eyes with the knuckles of both hands, letting his head drop back against the headrest.

"I didn't know," he said. "I didn't know how deep this was."

"And I still don't understand. Mama won't tell me. Daddy won't tell me. Marietta knows something, but she's hiding it fiercely. So…"

Corey shook his head. "He said he made a mistake. For the sake of argument, let's say it was a woman. He got tripped up doing it. Mama found out and that's all she wrote. So now," Corey glanced at his sister, "how long do you make a person pay?"

"Who's paying, him?" Bernadette snorted. "Money surrounds him, come on! Maybe somebody who knows that Daddy has all these children wants his money, and has to kill us first."

"Witt?" Corey asked.

"Didn't you say all he talked about was money and business? Doesn't one need money to do business?"

"Unless it's his mother behind this. One thing for sure, we know

Witt didn't kill our oldest brother. He wasn't born."

They both grew quiet.

"So, how do you bring Marietta into this, and throw her in Dad's face?"

"I don't know how, but I know there's something there. Did you see how red she was when we mentioned Daddy at the party? Did you see how much she was against finding him?"

"I was thinking she's just embarrassed about him. The way we've lived separately."

"I think she's embarrassed, but I think we don't know what she's embarrassed about. I think what makes the most sense is that somebody is being blackmailed. I don't know if it's Dad. I don't know if someone told him he would die if he continued to live with us. He said he'd been thinking about us a lot lately. Did he try to contact one of us? Is that what threatens our lives?

"It's the secret," Bernadette continued. "The reason why he left us. Somebody probably told him if he contacted us, the secret would come out."

"We don't know. We're guessing."

"Yes. But I do know one thing. Daddy did something awfully bad, and had to go."

"I don't care why he didn't stay. He's here now. He's risking it. That's what I'm glad about now."

"Well, I can't be glad until I know him. I have to find out what he did." Bernadette stared off into space, then snapped her fingers.

"I know what to do. I'm going to see Daddy's mother, Corey- Ms. Odessa. She's the woman who knows Witt's mother, the woman who knows Mama and Daddy, and the woman who was around through everything."

Corey looked at her.

"Then I'll see. If Mama won't say what happened, and Daddy won't say what happened, I'll go there. I will find out."

"You never stop, do you, Bernadette? If Marietta doesn't want it to be known, and Mama doesn't want it to be known and Daddy would just as soon not talk about it, why can't you just let it go? Why can't you just take people at their word, Bernadette? Leave them alone. Why do you have to do this to everybody? People have limits. Why do you like to push them?"

"Corey, three of us are dead, and the letter says killed. Dad says no, but I won't be number four. I can't stop your happiness, and if you don't care to know the real deal, that's you. Whatever I find out, I promise, you don't have to know. Okay? So you keep right on pretending. Make Alaina and your children happy."

"You don't want to go out to that old lady, who never contacted us and dig up stuff that's been buried for almost 20 years. She must be like 100 years old! She probably won't know you or won't remember. I'm sure she doesn't want to see you."

"That's just what the letter said. They don't want to see me. That's all the more reason I need to go. Somebody here does not want me to know what happened. And I'm going to find out."

# twenty-two

Am I doing the right thing?  Bernadette wondered as she sped across town in Corey's van early the next morning, negotiating piles of snowy slush as she headed for Bea's house. Bea knew something about this mess, something that made her want to see Daddy awfully bad. Bernadette had to find out.

She hadn't been able to sleep a wink the night before. Every time she closed her eyes, she saw either Daddy's face, sweating bullets, and making her feel badly, or Reggie's face, making her feel worse in a different way. Her body physically ached for Reggie and she felt her heart twist as she wondered whether he had walked away for good. She yearned to hear his voice, to know he wasn't that far. She thought about letting things go, and looking to the future, the way Corey had. But, she couldn't.

Even the threat of Colonel Chisholm's attack on her career seemed far away from this moment. There was no fighting him, or anybody else until she knew what happened to her family.

For now, she had to find out what Ms. O knew about them. It was obvious that she didn't want to have anything to do with her family, and didn't want them to have anything to do with her. But if she knew what had gone on between Mama and Daddy, she had a duty to tell her, didn't she?  She hadn't been grandmotherly in any other way.

Bernadette tried to pull up in front of Beatrice's house, but there were chairs strategically placed to reserve spaces where people had shoveled away the snow, so she parked down the block and jumped out. It was still early enough in the morning that, should Bea jump into some clothes, they should be able to catch Ms. O before she got up good.

She felt a rush as she rang the bell for her sister. To her surprise, the door opened up right away and Bea peeked out.

"Oh, it's you. Hurry up and come in," her sister said, a phone clutched in her hand.

Bernadette did and her sister slammed the door, then hurried away from her, putting the phone back to her ear and giving instructions to someone on the other end. Bernadette gave a sigh of relief when she realized the house was quiet. She followed her sister into the dining room, only half listening as Bea asked about times and wrote something down. Maybe Witt was already at work, which was what she hoped.

When Beatrice clicked off the phone, she told Bernadette that Toukie was at school and the baby was with one of her girlfriends, and she had but so many hours to do everything she needed to do.

"Not today. Look, drop that stuff and come with me. I'm going to see Ms. Odessa, and I need some backup."

Bea, dressed in stretch Levi's and a royal blue and bright orange Morgan sweatshirt, frowned.

"I can't go with you. I'm moving this morning."

"Moving?"

"Getting the hell out. And I don't have but so many hours to move."

Bernadette stared around, then looked at Bea. Not a thing was packed.

"I know it doesn't look like it, but Witt wasn't in on the plans. I had to wait until he left to get started. I won't get a lot of this shit, but I can take enough to get me and my children started, with what I have in storage."

"What happened?"

"It doesn't matter right now. I don't have time to go anywhere with you."

"Wait a minute, Beatrice," Bernadette said, putting her hands on her hips. "I have given you nothing but my time since you've been getting yourself in messes, worrying about Toukie, giving you money, taking my leave, and the one time I ask you to do anything for me, you tell me you don't have time?"

"Berni, you don't understand. I've got to get out, and I have to do it fast. I have had it with Witt, I don't love him, he doesn't own me, and besides, he's not what I thought he was."

Beatrice suddenly turned and walked quickly over to her china closet. She squatted, pulled open the bottom cabinet, moved some things around, then stood and faced Bernadette. In her hands was the jewelry box that Bernadette had only vaguely remembered as a child. Their promise box!

"You have it! I looked all over Mama's house for it, and you had it all along."

It was bigger than she remembered, with two small drawers on the front. Beatrice opened them, showing her sister the letters they had written were still inside.

"This was my surprise the night of my party. I kept this with me a long time, believing in it, but you know what? All the promises I thought would come true never did. And now I don't need it."

Bernadette took the box from her sister, and ran her hand across the top of it in disbelief. Then Beatrice added, "I guess I owe you an apology. All that stuff I said about Daddy being there for us, and Mama wasn't? Forget it. I guess it was possible neither one of them gave a good damn about us one way or the other."

Bernadette looked up.

"What?"

"Look through that stuff in there," Bea said, "You'll see. I wanted to believe Daddy was looking out for us even though he couldn't be with us. That nobody knew it, but he was making sure we were all okay, but he didn't. He swore to Nita and me that he loved us. He told me he would *always* be there for us. But you know what? He wasn't."

"How do you know he wasn't?"

"I came back to live with Witt because after Witt lost my money in his business deal, he promised he could get it back. I wasn't going to bother, but he hunted me down until he found me. He told me the city bought our houses, and we got some good money. I thought that meant he was going to join the business club and I was going to finally meet my Daddy.

"Well that wasn't happening. Sure, Witt did a lot of things to the house. This whole block will be used for professional buildings for the hospital, so he'll get good money for this. But he took the rest of the money he got and bought some old place in West Baltimore for his wood shop. And he stopped talking about joining the club altogether."

"Bea, you knew Witt was a fool before this. That's why you left him in the first place, remember?"

"But I didn't understand the plan. When I asked him for my 20 grand, he laughed at me and called me an ungrateful bitch. That's when he told me about Daddy."

Bernadette set the jewelry box on the table and pulled out a chair. "I knew it."

"I told him, no problem. I would find a way to have my Daddy get my money back, and Witt laughed, right in my face! That's when he told me Daddy didn't give a shit about none of us. He told me his mother had worked for Ms. O a long time ago, and when Ms. O got ready, she fired her, and kept money that belonged to his mother, for a large contract. He said Daddy and Ms. Odessa owe him and his mother, big time.

"I didn't believe him, but Witt is smart. He kept everything he could find on Daddy and gave it to me. I put some in that box. He told me if I knew what was good for me, I would stand by him and let him take care of me. But I'm through with him. It's over."

Bernadette held her arms around the box as she stared up at Bea.

"You'll see for yourself why I don't want to see Daddy. It's in that box. I guess you already got Ms. Odessa's address, but it's in there too. I stuck some other stuff me and Nita wrote in there. One letter I had to write over, 'cause her handwriting got so shaky."

"All these years, you hung onto this box. Even when you had nothing else."

Her sister shrugged, and looked away with a sigh.

Bernadette picked up her distress. "What is it? I mean, you're upset with Witt, but aren't you tired of running by now? You started running from the first time we lost Nita, and you haven't stopped yet. Can't you just make a decision that this is it? Just tell Witt you're leaving, and do it without fleeing? We're all here in Baltimore with you, we can help you move. Maybe Witt doesn't know Daddy like he's saying. He's lied before. Come with me now to Ms. O's. We'll come back and help you move."

"I've got to get the fuck out now, period." Beatrice started taking dishes from the china closet and placing them on the table.

"You will. Let me get Corey, Marietta and Alaina to help you. Bea, it's time to stop running. If you don't love Witt, you have to face him and tell him. In the meantime, can you please just come with me so I'll know you're safe?"

Beatrice started to pace. She took both hands and pushed the strands of her hair backward toward the ponytail.

"I don't know. You don't understand, Bernadette. I don't want to see Ms. Odessa. I hate them! I hate all of them! Those people are seriously crazy, and Witt tops them all."

Bernadette clutched the box even tighter. "What do you mean?"

"Haven't you figured it out yet?" Beatrice was crying now. "It was me, Berni. *Me.* I talked Nita into keeping the baby from Mama when she got pregnant. I told her we should tell Daddy, and he would help because we didn't want an abortion. And when I did write and tell him, I waited for him to answer. He never did and Nita got sicker. She wouldn't be dead if I didn't make her wait for Daddy. But he told me he loved us. He said he would always be there for us."

"Well, it wasn't your fault he didn't help you."

"I made her wait." Beatrice suddenly turned away from her sister, and started to pace, wiping tears.

"When I could see he wasn't coming, I didn't know what to do. I told Nita she couldn't get put out. Mama would put her out. So, I took her to this lady because she gave out pills that made girls have a miscarriage. And we didn't have enough money for the pills. So, she put this rubber tube up in her. She said it was all the way up to where the baby was, and the tube would make the baby come out if she didn't touch it."

"My God, Beatrice. Why not the hospital?"

"Who had money for an abortion, girl? Are you crazy? Everybody told us the pills always worked, but sometimes the tube didn't, because girls pulled it out. Nita didn't, but the tube caused an infection. I was so mad...so damn mad cause I thought, I believed Daddy tried to help us but Mama didn't let him. She hated him. She told us she hated him, and she would have nothing to do with him or anything he had. So, I thought she kept him away. I thought she just didn't tell us when he called.

"Nita died, and I was so mad, I went crazy.It took me a few years, but I went out and got Nita's boyfriend to have sex with me. I wanted the baby Nita was scared to have. I had Toukie, and I dared Mama to do anything to me. She told me I was nasty to do that with Nita's boyfriend, that I was a common slut like my Daddy and his whole family. But I did it for Nita—to show her I would stand up to Mama and have the baby she was scared to—but it was too late to change anything. It didn't bring Nita back. Look, Bernadette, I got to go."

Bernadette looked shocked at her sister's confession. Beatrice had held Nita back from telling Mama until it was too late. *Nita would be alive if she hadn't listened to Bea.* No wonder Bea wanted desperately for it to be Mama's fault.

"Okay, Bea," Bernadette said slowly, trying to digest the news. "We can talk about all this later. For now, just stay here and pack and I promise, when I come back, we'll all move you. But we're going to do this right. Don't just move out on Witt. We're not afraid of him, and all of us will be with you. You don't want him hunting you down again. We'll tell him it's over. Let me take care of this business first, Beatrice, please. Promise me?"

Beatrice looked at Bernadette, tears in her eyes.

"If you promise to get me out of here today."

"I promise. And when have I ever broken my promise?"

******

Bernadette pulled the van into the Edmondson Village Shopping Center just a few miles from Ms. O's and cut the engine. She was so nervous, her mouth was dry and her tongue kept sticking to the roof. Bea's information was surprising, and it had taken some wind out of Bernadette's sails. She needed to prepare herself.

A sub shop advertising tasty breakfast sandwiches, caught her eye, and she went in to eat and settle down.

It took a few moments to get her order of a large coffee and the breakfast special of eggs, bacon and cheese on a croissant. The woman behind the counter stared at the jewelry box Bernadette brought in with her as she handed Bernadette her order, but nothing was said as she made her way to the back table of the shop and sat.

She took a quick sip from the cup, and then reached over to open the little gold-handled drawer and pull out the letters they had saved. Finally she had them. *Their promises.*

There were just four pages, and when she saw the neat loops and swirls of her 11-year old handwriting, she smiled. She got a flashback of herself writing it, and settled on the words on the paper. Everything she'd written started with "I promise to," and Bernadette laughed. "Do well in school. Graduate from college. Become the president of my own company. Name my company after Nita." Company of what, Bernadette wondered now, then noticed across the bottom of her promises, and not in her handwriting, was more.

*I will not have sex, not have a baby, and not get married without the permission and approval of my sisters.* And under Bernadette's signature, there was Beatrice's, and Marietta's.

Bernadette pursed her lips wondering if Marietta thought she was still waiting for her permission to have sex.

She opened the next letter and stared at the signature at the bottom. Beatrice. She did not write neatly and Bernadette had trouble reading her promises. Clearly Beatrice had always had men on the mind as she promised to marry after she finished school and build a home and family that would make Nita proud. "And I will have girls," she had written, "that I will protect, keep happy and never scare them or make them afraid to tell me anything." Then, at the bottom Beatrice had written, "I promise that I will always love Daddy, and I will love him for both of us."

Even then, Beatrice was sure that Daddy deserved their love.

Then Marietta's promise: "To love and protect her sisters, to keep them alive, no matter what she had to do. And, to keep her promises to Mama until the day she died." This she promised in honor of Juanita.

Bernadette reread them. What was Marietta's promise to Mama? Once again, the Mama/Marietta connection that she couldn't figure out.

Another page, this time on yellow legal paper, was longer, and Bernadette pulled it out and turned it over to the end. Nita's signature was on this one. How did Nita get a letter in the box? Bernadette stared at the paper several seconds, not the words but the writing. Was this the last thing she wrote? Bea had kept it all these years.

A popular R&B singer moaned over the speakers of the shop about the love of her man as Bernadette steadied herself and started to read the very shaky script. No wonder Beatrice had to re-write Nita's letter before giving it to Daddy:

*Hi Daddy*

*I know I'm not supposed to write or call you, but I have something I want you to know.*

*Daddy, I am going with a boy named Otis Dent at school. We plan to get married when I graduate, but right now we can't. I need your help.*

*The other day I found out that I am going to have a baby. I know what I did was wrong, but I can't do anything about it. Mama told me and Bea that if we get pregnant, she would put us out. I don't want her to put me out. I want to finish school and get a good job and get married.*

*I tried to take care of it myself. Mrs. Lucille Lewis who lives on Caroline Street helped a pregnant girlfriend of mine, so I went to her. She tried to help me, but for some reason it did not work. I am still going to have a baby, but now I am so sick. I don't know what to do. Daddy, my stomach hurts so bad, it feels like somebody put a shovel of hot coal inside of me and it burns and aches and hurts. I almost can't breathe sometimes, it hurts me so bad, and if I tell Mama, I know what she will do.*

*Mama loved Danny and she still put him out when he was 18 because he didn't have a job and he wasn't in school or anything. But I'm too sick to go. Please help me. You don't have to tell Mama I wrote you because she will get so mad and I can't take it. I know you will help me Daddy. I miss you so much.*

*Then there was a paragraph in Beatrice's words--*

*Daddy, I'm bringing this letter to you because I want you to get it right away. Nita is so sick, she looks scary. Her skin is turning gray, and all she can do is cry and moan.*

*Please hurry up!*

*Love you, Beatrice and Juanita*

Bernadette crushed the hard paper napkin against her eyes and the tears fell. She hoped no one noticed or asked her anything. She just wanted to explode. How on earth could Daddy possibly not come after reading this?

She thought of Beatrice's words, that she had to re-write Nita's letter because it was so shaky, and was glad she had kept the original. Then she sighed and reached for the papers to fold them and put them back in the promise box.

She then opened the bottom drawer, the largest one, and pulled out a white envelope that looked too new to have been a part of the box over the years. Beatrice had said that Witt had proof Daddy hadn't wanted them in here. This had to be it.

She turned it over and saw Bea's writing: Witt's pictures. Curious, she peeped inside. A yellowed newspaper clipping was folded neatly.

Bernadette pulled it out, her heart thudding dully.

It looked like a society page notice. On it were groups of white people, dressed up and smiling. Bernadette glanced at the three photos. One was of a group, one was a couple, and another was a building with a group of people in the front.

She looked them over, and as she stared at the couple, she blinked. These weren't white people. The male in the couple was her father, and he was locking arms with a female who, on closer inspection, was probably not white at all, but very light. The caption read:

Daniel Windsor III and Helena Dowery,
stepping out for the White Rose Ball

The date:  October 12, 1985.

The group photo was of about 30 black men, and the caption read:
Sigma Pi Phi hosts commemorative dinner. Bernadette could not pick
out her father, hard as she tried.

The last was a building, backdrop for a small group of women
dressed formally in black. The caption noted that they were members of
the Minx, an all black women's organization that had recently bought
and restored a Catonsville mansion, the new home of the Blacks in Wax
Museum of Baltimore.

Bernadette's eyes shot back up to the photo of her father, and zoomed
in on the date. October 12, 1985. While he was grinning at the White
Rose Ball with this woman, Helena Dowery, his daughter was dying
alone in her bedroom. And he was ignoring her.

What was Witt doing with these clippings of her father?

Quickly she stuffed all the papers back in the box and jumped up.

It was time to see Ms. Odessa.

******

It was nearly 10:00 in the morning when Bernadette pulled into the
huge circular driveway of the house on Winans Way, just off Edmondson
Avenue. It wasn't quite the early morning surprise she'd wanted. A new
white Mercedes was in the driveway near the front door, and Bernadette
pulled Corey's van up beside it and cut the engine. She guessed that if Corey
was up, he was wondering where in the hell she had gone with his van.

For a moment she stood staring up at the imposing house and imagined her sister, years ago, book bag and all, standing around waiting for
someone to come to this door to save them. Just seeing the opulence surrounding her, she was sure Bea must have known she had done the right
thing by delivering the letter to Daddy instead of telling Mama. Only she
had been wrong. No wonder she had disappeared when Nita died. She
probably wanted to die too.

Bernadette marched up the walkway to the front door. Her eyes were on the stream of water running toward her feet from the slow melting snow, clinging everywhere to the grass and the trees. It was a spectacular backdrop, especially in this wooded section of town. The dwelling was huge. It seemed to spread all over the place the closer she got to it. She rang the bell, and looked around at the quiet, peaceful neighborhood. It was lovely. As far as the eyes could see, there were huge, snow covered lawns.

This was the kind of life for her, she thought as she looked about. Where did this kind of money come from? They weren't rich when Daddy was with them. When she was little, and they lived in the county just up the street from Ms. Monterey, she thought that house was big. It was a nice, small enclave of black property owners in Towson. It was filled with working class blacks, teachers, policemen, and government workers who were able to hold onto to the valuable land, though public buildings and malls sprang up within walking distance.

So, Daddy had money for quite some time. Why had they lived so differently?

Bernadette rang the bell again, then stepped down the one step and started walking around to the side of the huge house, as there was undoubtedly a side entrance. She saw several chimneys on this house, the one in the middle had a large fancy "W" made of black bricks near the top. Bernadette had noticed a black sedan driving around the side of the house just after she pulled up and maybe…

The set of double doors at the front of the house opened and Bernadette hurried back in time to see a middle-aged woman, maybe her mother's age, standing in the entrance. She looked expensive and well preserved and she looked at Bernadette without a hint of a smile. Her light brown hair was pinned up, and the woman had on a heather gray knit dress with gray suede pumps.

"Hello," Bernadette greeted, her heart beating hard as she made her way to the door. She smiled, hoping the face in front of her would relent, but it didn't. "I'm looking for Ms. Odessa Windsor?"

"May I tell her who's here?"

"Yes tell her it's Bernadette."

The woman arched a brow. "Bernadette?" she stretched out the name, as though waiting for something to follow.

"Yes. She should know me by that name. I'm family."

The woman's head tilted to the side.

"The Windsor family?"

Bernadette pressed her lips together. What other family could she mean, she thought as she felt her blood heat up.

"Yes, of course, the Windsor family."

The woman looked surprised, and her eyes roved over the goose down hunter jacket of Corey's, which Bernadette had also borrowed, the scruffy jeans and Nike boots that Bernadette wore.

"You're not here for the luncheon?"

Bernadette's brows lifted.

"No."

"Oh," the woman finally smiled. "At first I thought you were helping the photographer, then when you said Windsor...well, anyway, come in."

Bernadette walked in, pulling up her shoulders proudly. One thing about the military, it taught you how to look confident, even if you didn't feel it. Who the hell was this snobby woman anyway? Her skin prickled as she looked around the mirrored foyer, where a chandelier hung over her head in the hall. There was no doubt she would not be invited to this place. They would probably have people throw her out when they found out why she was here.

As the woman closed both doors, she said conversationally, "I pretty much know all the people in this family, and I never met you. What was your last name? "

"My whole name is Bernadette Renee Windsor."

The woman paused, and her eyes studied Bernadette's face. Bernadette stared back equally as hard, sizing the woman up in the same way. She wished she could read her mind, because if there was anything derogatory in it, she wanted to be ready.

"And I missed YOUR introduction?" she asked the woman pointedly.

"Melinda. Melinda Bauer. I'm a close friend of Mrs. Windsor."

A friend? She was nothing but a friend, and she looked down her nose at her?

"Is Mrs. Windsor expecting you? She didn't mention anyone but the guests."

"No, she isn't."

Melinda hesitated, and Bernadette could tell her mind was clicking. Was she waiting for an explanation? Bernadette didn't offer one.

"Then I gather this must be very important. You see, she has a big occasion today. She's being honored for her philanthropic work and nominated for a special achievement award by a group of close friends. She's always generously supported private education institutions for African-Americans, and she's being recognized for it. What she doesn't know is that the City of Baltimore and the State of Maryland will have representatives coming-- I heard it might be the Mayor himself. You know, she worked with the Abell Foundation helping to raise money to get the city schools out of the red. There'll be press here, and, well, a whole big party."

"Hhm," Bernadette murmured. "Well, it was important enough that I came here to see her about it."

Melinda looked like she was on the verge of asking what it was concerning, but she read Bernadette's expression and thought better of it. "Well! I'll just let her know you're here. Won't you have a seat? Maybe in the study, where you two can talk." She pointed to a doorway halfway down the hall. " Would you like some coffee?  I made a fresh pot."

"That would be great. Thanks."

Bernadette watched Melinda walk away from her, her eyes peeled critically on her every move. She seemed young to be a friend of Ms. O's. When she walked out of sight, Bernadette turned and walked down the hall, past the 'study', where she had been directed, and straight into a rather large, spacious room with cream colored sofas, beige carpeting, heavy wooden tables, floor lamps, a large aquarium built into the wall, a roaring fireplace, which burned cozily, and a smattering of chairs set up to face one direction.

What she couldn't miss were the many pictures Ms. O had on display, a gallery of photographs, paintings, and formal portraits. Bernadette perused the showing.

There were so many people, faces she did not know. Most of them were extremely light-skinned but the more she looked, she noted there were folks of deeper hues captured here and there. There were many professional poses, smiles, even on the old people she did not know but had a feeling she should have.

This was her grandmother's house, and she couldn't point to anybody in these pictures she knew. There wasn't one single photo of any of them, not even one of Mama and Daddy together.

But in seconds she found pictures of Daddy alone, or Daddy in groups of friends with his similar look. There was Ms. O's pride and joy, posing in a swank suit beside a black BMW. In another, Daddy was wearing all white, with a group of men holding tennis rackets. The same group was caught in another snapshot later hoisting beer mugs. These were long ago. There were no recent pictures of Daddy but Bernadette noted there was one of Melinda, the woman who opened the door, sitting by itself on an oak server.

Melinda had her hair up again in this picture, and she stared into the camera challengingly, or was it supposed to be seductively? Why would she give Ms. O this kind of shot? Somebody lied and told her she was cute. She had a prominent jawbone, thick enough to be a man's, and an arrogant slant to her chin, a familiar gesture. Did she know this woman from long ago?

Hearing Melinda in the distance, Bernadette started to go back down the hall, but stopped short. She wanted to see this house, to feel what it was all about. She would stay in here. Just as she thought that, her eyes swung to a large handsome portrait of a young woman, hanging on a wall to herself. Bernadette's breath caught. It looked remarkably like Juanita— just lighter skin, and hair. The small face, big eyes, and beautiful smile made you stare. It could have been Nita's smile. No doubt, this young woman was a relative of Daddy's.

She hadn't given Daddy's family much thought, any more than she did Mama's, nor any family other than hers, but now she wondered. She knew her father was an only child, and that Ms. O didn't like Mama for taking him from her. That had been Mama's story. She had also heard Ms. O was status conscious. Daddy came from a certain status, and Mama was a farm girl attending the University of Maryland on the Eastern Shore. That's where Mama met Daddy while he was in school at Howard University, doing an article on the school for his journalism class. He fell for her and married Mama right at the courthouse only months after meeting her. That, according to the little Bernadette knew, was what made Ms. O furious. And that was the most Bernadette knew of the old woman, who kept herself separate.

But what brought Daddy back?

Melinda came in with a silver serving tray, and walked into the large room carrying it regally, her face twisted with annoyance.

"I thought you'd be in the study," she said, and Bernadette shrugged and said, "I saw the bright lights down here and followed them." She glanced at the ritzy little tray with the china cup and saucer, silver sugar bowl and what she guessed were small containers for the cream and milk.

"Thanks," Bernadette said as Melinda set up on the coffee table near one of the sofas, poured Bernadette a cup, and then cleared her throat.

"I, uh, don't want to ask your business with Mrs. Windsor, but she does have a very tight schedule, and I hope this isn't something that will take too long or in any way wear her out. I mean, if it's urgent…"

"Oh, I can assure you, it's urgent, or I wouldn't have come unannounced."

"Urgent?" Again, Bernadette knew Melinda wanted an idea of what she wanted.

"Yes, urgent."

"Is there anything I can help you with?"

"No."

Melinda stared a second, then sighed. At that moment a short, white, balding man came to the doorway and called, "Ms. Bauer? About the books in the library you wanted me to set up?"

"Yes, I'm coming in a moment. I'll meet you in there after I let Ms. Windsor know her company is waiting."

The man nodded agreeably and disappeared while Melinda walked with long sure strides toward some stairs at the back of the room. Who the hell was this woman? Bernadette thought, wishing Corey, Beatrice or anybody had come with her. This wasn't going to be easy, especially with other people coming.

She heard voices at the top of the stairs and after a moment, Melinda came back down.

"She's coming. I have to take care of setting up some things. How long do you think this will take?"

"Not very long, I'm sure."

She nodded.

"Well, nice meeting you, Bernadette," Melinda said and gave a half smile. Bernadette watched her walk out, and as she did, she puzzled over what the woman's connection could be to Ms. O. Strangers were closer than her own family members.

At last a figure did appear on the staircase, looking curiously over the banister at her. Bernadette looked up, feeling her heart begin to race. There she was, Ms. Odessa Windsor. The way the woman stared, Bernadette was sure she had no idea who she was. It took some time, but the old woman made it down the stairs, cane and all, and walked over her.

Bernadette stood and walked to meet her.

# twenty-three

"Hello, Ms. Odessa," she greeted. Bernadette wondered if the woman would keel over if she uttered the word "Grandmother."

"Hello, I'm sorry, I didn't get your name, young lady. Melinda said something, and I really didn't hear." Her voice sounded querulous.

"Bernadette, Bernadette Windsor." She said it loudly and waited for the name to click. She was amazed that this little figure, dressed in a snazzy black silk dress with a big diamond brooch on one side, was the person she had to confront. She was so small. Even with her thin, beautiful snowy white hair piled high on her head, she still didn't reach Bernadette's shoulder. Bernadette expected to go up against something big and nasty. Evil should be big.

"You don't remember me, do you? I'm your granddaughter, Bernadette. Daniel's youngest girl with Ruth Ann Windsor."

The old woman's sunken gray eyes widened then.

"Oh!" Recognition lit her face. "Yes! It's been a long time. Bernadette? My Lord, child." She looked Bernadette up and down. "Give me a hug."

Bernadette obeyed, surprised at the request, but as soon as she pulled the frail woman against her, she released her quickly.

"How old are you now, Bernadette?"

"Twenty-nine, ma'am."

"My Lord, time does fly. And you remember me?"

"Not very well. I didn't get many chances to be around you, as I'm sure you know."

"Well, have a seat. They got all this stuff set up for one of my club meetings you know. But, if you've come to see me, I know it must be important."

Bernadette nodded, and positioned herself so that she could first help the old woman into a seat. Then she sat on the couch near her.

"How is Ruth Ann? Lord knows when I last saw your mother."

"My mother is doing fantastic. In fact, we all are. We just got together for my sister Beatrice's 32nd birthday party. I'll be going back home soon."

"And where is that?"

"I live in California. Anyway, I thought it was high time I came to see you, so here I am."

"Well, indeed! Now, what can I do for you?"

Bernadette was sitting close enough to study every thin strand of hair, every vein in her pale skin, and every beautifully manicured red nail that rested on the arm of her chair and on her cane.

"I want you to be so kind as to give me some honest answers. I know my mother and father tried, but they can't seem to tell me what I need to know. My father left my mother when I was only four, and I want to know why. I know something happened, but my father wouldn't say what. Can you please tell me what he did?"

She watched the old lady start to shake, as though the question rattled her. Her head rocked from side to side in small arcs.

"From what I understand," Bernadette continued, "you never wanted us, or even liked us. But my father loved us, so how on earth did he end up leaving forever? How did that happen? He seems to have so much remorse about it now."

"Oh, I can't take any of the credit for that," she said then. "Your mother put him out."

"As the last straw, I'm sure. That's what I can't understand. What on earth could he have done to make her do that? My father wouldn't just leave for no reason."

"Well, now, he had those reasons with your mother."

"And were they bad enough that he couldn't see any of us ever again? Ms. O, he had children that died, and we couldn't have anything to do with him when we needed him the most. Why not?"

Ms. Odessa looked down, her head still shaking. "That's some hard news, children dying off. That's some hard news to take."

"I lost two brothers and a sister. Did you know that, Ms. Odessa?"

"Well, I found out about it after they were dead! I didn't know until late--"

"Now, Ms. Odessa, with all due respect, I know my sister Beatrice came all the way to this very house to give my Dad a letter about what was going on way before Juanita died. You knew about it when she was just sick."

Ms. Odessa shook her head. Bernadette couldn't tell if it was voluntary or not.

"Lord, child, those were some terrible times. Terrible times for me, terrible for your mother and your father, terrible for everybody! But what can you do? You try to do the best thing to save everybody. You can't just save one person."

"Did my father get that letter, Ms. Odessa?"

"Mail would come to my house for Dan all the time. Mail came from your mother's house. Not just one letter. We kept getting letters, but it was over. The marriage was over. And Dan was to have no more contact with any one of you. That's what your mother wanted, but we got the attorney to change that. He told her she couldn't have that in the divorce, but I told Dan he would mess up if he kept going over there like he lived there. I told him that he had already uncovered a can of worms, and if he ignored it and went over there like he lived with your family, he would mess up everything. It was such a nasty mess. A bad mess, but what can you do?"

Bernadette frowned. "I don't understand. What did he do? I'm telling you that as children, we needed our father. We wrote him letters and asked for him. What do you mean he would make it worse if he contacted us? You mean he got the letter from Juanita and still let her die?"

"What I'm telling you now," Ms. O said, head shaking hard, blue veined hand raised with finger pointed, "he had to cut his contact, or he was going to ruin himself, me, everybody. I don't know what the letters said. Those letters you all kept sending to my house, I didn't read them. They came to my house from your mother sometimes, from the children sometimes. I didn't care. I burned them, threw them right in the fireplace. I didn't want Dan in more trouble. He was just beginning to do well. Getting interviews at the big magazines, you know, like *Life* and *Time*. He couldn't get involved. He didn't know about Juanita being sick. Didn't know until your mother called and said she died."

"But you took it upon yourself to throw out our letters? Even though you didn't know who wanted him, or needed him? Even though you knew he really wanted to see us?"

"Your father had written some articles, child. He had exposed people, writing about things some black families practiced, then he turned around and did it himself. It was too late then. Your mother said if he came back her way, she would write to the magazines he worked for and tell them. She would bring everybody down if he came near her children again."

The old woman turned her head away. Bernadette stared at her sallow complexion.

"It was such a mess, child."

"It must have been," Bernadette said slowly, moving a strand of hair back. Then she added in her most patient tone, "But, Ms. Odessa, I need to know what he started practicing. What made my mother keep him away?"

"Such a mess," the old woman continued to say and shake her head. "Do you have children, Bernadette?"

"No, ma'am."

"That's the best thing. They change your whole life, Bernadette. Everything they do! It's never the same. If they mess up, it falls back on you. If they do the wrong thing...I never talked about having children, you know, never even thought about having children when I was young. I was considered pretty." She paused and looked around. "A real catch, I was, and I just wanted to enjoy my youth. In my day, well, you didn't talk about how NOT to have babies. Course, far as we were told, good girls didn't have sex. And if you did, you didn't talk about it. At that time, when the time came to have sex, you just found out." The old woman gave a slight laugh. "That's what happened to me--when I had my first child."

Bernadette hesitated.

"Your first child?" Daddy was her only child as far as she knew. Was the woman really senile, as Corey warned?

"I had my first child when I was 17," Ms. Odessa said clearly. "My boyfriend, at that time, was a soldier stationed in Washington, DC. I was at Howard University back then—I still don't know why my granddaughter Jenny refuses to go there," she said, pausing to point at the portrait of the girl who strongly resembled Juanita. But anyway, black men in a uniform were just something to behold. You didn't see a whole lot of them. When you did, it just grabbed you, did something to you. Back when I was 17, a black man in the army was a big thing. He was a hero! Next thing you know, well, it happened to me.

"Back then, in my day, you didn't just have a baby like they do today.

It wasn't okay. I had my baby girl, and my mother made me give her away. Didn't too many people know I had a baby because she sent me away before I began to show. She gave my baby to a family we knew and I went back to school. And I forgot she was mine. It was like she never was. I never saw her, had nothing to do with her.

"When I got married a year later, to somebody my mother wanted for me, I had only one more baby, my son, Daniel. He has been my life since. All the life I had..." her voice faltered.

"And Dad disappointed you?"

"Lord, child, yes he did. Even to this very day. I never see him anymore. People say I didn't like Ruth Ann 'cause she was one of those black girls that had real dark skin. You know, if you wanted to move in the right circles, to be something in my day, you stayed in your color line. Black people had a color line, too. You picked your own color. For Dan, it would just make it easy for him to get on in life, you know, to move ahead in his color line. White folks days ago didn't listen to you unless you looked like they did."

"And you believe in that? You believe black people should choose to be with other black folks who are the same color?"

"I'm saying in my day you had to look close to being white for them to let you get anywhere. Otherwise, they didn't hear a word you said. Nowadays, they got Clarence Thomas on the U.S. Supreme Court, but back years ago you had Thurgood Marshall. It was like you didn't even speak English if you looked too different. I wanted what was best for Dan. He could have been anything. It would have just helped if he picked the right wife.

"That didn't mean I didn't like Ruth Ann. I did like Ruth Ann. She was one of those...those people that would make it no matter what. I knew that back then. She was going to be a nurse, I believe. Didn't have parents, just her grandmother, she said, who died her first year in college, but she was a farm girl with ambition. I didn't think Dan should marry her, I can't lie, but I still liked the girl. All I was trying to make him see was what it was like for him, what it could be like if he was with the right people.

"It took me years of getting to know the right people, getting the right contacts, giving the right parties and going to the right ones to make it where I got to. I did everything in my life to keep what my parents got for me. When I joined the Minx, Incorporated, you know, the club chapter that's coming here today, I knew my life was set. I would have the contacts to get my husband the backing he needed for his run for Congress, and everything my son could want, I could find a way to get it."

"What is that…the Minx?"

Ms. Odessa smiled slightly and looked at Bernadette.

"You would never hear about it. You couldn't be invited to join." She paused. "You have to be accomplished, a politician, doctor, lawyer…and if you had a certain look, then you were easily in. Our chapter doesn't have physical requirements anymore, like the light skin and straight hair. Oh, I know you all want that hair to kink up now, but when I grew up, it was not that way. We despised it. You all want the sun on your skin, but when I grew up, we hated it. But my group understands that you can do a lot in a sisterhood, the right group to back you. That's why I joined the Minx. It's all about making life comfortable for blacks with money."

Bernadette leaned back, stung by Ms. Odessa's statement that she would never belong. "Sounds like a bunch of exclusive snobs to me. How can that be good for blacks?"

"If it wasn't for organizations like ours, my darling, you wouldn't have the privileges you have today. You wouldn't have the opportunities. And that's all I wanted for my son. I wanted him to meet the right people, people like Melinda, people in the Minx or even the Girlfriends who moved in circles to make things happen. They could introduce Dan to the right people. I thought Melinda would help him meet girls like that, she was so pretty, and I asked her to…but I didn't know what I was doing."

Bernadette snorted and crossed her arms, glaring at the woman.

"Melinda was to introduce Dan to the right girls. That was my hope and why I pushed them to be together. The next thing I knew, your father was going with Melinda."

Bernadette looked her in the eyes. "The Melinda I just met at your door?"

"Yes. Next thing I knew, Melinda was pregnant by Dan. And then, it seems not long after, she had her baby, which was your sister Marietta."

Bernadette sighed and threw up her hands. Ms. Odessa was crazier than she thought. She reached down for the dainty little flowered china cup, sipped, and then set the cup down with a clank. This was going to be difficult if Ms. Odessa couldn't keep the people straight. She would never find out anything if the old woman didn't know who was who. How could Melinda have Marietta?

"I think you're getting it confused," she said patiently. "Marietta is my sister, from Dan and Ruth Ann."

For a moment, a long terrible moment, Ms. Odessa got quiet. She closed her eyes as if going to sleep, then said very slowly, "Now, listen to me and listen to me good. I am old, but I know what I'm saying. Melinda was raised as a friend of the family. She was given away, raised by another family. But Melinda is my first baby. She's my first born."

Bernadette stared horrified.

"You mean…she was your child that you had with the soldier? And my father was your child…and…they were sister and brother?"

"Dan didn't know a thing about that. All he knew, she was a friend of the family. They were raised as friends, even though they called themselves cousins. Melinda didn't know a thing either. The family who raised Melinda sent her away after that. She went to stay in Michigan, but I took that baby. I called your mother over here, and I told her this: Dan was a man and being so, he did wrong, but I would see to it that he didn't again. Here was his child, she could do right by taking it and raising it with little Dan, and not be bitter about it. I never told her who it was by. Melinda and Dan still didn't know they had the same mother at that time. I thought it would work if I took the child. She went to Michigan, Dan stayed with your mother.

"Ruth Ann was plenty bitter. She called me some of every kind of name you could think of, saying I put him up with other women." Here Ms. Odessa paused to laugh, a joyless sound. "She knew Melinda as his cousin, and she accused her of the same, and she said she didn't want that child. But then she thought about it, and I guess she realized it'd be better to raise up the baby with her own rather than let some other woman raise it and have to call on Dan whenever she needed something.

"And she must have forgiven him. She had more babies with Dan after that. She had a boy, then had three more girls. Melinda moved to Chicago, but then she came back to town. Her adopted mother wasn't doing well in her later years. One day your mother saw her. I don't know how. I don't know why, but she got it in her head that Melinda was back to cause her some trouble.

"She started checking up on Melinda. By now, Dan wasn't even seeing Melinda, or nobody else but your mother. He had a big family and he was quite the family man. He was doing well. Your mother went around asking questions, and one thing led to another. To this day I don't know how, but she found out that Melinda was not Dan's cousin, but my own daughter, Dan's sister. At that time, your father still didn't know, but when your mother found out, she told him.

"And that's when all the mess hit the fan. She said she was through with us. We didn't deserve to be around her children. She let him go for good. You were just a little thing, but it was bad."

Bernadette didn't realize she had both hands over her mouth. Her nose was pressed against her face and she had to gasp when she realized she wasn't breathing,

"My sister, Marietta? You mean…"

"Yes, the real light one."

There was silence. No words would come to her.

"Your mother believes I set Dan up like that." Ms. Odessa's head shook badly. "Like I would take my own two children, my son and daughter, and put them together like dogs to breed…" her words fell away. "Just because Dan had written about a family that did that, and got a lot of publicity behind it until it ruined them." Bernadette realized the old woman had started to weep.

"Oh, my God, Ms. Odessa!" Bernadette said, impervious to the silent weeping. "How can you speak like that about my mother, like she was wrong for feeling that way about you? How could you have let something so vile happen? Nobody knew, you say? You knew! You knew who Melinda really was. How could you not know their true feelings for each other?"

"They were raised as friends, more like cousins. You don't expect cousins to feel that way about each other. She would write to him and send letters to my house, but I didn't read the letters. I just gave them to Dan. I didn't know what they said.

"But your mother told him. He didn't need to ever know that about Melinda being from me, but she told him. She had the nerve to put it in the divorce—'incest' she said was the cause, even though he didn't know that's what he was doing at the time. She was wrong. My husband, Dan's father was trying to get into the Bentleys, the organization for professional black men. He had received an invitation and, since he was in politics, it seemed like he was going to be voted right in. Then this happened."

"Then my father is in a club? The Bentleys you said?"

"Oh, no. He's not in it, but his father, Daniel, Senior, is a member."

"But the ring he had, he used to wear with diamonds…?"

"That was my ring to him. It was my idea, to identify the sons of the Minxes, the women in my club. Dan liked the ring, and he kept it until we argued at the time he got married, and I told him to give it back. He didn't pursue anything like the Bentleys, not after what happened. His father and I separated not long after that, and I was afraid the whole mess would come out. Dan had a hard time with it after the mess your mother made for him. Bringing that up at the divorce hearing so everybody would know. And threatening to tell a story that he practiced having sex with his family to keep his bloodlines pure. She was a bitter woman and she made a bitter mess."

"My mother made a mess? You created the mess. You did all this, afraid we may come forward and mess up your perfect existence. So, you hired Witt to help you handle us? Is that what it was? As if things weren't bad enough, you wanted to do more damage?"

"Witt?"

"Witt Coleman. His mother worked for you, making quilts for your friends for years."

"Oh, Charlene's son?" Ms. O shook her head, and looked down to straighten out her dress. "He was something else. Liked to come here with his mother and get into everything. Yes, I was fond of him." She paused." I was not in touch with Dan. Then, when the family mess broke out, I dropped all my social work. I wanted things to die down."

"So, you didn't hire Witt?"

"Hire Witt for what? Last time I saw that boy, he was in school. I paid for him to go to a boarding school, then to Gilman. I liked his mother's work and I wanted to help her by paying for his school. Then I stopped when the trouble with Dan broke out.

"Well, now," Ms. Odessa paused, "that boy did call me some time ago. Called me about joining the Bentleys as a matter of fact. He wanted to know what he had to do, whom he had to see. I sent him the papers I had on them, for all the good it would do. My husband, Daniel, was in that club but my son didn't ever want to bother with it.

"I'll tell you, when that trouble with Dan broke out, my reputation was on the line. Your mother went simply crazy, starting all the trouble she could, telling everybody."

"My mother was crazy? What about you? Look what you did to her life. What did she do to you?"

"She ruined my life! My *life!*" Her voice became querulous once again and her body shook so badly Bernadette began to fear for the old woman's health. She quickly gave Ms. Odessa the set of napkins from the silver tray and helped her wipe her face. For a while neither said anything.

"Ms. Odessa, you brought this all on yourself. I mean, how can you now stand up and accept any award for philanthropic work and saving black children? You've destroyed as many lives as you may have saved. Look what you've done to us! My brother, Dan didn't have to go into the Army if it wasn't for you. My sister, Nita would certainly be alive if you had given my father those letters. You said my father doesn't have anything to do with you. Well, you have nothing to do with us. We aren't the right color. Yet you want to be presented as some great giver to mankind?"

"It's a fact of my life. It's how I was raised. It's not that I was against you. If it weren't for my organization, there would be nothing there for blacks who are wealthy like whites. We made a society to accept ourselves and to support each other, and it works because it's been around for years. We developed our own cotillions, balls, and clubs so our children would have others like themselves to socialize with. We are not working class blacks, and we have to maintain the accomplishments we've made for our race and for our class. We should be recognized."

"Maybe your organization did do some good at some point, I don't know, but there's no need for you anymore. You, on the other hand, have ruined your own life. You've made it impossible, and for what? To keep your color line pure? You've ignored my mother, ignored my family, for what? So people won't know there are darker Windsors in the family? What have you gained, Ms. Odessa?"

"I kept that mess about Dan out of my circles. I thought your mother would ruin everything for me, but I stayed in the Minx. I kept our chapter of the Minx strong. I survived the scandal of divorce, and I stayed involved, doing everything I could to help where I could. I gave my life to them. In return, I have their respect and their gratitude. And I've gained the respect of my daughter, Melinda, and her daughter and my grandchild, Jennifer."

"And what about us? What about our love and respect? I saw a portrait of Jennifer. She is beautiful, and she's lucky her heritage was acceptable to you, because she is no lovelier than my sister Juanita. Juanita should be alive and on that wall, just as well."

Ms. Odessa shifted her body uncomfortably.

"Young lady, I paid your mother good money to help her take care of everyone of you. I had six separate accounts set up, and sent her the bank-books."

Bankbooks! Bernadette sighed, remembering the big gold envelope in Mama's trunk with the books she'd thought were passports. Ms. O had sent Mama money. A buy-off for them, but Jennifer, she wanted.

"But of course, Jennifer's father is probably someone within the color line. Somebody acceptable. Am I right?"

"Melinda married a man from Harvard. And, I never had a thing against any of you children, Bernadette. Yes, you girls are pretty, all of you." Ms. Odessa paused when a small black woman, hair in a short afro came in with a duster in her hand and spoke politely, going into a corner and dusting the pictures.

"If you had nothing against us, Ms.Odessa, why is my sister dead? Why are my brothers dead?"

Ms. Odessa looked up at Bernadette. "It was in a letter you said. I never read those letters. None of them."

"But you had to! You wanted us gone and you wanted to make sure we couldn't ruin you. How did you do it? If not Witt, who? I know you wanted us gone, it's here! It's right here in this letter…" Bernadette reached into her pocket and pulled out the poem.

There was a noise from the corner, and both Bernadette and Ms. Odessa looked. The small cleaning woman cleared her throat.

Then she turned.

Bernadette's eyes widened.

"Mrs. Monterey?" She stared at Dina's mother without the colorful wigs. In a knit sheath and white apron, she stood with a feather duster in her hand. What was she doing here dusting? She'd always said she worked in the Village giving music lessons.

Dina's mother's face was expressionless, and her eyes went to Ms. Odessa.

"Excuse me Ms. O," she said. "I think you may be mistaken about that letter, what you just told this young lady. There might have been a letter from that young lady, Ms. Juanita, and there might not, but I was here the day she called. I was the one that brought the phone to you. I remember she sounded bad off, and asked to speak to her father first, then to you."

Bernadette stared in surprise. She was Ms. Odessa's maid?

"And you did take that call, Ms. Odessa ma'am," Mrs. Monterey gave a slight bow of her head. "And you never told her father. You never mentioned receiving any calls. I did not know she was dying. I had no place to say she had called her father, I didn't know it was life or death. But when I heard you say you never knew the girl called for her father, I wanted to remind you. You did know, ma'am. Now, if you will excuse me. Melinda needs more help in the kitchen."

She left the room walking slightly sideways, without acknowledging Bernadette in any way. After she left, nobody said a word. Bernadette closed her eyes tightly. The poem she had, that she'd been wondering about all this time, was from Mrs. Monterey. It was Mrs. Monterey who knew the color secret. Mrs. Monterey who knew that Juanita died needlessly. And now, with this award, did Mrs. Monterey suspect Ms. Odessa of harming her family? She must. But what did she know?

Ms. Odessa said nothing. Bernadette stood up slowly.

"Then you knew she was very sick, she would have told you that. So, what happened? Did you tell her to die? That you didn't need her kind muddying up your bloodline? Did you tell her she deserved it? Most importantly, did you ever tell my father that Juanita called?"

Ms. Odessa's head shook, but her small inset eyes pinned Bernadette, and to her surprise, tears started.

"I know you did nothing. You did nothing, and that was the problem. And for that, she died. You know what, Ms Odessa? You can't accept that award today. I don't care what kind of honor you think you deserve, you killed her. I don't care how many schools you supported or children you helped. When you could have helped us, you turned your back. And I'm telling you now, if you try to stand up here in front of anybody and take an award, I will tell it myself. I will tell anyone who will listen what you did. And if you don't believe me, try it. If I ever read anything about something you have gotten, for philanthropic reasons, I will tell. I can never repay what you've done to us, and I can't prove what you did to my brother Daniel, or to the baby, but for the years you have left, I will make you remember what you did to my sister!"

"My dear child, it takes a lifetime to build reputation. To open doors to a family never opened before. To garner respect and privilege and make life easy. It takes a second to bring it down. Bernadette, the Windsor name will bring you recognition you'd never get unless you married it, and it's because of the work I've done. You don't want to open your mouth against me. You're a smart girl, think what I can do for you."

"I can't forget all you've done. You let my sister die, and…my brother Daniel? How did you do it?"

"You give me too much credit. Your brother wanted a car to help him get home while he was in the Army. He came here looking for his father, but I was home. I gave him money and told him where he could go for good used cars, not inspected, but he could pay for that. He did not…"

"I don't want to hear any more!" Bernadette leaped up. "I have a lot to say to anyone who comes to give you any honor or award."

What happened next was unexpected. Ms. Odessa closed her eyes ever so slowly and rolled off the chair into the carpet face first. The next thing Bernadette knew, the old woman was in a heap on the floor, her cane beside her.

"Help!" she screamed dropping down on her knees beside the woman. She put her head close and noticed her breaths were shallow.

"Help! Somebody! Melinda! Mrs. Monterey! Call 911! Hurry!"

She straightened the frail body, checked her breath, and even as the others came running into the room, she hesitated, looking at the gaunt face of the hateful woman before she leaned over her and pressed her lips, giving short breaths.

She wanted her to live. She wanted her to know that now that she knew what had really happened, she would have no peace. Nor would all the little socialites that came after her.

As she heard Melinda on the phone, saw Mrs. Monterey rush out and back with a glass of water and some smelling salts, she could picture one thing in her mind, Beatrice's tortured soul. She thought she had caused it all, thought that Nita would have lived but for her. Only now she would know the truth. Ms. Odessa never told anyone about that call that could have saved Nita's life.

# twenty-four

Corey's loud laughter greeted her when she stepped into her mother's house late that afternoon and Alaina, seated beside him at the dining room table, jumped up, concern crossing her face. They were in the middle of having what looked like a late lunch.

"Well, look who's back!" Alaina said, taking a step toward Bernadette, then stopping. "Where did you disappear to for so long? Here, you can have my seat. You've got to have some of this chicken salad your mother went out of her way to fix for us."

They sounded so happy. Bernadette could only guess that Corey had given his wife a good report on meeting with his father, and they only expected the best to follow.

She glanced at all the food, feeling faint, but stopped when she noticed Marietta staring hard at her. She looked away.

"Where is Mama?"

"Upstairs, laying down."

"I think I'll have a nap myself." She had to go up and see Mama, now. How could Mama never tell them anything about Ms. O? What happened to the money Ms. Odessa and Daddy had given them over the years? What was Mama thinking?

Alaina insisted she take a glass of juice with her so Bernadette, trembling fingers wrapped around a glass of orange juice, went upstairs and down the hall. She stopped in front of Mama's room, her hand poised to knock. Bernadette hesitated, wondering how she would begin. She thought of Marietta.

First thing, talk to Marietta and tell her it was over. She now knew Marietta's big secret. Then maybe Marietta would tell her how Dan and the baby really died. After all, Marietta was just as guilty of knowing too much and saying too little. If Marietta wouldn't talk, then it would have to be Mama.

Yes, Bernadette thought, going into her bedroom and setting the glass aside, it should be Marietta. It wasn't until she sat on the bed that she realized just how big a morning it had been, and how exhausted she was. She still did not know what had happened to Ms. O, who was rushed to the hospital by ambulance amidst a shambles of a celebration. In seconds there was a quick knock and Marietta peeped in.

"Are you all right?" she asked. "When you walked in, you looked like you had seen a ghost somewhere."

"I did," she answered, then looked Marietta over. "Where are you going?"

Marietta was in dress black slacks and a burgundy tunic sweater. "Home," she answered briefly. "I have to go back sometime. I just want-ed to make sure that you were really okay first. You had this really weird expression."

"I'm fine." Bernadette answered, and Marietta shrugged, then backed out.

Bernadette stared at the empty doorway, and realized it was now or never. She had to tell Marietta. It took a few minutes to make herself go, but she found herself at Marietta's partially opened door. She knocked, then walked in. Marietta had taken over the back room when Alaina and Corey moved into the basement, once Reggie and Del had left. She was packing rapidly, and glanced up to look at Bernadette.

"Got a minute, Mari?"

"Sure. Come on in."

Bernadette did, sitting near Marietta's suitcase on the bed. She stared into it where Marietta had expertly folded and packed most of her things in a span of a few minutes. Military preparation.

"Getting out of here so soon?" Bernadette asked and wondered where she could start to approach Marietta about Daddy.

"It's time. It was nice, actually, seeing my whole family again."

"Marietta, you should have come with us to see Daddy. Why were you so angry when Alaina told us she'd found him?"

Marietta's slim hands moved quicker, rearranging the clothes in her suitcase.

She folded a shirt, answering, "I wasn't angry. I didn't agree with her, that's all, and I didn't agree that you and Corey should see him."

"Daddy was happy to see us, and we were absolutely right to go see him. Corey had a point saying what was between Daddy and Mama should stay there, and be separate from what's between Daddy and us. But what I didn't know before, and do understand now is why you didn't want to go."

Marietta stopped and looked at her sister. She put her hands on her hips.

"You don't understand anything. As always, you only think you do."

"I do, Marietta."

Marietta looked at Bernadette evenly. "You couldn't possibly understand. Daddy didn't tell you a thing. I *KNOW* he didn't."

"No, he didn't, but I still found out."

Marietta looked closely at Bernadette. She flushed bright red.

"Daddy admitted he made a bad mistake that cost him his marriage," Bernadette said.

Marietta sat on the bed, the suitcase between them.

"And I take it Mama told you what it was?" Bernadette asked quietly.

Marietta forced herself to breathe evenly, steadily. Bernadette stood up, concerned the way Marietta's chest heaved in and out. She pushed the suitcase back and moved closer to her sister.

"Are you all right?" she asked putting her arm around Marietta's shoulder. "Look, just take some deep breaths and relax."

Marietta leaned forward, put her hands on her knees and breathed deeply. In a few minutes, she had control. Bernadette waited, while she stared down at the floor.

"Oh, Bernadette," she said when she could speak. "I should have known, if anybody were to ruin my life, it would be you." She closed her eyes. "Mama ended up telling me, although she didn't want to. And I'm sure she never would have, if she didn't have to. I always thought Daddy was a little standoffish with me, but I would not have known there was a difference between myself and the rest of you. That is, until I started having these problems with my health when I was in my teens, terrible pains in my stomach, and oh, I can't describe it. At 16 I'd never gotten a period, and everybody else did, so I told Mama, and she took me to have things checked out."

Bernadette slid off the bed and walked over to the dresser, unable to sit still, leaning against it and looking at Marietta. Marietta's large eyes welled with tears.

"They said my female organs were stunted…atrophied was the term they used, and there were adhesions that weren't supposed to be there. From what they could tell, it looked like I would never have a period or be able to have children. They removed the adhesions and gave me some medication, but before the surgery, when they went through my medical background, it came out. Mama wasn't my mother, just Daddy was my Dad."

"So you were 16 when you found out Mama wasn't really your mother? That was well after Daddy left. You didn't know this when they broke up?"

"No, but I knew Mama was upset with Daddy before everybody else in the family knew. She said she believed he was having an affair once again, and told me she saw the cousin, the woman who was really his sister."

"Melinda."

"Yes. Mama didn't know Melinda was Daddy's sister when she agreed to take me in. She thought Melinda was just his cousin, and that it had been Melinda who set Daddy up with another woman. But, when she saw Melinda coming out of the office that publishes the *Afro-American* newspaper, Mama got suspicious. She wanted to know why this cousin was always around Daddy. And Mama is stubborn. When she wants to know something, she will find out. So, she tracked her down using her tag number of her car. She said she just wanted to approach the cousin and tell her to leave Daddy alone, and was shocked when the woman said she would never be out of Daddy's life. She admitted she was my mother, and that Daddy was her brother. That's when Mama threw Daddy out.

"But she didn't tell me the relationship between Daddy and Melinda until I went to the doctor at 16, when she had to. She didn't want to upset me."

Bernadette paused. "What in the world did you say when you found out?"

Marietta sighed. "I cried. I thought I was a freak. My parents were brother and sister. I didn't know what my life would be like. I didn't think I would have a normal life."

"When she told you, that your mother was Daddy's sister, did she tell you that Daddy didn't know Melinda was his sister?"

Marietta arched her brow and pushed back on the bed, pulling her feet on the spread. "How could he not know that?"

"She wasn't raised with him, or by his mother." Bernadette recited the story Ms. Odessa had explained, noting the surprise on Marietta's face. "So although he had an affair, it wasn't like he went for his sister deliberately."

"Oh, really? What about the research he had done on another prominent black family where he wrote that they practiced intermarriage to maintain some type of integrity in their bloodline? Mama said with his mother being so light, she believed these people practiced this anyway, and that influenced Daddy's decision."

"Ms. Odessa said she was very upset Mama believed that about her," Bernadette explained. "She said it was ironic that Daddy had done an article on that family, the Limonses, because Daddy knew nothing about Melinda being his sister. But, according to Ms. Odessa, she said Mama threatened to use this article and the fact that Daddy had you with Melinda to ruin him if he came around us."

Marietta stared silently. Then quietly, she said, "Mama made me promise to keep this between us, and to make sure that we didn't go around Daddy or his people. I think she believed that Dad and his family had no boundaries, and that he could easily cross the line, even with one of us."

"And it never occurred to you that Daddy may have a different story?"

"Well, why would it? The fact is, he did have sex with his sister, whether he says it was through ignorance or not. He willingly had a relationship with somebody other than Mama. And why would I think Mama would lie?"

"And so, are you planning to keep this a secret from Del forever?"

"It's not as easy to talk about when it's you."

"You don't think he should know you may not be able to conceive?"

"Yes, but that's not certain. There's a possibility I can, with all the fertilization techniques available. It will be hard, but we don't know."

"And you want to surprise him with this after you're married?"

"Well, I love him. I don't want to lose him."

"I can see you love him. And the thing is, that dude is crazy about your ass. And I don't know, 'cause I'm not Dear Abby, but if it was me, I would think about the fact that if it's true I may have a hard time getting pregnant, and I know this man wants children, then it's a good chance he'll walk anyway if I can't have them—if that's the type of person he is.

If he's going to walk later, why marry him first to see what he's made of?"

Marietta stared at her younger sister.

"Hell, you're already 38. It's conceivable your biological clock is striking midnight anyway!"

Marietta reached in the suitcase and threw a pair of underwear at Bernadette's head as she ducked.

"I mean, come on! Del isn't stupid. He can't want too many kids marrying you this late in life."

"Yeah, you really have some good points, Bernadette, but it's not easy. I'm living with this."

"You've lived with a lot, too much. I can't believe you never told us about Mama's first baby. Michael."

Marietta stared unbelieving. "You know about that too?"

"Why did you keep it a secret? What happened to him?"

"He died at birth. That was the first year Daddy and Mama were married. Ms. Odessa was always invited to dinners and balls and other big social affairs and she always wanted Daddy there. Well, she didn't know Mom and Dad were married in the beginning, and she had invited him to escort some girl, but Daddy was taking Mama. Mama knew how dressed up everybody would be, and she wanted to look good. She took on this janitorial job at night doing manual labor. She told Daddy she was nursing an old patient, but it was doing heavy cleaning, and she ended up lifting something and having the baby early, and he died. That was actually how Ms. Odessa found out about Daddy being married, and it was all such a mess. She insisted on burying the baby with her family, the rich Windsors, but she wanted Mama to promise to go away, as if Mama would."

There was a hard knock on the door, then Corey called out, "It's me."

"Come in, it's open!"

He stepped inside. "Beatrice wants to know when you're coming back. She says Witt's on his way?"

Bernadette jumped up. "I almost forgot! Come on, I'm going to need the both of you with me for this one."

******

Witt's big truck was pulled toward the curb, back-end sticking out as though he had jumped out in a hurry. When Corey pulled up in his van, Bernadette asked them to sit still and wait a second. She shook her head.

"It's not right. Maybe you should stay in the van, Marietta. Just Corey and I will go to the door and see what's going on."

"Why?" Marietta said. "I want to see what's going on, too!"

"No, trust me, it's more than that. I need you to stay here in case we need you to call 911. Come on, Corey!"

They knocked on the door and rang the bell but couldn't get an answer.

"Maybe they went out in another car," Corey suggested.

"Corey, I have so much to tell you, but for now, trust me. He's in there. Bea is leaving Witt, and he's not taking no for an answer. I don't know what he's doing in there, but it isn't good."

She glanced around thinking again of hurling something at the windows, calling attention to the house, as Corey was stuttering something about the police.

"School is out, so Toukie would have to be in there, too. We may have to break in," Bernadette said decisively, backing up to examine the door.

"What do you mean? We should call the police, Bernadette."

"Do you know where you are? You are in the middle of Baltimore City. You are in the heart of the ghetto. You are going to report that you cannot get into your sister's house, and you think they're going to send in S.W.A.T?"

"They'll send them after they talk to me." Corey walked back to the van while Bernadette leaped to the steps next door. Mrs. Jones kept the baby, she remembered. She could get in from a back window maybe, or from Mrs. Jones' rooftop.

Mrs. Jones opened after one ring and remembered Bernadette. To her surprise, Mrs. Jones had a second key that Beatrice had given her in case Toukie needed it.

Bernadette quickly took it and quietly unlocked the door. Corey came running in behind her.

As they entered through the small foyer, Bernadette spotted boxes lined up in the hall. Beatrice must have been in the process when Witt caught her.

That's when they heard the bumps upstairs and a door open and close. Several seconds later, Witt came downstairs.

"How did you get in my house?" he sounded breathless and surprised.

Corey stepped forward. "Look man, we didn't get a response when we rang, and I know my sister is in here. All we want to do is take her with us."

"I can have you arrested for trespassing. Now, I want you, and your sister to turn around and get the hell out."

The bumps overhead started again, this time louder.

"Is that Beatrice?" Bernadette demanded. She was glad Corey stepped in front of her. It gave her a chance to look around to see what she could use as a weapon on Witt, if she had to. Glass picture frames, the poker in front of the fake fireplace, and the lamps looked good, if needed. That's when she noticed that Toukie was here. Her bookbag and keys were spread on the floor. Where was she?

"She's not going anywhere. We had this talk, Bernadette, and I thought you understood. I believe you promised not to interfere in my family again."

"I talked to Ms. Odessa, Witt. The game is over."

"I don't know what you're talking about."

"I know what you're after, and this isn't the way to get it. Beatrice doesn't want you. You've never been honest with her. You've been taking from her and Ms. Odessa. I know you've been cruel to Toukie. And we can't let this keep going. Let's just call it even and everybody walks away."

"You don't know what you're talking about, and I want you out."

"Ms. Odessa gave you the ring, Witt. Then she later told you everything was over. She didn't want to help you anymore. What more do you want from us?"

"Ms. Odessa does not get the chance to call anything off. Not when she took all the quilts and custom made drapes and curtains my mother made for her club members and left my mother hanging. Not when she promised me, she *promised* me I would be as big in business as I wanted to be with her help. You don't do that to me, and then stop taking my calls without telling me why."

"But you aren't hurting Ms. O. You're hurting Beatrice and the children!"

"I'm giving you one more chance to walk out of here."

Bernadette stared in his eyes. He was crazy. He must have a gun. Beatrice must have told him about Derrick. Or did Derrick call? Or was Derrick upstairs with Beatrice, tied up? Somebody was upstairs banging.

"Okay," Bernadette said quickly, not wanting Corey to challenge

Witt. She could see the expression that crossed Corey's face, tell by his stance that he was prepared for a physical battle. He was ready to jump on Witt. Instead, Corey grabbed Bernadette's arm and pulled her back."

"You're right," Corey said. "We are trespassing. Let us see Beatrice and we'll go."

Witt reached behind his back and pulled a small gun that looked like a toy.

"Okay, throw your cell over here, Corey. You throw yours, too," he said to Bernadette.

Bernadette and Corey both looked shocked.

"This isn't going to help you, Witt. You hurt us, and you definitely won't get Beatrice. You won't get to raise your son. You won't get anything," Bernadette said.

"I don't plan to hurt you. I just want you out. Give me your phones, and then you're going to walk out of here like I asked you to. Beatrice is staying with me."

Corey tossed his over, and Bernadette shook her head throwing her hands up. "I don't have my cell phone with me."

"I don't believe you," he said, and just as he started over to her, they all heard a barrage of loud raps at the door, and the words, "Police! Open up!"

Witt looked surprised.

"Put it away man, it's not worth going out like this," Corey said in a quiet voice.

"Mommy!" Toukie's voice was outside. What was she doing out there?

Bernadette felt her heart leap. At least Toukie would not get hurt.

Then things happened fast.

Corey turned toward the door, and Witt turned to go up the steps with the gun still in his hand. That's when Bernadette jumped on him. He was not going to hurt Bea, not when she had things so nearly pulled together for everybody. Not when she was finally able to understand.

Witt flipped her over hard and fell on top of her.

"What are you doing?" he asked, grabbing her arm and twisting it hard up behind her, between her shoulder blades. She screamed out in pain, and he leaned down closer. "Didn't I tell you to keep out of my family?" he whispered and jerked her arm even harder.

That's when she heard what sounded like a pop, then felt her body, face first, push into the carpet before she realized he was off her and against the wall with Corey's hands around his neck. The two men clutched each other, Corey had Witt's neck, and Witt had Corey's collar. The banging on the door started again as the men slammed into the wall, then into a table, knocking over a lamp, but before Witt could slip out of Corey's hold, Bernadette, rising slowly, realized the gun was under her leg.

She grabbed it and aimed.

"Witt, I'm warning you, hold it!" she said getting up on her knees.

The next sounds she heard were gunfire. As she turned, she saw the front door blow open and the police storm in, screaming at her to drop the gun. She did and struggled to put both her hands up. In that minute, she saw Toukie run into the house with tears streaming down her face.

"He killed my Mommy! He killed my Mommy!" she screamed as she ran toward the stairs. Faint with the pain from her shoulder, Bernadette pulled herself up and took off up the stairs behind her.

he'd approached Reggie's friends to find corroborating evidence of an improper relationship, but it didn't mean he got it. The only thing she knew was he had something, or he wouldn't have gone this far. She knew he wanted her out. Still, she made up her mind that she wasn't going out without a challenge.

What she also knew was that he had thwarted her mail. There had to be an official memo to change her APO, the overseas mailing postal system used by the military, because only the mail sent to her from the base was misdirected. Only an officer could change that. However, she could not find any evidence that such a memo existed.

The thing that amazed Bernadette most while her career hung in limbo was she no longer felt scared about what would happen to her. She had always believed that without the Marines, she would whither. Instead, she found herself feeling stronger than ever everyday as she waited to find her fate. She had succeeded in finding the pieces she needed to put her family back together. She had made it back from the Middle East, sane, in one piece, and in a stronger spirit than she'd ever known. Despite the accolades she had received for her superior work overseas, she now knew she was more than any medals or letters the Marines could give. She felt there was more to her life, and she was ready to make changes if she had to.

She no longer had that burning desire to defeat and control everything. A sense of peace had replaced it now that she had Marietta, Beatrice and Toukie back in her life. A sense of order was there now that she knew both her parents and all the secrets had come out. There was a calmness she hadn't felt since the afternoon at the cemetery beside Nita's grave. There was peace inside her. Everything in her life had fallen into place except for one thing: Reggie.

She loved him. Officer or not, she could not pretend she didn't want that man. Every night as she waited for her hearing, she found herself looking out the window across the bay, where she would see the lights flickering on the water's surface, listening to the SOS CD he'd given her, especially the song "Tell Me That You Love Me." Maybe he would feel how much she missed him, and would come to her. Her heart would leap when the phone rang, hoping it was him. But she quickly realized, he was not trying to see her. She had left him thinking he was not the most important person to her, and to Reggie, that was that. Not even calls to Nancy and Lonnie could make him contact her.

She remembered the events of the hearing as though it were yesterday. She recalled that the two long months from the time of Beatrice's party to April last year had seemed like two years, but when April finally came, Bernadette couldn't have been happier. She had been at her desk, trying to work around the sling she had to wear for her dislocated shoulder, thanks to Witt, and trying to keep her legal problems in the back of her mind, when Major Whitaker had called...

The Major barked through the phone that Bernadette was to get herself over to the Administration Building, ASAP. The gruffness in the major's voice let her know this was it.

She reported right away, about a five-minute walk, just to find she had to sit outside a closed door in a room with several wooden benches and wait. An informal meeting was underway between Colonel Chisholm, Major Whitaker and, to her surprise, the major's superior, Colonel Snucker. When she learned that an undisclosed fourth party was in there, she could only close her eyes. It couldn't possibly mean anything good for her that a witness had come forth, even though she was sure Major Whitaker would try. She had to prepare herself. What if they had Reggie as the witness against her?

Just as she thought she couldn't sit and wait another minute, the door to the hearing room opened, then slammed behind Major Whitaker, who had come striding out, and heading straight for her. Bernadette rose and saluted, then waited, trying to read her face.

"I knew it!" Major Whitaker had chortled loudly. "I knew it was the biggest crock I ever heard. When we got him in there, he folded like a sliced beach ball."

"He, who?" Bernadette asked.

"Lance Corporal Weeks. He was the witness Colonel Chisholm called. He tried to explain how he knew your relationship with Corporal Taylor was out of bounds, but he couldn't corroborate it with anything that could be used as evidence. He acted as though he thought the colonel was going to be his back up, and corroborate his statements. Maybe that was the agreement, but it didn't happen. So his testimony was out.

"Then Colonel Chisholm started, with his phony statements about how he had only your best interest at heart, as well as the best interest of the Corps. He kept saying how his aim was to shape you into the kind of officer worthy of the Marines. He said he wants you to know there was no malice, nor intent to discredit you in any way. Blah, Blah.

"And then I brought up the mail tampering you told me about. It was just an informal hearing, and he knew he wasn't on trial, so I asked him, if his efforts to shape you up had anything to do with tampering with your mail. He jumped up and turned two shades darker spitting his denial, but I said I might be able to produce the original memo, if he couldn't remember, authorizing the change in your APO. It wasn't signed, so it should not have been followed, but the person who received it firsthand, knew who had given it.

"It was the same person that you mentioned had refused to walk anything over to Colonel Chisholm, or help your project in any way."

"Private Winnie Sugar?" Bernadette had asked.

"Seems she had some type of "inappropriate" run in with him, she would not say exactly. But just that memo alone that she'd copied had him singing a different tune.

"He's now interested in meeting with you one-on-one to clear up any misunderstanding."

Bernadette remembered how her knees had buckled from relief, and how she bent over, covering her face, laughing and crying at the same time.

"But what now?" Bernadette managed to ask.

"You're free to go on, Lieutenant. Your file is expunged of all accusations."

Bernadette swallowed. She hadn't been prepared to tell Major Whitaker anything about Reggie right after her tour in Saudi Arabia, because she wasn't sure what to tell her. She hadn't heard from Reggie in over a year, and she didn't know if there was a relationship to which she should admit. Though she had no proof from Reggie, her gut told her there was something between them worth fighting to keep. Something she wanted. She remembered that she cleared her throat.

"Major, I want to explain something to you. If you don't mind, ma'am," she'd started, but the major's intense stare stopped the words cold on her lips.

"Listen, Lieutenant, I didn't just sit in there and defend something that I wasn't sure was a benefit to the Corps. Whatever it is you feel you have to tell me, before you do, understand this: I will uphold my responsibility to the utmost. Now, if anything about your situation is different than it was when we spoke earlier, I advise you to consider carefully what you want to say to me, and what you want to do about it. With that in mind, I am willing to hear you out."

Bernadette had looked away, wondering what she was doing. She was clear. She could walk away. It was April, and Reggie hadn't contacted her in the two months since Beatrice's party. The investigation was over. What would she prove by admitting anything about him now?

"I want to thank you. I just want to make sure the colonel is not going to interfere with my tours of duty or future promotions."

Major Whitaker's eyes had narrowed. "You're free to continue as you were Lieutenant, unless there is something more you want to tell me. Hell, I wouldn't have gone in there and wasted my time if I thought he had a leg to stand on. And I believe he did all those things you said, discarding your work on the project, but you know what? If he does anything more than glance at you, I'd be willing to pay you money. He was guilty of messing with that mail and he knew he was guilty, and if he didn't want us checking him out, he thought better of pushing his way with you."

Bernadette heaved a big sigh, surprised that she would walk out the door still a Marine. Surprised he had actually let her go.

"Is there anything further I need to know now, Lieutenant?"

Bernadette looked the major in the eye. Major Whitaker did not blink, staring hard at her. She must know something, Bernadette thought. But maybe not enough. She didn't want her superior thinking she had defended her in vain. Yet, she didn't want to continue sneaking with Reggie, because for sure she would now get caught.

"Thank you, ma'am." She'd whispered to her commander, still feeling weak in the knees.

"I suggest you take the rest of the afternoon off, and report as usual tomorrow morning," Major Whitaker said. "You deserve it."

Bernadette gave her a final salute and hurried out. Down the cement steps, around the brick building she walked, heading to the parking lot and to her car. Inside, she rolled the window down, and burst into tears.

This hearing meant she was clear, if she stopped seeing Reggie. This was not what she wanted, but what could she do?

She had driven back to her apartment feeling her stomach flip. She should be happy, but all she felt was sick. Reggie had cut her off. Even he knew it wouldn't work. She now had her career back. She had her family. She had what she wanted. But she wasn't happy.

Bernadette remembered as she turned off the motor, and sat in front of her apartment building, how crazy she felt. She had won. But so what if Reggie didn't love her. She would get her promotion. Wasn't that enough? She knew it wasn't. She loved him, with everything she had. She needed one more time where she could tell him. Where she could explain…

Then she remembered her head against the seat, and seeing something move out the corner of her eye. She looked up and saw a familiar figure standing on the landing, looking in her direction. She sat up straight and peered in the distance. Then a smile tugged her lips.

He saluted her, and walked over to her car, pausing at the passenger's side.

"How did it go, Lieutenant?" Reggie asked, and she leaned over to unlock the passenger door so he could slide in. She looked at him in disbelief.

"It's actually over. The investigation is closed."

"Can we go inside?" he asked, and she laughed, wiping at her face and jumping out the car, leading him up to her apartment. As soon as the doors closed, she fell against him in tears.

"It's all over, Reggie. I told Major Whitaker that I was not guilty, and even though I think she has her doubts, she's giving me a chance."

Reggie was quiet at first. Then, holding her tightly, he moved his lips next to her ear, and whispered, "I knew it would be. I knew it was going to be okay. If they didn't trip us up and catch us right before the hearing, I knew there was nothing. So, I made myself not call you. I made myself not come. But I missed you. I missed you so bad," his voice was husky and low.

She looked up at him, and his full, perfect lips met hers hungrily. When he pulled away, she'd looked in his eyes.

"I'm not staying in," she remembered telling him then. "I can't. This life was perfect for me, and I would have died for this outcome. But I don't feel it anymore. I can't go on like this, Reggie. I can't stop the way I feel about you and I'm not prepared to keep lying."

"Feel about me? You want to tell me now you have feelings for me, Bernadette?"

"I love you, Reggie. I love you so much. I love the way your short hair curls up after we make love for a long time, I love the way you look at me whenever we're alone together, I love the way you say my name, I love the way you feel against me, I love the way I feel when I'm with you, I love that you want me...I love you, Reggie."

He'd kissed her long and deep, then looked at his watch.

"I have to get back, in fact, I'm going to be late. I took an hour personal time, but you took a long time to get here."

"Oh, Reggie, I have so much to tell you. First, Del and Marietta are getting married next year."

"Tell me about them when I get off duty. In the mean time, I want you to tell me what you think of this..."

\*\*\*\*\*\*

That was last year. Now she had Reggie beside her at the wedding, sitting between her and her father, and she looked over at him as Marietta and Del were pronounced man and wife. Feeling her eyes on him, Reggie turned and covered her hand with his.

His fingers touched the one-carat diamond he had placed on her hand just before he left her apartment the afternoon of the hearing. Now she squeezed his hand.

"Am I supposed to wait until the reception to let them in on everything?" Bernadette whispered. "They know about the engagement, but you know I'm dying to read this letter about your deal with Arista Records. Can I tell them they bought five of your songs, and want you as one of their new music publishers?"

"Of course, you can."

"I can't wait for your enlistment to be up," Bernadette continued, "and for you to start doing something you really love. Do we really have to go back?"

"I only have three weeks left in my tour, and I don't plan to re-up, but now you. What with this money your family put aside," he whispered, "you got to decide. "What are you going to do?"

Bernadette smiled at him thinking of Mama's words. After all the years Mama had never mentioned Daddy or what she put up with, the day Witt was arrested, Mama opened up the floodgates.

"Remember, Bernadette, with women, it's all about love. We give everything up for love. With men, they just don't love the same. How easy is he getting you? If he's getting you easy, it ain't going to last. I learned the hard way—the more I loved your father and gave in to keep him, the more I lost. If you ain't easy to get, you ain't going to be easy to give up, just like anything else in life. Make sure of that."

"Well," Bernadette said in a whisper, "Maybe we'll decide that together." She winked at him before glancing over at her father, feeling very relieved that her grandmother hadn't died and there would be no guilt accepting the money Mama had kept from them for years.

The family stood as the pastor introduced the newly wedded couple as Mr. and Mrs. Delaney Peterson, and the bride and groom faced the crowd to thunderous applause before starting down the aisle.

"How long are we going to stay here this time?" Reggie whispered. "You know you promised I could have some on the East Coast last time I was here, and you never paid up."

She smiled, leaned up and kissed him full on the lips, as though there was no wedding going on, and no one was around to see them.

"Okay, Reggie, just one dance. One dance at the reception, and this time, we can leave together. I promise."

## The End

# Discussion Questions for The Promise Box

1. How rational is Bernadette's decision to follow-up on a letter that hints someone in her family is a danger to them?

2. What does Bernadette's mother's question: 'Have you fallen in love yet?' have to do with what happened to her daughters? Why does Mama blame 'love' for what happened to her family? Is she right?

3. Is Beatrice's relationship with her daughter responsible? What should a woman consider when she finds herself caught in a conflict between her children and the man in her life?

4. Is Witt just a misguided good guy?

5. Is Marietta's behavior toward her family rational?

6. Did Mama handle Ms. Odessa in a reasonable way? Did she handle Bernadette's father in a reasonable way?

7. Who is more to blame for the family strife: Mama, Daddy or Ms. Odessa? Why?

8. How important is it for family to stand strong for each other, even in adulthood? How do you balance the love of your family with the love of your significant other? What happens when there is a conflict?

9. What value, if any, is there to keeping family secrets?

10. What do you think was the purpose of the promise box? Did it serve its purpose?

# the promise box

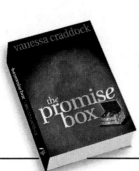

## Order Form

| | |
|---|---|
| The Promise Box | $15.00 |
| Shipping/Handling (one book via U.S. Priority Mail) | 3.85 |
| Total | $18.85 |

\* MD residents add $.75 sales tax
  for each book before S/H

### Purchaser Information

Name_____

Address_____

City_____ State_____ Zip_____

Total number of books ordered _____ @ $15  =_____

Shipping charges for 1 book ___1___ @ $3.85 = _$3.85_

\# of each additional book with this order _____ @ $1.00 =_____

TOTAL amount enclosed  $ _____

*Acceptable forms of payment:*
*Checks/Money Orders made payable to address below.*

SmartGirls PUBLISHERS

P.O. Box 11492
Baltimore, Maryland  21239
smartgirlspublsh@cs.com